W9-CFY-259

Who'd said Hell was murky?

I stood transfixed. The lights were a kaleidoscope gone mad, shifting down the long dark tunnel, rushing closer as though space itself were collapsing. The back of my brain whispered a warning to the front, but I wasn't listening. What could it *be*?

I stood there beside the fissure with my mouth hanging open, staring as the flood of lights and noise rushed at me out of the darkness, and didn't have the sense to get out of the way. My ears popped again and a freight train noise roared in my ears, its thunder shaking the very walls. My teeth rattled and I squinted against brilliant light. It leaped off the floor as high as my head, showering in fountains and spurts like molten steel.

With the air a solid wall of sound beating at me, instinct finally took over and shoved me into the fissure, bruising ribs and tearing open my injured back and knees again. I yelled and heard nothing but the roar permeating the rocks. I found myself panting as terror took hold. Then I forced myself to face whatever it was that came sweeping down the cave.

Thunder hurt my skull. Stone chips stung my face. Then I saw the eyes.

SLEIPNIR

LINDA EVANS

SLEIPNIR

This is a work of fiction. All the characters and events portrayed in this book are fictional, and any resemblance to real people or incidents is purely coincidental.

Copyright © 1994 by Linda Evans

All rights reserved, including the right to reproduce this book or portions thereof in any form.

A Baen Books Original

Baen Publishing Enterprises
P.O. Box 1403
Riverdale, N.Y. 10471

ISBN: 0-671-87594-9

Cover art by C.W. Kelly

First printing, March 1994

Distributed by
Paramount Publishing
1230 Avenue of the Americas
New York, N.Y. 10020

Typeset by Windhaven Press, Auburn, N.H.
Printed in the United States of America

Sleipnir is for

My family, because Lois, Don, and Michael Evans,
Darrell Walton, Ron Walton, Frances Walton, and Zella
Evans all believed in a skinny, awkward kid . . .

Susan Collingwood, because she always tells me when
I'm wrong, and believes in me when I despair . . .

David R. Palmer, because he taught me craft and went
above and beyond the call of friendship doing it . . .

Marj Schott, because she gives of her soul . . .

Ms. "Mom" Wiley, Dr. Constantine Santas, Dr. Andrew
Dillon, Dr. Gail Compton, Mrs. Bushong, Mrs. Hill,
and all teachers everywhere, because
they create our future . . .

Doyle Pope, because so long as we remember, his Manta
Ship will fly the stars . . .

Dr. John Boyle, because good doctors are worth
their weight in diamonds . . .

Toni Weisskopf and Jim Baen, because they
made my dream come true . . .

Debbie Anderson, Mary Ann Emerson, Bill Brand,
Brenda Long, Kathy Lyons, Amy Repasky, Daryl
Finnegan, Jenny Bruno, Sandra Kay Haile, Robert
Berger, Kathy Rath, and all my many, dear friends in the
North-Central Florida Sportsman's Association and the
NRA, because without good friends, we can accomplish
nothing, but with their help, we can work miracles . . .

but mostly, *Sleipnir* is for Bob Hollingsworth,
and all the heroes who fought the Cold War, because
some of them never returned to tell the tale.

Chapter One

Pushing a cave isn't a job for amateurs.

But then, neither is hunting gods. Especially in their own stomping grounds. Predictably, I was doing a lousy job of both.

Considering my past history—I never took advice I didn't like—it wasn't too surprising my spelunking guide was so mad at me he wasn't speaking. Now, nobody has ever accused me of possessing tact, but in Klaus' case, it had taken a lot of effort to get him to the stage of silent jaw-grinding. Klaus had several thousand reasons—all of them deliciously green—to put up with my demands, but even poor old Klaus had finally reached his limit.

Every morning for the past three days he had insisted we turn back for the surface. I insisted we keep going. Klaus was stubborn; but I've been called less flattering names than a bullheaded, mule-eared horse's backside. I got my way.

When I woke up that morning, I knew Klaus would try again. I braced myself for the inevitable, and wasn't disappointed. Even before I'd crawled out of my sleeping bag, he looked me straight in the eye—which left me half-blind, since he was pointing the carbide light on his helmet right at my face—and muttered, "We go back. *Now*."

The moment was fast approaching I'd either have to tell him what I was really doing down here, or hit him over the head and go on alone. So, trying to delay the inevitable a little longer, I snapped, "Tonight! We got one more day to go before I turn around. Read your contract if you're not happy about it. And get that light out of my face!"

Nobody should have to argue with an angry Norwegian before breakfast. I'm not human until I've had coffee—which probably explained my mood, since it'd been a week since I'd had any. I got myself clear of the sleeping bag, and flexed my knees, trying to limber up before we came to blows. He was older than I was, but probably in better shape. My leg still hurt from the gunshot wounds, and a slithering fall down a sharp rockface two days previously hadn't done the rest of me any good, either.

Klaus scowled. His round face took on the look of a satanic elf. "Damn it," he growled, making two words of it, "we have walked deeper than anyone. You have the record, Herr Barnes. We have pushed Garm's Cave far enough. We turn back *now*. Our supplies are low—"

I nudged to see how far he'd give. "Tonight, Bjornssen! Or didn't I pay you enough?"

He looked for a moment like he wanted to punch me. In fact, when his fists tightened down I set myself to feint to one side and end this the hard way. Then he just turned his back and slammed his gear together. I let tense gut muscles soften, and started breathing normally again. Another day gained . . .

Given the white-lipped set of his face, I halfway expected him to march back toward the surface—alone. But he didn't. He just slouched down with his back to me, and started wolfing his breakfast. For all the attention Bjornssen paid me, I might have been part of the rock under his khaki-clad backside.

I thought about apologizing, but I wasn't about to go back now. Not after the price I'd paid—money and blood—to get this far. So I kept my mouth shut and let him stew in silence. When I was ready to go, I stood up and shrugged into my pack.

Bjornssen glanced back and eyed my unorthodox gear. He scowled again; then deliberately reached for another handful of dried apples from his own supplies. I shrugged metaphoric shoulders. Klaus Bjornssen had known what I was carrying from the outset. That gear was partly why his fee had been so high. Besides, he was the only guide I'd been able to find willing to take a rank amateur into a cave only professionals had dared "push" before.

Part of the reason I'd been riding him so hard was the hope he'd finally blow his temper and leave me to get back out the best way I knew how. To date, that part of the plan had failed. Call it professional ethics or masochism, Bjornssen had absorbed all the punishment I could dish out, and was still with me. All things considered, Klaus was entitled to a sulk. So while he finished his meal, I lit my carbide lantern and explored the passageway out to the limit of Bjornssen's helmet light. My footsteps sounded hollow against the muffled sounds of Klaus reshuffling gear and readjusting straps.

I glanced back as Bjornssen marked the wall with a strip from his ever-present roll of surveyor's tape; then I moved on as he turned to follow. A whole series of hundred-foot dropoffs, which had required ropes and rock-climbing pitons to traverse, had given way to another long, low cavern with no apparent end. The rock no longer looked entirely like limestone; or maybe it was just my eyes. I'd been looking at nothing but grey rock for days, now. The only genuine difference I could pinpoint was the absence of water.

After a good bit of beard-scratching, I decided that must account for the almost subliminal changes I was noticing. The lack of water worried me—we were lower on water than anything else—but it shouldn't have surprised me. It was predictable that the immortal bastard I was hunting would dry up the water supply when I needed it most.

Bjornssen's footsteps stomped up close behind me. He was muttering to himself in Norwegian. From the sound of it, he probably wanted to tear my head off and serve it to me for lunch. I started to step out of his way before he could shoulder past and take the lead—

—and he yelled. The light from Bjornssen's lamp swung crazily. He smashed forward into my back and kept falling. I stumbled, and windmilled for balance. A loud, sickening scrape reached my ears, then he grabbed wildly at my ankles. I crashed to the floor and bruised face and ribs on rough stone. The impact extinguished my lamp. Stunned, I tried to catch my breath. Bjornssen gabbled hysterically. His weight was pulling me backward over a lip of rock. Both of us slid out over nothing at all.

I yelled—and all that came out was a gurgling croak. I left skin behind on the rough stone, and tried to lift my face. We were still sliding. I grabbed for any available handholds to brake our fall, and didn't find any. His whole weight hung suspended from my ankles. The only light came from his helmet. It swung crazily as he struggled. Wild, distorted shadows left me grabbing for handholds that were nothing but illusion.

"Hang—on—" I gasped. He made a lunge for my knees with one hand—and missed. I slid backward another six inches, and dug in with my fingernails. The rough lip of stone caught my crotch. "Dammit"—I used elbows and hands, hugging stone in an effort to stop our fatal slide—"get your—hands around—my knees—"

My feet jerked hard. I gave an involuntary yell as I slid backward clear up to my chest. My legs dangled in empty space. Even without looking, I could sense how long a way it was to the bottom. Bjornssen screamed and cursed and hung on by my bootlaces.

Then he was gone.

The light faded swiftly below me. His screams echoed, dropped rapidly away until I couldn't hear him anymore.

For long moments I hung absolutely motionless, halfway to falling to my own death. Then, in the process of scraping myself painfully forward, gasping and flailing until most of me was on solid rock again, it occurred to me I hadn't even *seen* a hole big enough for a man to fall into.

I scooted backward until my back touched solid rock, and wished there'd been a way to back up even farther. That hole hadn't been there. It *couldn't* have been there. I listened for a moment to my heart pound in my ears. I thought about letting go of the rock floor to strike the sparker on my helmet; but my lizard brain wouldn't let my hand relax its deathlike grip. *Okay, I thought, I'll just sit here and think for a couple of minutes*. My thoughts weren't pretty.

I'd seen men die before. Had killed a few, myself. But this . . . I felt sick all over, like I'd tricked a puppy into the jaws of a killer wolf. Dammit, I hadn't liked the man much; but he had been a good spelunker, a loyal guide, and a decent enough human being. He certainly hadn't deserved to die, especially when he didn't have the faintest idea what I'd dragged him into.

I was hunting Odin by my own choice. My own pride, combined with the recognition that I needed to hire spelunking expertise, had contributed to Klaus' murder as certainly as though I'd shoved him down the chimney myself. Guilt ate up whatever comfort could be found in the knowledge that I'd always done better when hunting alone in the dark.

I swore bitterly and breathed deeply for a moment; then listened to my pulse rate gradually slow down and fade from the foreground of my awareness.

Klaus Bjornssen had doubtless gone to his death convinced I was the biggest asshole this side of hell. I snorted. If I were right, he was there right now, probably still calling me every name he could think of, to every poor, dead soul who'd listen. I hoped it made him feel better.

No more innocents in the way. Odin had another think coming if he and his buddies thought they could stop me just by pulling the ground out from under my feet. . . .

Well, it wasn't going to be the last time he'd try it. And he had at least as much to lose as I did; maybe more. I swore aloud; then grinned, although the wobbly effort felt a little sickly. I might be shaken, but I must have managed to put a serious dent in Odin's confidence. That counted for more than a little in the deadly game I'd found myself caught up in.

And since the only score which mattered was survival, that left me on top. So far, anyway. Somewhere at the bottom of this cave, Odin must be spitting ten-penny nails.

Gary would've been proud. Well, maybe he would; then again, maybe not. Gary Vernon had wanted me to go Stateside when my discharge came, find myself a decent job and marry some freckle-faced kid with a down-home Cracker accent. But if I had, I would never have been able to look myself in the eye again. Gary Vernon was the reason I was here, stranded on the lip of a bottomless chimney in a freezing Norwegian cave. And no one-eyed, oath-breaking, cold-blooded killer was going to divert me. Of course, nobody'd ever accused me of having too many brain cells; but Randy Barnes wasn't, by God, a quitter.

I can't speak for the rest of humanity; but having my life wrenched inside-out by assholes really pisses me off. I never could tolerate an asshole. (Despite a sneaking suspicion that I was one.) I let out a bark of laughter. They do say the only creature on this green earth stupider than an infantryman is a Marine. Not even a *leatherneck* would have walked into this mess.

There were only two things I could see that I might have done differently. I should *not* have opened my big, fat mouth and told Gary Vernon to go to hell. And I certainly shouldn't have made a pact with *Odin*.

Hindsight is a mother.

It's also a waste of time. I muttered something ugly into the darkness and my words echoed oddly in the close air. I growled out something even nastier, hopeful the curse followed my dead guide all the way to Odin's ears. I'd learned the hard way that you never knew who—or what—might be listening when you cursed, or took an oath, so I cursed away, because sure as worms eat little green apples, nothing I said now could possibly get me in deeper than I already was.

"Okay, Barnes," I muttered. "What next?"

My lips and throat were dry. I fumbled for a canteen and swallowed a sip. I didn't dare drink more; no telling how long this half-full canteen would have to last. Once it was secure again, I leaned back and blew out my breath in a gusting sigh.

"What a mess."

Most people in my shoes would've had the sense either to go quietly mad, or to forget the whole thing had ever happened. Johnson would have cracked—and, in point of fact, had. Nobody else involved had even come close to admitting what was going on, probably not even to themselves. Gary . . .

I swore again. Gary might have believed me. Had believed, in fact, even before I met him.

Not that it had done him any good.

Regret was also a waste of time. I needed to get my carbide lantern relit, see what I was up against. I hadn't just spent three years guarding nuclear missiles—and playing pussyfoot with half the terrorist groups in the world—for nothing. I had survived everything the Army and the ragheads and Odin could throw my way. I owed myself—not to mention Gary Vernon—something better than sitting in the dark.

I *owed* Gary Vernon an apology. And my life.

Chapter Two

Of all the gutless wonders, greenhorn newbies, dopers, and fools who joined the Army and somehow got themselves assigned to Pershing, only a pitiful few were competent to handle the job of guarding nuclear missiles. Among those few were guys like "Wally" Wallenstein, and Charles "Chuck" Norris, and Crater, who, as far as I knew, had never been called anything else (although I'd heard it rumored that his real name was Haversham).

They'd been among my closest friends.

But head-and-shoulders above the whole crowd—in *everyone's* opinion—was Gary Vernon. The best of the best. An all-around nice guy, who'd lend you beer money when you were short, and watch your back on patrol. Which was good, since he was generally acknowledged to be the luckiest man alive. And since his luck seemed to rub off on whoever pulled patrols with him, everybody wanted to be teamed with him.

Gary always laughed it off, attributed it to a pact he'd made with Odin. Whatever the cause, it seemed to work. And the closer I got to discharge, the happier I was that Sergeant Brown and Lieutenant Donaldson teamed us

9

up a lot. We worked well together, and nothing got past us.

Being teamed with Gary got a whole lot more attractive once the brass sent down their no-ammo-on-patrol policy. The official explanation sounded like an updated version of Mom's "You'll shoot your eye out" excuse for never buying BB guns for Christmas—and made just about as much sense. We were sitting on several megatons of nuclear warheads, and incidents with terrorist groups running "training missions" in our area had been up at least three hundred percent over the previous three months. Yet brass decides out of the blue we ought to go sneaking around in the dark with empty rifles? Go figure.

It wasn't *our* fault some goddamn fool of a civilian had gotten himself shot on one of the other sites. The way we had it figured, he'd probably been point scout, anyway, and got caught. But brass up at HQ had had a royal cow, so we got stuck with the cow patties. The *tower* guards got live ammo; just not us poor, dumb fools assigned to patrol the perimeter.

Being GIs, we found ways around it, with nobody the wiser, and none of us ending up casualties. We had the situation well in hand—until that inevitable, bitter night under a full moon when I turned to Gary and whispered, "You got any spares?"

He shot me an incredulous look. "You don't?"

"No—Wilson borrowed 'em last night. He's running scared. You know, his second kid's due in a couple of weeks, and I felt sorry for him. Besides, I knew you always carry."

Gary snorted, visibly disgusted. His breath steamed.

"Great. I dumped mine back into my gear while you were in the can. Brunowski almost caught me when he poked his head in the door. I knew *you* always carry."

I wasn't sure which of us was more dismayed. Neither of us had any illegal personal ammo; which meant we now carried what amounted to clumsy plastic-handled clubs.

"Well," Gary muttered philosophically, "I guess it's you and me and the gods tonight, good buddy."

As we started down the access road that led up toward the main missile site, I growled morosely, "Odin help us if we run into trouble."

"Odin, huh?" Gary's ugly face broke into a lopsided grin. "The fledgling pagan speaks."

"You're a good one to talk about pagans, Vernon."

He laughed. "Yeah. Well . . ."

The little gold Thor's hammer I wore beneath my shirt moved on its chain as I shrugged. "I wish more of those old stories had survived. It's really great stuff. Whoring, drinking, fighting off the bad guys against all odds—our kind of guys."

"Kind of thought you might like that," he laughed.

I grinned; then we headed into the woodline and fell silent. It hadn't snowed yet. The iron-hard ground was littered with leaf debris, all of it tinder-dry. It was tough to move without making enough noise to wake the dead. Thanks to the full moon, ghostly white light fell in odd bright patches. The forest floor was a nightmare of shadows and light. Where moonlight cut across low-hanging branches, hard black lines ended abruptly in a tangle of silver limbs, confusing the eyes and distorting depth perception. Patches of shapeless grey where low-hanging pine boughs brushed the ground made it hard to see what was pine tree and what might be a foreign object under it.

With this lighting, we could run across anything from a wild boar to a Soviet Spetznaz platoon, and not even see it. Of course, realistically speaking, we'd probably either run into ragheads or nothing at all. I figured it was just a matter of time before one of the groups hit a nuke site. They didn't even need to carry off any warheads—

just blowing up a Pershing or three would generate the desired effect, and be much easier.

I could see the headlines now—U.S. NUCLEAR MISSILE EXPLODES. Ought to do wonders for our political and military presence in Europe. Not that any of the little incidents we'd had with terrorists over the past few months had made it into the press. They hadn't. Not one. And we soldier-types were expected to keep the world safe for democracy—without bullets? I shuddered. Stupid peacetime army . . .

One of these nights I was going to get backed into a tight enough jam to make a pact with Odin myself, and see where it got me. All I'd ever gotten from Jehovah was a great big, fat silence, leaving me to figure out ways to save my own rear end. That was the trouble with gods—

Gary froze.

Instinctively, I did, too.

He stood slightly ahead of me in a deep patch of shadow. I was near its edge, and had just been about to move out of it. I held my breath and scanned the moonlit woods, although I knew what I'd see even before I spotted them a heartbeat later.

And there they were.

I swallowed: half a dozen ragheads in black, hugging the shadows under the trees, their AKs held at ready.

And I'd almost stepped out into that bright little patch of moonlight, straight into their line of sight. . . .

We went to ground, flat on our bellies under rustling pine branches, and watched them slip through the deep gloom between the trees. They were headed away from the site, from the direction of Tower Three. A scouting party that meant trouble later? Or part of a team sent to eliminate the patrol?

—Us.

I clutched my empty M-16 in sweaty hands and

listened to Gary's breathing and the ragheads' careful footsteps. I was surprised they hadn't heard us. Of course, I hadn't heard them either, and I *knew* better than to spend patrol time woolgathering, dammit.

The ragheads stopped within spitting distance and began to whisper among themselves. It sounded to me like an argument. The evident leader said something really foul-sounding. The man who'd raised an objection backed down. Then, just as they were turning to go, a brittle, snapping sound loud as gunfire cracked through the darkness from almost next to my ear.

Sweat popped out all over my belly and thighs. The ragheads whirled and stared straight at us. Rifle barrels swung around into a deadly line aimed less than a foot above our backs.

I *willed* the bright moonlight to blind them. . . .

Another loud snap came from near my right ear. *What the hell was it?* I didn't dare look—didn't even dare breathe.

At a whispered command, the last terrorist in line started toward us, his features lost in the smear of camouflage lampblack rubbed into his skin. His rifle—it looked like a Rumanian copy of the Soviet AK-47— glinted in the cold moonlight. I watched the terrorist's boots walk straight toward my face. Saw him begin to stoop down to peer under our tree . . .

I swore solemnly that if I got out of this patrol alive, I'd blood a good steel knife and leave it under an oak tree for Odin.

It seemed to work for Gary.

Abruptly a small hedgehog, about the size of a well-grown box turtle, waddled out from beside me into the patch of moonlight. The terrorist stopped and grinned, teeth gleaming whitely for an instant. Then he raised his rifle and aimed for center of mass on the spiny little body. An angry hiss came from the trees. The would-be shooter snarled something in reply. The hedgehog reacted to the voices and snapped into a tightly curled ball, spines bristling.

Another whispered argument broke out. The leader strode over and grabbed his man by the arm. He gestured angrily toward the missile site, then off toward the little village about two klicks away through the forest. The subordinate shrugged and kicked viciously at the hedgehog. It squealed and curled up tighter than ever, skidding to a pathetic stop a few inches from our noses.

My knuckles went white gripping the useless rifle. If it'd been loaded, I wouldn't even have stopped to think about it. Hurting a hedgehog brought unthinkably bad luck. Not that *I* was overly superstitious—

The two terrorists rejoined their group, and the three of us—hedgehog, Gary, and I—lay frozen in place, waiting. If they searched the immediate vicinity for good measure . . . Fighting it out under halfway decent odds was one thing. Given three-to-one their favor, Gary probably would've charged in and let Odin sort it out. But getting shot to pieces because all you had was an empty tube with a flimsy plastic stock on one end was not my idea of a good time. Even a Berserker would've prayed they just turned around and walked away.

For once, something came out the way I wanted. The black-clad Palestinians—or whoever they were—disappeared into the darkness. Gary and I waited until the sound of their footsteps had died completely away; then I rested my forehead on my arm and started breathing again. I tried not to shiver too loudly in case the sound carried.

Then, noticing for the first time the wonderful, Christmasy smell of the pine tree, I squeezed Gary's arm in silent thanks. I nodded when he made a motion with his thumb. We crawled cautiously out from under the pine tree. The hedgehog still hadn't moved. Poor little guy . . .

Then, like a swimmer coming up from a long dive, I took a deep breath and let it out again silently.

Looked like I owed Odin a knife.

And Gary my life.

Chapter Three

I finally managed to get the sparker going. The carbide lit with a hissing pop. The cave was so quiet I could hear the silence listening to me, waiting for me to make a move. So I just sat still for a moment and let my eyes adjust to the grey light pouring from my helmet. There should've been a warm yellow glow; but the walls swallowed the color, leaving only an eerie, dead grey to light the low-ceilinged cavern. Even my skin looked grey. The only exception was that deep black hole beside me.

When I got a good look at it . . .

There was literally no way I could have avoided stepping into that hole.

It was a good four feet across, nearly round, and smack in the middle of the passage Bjornssen and I'd been following. If it had been there, I would either have seen it or fallen into it. No question. But a hole that size couldn't have opened up between us without either of us noticing—a cave-in is not a quiet phenomenon. If it was an illusion, it was a damned good one.

I leaned cautiously forward. The walls were absolutely perpendicular. No ledges, no bumps, no projections—it plunged straight down like an enormous sewer pipe farther than my light could penetrate into the blackness. I hadn't heard Bjornssen hit bottom. I sat back again, knowing that I had to stand up, move, do something; and wished intensely for a cigarette. I hadn't smoked anything in three years.

My lamp flickered; then flared bright again, and sent shadows rippling across the walls. Odd kind of rock in this part of the cave. Stranger yet, hadn't I just been thinking that when Bjornssen disappeared? My brows puckered and I chewed at my upper lip, moving my head to play the light across the opposite wall.

The surface was jagged, and unused to light. Even the shadows it cast were wrong. Nothing I could put my finger on, exactly . . .

I got to thinking about the marks Bjornssen had made with his surveyor's tape, and a feeling I didn't stop to analyze hauled me to my feet. I piled my gear in a heap and went back to verify the last marker, which my guide had made about ten feet the other side of the chimney.

Jumping over the gaping hole gave me a case of serious sweats—which was stupid. I was too smart—or too well trained, anyway—to let fear get the best of me like some half-brained Stone Age savage. So I worked harder at reminding myself that I was a modern, civilized, highly trained combat soldier on a very simple recon mission. Christ—it was only a ten-foot recon at that. In a totally empty cave. No problem.

After two full minutes of steady hiking, I still hadn't found it. I looked back the way I'd come, and absently scratched my elbow. Odd, I didn't think I'd walked that far from the spot where we'd spent the night. I went back to the chimney and started again, watching both walls this time and paying closer attention.

It still wasn't there.

Just when and where had Bjornssen made that last

mark? I knew he'd put a marker along the straight stretch here, and Bjornssen always plastered a bit of tape at *every* turn. I'd watched the "mark-the-trail ritual" too many times to doubt that. We'd come through a whole series of turns and side tunnels fifty feet back, or so. I'd miscalculated, was all.

I started from the chimney again. Sixty-five feet of carefully measured steps later, I stopped. Nothing. Not a trace of where we'd spent the "night." Not even a hint of old adhesive on the walls. And while I never actually saw them change, the shadows looked different every time I glanced away and back.

Worse, the side tunnels were missing. As far as I could see, ahead and behind, there was nothing but unbroken grey rock wall.

At one hundred twenty feet I stopped again, breathing hard. My shirt was soaked and sweat trickled down my skivvies (I hoped it was sweat) to run past my knees and into the tops of my socks. It tickled like blazes—and I was too worried to scratch.

Those tunnels couldn't be gone. They *couldn't*. But they were. Suddenly I wondered what else might disappear—

Goddamned one-eyed son-of-a-bitch!

I broke and ran like hell for my pack, leaping the chimney like a running longjumper. My gear was still piled where I'd left it, complete with food, canteens, carbide—and the Armalite AR-180 assault rifle strapped across it. . . .

I slid down against the wall, barely feeling the needle-sharp projections that scraped my back, and sat swearing at the wall opposite me. Odin was playing games again.

I scrubbed my eyes with the heels of my hands and tugged on my hair for a moment, and wondered with a nagging sense of futility what would have happened if I *hadn't* kept my half of that misbegotten bargain with

Odin? Surely it couldn't have been much worse than what *had* happened. I laughed aloud, and shuddered at the same time.

It was far too late, of course, but I couldn't help wishing I'd kept the knife and said the hell with Odin and every other god ever invented. What a waste of a perfectly good blade . . . and a pile of money, not to mention my time, and Gary's.

I even found myself wishing for Frau Brunner's company. Odin himself would've thought twice about crossing *her*.

Frau Brunner—a shrewd old woman who had survived everything from the Allied Blitz to navigating landmines at the East German border—was known throughout town as a shark.

Her standard sales-floor expression was a scowl that routinely cowed GIs, tourists, and rabid dogs. By the time I'd bargained my way to a final sale on the Mauser K-98-k bayonet I'd chosen, I was sweating into my uniform, and was convinced that Frau Brunner was a throwback to the original Viking traders she was descended from. She might have been closer to eighty than seventy, and was homely as a bald crow—but the lady was *sharp*.

Which made the compliment Gary paid me when we walked out the door even sweeter.

"Pretty good, RB." He grinned. "Most of the officers on base warn guys away from her; but you got a good price on that. Nice blade, too." Then his grin turned nasty. "Too bad you can't bargain like that when it really counts. If you could talk like that to the brass, you wouldn't get yourself in half the jams you end up in. And you might just get yourself *out* of the other half."

I grunted and didn't deign to respond.

He chuckled. "Cat's got your tongue, eh? Well, you

did a good job, anyway. Sometimes Frau Brunner reminds me a little of my grandma. She used to make me bargain for cookies when I was a kid. Nobody ever got anything over on her. You'd love her."

"I'd like to meet her," I said, thinking about the lonely old woman who'd cried over the letter Gary'd shown me. "Think you could talk her into visiting you over here?"

Gary shrugged. "Don't know. She's kind of funny about traveling. Says the men in the family have done enough traveling for several lifetimes. She's got a point, I guess, considering the odd corners of the world we've been sent to fight in. Grandpa, Dad, and now me. She never figured on a bunch of ragheads shooting at me over here. Poor Grandma." Gary shook his head; then got an evil glint in his eye. "One of these fine nights, you know, those bastards are going to overrun the site, and leave brass holding a bunch of bodies in the bag. Ought to be some fight, huh?"

I regarded Vernon with a jaundiced eye. Gary—and his dad, and his granddad—had been raised with this pagan thing about fighting for glory because that's what life was for. Both his father and grandfather had been decorated in their respective generations' wars before they died together, pointlessly, in a car wreck. I guess Gary was just intent on continuing the family tradition.

I admired Gary's heroic attitude; but it was going to get him killed, and then where would he be? Pact with Odin notwithstanding, sometimes Vernon had carried this Viking stuff a little too far. You did a whole lot more damage to the enemy if you shot twenty or so with a sniper than if you took out half a dozen in a suicide dash—and you generally didn't lose the sniper, either. Patton had had the right of it as far as I was concerned— make the other poor, dumb son-of-a-bitch die for his country.

"You know, Gary," I said as we headed for the railway

station, "I figured out why there aren't any more Berserkers. They killed themselves off before they could reproduce. What was it Niven and Pournelle said? 'Evolution in action'?"

He gave me an enigmatic look from under his eyebrows. "Never thought of it quite that way," he said quietly. "Maybe that's why Grandma asked me to quit Special Forces." His voice trailed off quietly and I winced; I hadn't meant to rake up bad memories. He'd once admitted—somewhat shamefacedly—that he couldn't say no to anything his grandmother asked, because he was all the old lady had left to live for.

Our train ride was short, and soon we were back at the little village near the missile site, headed into the surrounding forest. Within minutes, streets and houses were out of sight. It was hard to believe, sometimes, that you couldn't get farther than a couple of kilometers from civilization anywhere in Germany. The forests were so dark and forbidding, you could almost convince yourself you were living a thousand years in the past—then a group of school kids would come trooping by, waving and shouting and playing radios or something. . . .

"Uh, Gary?" I was careful to keep my voice low-pitched. That wasn't reverence for the forest; just ingrained caution and leftover paranoia. One couldn't always count on hedgehogs. I hadn't told Gary any details about my oath, and hadn't planned to—but the towering silence of the trees left me looking over my shoulder for . . . something. I didn't know quite what. Abruptly I wanted to share my thoughts.

"Yeah?" He glanced back.

"Anything strike you as, well, strange about that hedgehog the other night?"

Gary turned to look at me over his shoulder. "Like what?"

"Like why it didn't just roll up into a ball under the

pine tree? It was close enough to me, it must've heard my heart beating, never mind smelled me, and you know how shy they are about people."

"You weren't moving, Randy."

"No, but . . ."

Gary glanced back again, one brow cocked quizzically.

"Okay, I'd barely taken that oath when out he strolls, maybe saving our collective bacon."

He stopped walking. "So you wonder if Odin heard you?"

I grimaced, falling silent again, and Gary nodded silently, as if to himself. We kept walking. It was stupid, and I was probably just as superstitious as Brunowski—who at least was honest enough to admit it—but I couldn't help wondering, at least a little. Kind of nifty to think of a genuine god answering my oath . . . but then again, maybe not. What might a god consider a "marker"? And what would a god do if he called it in and I couldn't pay?

Well-l-l, either way it couldn't hurt to just cover my bets—which was, after all, the reason I was out here, and not sleeping late. At least Gary hadn't laughed at me.

A few minutes later he found the spot we'd been looking for, an enormous oak tree that looked old and twisted enough to have seen the Germanic tribes sweep the Romans before them on their drive south. Well, maybe not that old—but it might have been old enough actually to have had sacrifices made to Odin in it. How long did an oak tree live?

Gooseflesh crawled along my back. I shook myself mentally and hastily removed the bayonet from its wrappings and steel sheath. I shucked off my heavy jacket and handed it to Gary, and shivered in the cold air as I rolled up my sleeve. Holding out my arm, I firmly took hold of the bayonet's grip and drew the edge of the blade lightly along the inside of my forearm.

I suppressed a gasp as the cold steel opened my skin. As blood dripped down my wrist and fingers to puddle on the frozen ground, I said, "May it please the one-eyed god, the Valfather who sits in Hlidskjalf, where he sees and understands all: this offering of a new-blooded steel blade is given in fulfillment of my own oath given in promise of blood."

I'd memorized the words in German, having looked up some of them to be sure. After I finished speaking them, I knelt at the base of the tree and drove the blade up to its grip into the hard ground. I rose then, and found Gary standing behind me. Weak winter sunlight turned his sandy hair to gold, while I shivered in shadows under the gnarled old tree. His eyes had a faraway look. I wondered what he was thinking. Or dreaming . . .

I wasn't sure why, but the moment reminded me of Hohenfels, when we'd been out one damp and shivery late autumn day, on a week-long field problem. Gary and I had been ordered to secure an observation post on one of the hills, so we dug in—and discovered it wasn't a hill at all. Under the moss and leaves and gnarled tree roots there were crumbled blocks of stone.

"Holy Mother of Odin," Gary had whispered into the silence. "It's a burial mound, RB."

"I didn't think they were found this far south."

"They aren't."

I don't know why we whispered; but we did.

The sun was so low and the mist so thick we nearly missed the hole broken into one side. Right outside that hole, almost as though someone had planted it there when those stones were still raw from the cut earth, stood the blackened skeleton of a huge oak tree. A stray breeze opened a rent in the mist and the dying sun bathed the mound in light the color of blood; a cold, bitter draft eddied from the hole.

"Jesus, what's that smell?"

Gary hadn't heard. He took three steps toward the gaping hole and stopped. Only the luminous dial on his watch, flashing in the gloom, reminded me this was the twentieth century.

"They used to perform sacrifices on trees like that," Gary murmured. "They'd take a warrior and strangle him and spear him in the heart while he choked to death. Then they'd hang him in an oak tree for Odin, who would send a valkyrie, or maybe his stallion, Sleipnir, to fetch the sacrifice to Valhalla."

Gary stared at the tree; then gazed off into the mist, where disturbing shapes loomed indistinctly and tricked the eyes. "You can almost see Sleipnir coming—"

"Shut up, will you?" I spoke louder than I'd intended. Gary started and swung to face me; then grinned. "Sorry. It gets to you sometimes, you know?"

I knew. But we had to sleep on the cursed mound.

For a moment he looked as sheepish as I felt; then we grabbed our shovels, and got busy with the army's observation post.

I'd forgotten all about that day; until now. Gary looked really eerie, with that golden light touching his face, and a stark shadow from the naked oak branch over my head cutting across him. I shivered without quite knowing why, and wondered if burying that knife had been such a good idea after all. Blood still dripped down my arm, warm and sticky.

"Gary, you got that lousy bandage?"

He blinked a couple of times; then walked over and bent to look. "Good cut, Randy. Not too deep. Yeah, it's right here." He pulled out the gauze and wrapped my arm securely, stemming the flow. I wiped my blood-stained fingers on an extra cloth I'd brought along and rolled my sleeve down and buttoned the cuff; then put my coat back on, feeling a little foolish.

Now that the ceremony was over and I'd fulfilled my half of the bargain, I found I couldn't get away from that tree fast enough, and led the way until we were out of sight of it. I slowed down, then, hands thrust deep in my pockets, and worked at ignoring the slight burning in my left arm. Gary walked beside me, uncharacteristically silent.

I spoke without looking directly at him. "You think I'm crazy?"

He shook his head; but the corners of his mouth twitched.

"Nope. Sacrificing to Odin is pretty sane behavior for you, Randy."

Sometimes I really hated the fact that Gary could outrun me.

I finally gave up the chase, and with my remaining breath, yelled, "If you'll stop running, I'll let you live. . . !"

He stopped—grinning—and waited for me.

"You know," I mused, once I got my breath back, "those old Vikings, they weren't far wrong, I guess. Good friends, good sex, good fights, plenty of gold—hell, at least they had something to believe in."

Unexpectedly irritated, I kicked at a dead branch and sent it scooting off through the dead leaves. "Some nights on those towers I'd give a lot to have something I could really believe in."

Gary nodded. "Yeah. I guess what I hate worst is the idea of dying for nothing. I don't know, Randy. I guess if I were to die, I'd want to go the way they did. Take off for Valhalla in a blaze of glory; then more good friends, more good sex, more fighting and gold, right up to the end of everything." He laughed. "Who knows? You game to find out with me?"

I blinked. Sometimes Gary overdid things. "Be serious, man. We got plans for tonight."

He laughed. "And you're buying, right?"

"You bet. So let's get back to town. I'm freezing my ass off out here." The undefinable feeling I'd had since the moment that hedgehog had strolled out into the open had finally evaporated.

Well, almost.

As we'd headed toward town, I hadn't quite been able to suppress the urge to glance over my shoulder. . . .

Months later, I was still glancing over my shoulder, in a cave that Somebody was rearranging like a con man's shell game. I dropped my hands against my thighs and deliberately uncurled my fingers. Brooding on the past wasn't going to get me out of this fix. I had to figure out what to do next, and I had to make the right decision on the first try. Odin probably wouldn't give me the luxury of a second chance.

It was pretty obvious that I couldn't go back, even if I'd wanted to—which I didn't. What wasn't at all obvious was *why* I couldn't go back. If Odin had simply wanted to get rid of me, it would have been far easier just to drop me quietly down that hole. Bjornssen certainly wouldn't have wasted any time making tracks out of here to live off my money if I'd died. Not only would I have been out of his hair, there would have been no one left alive with any reason to discover the truth behind the legends about Garm's Cave.

Odin was just toying with me. Or maybe he had something even nastier planned. Ugh. Something worse than pulling the earth out from under my feet? I glanced down at my pack and grimaced. If I didn't move very, very carefully, I was a dead man.

Or worse . . .

I snorted and listened to the sound disappear, swallowed up by the blackness. Since "back" was out of the question, my two main options appeared to be "forward" and "down"—down the hole after Bjornssen, that is.

Right. Odin would love that.

Some options.

Maybe, in the final analysis, that was why Odin had killed Bjornssen. This way he knew exactly where I was, stumbling around blind in his territory, not mine. The idea that a god might consider me too dangerous to leave running around loose didn't exactly comfort me; but it did kind of stroke the ego. . . .

Frankly, I could do without that kind of ego-boo.

I considered my supplies. I had food (some), water (less), carbide (not nearly enough), and cyalume chemical lightsticks (mostly half-hour shorties). Bjornssen had been packing most of the carbide and a good portion of our food—which did me no good at all—so I gritted my teeth and stopped wasting time wishing I had his gear. I also didn't have time to waste backtracking for water, since I wasn't at all certain it would be there anymore.

I had plenty of ammunition in my pack—but on further reflection I remembered you can't fuel a carbide lamp with smokeless powder. Besides, what would I do afterward with all those iron-jacketed pistol bullets? Eat them? The idea of starving did nothing to lighten my mood—and if I didn't find Niflheim soon, I quite likely *would* starve to death.

What was it the sergeants were always telling us—prior planning prevents piss-poor performance? I laughed aloud and began stowing my ammo again. The way things were looking, I should've packed in a whole lot more food, and a whole lot less "insurance." I was going to be an awfully embarrassed ghost if I showed up as an emaciated corpse in Hel's death hall while lugging around enough hardware to storm Grenada . . . again.

I shook my head and finished stowing my arsenal. Poor Klaus . . . He really hadn't been able to figure out why I'd brought all this stuff along. His *first* question to me, back in the world of sunlight and wind and rain, had been why I wanted to pick the most dangerous, least explored cave in northern Europe and explore it as far as I could get, when the only time I'd spent in any cave was the night I'd bivouacked in a genuine prehistoric site in the Neanderthal Valley while on military maneuvers.

Being me, naturally I'd said, "That's a very good question," and then had proceeded to lie for all I was worth—while plopping hundred-dollar bills down in front of him. Fortunately he had run out of questions before I ran out of money. His *second* question had been why in God's name (his God's name, anyway) I wanted to carry a bunch of guns on a spelunking trip. My answer— more hundred-dollar bills—hadn't satisfied him until his stack was a whole lot taller than mine.

I just hadn't seen any sense in trying to explain that facing down Niflheim's permanent residents was probably going to call for all the firepower I could lug with me. So call me paranoid. Apparitions like Sleipnir aren't that easy to explain. Or believe, for that matter. Quite probably I was the only person left alive in the world who *did* believe.

I hadn't packed that AR-180 assault rifle for target practice.

But I didn't tell Klaus that. I just said I had no intention of dying slowly at the bottom of some cliff, if I happened to fall and shatter half my bones, then laid down more money until he shut up and agreed. It'd cost me nearly my whole severance pay, but he'd bought it. I glanced at the bottomless chimney. He'd bought it, all right.

I unholstered my P-7 pistol, and balanced it across my palm. Its lines were sleek, deadly. So was Gary's sheath knife, strapped to my calf. What if I were fooling myself? Even if Niflheim were as real as the gun in my hand— and I'd seen the proof of that—what if a living man couldn't get there? All the myths and sagas were pretty consistent on one point. The gods did the choosing, not men. It was more than possible I'd just wander around down here until I died, without ever seeing anything more interesting than grey rock walls.

I reholstered the P-7.

It didn't matter.

Odin was breaking the rules ten ways from Sunday— I'd seen the goddamned proof of that, too. And if he could cheat the Norns, then I could get to Niflheim. Without dying. I hadn't doubted it before, when there was still a chance to back out, and I wasn't about to doubt it now.

I looked down the long stretch of bland grey tunnel, and listened as the silence echoed in my ears. The cave twisted into the bowel of the mountain like a wormhole burrowed into the core of a rotten apple. Feeling some sympathy with a cockroach about to be squashed, I shouldered my gear, stuck an emergency cyalume stick in my shirt pocket, and started down the jagged slope.

Chapter Four

Ever notice how assholes just have to show off, even when they know better? I haven't yet met an exception to that rule—and I figure I know myself as well as I'm going to by now.

Most of the time, nothing serious happens when some idiot shows his true colors. People nearby mutter, "What an asshole" and that's an end to it. (Of course, kids kill themselves all the time pulling stupid stunts like falling off hotel balconies while they're drunk, and driving off bridges at a hundred miles per hour, and doing enough crack cocaine to give the entire Rams front line a buzz. Dumb schmucks.)

But for those of us who survive puberty, being an asshole is generally limited to minor idiocies like proving that your dick won't fit through a toilet-paper tube, or ordering the meal in French just to prove to her that you can pronounce it (whether you can or not). If we all stayed as stupid as we are when we're young, the species wouldn't continue breeding very long. Despite the reputation most infantrymen get, I know perfectly well that women are one hell of a lot smarter than men. (I can

30

prove it—act like you did when you were seventeen, and see how many second dates you get.)

Unfortunately, showing off—adult asshole style—generally means that the damned fool involved is getting careless.

And when men get careless, the gods take advantage.

After nearly three years on Pershing duty, I *knew* better than to show off in front of an L-T. But some things are like trying not to scratch an itch. And besides, it was something I was really good at; and inordinately proud of; and who would have figured that something so innocent would prove to be the catalyst that led to my hiking solo through the middle of a Norwegian mountain, looking for a god, just so I could strangle him with my bare hands?

What hurt worst was the fact that damned near everything which had happened had been avoidable; but I'd never been one to avoid anything I could go out of my way to step into. (Witness my presence in this cave. . . .)

It had begun, innocently enough, when Sergeant Pritchard stomped into the barracks mess room. He stamped his feet, shook snow off his clothes, and began to unpeel.

"Gentlemen," he nodded, carefully avoiding looking at us.

It occurred to me that he looked uncomfortable, and not because of the weather. I'd been in the Army long enough to know that a sergeant with a problem is like the common cold—he doesn't get over it; he gives it to somebody else. And there was nobody here but us. . . .

Pritchard snagged a coffee mug and poured himself a cup. He sighed and drank again, letting the brew warm him up slowly.

"What's up?" Wally asked suspiciously. Bright boy, Wallenstein . . .

Pritchard cleared his throat self-consciously. "You gentlemen are scheduled for qualifying next week."

"Boom, rat-tat-tat!"

"Hot damn, we get to shoot next week!"

"Brrrup, brrupp-upp!"

Maybe I was just more paranoid than the rest of the guys, but instead of contributing to the general nonsense, I found myself waiting for the other shoe. Pritchard waited for the silly-season furor to die down before continuing.

"I don't have to tell you the political situation we've got here. Brass doesn't want any incidents with unqualified troopies, so we'll have one hundred percent qualification from this outfit—and I mean *no* exceptions. I don't care how long it takes some of you to do it."

Without exception, we glanced at Butler's half-closed eyes. He was struggling to stay awake, at least while the sergeant was in the room.

"We pull out at oh-nine-hundred Monday, after your shift, so be ready. Well, snowbunnies, carry on. I'll be expecting a good qualification round from all of you."

He pulled on his snow gear again and disappeared back into the blizzard. Probably had a warm truck waiting for him down at the gate.

He was no sooner gone than the discussion broke out.

"What'll we do about Butler?" Crater wanted to know.

"Get him off the damn Quaaludes for starters," Chuck replied.

"We'll have to nursemaid him, all right," Gary said. "I hate to admit it, but brass does have a point. We've got to be sure all of us qualify. With the number of incidents up, we've *got* to have guard personnel on the towers who can use their weapons."

"Damn straight," I nodded. "And anyone who can't qualify should have his ass kicked right out of security clearance and back into rock-painting duty, or wherever it is they find some of these losers."

I noticed that Gary was carefully avoiding my eye, and I knew what was coming.

"You know we're too short-shifted to do that," he said quietly.

"Dammit, Vernon! It's our lives on the line out there. If a guy can't cut it after a fair chance to qualify, he doesn't need to be out there bumbling around in the dark. And you know blessed well those qualifications are so simple a chimpanzee could do them."

"That's not fair, and you know it." Gary's tone was calm, assured. Sometimes that knack of his, never losing his temper in an argument, really drove me crazy. "If a guy comes from the city, never has a chance to practice, maybe never even sees a rifle, how is he going to compete with those of us who grew up with them? We need all the qualified personnel we can get, and if a man can't qualify right away, he ought to have another chance—because we might need him to give us a chance out there."

He pointed into the blizzard outside. I glared at him. It was an old argument, one of the rare points we didn't agree on. He was all for fixing the screw-ups, while I felt screw-ups shouldn't be allowed to happen in the first place. For me, it was perfection or nothing, because anything less could make you very dead when the brown stuff hit the fan blades. We weren't going to solve this today—and from the unease on everyone else's faces, our argument wasn't helping already bad morale.

"Good of the unit, huh?" I said finally. "You know what I think, and I know what you think, so we'll just let it go at that, okay, Vernon?"

He relaxed and nodded, and I felt relief sweep through the rest of the room. It made me very uneasy to realize that Gary Vernon and I were holding the morale of A-Shift together practically by ourselves. The situation could get worse real fast if our next patrol together wasn't quite as lucky as the other night's had been.

Monday's qualifications were held on one of the German Army's "million-mark" rifle ranges, which they rented out to the Americans on an as-needed basis. Snow covered the ground under a weak winter sun. At least the high protective dirt berms kept the worst of the wind off us. We had to shoot a combination course of bull's-eye targets at one hundred meters, and pop-up targets at two and three hundred meters. What made the morning's shoot interesting was that we had ridden two hours in deuce-and-a-halves to get here, directly after coming off of twenty-four hours of guard. Most of us hadn't had more than about four hours of sleep. I'd have been surprised if guys like Butler could even have *seen* the targets, never mind hit them.

"Man, this snow is a real pain," Crater complained, lying prone in the freezing stuff.

"Just shoot, Private." Lieutenant Donaldson frowned.

I got a good sight picture on my first target and was just beginning to squeeze the trigger when I heard the L-T's voice above me: "Your head's too far back, Barnes. Get it down there where it belongs; see all you can through that rear sight aperture."

"But, sir, I always shoot like this."

"The Virginia Military Institute taught me how to fire a rifle, Private. I'm not interested in how you shoot; I'm interested in seeing you shoot correctly."

I cast a pained look up at Donaldson. "Sir, I've made Expert every time during the last two years." Briefly I debated adding that I had just placed in the top five in the German National Match competition but decided against it. An enlisted man can only get away with being right when doing so doesn't prove an officer wrong.

Fortunately at this point Sergeant Brown approached.

Closing in on retirement, he was our platoon sergeant. Like most good noncoms, he was more interested in results than gold braid, and he knew my score at the Nationals.

"Lieutenant . . ." It's always heartwarming to watch a professional in action; Brown sounded genuinely respectful ". . . Private Barnes is the best shot in the platoon. Hell, half the time he's the best shot in the company. Tell you what, L-T, if anybody in this bunch outshoots him, you can teach him to your heart's content. Otherwise, please let the man do his job."

Donaldson's lips thinned. "Okay, Sergeant, I'll do just that. But if he shoots less than an eighty-five on these bull's-eyes, for the next month you and he will have an opportunity to explore a theory of mine that suggests that the amount of time spent pulling grounds maintenance is directly proportional to a man's level of small-arms proficiency."

From somewhere down the line I thought I heard the beginnings of a snicker, muffled instantly.

"Yes, sir," replied the sergeant, sounding more confident than I felt. (I wasn't looking forward to a month of shoveling snow and rearranging rocks any more than he was—but the potential consequences of having caused it for him thrilled me even less.)

Now, shooting accurately with somebody standing behind you slapping his own leg with a cleaning rod as if it were a riding crop isn't as easy as it sounds; but I managed to get off all ten shots well before the time limit.

It didn't take any longer than usual for the range phone to ring, I'm sure.

However.

I did have to suppress a start when it rang, and remind myself to look disinterested as the scores were read. Simpkins, down on Lane One, had his usual sixty-something, and Crater barely beat him out.

Then the sergeant turned to me. In bored tones, he said, "Barnes, you're letting your group drift a little into the nine ring, low at six o'clock. You only scored ninety-seven. I don't know what's wrong with you today."

I grinned nonchalantly. "Must be the cold, Sergeant." —and belatedly resumed breathing.

After all the scores had been read off, the lieutenant said, "Very well, Sergeant, I'll talk to both of you later about this."

He favored me with a level stare. "Be glad we didn't conduct this exercise with those damned forty-fives."

"What do you mean, sir?" I asked. (I never knew when to keep my mouth shut.)

"Well, everybody knows how inaccurate these forty-year-old pistols are."

"Oh. Uh, right." And barely remembered to add, "Sir." It never fails to amaze me how many otherwise knowledgeable people have bought that particular myth. The forty-five automatic is one of the finest combat pistols ever made.

The sergeant caught my eye. "Say, Lieutenant," he interjected, his face a mask of deadpan sincerity, "are you a bettin' man?" I didn't know what he was up to; but sometimes even I know when not to jostle somebody's elbow.

The lieutenant looked puzzled for a moment. "I only bet on sure things, Sergeant."

"Well, would you be willing to bet me twenty dollars that Barnes can't knock down three out of five of the pop-up targets from here with your forty-five?" Suddenly I understood. Quickly, though not without effort, I affected what I hoped would pass for a worried expression.

"Sergeant," drawled the L-T, "I don't as a rule steal money from subordinates; but I will pick it up when I find it thrown away."

He pulled out his forty-five, shucked the top two rounds out of the magazine, turned to me, and said, "You know how to work one of these things, boy?"

"I think so, sir." I took it from him with both hands and turned it over and around like a chimpanzee inspecting a new toy. I didn't quite stare down the muzzle; I thought that might be overdoing it.

I glanced up at the lieutenant. "Uh, sir, could I get Gary Vernon to spot for me?"

By this time Lieutenant Donaldson was visibly having trouble restraining a smile. "Sure, why not. Sergeant, have 'em stand up a target on this lane and set it for automatic reset." (Who says the gods don't have a sense of humor . . . ?)

I took up my stance. Rather than the wimpy one-handed pistol stance shown in "the book," I use the solid two-handed "Weaver stance." The first round thumped into the backstop one hundred meters away, a little high, I knew, because I saw the dirt fly.

Gary called out, "Looks like it was just over the shoulder on the left."

So I dropped the sights to the lower right-hand corner of the target and squeezed again, and this time when the pistol came down from recoiling the target was falling. Three seconds later the target had reset; in another three, it was down again.

While waiting for the target to reset for the fourth shot, it occurred to me that I had a golden opportunity to correct not only the lieutenant's misapprehension; but potentially even to send a message concerning common-sense methods back up the chain of command.

Twenty dollars isn't much of a lesson. . . .

Carefully I planted the fourth shot in the backstop to one side of the target; then pushed the safety up and lowered the pistol. Glancing over my shoulder, I said,

"Sergeant, you *are* splitting that twenty dollars with me, aren't you?"

The sergeant's smile reminded me of a TV minister reviewing his ratings. "Long as you share it with the boys."

"Lieutenant, sir, how much is it worth to *you* for me to miss this next one?"

Donaldson snorted. "Soldier, I hardly think two hits out of four are reason to gloat."

"Double or nothing, sir?" Richard Nixon would have been proud to claim the look of wide-eyed innocence I achieved at that moment.

"You're on!"

I let my face relax into a grin. I slipped off the safety, took careful aim, and pulled the trigger.

While watching the lieutenant dig out his money, I noticed that Crater was handing a few bills to Simpkins. "You asshole," I blurted indignantly, "you bet against me!"

He grinned. "No, you sorry shit. I bet you'd hit four."

The lieutenant watched the sergeant hand me a twenty. He looked around thoughtfully; then said, "You know, back at Virginia Military Institute, Captain Proctor was fond of saying that hard experience had taught him that the book didn't have all the answers. He regularly advised us to keep our eyes open in the field. Maybe this is what he meant. I guess a second lieutenant *can* learn from his platoon sergeant. And an occasional private."

Brown's eyes twinkled as he said, "Good thinking, sir."

The lieutenant was actually grinning as he walked off.

Unfortunately, I didn't have long to gloat. A day and a half later, Sergeant Brown walked in on us as we packed our gear to head out. Wally had been telling Crater that he was flying his wife, Annie, over for the holidays, and Gary and I had been making our final plans to go on the

annual tour of the HK firearms factory over in Obern-
dorf am Neckar next weekend, something we'd been
planning for at least ten weeks.

When Brown shut the door and didn't say anything at
all, I got an itch between my shoulder blades that
wouldn't go away. Something about his expression made
it worse.

Crater missed it. "So, how did Second Relief do on
the range yesterday?" he asked breezily.

"Not bad. We got back early, too—we didn't let them
use the 'French PX' after you guys and Sergeant Pritchard
bought that case of French wine yesterday. By the
way"—his mood lightened momentarily—"how was it?"

"Most likely just like the bottle we left in your room,
Sergeant, sir," Crater said innocently.

"Oh. —Oh! That's where that came from. Thanks."
Brown's flinch was visible this time; the news must be
really bad. "The lieutenant didn't think Captain Jones
would appreciate it if he let you guys keep buying black-
market booze from the back of a deuce-and-a-half."

Then he turned to me. I could see in his eyes that he
was about to drop a shoe—first or second didn't matter;
I knew I wasn't going to like it. Diffidently he said, "Say,
Barnes, didn't you spend some of your time off this past
week teaching Johnson how to shoot?"

Uh-oh. "Yeah, Johnson and all those other no-gos on
that relief. Why?" (Never *ever* show off in front of second lieutenants: they'll either bust your ass—or put you
to work. Donaldson was the latter type. I'd spent hours
out in that freezing snow drilling those idiots, showing
them how to hold their weapons properly, how to read
their sight pictures accurately, how not to jerk on the
trigger or take a deep breath for luck just as you're
squeezing the shot off. . . .)

Brown grimaced. "Well, all the others did okay; but
Johnson didn't even qualify."

"That's no surprise," Wally groused. "He doesn't qualify to be a human being."

"Well, damn." So that's what had been dripping off the fan blades. "I knew he wasn't paying attention; but I've never had *any*body not qualify." To the astonishment of nearly everyone, I'd even managed to nurse Butler through his qualification.

"Well, you have now," Brown said. "Fortunately, one of the other platoons in training has the range today and the L-T wants you to take Johnson over right now and get him qualified."

Now? As in *right* now?

Great . . .

I truly loved this guy—I hadn't had any real time off in a week, and now I got to play wet nurse. I sighed. "So who's coming off our shift to take Johnson's place on the other relief?"

Johnson's relief worked opposite us on the missile site; when we were on site, they were either off duty or pulling patrols, and vice versa. We rarely saw the guys on the other relief (except when we changed reliefs), unless someone changed shifts and they shuffled people around.

Brown wouldn't meet my eyes. I knew then that my suspicion had been right on the money. Another shoe *was* falling and it had my name on it.

"Well-l-l," Brown drawled, gaze glued to the ceiling, "we don't really have anybody on slack. Peters fell and sprained his knee on the ice yesterday, and the L-T let Wilson go in this morning 'cause his wife's having a baby, and Whitney has pneumonia. One of you guys is going to have to pull forty-eight hours straight and be on the other relief for a while."

"I wouldn't take his place if his life depended on it!" Wally exploded.

Fuck. I hate it when the handwriting on the wall conflicts with my plans. I avoided looking at Gary. I was already seeing red, and he hadn't even said it yet. Good of the unit . . .

"I'll do it," he said. Just as I knew he was going to.

Wally and Crater made outraged sounds: "Hey, man, you can't—" "Sheeiit, Vernon, what're you doin'; you crazy all of a sudden?"

I lunged to my feet. "Damn you to hell, Vernon! You know goddamn well if you switch with that little prick-head, the HK tour is screwed—"

Gary met my eyes squarely. "Randy, hang on to your temper a minute—"

"Fuck you very much, Vernon."

I turned without another word and left with my gear slung across my back, not even stomping or hurrying. When I got to the door, I slammed it open and stalked out into the cold.

Dammit! It was about time Vernon let somebody else take the shit for a change. *Screw* morale . . . along with everything else about the goddamned Army. . . .

As I stormed toward the waiting jeep—where Johnson already huddled, looking less miserable than he was going to by the time I got through with his ass—I wondered if I'd get any sleep on the drive over.

Johnson grinned at me and said, "Hey, man, you know how it is . . ." with that stupid look of his pasted all over his bony face.

I wanted to shoot him.

Instead, I drove out to the goddamned range with him, and got the misbegotten little shirker qualified. By the time we finished, Johnson wasn't smiling anymore. Hell, by the time I finished with him, I wasn't sure Archibald Johnson would ever smile again, and didn't give a bald rat's ass one way or the other. It didn't help my temper any to realize that while Gary Vernon's pact with Odin had brought him nothing but good luck, mine seemed to have brought nothing but bad.

Chapter Five

My footsteps rattled around the cavern like angry wasps inside a falling nest. Whoever said to beware asking the gods for gifts knew what they were talking about. (Which made me wonder how many other mortals had been royally screwed down the ages.)

I hadn't asked for much; just something to believe in on those endless nights in the missile site's guard towers, where hours and hours of deadly boredom alternated with occasional moments of lethal peril. Just something to believe in, for those excruciating seconds when all hell would break loose, and a man didn't know which direction death might come from next.

Well, I'd gotten exactly what I'd asked for. Odin had let me have it, both barrels.

And in all the chaos, I hadn't apologized to Gary.

He'd only done exactly the kind of thing I'd always admired most about him. Given his silver tongue, I should have realized he could talk his way back onto our shift again before the scheduled HK factory tour. I certainly should have realized that morale really *was* that important. Soldiers who don't give a damn anymore make mistakes that get people killed. Both of us had ended up mad enough at each other—and at the system in general—to be just that little bit less cautious than normal. When the gods are watching, that's all it takes.

I should have apologized.

Archibald Johnson took Gary's place on Tower Five. I hadn't said much. The guys understood, and let me stew in silence. As though echoing my mood, ice formed on the tower's windows—from the inside—and blocked my view. Double chain-link fences and a treeless perimeter were all I had to look at for the next few wretched hours, but they beat looking at Archie Johnson.

I rubbed the windows with a scrap of dirty toweling, and muttered obscenities at the heater. I couldn't really fault it. Whoever had ordered it, back Stateside, they hadn't taken into account the plywood-and-glass box on stilts where it was going to be used. The idiot obviously hadn't figured on German winters, either. The heater was doing its best, faced with impossible demands.

I winced. I'd made some pretty impossible demands of my own, then ended by telling my best friend to go to hell.

I was not proud of myself.

So I scrubbed the windows and scowled out at the perimeter, with a black sky and black thoughts and glittering ice for company, and wondered how to apologize. My breath froze into little slivers of ice on contact with the glass. Tomorrow morning—first thing—I would put on my best hangdog expression and go find him.

Earlier, Wally had said that Gary was going into town tonight with some of the guys: Hill and Rosetti and a couple of others I didn't know very well. Wally had also said he'd looked mad as a two-dollar whore stiffed by a fifty-cent john. Which hadn't sounded at all like Gary Vernon, and made me feel even lower and slimier than I already did. A night off ought to leave him in a better mood, anyway; maybe good enough to accept an apology from a first-class asshole.

I sighed, and used my sleeve to wipe away ice crystals. Deep shadows lurked beneath the trees out beyond the perimeter. They hid secrets from the stars. Too quiet out there. Some nights silence was a relief; but others . . . Nights like *those* a man was glad when the sun came up to find him still breathing.

I decided to listen in on the phone, just to hear human voices. Chuck had just delivered the punchline of a joke. I winced, and wondered what had led up to "—so she sucked his apples!" Laughter erupted over the line.

When the chortling died down, the platoon's Clark Kent finally decided to include me in the conversation. "Say, Barnes," Wally asked, "what are you planning to do after you leave us behind? You're getting pretty short, now, aren't you?"

"Me?" I forced a rusty-sounding laugh. "Anything but re-up." For some reason, that earned laughter.

"What, you're not tired of the Army life, are you?" Crater snickered. "How about Vernon? He's due to re-up or *didi* out pretty soon, too, isn't he? Do you know what his plans are?"

I sighed. "Yeah. He's going to give college a try, go ROTC, and come back to haunt you bums as a butter bar."

"ROTC?"

"A second lieutenant?"

Chuck's response was even more eloquent: "An effin' *officer. . . ?"

"Sure. First a grunt, then a Special Forces officer, then a state rep, then a congressman, then president— and pretty soon he'll be running the whole show." Laughter greeted that assessment.

I wasn't kidding about Special Forces, though. Just

because he'd resigned from the program as an enlisted man did not mean the door was closed—at least, not for Gary Vernon. For just about anybody else, yes; but not for Gary. Sneaky Peek, that was his goal, and I wished him all the luck making it to Special Forces. He probably would, too. Gary could work within the system, or at least get around it on the sly without getting into trouble.

I envied him that skill. When I saw something wrong, I needed to fix it right then. I'd already gotten busted for doing the right thing when an officer had told us to do the wrong thing. And, knowing myself, I figured I'd do the same thing again if it came down to it; which was why Gary had a future in the Army, and I didn't. At least he *had* a goal. The only thing I knew for sure was there was no way I was going to re-up into this Army.

"Shit, sounds good to me," Crater muttered. "Maybe things'd get done right for a change."

A grim silence followed that cheerless observation, and not even Wally seemed able to steer the conversation into something less depressing. Everybody fell silent for too long. When the phone beside my hand finally crackled to life again, I actually jumped.

"Hey, Barnes," Chuck said into my ear when I answered, "commander of the relief is coming around."

"Thanks."

That was part of our ritual. When the commander of the relief walked the perimeter to check on the towers, you warned the next guy down the line he was on the way.

Sergeant Pritchard was on tonight; he walked into view between the fences and I challenged him. He issued the countersign and I waved him on past; then, as Pritchard walked under my tower and headed on toward the next one in line, I picked up the phone and warned Crater. He acknowledged and I cradled the phone again.

And was startled stiff when gunshots rang out over toward Tower Five. I grabbed my rifle and checked the magazine as voices erupted over the phone.

". . . Johnson, you stupid shit-for-brains moron!" Wally was snarling, which surprised the hell out of me. He never used that kind of language. "You shoot at Count Dracula again and I'll rip your balls off and beat you to death with them!"

Uh-oh.

"Be cool, Johnson"—that was Crater's voice—"it's just an owl. Put the rifle down. Pritchard's on his way over, you don't want to shoot him."

"Goddamn huge—no bird that big—" Johnson sounded terrified.

I grimaced. Maybe it wasn't so bad that Johnson couldn't shoot worth crap. More than one newbie had gone screaming into the night when our resident eagle owl swept down out of the dark on his five-foot wings. The Count hunted by our perimeter's lights; we'd sort of adopted him as a mascot. The largest owls in Europe, eagle owls had been extinct in Germany until recently, when the Frankfurt Zoological Society had helped sponsor a reintroduction program. Ours was one of those released into the wild, and it had been a big story in the local press.

We were all pretty proud of the bird, which we'd immediately dubbed Count Dracula; but Wally—well, hell, Wally thought of that bird as his personal friend, and had even looked up the local equivalent of the game warden to learn more about it, and find out how well it was adjusting to its new home. If Johnson shot his bird . . . hell, Wally just *might* kill him.

I'd be more than happy to help.

"Johnson!" I snapped into the phone. I heard a gulping wheeze on the other end and knew I had his attention. God alone knew he ought to listen to me by now. "It's a goddamn owl, Johnson; are you listening to me? An owl! And if you shoot it, every man on this shift will help Wally rip your brains out. I said, are you listening?" Another burbling sound indicated that he was. "Good. Pritchard is going to be coming around any second now. Have you put that rifle down yet?"

"Yes."

"Good. Don't shoot at shadows, Johnson. If you can't see what it is, call somebody else."

"All right, you made your point." His whining snarl was almost back to normal.

I gave him an inarticulate growl of disgust. Wally's voice was quiet when he spoke. "Thanks, Barnes."

I hoped I didn't sound as curt as I felt when I growled, "Sure, Wally. Any time." I probably had—nobody spoke to me for the thirty minutes it took to straighten out the mess with Johnson and do the stupid paperwork to log in the shots fired.

That suited me fine . . . at first.

Unfortunately, after the ruckus over the owl died down, nobody said much of anything to anyone else, either. The feeling in the air was wrong, somehow. More wrong than just bad tempers and low morale. There'd been no sound from the phone for over fifty minutes before I really noticed the change in the quality of the silence. It was almost as though the darkness were listening to us sweat. An uneasiness I couldn't define crept over me as I stood listening to my lungs in the bitter air.

The night was amazingly clear, full of stars and sharp shadows. Nothing stirred anywhere on the perimeter. Even the trees stood motionless, tall black spears stripped of their leaves. My watch dial read a quarter to midnight. For some reason, that observation worsened the tension I was feeling.

God, I was in a hell of a mood tonight.

A spurt of static startled me into glancing at the phone.

"Hey, uh, anybody out there?" Crater's voice crackled through static.

The silence held. I started to move toward the phone; then shrugged and turned back to the window. I didn't feel like talking; hadn't felt like it since yesterday's fight with Gary. Instead I wiped off more ice crystals, and let my gaze drift across the grass, down to the treeline.

Last summer we'd chased a couple of kids out of those woods. They'd been going at it pretty hot and heavy when we showed up. The boy had said something about a bet while they pulled their clothes on; then they'd disappeared without another word.

The woods had been quiet that night, too, but peaceful. . . . Hell, I didn't know what was wrong. It was probably just me, and my sulks had finally affected the rest of the guys. The silence in the tower grew in my ears until the skin on my back began to crawl. I rubbed both arms in an unsuccessful attempt to get the hairs to lie down flat. Finally I turned and tried my own luck.

"Hello? Anybody listening?"

I started to say more; then stopped. Fortunately nobody answered me. I was embarrassed that I'd let myself get so spooked. Christ, I could handle a little silence better than *Johnson*. I paced back to the window, uncertain and edgy, one ear tuned toward the phone. Over the next ten minutes three more guys called hesitantly over the line; but I didn't answer. Nobody did. There was an odd prickling at the back of my neck, and the uneasiness I couldn't explain left me in no mood to discuss anybody else's jitters. This was much worse than that afternoon at Hohenfels—

A burst of raw sound from the phone sent me six inches off the floor. My scalp tingled; the hairs stood on end. There was noise coming from the phone, like nothing I'd ever heard coming over the line before. I picked up the receiver to hear better. Metal grated and clashed against metal, and men's voices shouted hoarsely; but I couldn't make out the words. It wasn't English, or German, exactly. . . . And screams, too, faint but unmistakable through the static.

I thought of late-night war movies and decided someone was playing an elaborate hoax. They'd probably taped an old movie, messed with the sound a little, and were playing it back over their phone to freak Johnson a little closer to cracking. It was something Chuck could have put together in his sleep—the man was a true artist when it came to messing with people's minds.

I backed away, holding down an involuntary shiver, and told myself to ignore the weird sounds, since there wasn't anything I could do about them now. I looked out the window again—and almost fell down.

I grabbed at the heater and singed my hands in the process. The phone banged against the floor and hung from its trailing cord, forgotten.

There were no stars.

A huge patch of sky was utterly, hideously black.

And the thing that stood between me and the night sky . . .

I tried to swallow and couldn't; tried to blink, and couldn't. It stood multiple yards higher than the treeline. The fact that I had often seen heads shaped like that, held proudly on muscled necks arched in precisely that manner, only increased the horror. It hulked above my tower, its very size making it appear misshapen against the night sky. Flaring nostrils steamed in the frozen air, well above the topmost branches as it tested the wind for scent of its quarry.

Odin's death stallion was hunting in the darkness beyond the perimeter lights.

But who was Sleipnir hunting?

A massive cold shudder that had nothing to do with the temperature seized me.

His ears twitched, blocking out more stars as they moved. The part of my mind which functioned on that level—no matter what else I was doing—took the measure of the angle from the lowest part of the neck to the tips of those silky ears.

Assuming all eight feet were firmly planted on the ground, Sleipnir stood two hundred feet tall.

All six-feet-plus of me shook in the darkness.

His gaze swept across the ground far below, peered through the barren trees, passed across the frozen grass and glittering chain-link fence—

—and rested on me.

Time slowed. We stared at one another while the constellations watched silently. His eyes blazed with an intelligence far greater than any animal had a right to possess. He bared his teeth in a perfect imitation of a wicked grin. . . .

My hand came to life, groping for my rifle. I didn't give a damn what I'd told Johnson. *Could I kill a thing like Sleipnir with an M-16?*

Behind me, the sounds of screaming men and ringing metal shrieked, filled the tower . . . and still Sleipnir held my eyes.

He moved one step closer; if he'd stretched his neck, his teeth could have ripped the flimsy wooden roof off my tower. His head bobbed lower in the starlight as though he'd heard my thought. I threw myself onto the floor behind the big heater. Burning my arm on the back of it had very little to do with the yell I gave out as his enormous head filled the glass windows above me. . . .

My hands worked the rifle bolt and I crouched lower. My pulse pounded against throat and temples.

He'd come for somebody. Goddammit, he'd come for somebody—

Well, it wasn't going to be me. Not without a fight.

The stallion tossed his head against the blackness of the night sky, and half reared. A massive, misshapen chest surged momentarily into view. Then he subsided and peered intently into my tower again. His nostrils flared wider, and his coat rippled and shuddered as muscles bunched smoothly under it. He sidled to my right, treetops whipping violently aside as he moved. He bared glinting teeth and snapped at the air above the double fences; then snorted. The walls of my tower shook as fog engulfed the windows.

I started praying—I didn't even know to Whom.

The glass cleared, and again I saw his eyes, wild and angry. Then he reared up above the trees, and two sets of flailing forefeet raked the treetops. Snow went flying in an explosion of white powder. When he subsided again, he shook his head. Rippling mane hair went flying wild in a sudden wind that roared down across my tower with gale force. The stallion's eyes held mine for a long moment more; then he turned his head away and began scanning the ground, peering off in the direction of town.

I flexed my fingers. Tried breathing again. My lungs rasped once; then started to work. I noticed my shorts were suspiciously warm and damp. Damn.

My pulse still pounded fiercely in my ears, and I blinked sweat out of my eyes despite the intense cold. I eased cautiously to the windowsill, and peered up over the edge as the apparition moved one step away from the site, then another.

The phone fell silent behind me. I started, and glanced around at it. When I looked out again, I saw the stallion rear again. His front legs raked the night sky. I half expected the stars to explode in a shower of sparks as his hooves caught them. There was something—I couldn't tell what—held in his teeth.

Then he was gone.

He didn't fade away. Or disappear. He just . . . wasn't *there*. A rumble of thunder struck the tower; then everything fell silent.

Slowly I eased my rifle down; slowly wiped my hands on my pants.

My watch said midnight exactly. I looked at the phone, expecting it to burst into life any second; but it didn't. The silence lasted right up to the end of watch.

I spent the rest of that watch staring out at the snowless treetops and fighting shudders that insisted on crawling up my spine every few moments. I studied the night, traced its frozen patterns from sky to ground and back. It was different, worse than before, tainted somehow with the scent of blood.

Which was crazy.

Count Dracula dropped from the night sky, so close to my tower windows I actually yelled and brought my rifle to my shoulder before I got control of myself again. The Count struck a mouse and devoured it while I struggled to get my heartbeat back down under 120 again. Reluctantly, I had to admit that I now understood—at some primal level I'd never experienced before—why Johnson had shot at that owl. My fingers gripped my rifle so hard I looked later for dents.

When my relief finally arrived and I climbed down, I moved so slowly I felt like a geriatric case; except that I kept trying to look in all directions at once, which I couldn't have done if I were genuinely as old as I felt. I glanced briefly at the guys as we made the round of the towers; but carefully met no one's eyes.

No one seemed anxious to meet mine, either, and none of them appeared to be in any better shape than I was. Crater was determinedly ignoring the sky altogether as he slouched up to the silent group. We assembled in the dark, and no one broke the silence as we trooped into the psychological safety represented by the mess room.

Johnson was a basket case. It took Wally, Crater, and Brunowski to get him into his bunk. When Wally and Crater returned, leaving Johnson in Brunowski's care, we gathered around the coffeepot. No one seemed willing yet to meet anyone else's gaze.

Crater spoke first. "Did, uh, anybody hear anything kind of, well, weird—"

"Yeah," Chuck cut in, his ruddy face sweating. "Kind of like screaming and shit, and metal hitting or scraping or something—"

I didn't want to listen to the half-whispered comparisons of what I'd heard over the phone tonight. I didn't like thinking about it; it soured my stomach thinking about it.

Nobody mentioned Sleipnir, and I sure as hell didn't either. There's a reason pilots who report UFOs get the rest of their careers scrubbed. I scowled into my muddy coffee and saw those impossible eyes staring back.

The door flew open with a bite of ice in the wind and Pritchard staggered in, pulling off gloves with hands that shook. He drained a cup of coffee in one gulp and poured a second, then let out a sigh that was mostly shudder. We waited.

"Bad wreck," he muttered, his voice choking.

"Say again?" Wally asked.

"Bad wreck. Somebody go find Brunowski."

Nobody moved.

"What happened, Sarge?" Wally asked quietly.

Pritchard stirred, looked around, saw we were waiting. He seemed to brace himself. I knew, without a word spoken, that the biggest shoe of all time was about to squash us flat. I found myself gripping my coffee mug until my knuckles showed white.

Pritchard finally spoke. "One of our trucks missed a curve; hit the trees doing sixty-five."

The ensuing silence was broken by a reverent whisper.

"Fuck . . ."

"Rosetti's got a busted skull and no teeth in front. Hill broke both his arms. A couple of guys in the rear broke damned near every bone you can break. —Shit!"

He'd spilled coffee on his shoe.

"Gonna be hell on you guys, 'til we get a full complement again on the other relief."

Pritchard still wouldn't meet anyone's eyes—he had more to tell, and didn't want to spill the really bad news. Memory of Sleipnir standing taller than the trees, something grasped in his wicked teeth, hit me hard. I felt sick, didn't want to think it, wanted to throw up, rather than ask . . .

"Gary Vernon?" I barely recognized my own voice.

Pritchard looked up again. He met my eyes for a second, then let his gaze slide away.

"He bought the farm, Barnes. Dead before the pieces quit bouncing. Sorry."

I slammed my fist down on the table. I never noticed the hot coffee that sloshed over my hand as the mug I was holding shattered. I just stumbled outside. The stiff breeze from the north compounded the effect of the sub-zero temperatures to freeze the moisture on my cheeks instantly; but after the skin froze I hardly noticed.

The air smelled like more snow. I didn't care.

He'd come for a warrior, bloody goddamned monster. He'd gotten one.

Chapter Six

I heard water long before I found it. Sound travels almost forever in a cave; and this sound wasn't a quiet dripping splash, it was a running, rumbling roar, loud and wet through the darkness. The floor began to slope sharply downward; I had to brace with both hands as I picked my way carefully along a sixty-degree slope.

The air was moist, and the walls were damp to the touch; but there wasn't any visible seepage yet. Just the noise, much louder now, beginning to sound almost like the roar of a waterfall—although as long as it had been since I had heard anything but the sound of my own footsteps, my perspective was, perhaps, suspect.

Finally the walls began to curve around in a tight, left-hand, downward spiral; before I was completely around a final, sharp corner, cold, wet spray hit my face. I dug in along the very edges of the slope and stopped.

It *was* a waterfall.

A dark spout thicker than my torso shot straight out of a hole in the "cliff face" fifteen, maybe twenty feet above my head. The water tumbled down into the same crevice where I stood, pouring away downslope in an honest-to-god underground river as it followed the bend. Wet stone glistened in the lamplight. The surface surrounding the falls rippled in a beautiful formation Bjornssen had identified as flowstone, which glistened in the light with stunning shades of ruby and fiery orange from whatever minerals had been dissolved in the water. The opposite wall remained the dirty, ugly grey that had characterized the rest of this passage so far.

And then I saw that a good-sized side passage led off to the right, also sloping down, just this side of the waterfall.

For a moment I just stood there, staring stupidly from one passageway to the other.

Crossroad.

Finally my brain kicked in like a rusty carburetor, and I got busy doing first things first. I unstrapped my pack and broke out the filter pump. Since the water was moving fast enough to pick up all kinds of sludge, I didn't want to risk drinking it unfiltered, despite a raging thirst. I filled both canteens, slaked my thirst, refilled the second canteen again; then repacked my gear and contemplated the two possible roads.

There was no telling how far this "river" flowed, or how deep it got. If the floor continued to slope down much farther at this angle, the water would be above my head in no time flat.

Scuba gear was one item I hadn't brought with me on my journey to hell.

On the other hand . . .

I took off my helmet and held it as far down the right-hand passageway as I could. I flashed the light around, and studied the opening. The floor fell away at a slightly smaller angle of slope. It appeared to be completely dry, and it didn't appear to narrow down at all.

It looked like a much easier route, and probably a

survivable one. I jammed the helmet back onto my head and studied the river passage again. My Sunday-school teacher had always said the road to hell was an easy passage; but I didn't think Christian ideals necessarily applied here.

As I squatted there at the very edge of the black river, I felt an almost subliminal humming along my calf. The knife strapped to my leg seemed to quiver in anticipation.

That wasn't necessarily a good sign.

Involuntarily I glanced down; then wished I hadn't. I spat and watched the tiny blob of spittle vanish as the tremendously swift current swept it away.

Hell, I still didn't know what to make of that knife.

And, though part of me wished bitterly that I'd never laid eyes on it, another part of me knew that nothing in the known universe could have prompted me to refuse accepting it. Call it guilt; call it cowardice. Hell, a case could even be made for compassion. . . .

I wondered what Gary's grandmother would make of me if she could see me now. I snorted. Probably ask to borrow the knife back, then call the cops to come and lock me up once I was unarmed. She'd seemed an extraordinarily capable old lady. Granted, we hadn't met under the best of circumstances. But then, they do say stress and grief tend to bring out a person's real personality. Which said a lot about her—and even more about me.

Even through the numb shock and the sick anger that had gripped me, once I had met Gary's grandmother, I'd discovered I envied my dead friend every minute of the time he'd spent growing up in her house. I'd never met anyone quite like her and knew I never would again.

Either the Vernon family had been a rare breed, indeed, or my life had been emptier than even I had thought.

I rubbed my eyes with thumb and forefinger, then tried to ease a cramped knot in the back of my neck. If

I'd had any doubts *before* the funeral about Who—or What—had killed Gary Vernon, I certainly didn't have any afterward. I probably shouldn't have been surprised; but the last place I'd expected to encounter more of Odin's legacy was at Gary's funeral.

The weather at the cemetery wasn't any better than Germany's, just warmer. Thick, drizzling mist threatened to become cold rain at any moment. I'd flown halfway around the world—threatened to let all hell loose if I didn't get the leave time I was owed, and get it right *then*—only to get rained on at my best friend's funeral.

I watched the grim procession crawl through the rusted iron gates and move toward me. Nothing could have induced me to set foot inside the funeral home; it was bad enough out here under the miserable sky, with the miserable mountains glaring down at me through the miserable mist.

This stretch of godforsaken Oregon coast ended at a cliff, dropping a sheer hundred fifty feet into crashing surf. The cemetery clung to the edge of the cliff, shivering in heavy, cold fog. The few markers were granite, some very old, three with the same date of death.

The Vernon family was almost completely reunited.

I didn't have to wait long for the line of cars to crawl through the gates and stop near the open grave. Small towns didn't have many mourners in them. I stood at some distance while they gathered, and knew I was almost invisible to the mourners through the fog, which suited my mood. Then, when the minister took his place, I shouldered my way closer. Friends of the family stared, wondering who the silent uniform belonged to. I was obviously too late an arrival to be a member of the honor guard who would give Mrs. Vernon that terribly expensive flag after they lowered Gary's box from under it.

The mist thickened, creeping between the tombstones and around the mourners, until I could barely make out the casket. It wasn't the right sort of mist; not tangy with salt air and the fresh sea scents of a living coastline. It stank of blood and bodies long dead. The cold, slimy feel of it clinging to me was the feel of the grave, the touch of Sleipnir's cold eyes. I shuddered, wanting to tear at the smothering mist and rip it to shreds with my fingers.

The preacher droned on about the mercy of God and I ground my teeth. There was no merciful God; just a bloodthirsty old bastard with one eye who wouldn't be satisfied with the dead he already had.

No one here would believe what had really happened; but the memory of that tiny shape swaying in the grip of Sleipnir's massive teeth was so strong, it was all I could do not to fling open the coffin to see if Gary's body bore teeth marks.

The sharp report of the first rifle volley snapped me back. Two more followed, echoing off the shrouded cliffs.

The woman beside me closed her eyes; but didn't flinch. I'd seen Gary's photographs enough times to know this was Mrs. Vernon. Gary's grandmother was a solid woman, built to live forever. In the wreck of a face made old by more than time, I could see she'd once been beautiful.

Gary's grandfather must've been crazy, to leave her to go off to war. Her hair was silver and diamonds in the mist, and her chin was firm and high.

The only movement anywhere about her leaked from the corners of her eyes. She never sobbed once; but the tears didn't stop or even slow down, and there wasn't enough courage in my whole body to meet her eyes. I wasn't sure she'd even noticed my presence when I'd nudged my way between her and a disapproving neighbor.

The bugler began taps amidst an unexpected growl of thunder from the Pacific. The service wasn't over yet when a violent squall swept in off the sea and shredded the mist, sending it flying before a sharp, salty wind. Rain tore at the mourners, cleansed the casket; the stars and stripes draped over it blazed when the lightning flashed. I pulled off my overcoat and held it above Mrs. Vernon's head while the gathering broke and ran for parked cars, leaving a mere handful to finish out the graveside service.

Rain and wind slashed through the graveyard, battering at us. My arms shook slightly, holding up the sodden coat. I peered intently through the storm, half expecting to see the monstrous, deformed shape of that eight-legged hellhorse rise up out of the stormy sea to tower above us.

Except he'd already come and gone, his dirty work done.

I found myself standing between Gary's grandmother and the wind, shivering, but determined to protect Mrs. Vernon. She was the only bit of Gary left alive in the world.

"You'd best go on now, Ingrid."

One of the gravediggers had appeared. Mrs. Vernon was holding the folded flag. The service had ended while I was watching the rotten storm. Mrs. Vernon and I were the only two mourners left at the gravesite.

"I'll go when my boy's home, none sooner."

Not a quaver; but her tears came faster. Either that, or the wind was crying, too. I edged closer to her side, not quite daring to put an arm around her, and faced down the gravedigger. He looked at my bedraggled dress uniform and shrugged.

They lowered Gary into the earth, their grunts and oaths barely audible above the storm. The splunk of mud against dark, wet steel settled all argument. A moment later we turned to go.

Mrs. Vernon looked me up and down, and my heart jumped into my mouth. I was a good half-a-foot taller than she was, for all that she was impressive; but she could've knocked me into the mud with a look.

"You'll be coming to the house." It wasn't a question, but I made noncommittal noises.

"Mr. Barnes, you've come all the way from Germany, as none of the rest of them have, and I'll not see you turned out into a storm for thanks. You follow my car back."

For a moment I was puzzled that she knew my name; then it occurred to me that I had no idea what sort of letters and/or pictures Gary had sent home. I nodded and helped her back through the mud and rain to the waiting limo.

The limousine dropped Mrs. Vernon off on a tree-lined street, in front of a small stone home. I parked my rented Mustang and stepped out into a deep puddle that soaked coldly through my already drenched shoes.

Mrs. Vernon ushered me onto the porch and into an unfashionable living room filled with unmatched, comfortable old furniture, and family pictures in heavy gold and wooden frames. I dripped muddy water onto her throw rug, and tried not to look at the laughing faces in those photos. Across the room a few brown pine needles and a stray "icicle" on the carpet showed where a Christmas tree had stood until recently.

Merry Christmas, Ingrid Vernon.

She spoke then, while pulling off her coat. "Sit down, make yourself comfortable, Mr. Barnes. I'll be just a moment."

She disappeared into the back of the house. I stayed where I was. I'd already ruined the seat of the rental car.

She returned sooner than I expected, having left the sodden coat somewhere, but she still wore the muddy shoes and bedraggled black dress. Her hair dripped onto her shoulders. She held before her, on outstretched hands, a long narrow box wrapped in an old, faded bit of gingham cloth.

She glanced down at it for a long moment; then met my eyes.

"You were special to my boy."

I didn't know what to say, so I kept my mouth shut.

She unwrapped the gingham and held out a slim wooden case. "The men who carried this are all gone. Gary wouldn't take it with him over there; he said it would just get stolen some night. And maybe—maybe it would have, at that. There are *those* . . ."

She faltered; her eyes closed briefly, then opened. Her chin came up resolutely and she stared into my eyes, apparently searching for something—and whatever it was, I couldn't have explained why, but right then, for just an instant, I'd have been willing to die to give it to her.

And then the moment was past. Mostly.

Softly Ingrid Vernon said, "I'd be proud if you would have it. It was meant for Gary, at least I'd hoped it was; but that wasn't to be. None of what I'd hoped for was meant to be. . . ." Her eyes held unshed tears. Her expression, while utterly bleak, somehow conveyed an impression of frustrated rage and a sense of personal betrayal. "But life is as it will be," she continued, and finished grimly, "regardless of pain."

Barely in time, for a change, I managed to bite back my response. It would have been entirely too heartfelt— I'd heard the same line from Gary too many times. But however much I wanted to rage at her—to tell her it was her fault; that she'd made him the way he was, and that's what got him killed—I couldn't have said a thing like that to my worst enemy, let alone this proud, stubborn old woman trying not to inflict her grief on her grandson's friend.

Reverently she handed me the box. "You are *chosen*."

I blinked but carefully said nothing. It seemed likely that she would explain further. (And oddly enough the prospect sent a chill up my spine.)

"For generations, it has always *chosen* its keeper from the males of my family. Now there are no more. You are the one it wants."

I opened the lid. For a long moment, my eyes refused to focus on the object inside. Black as Sleipnir's eyes, a long, somehow menacing shadow crouched between folds of crimson velvet. From needle-pointed blade tip to end of pommel, absolutely no light reflected from the knife. It wasn't coated or plated to look black; it *was* black—even the razor-honed edge, which should have reflected silver; but didn't. A dragon's-head guard and tail-shaped haft curled into a belt or thong clip. It might have been gaudy—should have been—but it wasn't.

Not at all.

Without quite knowing how it got there, I found my fingers closing about the haft which lay on my abruptly sweating palm. It was soft and warm to the touch; it felt almost like living flesh. Something, no doubt feedback from my inexplicably pounding pulse, created a sensation within my fist that felt oddly like the purr of a smugly self-satisfied cat.

I looked at it more closely. From its appearance, I couldn't hazard a guess as to what it was made of. Obviously it was very old (possibly even ancient). It was certainly utterly unique, and unmistakably priceless; somehow I knew instantly that the last place it belonged was a museum—or maybe, as I became aware of my surroundings once again, the next-to-the-last place. . . .

Hastily I dropped the knife back into the velvet, snapped the lid closed, and met Ingrid Vernon's unfathomable gaze.

"I can't accept this!" I sputtered.

She held up a hand. I shut up.

"It *chose* you," she stated flatly, "and that's all there is to be said. Keep it, Randy. For his sake."

I gave up. Briefly (and without notable success) I tried to say something appreciative. Eventually I fell silent.

Presently she said, "It was good of you to want to come."

"I always wanted to meet you," I fumbled.

She offered a wan smile. "Thank you, I see you mean that, and I wanted to meet you, too. But I didn't want it to be . . ."

I couldn't answer. She seemed to understand.

Finally, after a timeless interval, I broke the quiet that had settled over the room. "I, uh, guess I'd better be going. Have to get back to Portland, to the airport. . . ."

Flushing, I made an awkward farewell.

I could feel her eyes on my back all the way to the rented car; then I was alone with the knife. I opened the box again, and stared at the dead black shape for a moment. It occurred to me that Gary probably had been right. This little number was thief-bait. Even if I hadn't had a job to get back to—Uncle Sam still wanted me—I probably wasn't going to want to look at it again for quite some time. If ever. Too many memories. It would have to get used to its dark little box until my discharge.

I experienced an inexplicable flash of anger at the thought. The feeling grew stronger as I snapped the lid shut and rewrapped the gingham. It intensified further as I began to think about getting back to duty. The feeling persisted all the way back to Germany, where I asked that it be logged in and locked up safely in the arms room. As I walked away, I received an indelible impression of frustrated rage.

Chapter Seven

A dark swirl of water raced away from me, down into the heart of the mountain, as cold as my gut. The next choice I made might well be my last. I had to decide not only whether I went left or right; but also whether or not to trust the knife which now hung poised along my calf. A grimace tugged at my lips.

The immortal Juliet had begged Romeo not to swear by the "inconstant moon" lest his love prove just as changeable; the risk that this knife would be just as fickle loomed in the foreground of my awareness.

I eyed the blade uneasily; then reached down and felt the grip slide smoothly into my hand. Instead of holding it by the haft, I simply laid the knife across my palms and stared at it. It was heavy and reassuringly solid to the touch; but—as I had learned shortly after acquiring the damned thing—I had ample reason to be wary. I glanced at the river again. The fall of black water churned its surface with endless boiling motion.

Black knife, black water . . .

The knife lay cold and dead against my palms, giving me no clue. But then I didn't really need the knife to make my decision. The Christian hell might be notoriously easy to get into; but I was betting the Norse one wasn't. I thrust the blade back into its sheath and came briskly to my feet. I cast one last longing glance down that dry passageway. . . .

Then strode forward into black spray.

Gingerly I tested the footing along the edge, as far away from the cascading waterfall as possible. In seconds I was drenched to the skin, and the bottom continued to slope away, leaving me hip-deep and sinking in next to no time. The water was *cold*, nearer the temperature of an ice cube than liquid water. I gritted my teeth and kept going, trying unsuccessfully not to shiver as the icy water filled my boots and chilled my bones.

The bottom slowly leveled out, and I found myself waist-deep, struggling to stay upright in swift current that tugged at my pack and threatened to drag my feet out from under me. Gradually the current slowed as the walls widened out. Unfortunately, that made hanging on more difficult. Soon I couldn't reach both sides at once. After the roar of the waterfall died away, the only sound was that of the river itself, softly hissing over and around rocky protrusions.

I began to shiver in earnest as my frozen body tried to warm itself. Dying of hypothermia hadn't occurred to me; but it was entirely possible. Somehow I didn't think freezing to death qualified a hero for admission into Valhalla. Not that I felt much like a hero; I was just too goddamned mad to lie back and enjoy what most people would have considered inevitable.

I actually laughed aloud. The sound skittered across the black river and vanished downstream. Odin was probably very unhappy that I wasn't most people. I hadn't been, even before Gary's death, and afterward . . .

Afterward, I had felt a bitter kinship with the poor guy in Heinlein's *The Unpleasant Profession of Jonathan*

Hoag, who had started sleeping nights handcuffed to his wife. But that guy's solution to his personal nightmare had been to run away and hope it didn't get any worse.

I didn't do things that way.

It had eventually occurred to me that Gary's murder had been—mythologically speaking—impossible. Gary Vernon had been "collected" by Sleipnir, Odin's personal courier for fetching to the Valhall those warriors *killed in battle*.

Gary Vernon had died in a traffic accident.

Sleipnir did not collect—and never had—traffic-accident victims. Those who died accidentally ended up in Niflheim, not Valhalla. That realization had stopped me cold in my tracks for a couple of days; fortunately, they were *quiet* days, because an entire division probably could have rolled through the fences next to my tower and I wouldn't have noticed. I'd been too busy with thoughts that leapfrogged across all the old stories I'd ever read as I tried to make sense of something even more impossible than the impossible.

And then, when I couldn't make sense of it, I'd gone out and done additional research. Lots and lots of additional research. My new obsession might have made me the butt of endless jokes; but nobody razzed me much. Of course, Rosetti's new orthodontia, compliments of Uncle Sam, might have prompted some of that reluctance. Somehow word had gotten around to leave me and my pagan gods strictly alone. . . .

Beneath the trappings of glory and drinking and whoring it up, the old Viking religion was damned vicious. Three old hags called the Norns made all the rules—including the ones the gods themselves lived by. These three witches made the Greek Fates look like Sleeping Beauty's Good Fairies. Their rules for living—and dying—were ugly, cruel, full of blood and torture and death. Nobody, including Odin, spat without those three old hags' by-your-leave, and *nobody* broke the rules.

Warriors—those who died in battle—and accident victims did not share the same afterlife. Not ever. And yet there Odin was, apparently throwing everybody into one stewpot, willy-nilly. Odin wasn't *allowed* to collect victims of accidents—or disease, or old age—for his great battle hall. But he'd collected Gary. And apparently the Norns were letting him get away with it.

That had left me with two possibilities. Either the army had lied about the accident—which was not only entirely possible, but highly probable, if ragheads had been involved—or something really screwy was going on here. Why would Odin start stealing men wherever he found them? And why would the Norns let him?

To answer my first question, I'd collared Hill, the driver, and Rosetti—separately—and had done my best (or worst, depending on your viewpoint) to get the real story out of them. They had agreed on every detail. Gary had died in a plain-and-simple truck wreck. No raghead ambush, no sabotage of the truck, no nothing. Just one blind-drunk muther at the wheel and one dead GI. I think they had to rehospitalize Hill after I got done with him. . . .

Meanwhile, Odin had gotten away with murder. And probably would again—maybe even mine. I bitterly acknowledged that fact, and, somewhere in the process of getting drunk and ripping up a German bar and a few dozen of the Palestinian "Turks" who hung out there, I felt like I finally understood why Oedipus—who had also fallen afoul of a divine joke too cruel to bear—had stabbed out his own eyes.

And then, quietly and clear-headedly, I had vowed that Odin would pay. No matter what it took. Which left me with figuring out *how*. A mortal doesn't just hop a bus for the home of the gods. . . .

Not even dying was a surefire way to get to him. Most of the dead went to the goddess Hel's hall in Niflheim, and a full half the warriors killed in battle were claimed by Freyja for *her* hall, wherever that was. Besides, I didn't want to die first just in order to get to Odin. Dead men don't get much done, and I had a lot to accomplish.

The only reliable way to get to Odin without dying was to cross the rainbow bridge Bifrost, into Asgard. Problem was, it bypassed Earth without stopping. Besides, no mortal could cross it anyway; it was too fragile. I had to come up with another way to get to Odin.

A really convoluted, arguably crazy way.

According to the old stories, a man could find his way into the underworld—without dying first—by locating a very deep cave, and following it down to the echoing bridge that led from Earth into Niflheim, the "underworld"—not precisely hell (since *that* was called Niflhel); but certainly not heaven, either.

The old stories also said that Loki was chained in the underworld as punishment for killing Baldr, Odin's favorite son. He would remain there until the twilight of the gods and their final battle at Ragnarok.

Sleipnir—through a biologically improbable series of events—was Loki's son.

And Sleipnir—bless his big black heart—was the only creature in the combined nine worlds able to cross between any two of them at will.

Voila: All I had to do was catch Sleipnir and ride him to Asgard. Once I got Odin within arm's reach, I would wring his cursed neck for him. Piece of cake. Always assuming a human being could kill a god, of course. . . .

The one thing I *couldn't* do was just sit and do nothing. I *had* to believe one man could change what was happening, because to believe in predestination—that everything was fixed and immutable, that nothing you did meant spit in the long run—was to believe that Gary and I, the rest of humanity, everything we'd accomplished as a species was worth nothing. It meant we hadn't done anything more meaningful than run headlong down Somebody's elaborate rat maze. I wouldn't buy that.

I might be an asshole; but I sure as hell wasn't a rat.

The gods were mortal, after a fashion. They were all slated to die at Ragnarok. If everything were foreordained, and ran according to rules as immutable as the physics that governed nuclear fission, then Fenrir would kill Odin, Thor would die of poison blown by the Midgard serpent, and traffic-accident victims would always end up in Niflheim, not Sleipnir's teeth.

But if everything *weren't* foreordained . . .

I didn't know if I could kill a god; but I knew I had to try. If he could snatch victims from insignificant traffic accidents, who could guess what bigger and better "accidents" he might arrange? It wouldn't take much meddling to blow the lid off the uneasy peace we had going at the moment. That would sure as hell give him a steady supply of bodies. He had to be stopped; and there just wasn't anybody else I could think of in any position to stop him.

The Norns—hiding under the roots of the world tree, where the great rainbow bridge spanned the gap between Asgard and the Norns' shadowy hall—made the rules Odin had been breaking.

I didn't much care.

I was not only going to break the rules, I was going to play another game altogether. Which left me waist-deep in a freezing river somewhere in the middle of a Norwegian mountain.

I don't know how long I slogged through the cold water, putting one booted foot carefully ahead of the other and forcing my shivering body to keep moving. My watch had tritium-coated hands and numbers, which meant I could see them even without the carbide light; but my brain wouldn't register the time properly. I knew I had to get out of the water soon or I would freeze to death.

Unfortunately there was no end to the river in sight. The walls began to narrow down again, causing the current to pick up. My legs were so numb I was having trouble keeping my footing, and the only thing that saved me from falling a couple of times was grabbing for the walls. The rough stone cut my hands, so I braced myself long enough to dig a pair of wet gloves out of my butt pack. They were cold and soaked; but saved the skin of my palms several times during the next few minutes.

I was shivering so hard now, it was a race between the numbness and convulsions as to which would dunk me in the end—

My footing disappeared without warning. I dropped off a shelf and floundered, choking with icy water up my nose. The weight of the pack dragged me under. My waterlogged boots hampered my efforts to kick toward the surface. I flailed desperately and managed to get my face above water long enough to gasp.

I stared wildly into utter blackness. Not only had the carbide lamp hissed and gone out instantly; but the current had dragged my helmet away into the darkness, gone before I could even think of grabbing for it.

A low rumble grew ominously in my ears. The current—which had picked up sharply—dragged me mercilessly along. Blind, half frozen, I flailed both arms, and scraped my hand against the wall. I tried to grab hold; but only managed to scrape up my arm without finding purchase. Kicking hard slewed me sideways in the heavy current, then smacked me hard into the wall, sooner than I expected. I tried again to grab hold, scrabbling with hands and feet.

The roar grew louder and the current picked up more

speed. Try as I might, the river scraped me along the wall (leaving bits of cloth and skin behind) toward a dropoff—a cliff, or chimney, no doubt—which certainly lay ahead. When my feet bumped into something, it took my brain a couple of seconds to register the impact.

When realization sank in, I kicked hard. There was a shelf of rock, very narrow, under my feet. I tried to brace myself on it; but the current was too swift. I ended up sliding sideways on tippytoes, trying to maintain contact with the ledge.

The roar had grown to a deafening thunder, and the current dragged at my clothes and pack, trying to drag me bodily off the tiny shelf. My head bumped into something extremely hard and I ducked instinctively.

I almost lost my balance, and flung both arms upward. My hands smacked against the ceiling. Primate instinct took over from the lizard brain. I jammed my feet against the bottom and braced my hands hard against the ceiling, and halted my slide toward doom. Thus supported, I was able to hold my position; but I wasn't sure how long I could maintain my stance, shivering as hard as I was.

There was obviously one *mutha* of a hole somewhere up ahead—and very close, from the sound of it. My tunnel was narrowing down so fast I'd be completely underwater soon—if I didn't get dragged down the hole first. I was so cold I couldn't think what to do; trying to reason felt like trying to swim in Jell-O. The only coherent thought I could dredge up wasn't particularly useful. To wit, if I let go of the ceiling, I was going to drown, assuming I didn't first hit the bottom of the hole into which the river was pouring.

The germ of a thought percolated into my numbed brain and I braced myself carefully, letting go with one hand to fumble inside my shirt pocket. Sure enough, my emergency cyalume stick was still there. Ripping the foil off with my teeth, I held one end against the ceiling and applied pressure to the other end. The plastic outer tube bent until the glass vial floating inside snapped. I shook vigorously, and was rewarded with a cool, chemical glow which lit my surroundings.

I stood jammed against one wall of a six-foot-wide tunnel, with dark water racing by so fast it made me dizzy to watch. The cave ceiling arced down to meet the water some fifteen feet ahead. Either that, or that was where the river dropped off into the hole, and the tunnel dropped off with it.

Somewhat desperately I scanned the wall and saw a roundish patch of darkness maybe two feet this side of the dropoff point. A side tunnel? Big enough for me to get into? Or just a small hollow that led nowhere? Even if it were a tunnel, could I hang on against the current long enough to drag myself into it? Not that I had much choice either way.

With nothing to lose but my life—which I figured was long since forfeit anyway—I clenched the cyalume in my teeth and inched forward, fighting the drag of the current, until my arms ached with the strain of pushing against the ceiling. The current tore at me so strongly, I didn't dare raise my feet. Instead I shuffled along, scraping my boots against the rock riverbed.

Closer, and I could see the opening: hole, all right, and big enough for me to squeeze into, even with the pack. The edges and inside surfaces were rounded and worn smooth from water, suggesting that the level of the river was considerably higher at times, bleeding off part of its flow into this side chute.

The side passage floor was at chest level. Could I drag myself up into it, with muscles frozen stiff and trembling from exhaustion, before the current dragged me into that bottomless pit? I didn't give myself odds on that one; but again, there wasn't much choice. I thought briefly about easier roads to Hell, and muttered something obscene around the lightstick clenched in my teeth.

I was *not* going to dive down that waterfall.

I reached the opening and braced myself. I was going to have to let go with my right arm. I shut my eyes, and drew a deep breath around the cyalume; then grabbed the edge of the hole. The current slammed me sideways. I bashed my elbow against the side of the new tunnel; but I wasn't swept away. I fought to shuffle back against the current, while pulling against the edge of the tunnel as hard as I could with my right arm. I gained about six inches, which put me more or less back in front of the hole again.

Walking my fingers along—while maintaining pressure against the ceiling with my palm—allowed me to reach the edge of the tunnel. I tensed and tried to ready myself for a lunge that would be my one and only chance. Bearing in mind Yoda's immortal words, "There is no *try* . . ." I emptied my lungs, filled them again, and emptied them once more (which wasn't easy with a cyalume stick in my mouth). I attempted to calm myself and closed my eyes to concentrate. . . .

Water yanked my feet sideways. I landed with nearly rib-cracking force against the right wall. My breath slammed out in a guttural grunt and I almost dropped the cyalume stick. My right arm was crushed against stone. I dragged myself forward half an inch, an inch, two inches. . . .

The river pulled madly at my legs, dragged me back again. I clung sideways, face jammed against rock, left hand scrabbling for purchase, and thought wildly about the knife in my boot sheath, where it did me no good at all. . . .

I cursed; then dragged my right leg painfully up out of the water. I worked my knee up along the wall while I tried to find some sort of toehold with my other foot, and did it the hard way. I clung with my left hand; then made a grab for the knife—

My fingers closed around it. And as I twisted and slipped and started to fall back into the river, I jabbed the blade into solid rock. It sank straight into the wall. And held.

I pulled myself up two inches; got my other knee out of the water; felt the strain in the knife as it began to bend under my weight. I collapsed forward onto the ledge with startling suddenness. My feet hung out over space, clear of the water.

I rolled flat onto my stomach across the cyalume stick, and felt my hand drop. The haft quivered as my fingers slid away. I lay in utter blackness, my feet barely clear of the water.

I was still alive.

I tried to smile. Good old knife . . . it had even managed to get rid of Johnson for me. My eyes closed all by themselves. Poor, stupid Johnson . . .

The day had begun decently. It graduated to miserable in short order, and left me convinced to my socks that Somebody Up There had taken very serious notice of one otherwise insignificant GI.

It was supposed to have been a classic ambush. Things had started out well, in fact, despite the conditions. After a bad blizzard, the weather had turned clear, with bitter temperatures and worse wind chill. Hauling sixty-five pounds of gear, I had slogged through snow that drifted knee-deep in places. Johnson stumbled ahead of me, muttering incoherently. After the rainy warmth of Oregon, returning to Germany's biting cold had been a shock.

With Lieutenant Donaldson in charge of the exercise, Staff Sergeant Myers as our squad leader, and Wally as acting fire team leader, we had experienced, trustworthy personnel running the show. Which was something of a relief.

Donaldson barked orders into the freezing air and we got moving. Setting up the ambush beat standing around freezing to death. We positioned ourselves in a crescent-shaped deployment back up in the trees on a fairly steep hillside.

Below us a small road snaked along the edge of the hill; we centered ourselves on the outside of a ninety-degree turn, far enough from the crest not to be visible against the skyline if we stood up, but close enough to the top to scramble over it quickly. We'd spring our hit-and-run ambush on the convoy expected through sometime during the next two hours, then melt away over the ridge.

On the far side of the road, twenty yards or so distant, was another stand of woods. On our side, a snow-and-stubble covered field stretched away to the right, toward another woodline. We were in a good position; Donaldson knew what he was doing. Down on the far end of the crescent, Simpkins' squad had set up their M-60 machine gun to command a clear view down the road as it departed from the corner. At the other end, the weapons squad was setting up another M-60, positioned to rake the road in the other direction.

The result was the classic crossfire pattern, which in combat would have forced the enemy off the road in our direction, right into the fire of four eight-man rifle squads lying in ambush between the machine guns. In addition, my squad had two 90mm recoilless rifles, which looked like old-time World War II bazookas, but had more range and carried a lot more punch.

None of this impressive array of weaponry was, of course, loaded for our training exercise. The brass, in their wisdom, had determined there was enough chance of us dumb troopies hurting ourselves on a training maneuver, without the added risks of live ammo. Given the presence of troopies like Johnson, I was, for a change, inclined to agree.

All of which meant the three guys carrying 40mm grenade launchers attached to their M-16s didn't even have dummy grenades with them. The only "weapons" we had with us were blanks for the M-16s and the M-60s, a collection of pocket knives, and the ubiquitous entrenching tools that infantrymen since the days of Julius Caesar have carried with them in order to dig fortified emplacements. (Which was the only way to get your ass out of the hand-to-hand stuff without succumbing to cowardice.)

The major complaint I had about the setup was being ordered to take cover in two-man positions. Under battle conditions, one man would rest or sleep while the other kept watch. But . . .

I'd been teamed with Johnson.

To give him his due, Donaldson probably didn't know.

For my position, I'd chosen a tangle of bushes that concealed me from both the road and the hilltop. About ten feet to my left, Monroe fed a belt of blanks into the M-60's tray with a minimum of clanking and rattling. Then as he and his partner concealed themselves, I settled into the shallow trench I'd dug between my chosen bushes. Since I'd carefully distributed the excess dirt and snow smoothly beneath the bushes where it wouldn't show, I was nearly invisible from every direction.

Johnson was directly to my left. I could just see Wally and Crater over beyond Johnson, between him and Monroe. Gradually things got quiet as everybody settled in; within ten minutes the only sound I could hear was the wind and Johnson squirming in the snow. *Moron*. We waited, got colder, then colder still. At moments like this I understood why Uncle Sam wanted *me*. Nobody with brains would confuse this sort of thing with the patriotic satisfaction all the recruiting posters prate about.

That made me think of Gary again. I felt like a broken record, stuck on "raging mad." But if I let myself dwell on it, they'd end up locking me up in Leavenworth for life, because Johnson wouldn't come out of the ensuing brawl alive. That misbegotten little idiot had actually protested that the relief would be too short-shifted if I left for the funeral. Amazing, how strong nine healthy infantrymen can be. . . .

I'd almost gotten to his throat anyway.

Johnson shifted around again, so that snow crunched loud as a rifle report under him.

"Keep still!" I hissed viciously.

He flipped me the bird, but subsided.

I forced my concentration back onto my job. No convoy in sight. No trace of advance scouts anywhere. I held in a sigh.

Damn, it was cold.

As we lay there, waiting for that stupid convoy to show up so we could shoot the theoretical shit out of it and then get moving—and somewhat warmer again—I found myself uneasily wanting to glance over my shoulder. For reasons I couldn't fully explain, the skin on the back of my neck prickled, and my right palm itched. As the feeling worsened, I began wishing I had a loaded pistol, or even a decent knife. I would even have welcomed holding that weird black thing Gary's grandmother had given me.

I tried to shake myself out of my mood. Maybe I should have taken more leave time, after all. Here I was on routine winter maneuvers, and I felt as jumpy and disquieted as the night Sleipnir had—

Snow crunched, from somewhere behind us. I stiffened. Then it came again: a stealthy footstep, almost silent, from behind and to my right, in the trees farther up the hill. . . .

I swore under my breath. Wouldn't it figure the aggressors would come scouting through the woods ahead of their column? It occurred to me that—since I seemed to have more acute hearing than the rest of the guys—probably no one else had heard it.

I did a lightning-fast review of our tactical situation. Our primary objective had been concealment from the road; but as far as I could tell, we were concealed from the direction of the hilltop, too, unless someone moved, betraying our position. We were pretty good at what we did.

Abruptly I swore under my breath. Archibald Johnson *wasn't.* . . . Then I had two of them in sight, all but invisible in snow-and-winter-tree-bark camos. They were moving down between the trees, toward the field. My glance fell across the rifles they carried—

—Ahh, *shit*.

Those weren't rubber training AKs they were carrying. They were as real as the sudden fear-stink in my nostrils. I focused my gaze, and saw dark faces, thin noses, black Palestinian eyes. . . .

Ragheads.

They were already among us, still without having seen a thing. From my position I could see Wally's eyes; but only because I knew exactly where to look. I could tell he'd seen them, too; he looked as scared as I felt.

I glanced at my rifle—loaded with nothing but training blanks—and speculated upon the kind of stopping power blanks might have if things got hot. The M-16 didn't even produce a useful muzzle blast; most of the gas vented to the side. I eyed the entrenching tool lying close beside me, and swore under my breath. Great, a useless gun and a shovel. That made me feel *much* better.

Intent on their own movements, they still hadn't seen us. I uttered a tiny prayer—but *not* to Odin—that they'd just keep going, never seeing or hearing a thing, like ships in the night.

And they might have; but for the contribution of Mr. Model Soldier. Two feet away, Johnson shifted again. Snow crunched under his damn belly. The ragheads spun, crouched—and Johnson saw them for the first time.

I held my breath. Johnson gave a grunt of surprise and—

SHIT!

—made a reflex grab for his M-16.

Bark exploded from the trees. Bullets tore past my head and a cloud of snow erupted from the ground. I heard Crater yell, and suddenly Johnson was cowering behind a tree trunk. I fired the blanks in my rifle, with exactly the results I'd expected—none. The M-60 was blazing away, too, with no more effect than I'd had. If it had been closer to the bastards, the bigger blanks might have done some damage—but this wasn't horseshoes.

The only cover between me—flattened out in the snow—and a hail of live bullets was an all-too-thin screen of low bushes. Fortunately, on full-auto, their fire only lasted about two endless seconds; then their last hot brass sizzled into the snow.

I took a quick personal inventory.

I wasn't hit.

I knew I was going to be surprised about that when I got around to it.

Instantly, I launched toward the nearest raghead, entrenching tool in hand. He saw me coming and tried to hurry home another magazine but jammed it. He didn't get another chance.

Midspring, something warm—*something that felt like flesh*—wrapped around my wrist. Before I could react, the death-black blade of Gary's knife had buried itself in the raghead's belly. It sliced upward through cloth and flesh like so much soft cheese. A scream split the air—

Followed almost instantly by a curse from the other raghead. In his haste, he'd managed to drop his second magazine in the snow. I grinned in his face and the knife slashed out. A greenish aura swirled within the very substance of the blade as it severed the raghead's hand. His rifle—and hand—dropped to the snow. Without slowing, the knife continued upward through the raghead's throat, and cut short his scream.

I whirled and stopped. It was over. There had been only two. I found myself on my knees, panting hard, staring in abrupt amazement at the impossible knife clutched in my palm. The heavy blade was streaked with red against the snow; so was most of my uniform. Only now did I realize that the long, curved "tail" of the haft was somehow wrapped snugly around my wrist.

Twice . . .

Likewise—now that it had my undivided attention—I could tell that the flesh-textured surface of the haft was indeed radiating a perceptible warmth against my frozen skin.

I looked more closely. Call it a hallucination, but those damned eyes were *twinkling*, visibly—and the haft *moved* within my grasp. Somehow, from somewhere, I was getting the impression of laughter. . . .

But even as I stared, the eerie glow died away, and the knife was flat black again. I yelled and shook my hand violently, trying to shake the thing loose. It fell to the snow, and blurred—or maybe it was my vision—

I shut my eyes. When I opened them again, a bloody entrenching tool lay in the snow before me.

"Hey, Randy—"

A hand fell on my shoulder. With a shout I convulsed sideways. I landed sprawled in the snow and my cheek touched something warm and wet. I jerked away and looked down. It was the raghead's severed hand. Still twitching in the snow.

"Man, you okay?" Monroe looked scared and worried and awestruck at the same time.

"Uhng. . . ."

The guys crowded around. I sat up slowly. Someone was yelling for the lieutenant, and someone else was yelling for the medic. Everyone was talking at once. I felt sick and dizzy; it was difficult to follow what was going on.

Sergeant Brown shouted for order and formed us into a circular defensive perimeter—fat lot of good that would do, but it *felt* right—while Lieutenant Donaldson radioed Captain Jones that we'd had a real incident, somebody trying to steal weapons, and that shots had been fired. The L-T was also bright enough to call for another platoon—an *armed* one—to search the area for other terrorist patrols.

"How many down, Sergeant?" I heard him call.

"Two enemy dead; one of our boys down."

Donaldson relayed that and requested an ambulance. Wally was yelling for the medic to shag his butt. Crater swore nonstop, propped against a tree, his pants covered with blood. Wally held a compress against the wound. The medic pushed Wally out of the way and took over.

"Crater," I called shakily, "you okay?"

"Yeah, dammit, I took one across the back of my effin' thigh—ahhhh!" The medic had ripped his pants open. "Keep that asshole away from me or I'll kill the son-of—ahhhh—" He yelled again as the medic did something else to his leg.

"Clam it, Barnes!" Brown barked. "Watch the goddamn perimeter!" He then turned his wrath on Monroe, who'd left his position.

Chuck stood over Johnson and clutched his useless M-16. Chuck made a good show of watching the perimeter. He was also effectively holding Johnson down. *That* worthless dildo lay shivering in the snow, looking utterly wretched. No one had to ask Crater who the "asshole" was.

The ambulance showed up seconds before three jeep-loads of MPs skidded to a halt. It would have been hard to decide which we were happier to see. The ambulance meant help for Crater; but the MPs had *bullets*.

They landed spitting orders.

"Get these men out of here."

"Anyone touch that evidence?"

"Search everyone—I don't want any goddamned souvenirs walking off this site!"

"Who was directly involved in this?"

The latter question was from the MP Captain in charge of the investigation. Lieutenant Donaldson had the two ranking MPs in tow, moving purposefully toward Sergeant Brown. The MPs patted down the platoon for souvenirs, then sent us out of the area they had already roped off as the "crime scene."

Brown reported succinctly who had done what to whom.

Donaldson glanced at me, then looked at the ragheads closely for the first time. His eyes widened. Then he turned on me, his expression grim, and noticed the condition of my uniform. "Spill it, son."

Not wanting a court-martial for insubordination, I chose not to reply that I already had spilled it. In quantity. Not wanting a Section Eight, I was not about to mention Gary's knife. I did describe Johnson's giveaway of our position; then toe-danced selectively through the details of my role in the fight. The MP Captain listened intently. I watched him even more so. My blood pressure began to subside as it became apparent that he was not more than normally suspicious.

"This is the weapon?" Donaldson asked into the silence that ensued when I finished. He pointed toward the bloody entrenching tool with the toe of one boot.

"Yessir. It was the only thing I could think of grabbing, sir, when the blanks didn't have any effect."

The MPs examined the dead terrorists while Donaldson eyed the severed hand. "And just how did you inflict this kind of damage with an entrenching tool, soldier?"

I opened my mouth on empty air when Johnson broke in. His voice was shaking almost as hard as the rest of him.

"It wasn't the shovel—he had a *knife*, dammit, a huge knife! I saw it—it was about a foot long and black. . . ."

He gulped and shut up under the L-T's withering stare.

Donaldson regarded me quizzically. I shrugged, forcing myself to meet his eyes. "I don't know what he's talking about, sir. I haven't got anything more than a pocket knife on me. And"—I indicated the entrenching tool with a jerk of my thumb—"there's blood all over the shovel. I keep it sharp, sir. I just swung hard and thought about it afterward."

"Maybe Barnes used shovel judo," Chuck suggested helpfully into the silence.

Donaldson glared at him; then had me strip in the snow. Of course there wasn't a knife anywhere to be found, other than my little three-inch folder.

"There will be an inquest, soldier," he said, skewering me with his gaze while I got dressed. "Everyone involved will be questioned by Captain Plunkett." He nodded toward the MP Captain concluding his notes on my report.

Plunkett finished scrawling in his notebook and looked up. "I want this site left untouched, and I want all of you back at the base immediately. Out into the road, all of you. Detriech, make sure you get all the brass. Half of it's going to be under the snow."

After being dismissed, we trudged down to join the rest of the platoon on the road. There we waited for the truck Lieutenant Donaldson had radioed for. We stood around in the snow and carefully avoided meeting each other's eyes. Especially me. I had more reason not to want to talk with anyone than all the rest of them combined. Being a hero is embarrassing. Plus, I really needed to get back to the base armory and look inside that damned box. It was there, of course—it had to be there—but I needed very badly to *see* that it was there.

Though I wasn't certain I could trust my own eyes anymore. . . .

Several hours of intensive grilling later, the MPs were satisfied and I was free to go, the last member of our squad released. The others were waiting outside, questions written all over their faces.

"I dunno," I said. "They pumped me for all I was worth; then shut up like clams. My guess is they'll hush it up like usual."

Wally nodded.

"How's Crater?" I asked.

"Okay. The medics are holding him at the infirmary overnight; then he'll be back with us for light duty. They're sending us back to the field, I guess."

Wally didn't sound pleased.

"At least we're still around to go back," Chuck said quietly. "I never saw anything like it, man," he added. "Jumping them like that, with nothing but a goddamn shovel. We were lucky they didn't hit us worse before you got them. How'd you do it?"

I looked off into the distance, uncomfortable over the awe in his voice. I had pulled a suicidal-seeming stunt with a shovel and they all figured I was some kind of hero who'd saved their lives, or something.

Well, maybe I had at that, but it sure wasn't because I was fearless in the face of death.

As for *how* I'd managed it, I couldn't admit to them or anyone else what'd really done the killing. Only Johnson had seen that knife, and he'd been ridiculed for blurting it out; would probably get cashiered on a Section Eight, if he stuck to his story. Not that I'd be sorry to see him go.

"I don't know. Honest, I just don't know. Blind dumb luck, I guess. Have I got time to head over to the armory?"

"Armory?" Chuck laughed. "What're you going to do; ask if they've got any more of those deadly entrenching tools?"

"Or something." I forced a grin.

Wally nodded. "Okay, meet us in twenty outside the mess hall. Truck's supposed to be waiting there."

I left them and made my way reluctantly back to the armory. The armorer looked annoyed at my request; but went and got the box. He tossed the wooden case onto the table between us with a solid thunk, and buried himself again in his spy thriller.

It hadn't changed in the twenty-four hours it had sat in the locked safe. It was still a slim wooden box, still wrapped in faded old gingham. I stood for a long moment just looking at it; then made my hands open the lid, quickly.

It was still there. The light from the overhead bulb glinted coldly along the nonreflective black blade. Irrationally, I had the feeling it was looking up at me. There was no trace of blood anywhere. The curve of the haft was precisely the same as when I had first laid eyes on it. I attempted to flex the "tail" with both hands. Reason told me that nothing that solid could bend.

But it had. . . .

From somewhere came an impression of unheard laughter.

I glanced up at the sergeant. He was still oblivious to the world. Okay. Symptom or fact . . . we'd see.

I picked up the knife and held it in a battle grip. It still felt warm under my palm. Feeling a little foolish, I dared it to move.

It *did*. Faster than my eyes could follow, the tail whipped around my wrist and gripped firmly.

I bit off an exclamation and forced myself to stand still. Nothing further happened: no glowing green light, no glittering eyes. The knife just lay quietly in my hand, its tail curled impossibly around my arm.

As the initial shock wore off, it slowly occurred to me that this could be a real helluva useful knife—if any of this were really happening, as opposed to a warning that my load might be shifting.

Gary's grandmother had said this thing had *chosen* me. I had almost talked myself into believing that was her way of saying, "I want you to have this." Now I wasn't so sure. How in the nine worlds had a little old lady in Oregon gotten hold of this thing? Had she known what she had?

It struck me, standing there in the armory with a supernatural knife wrapped around my arm, that if Gary'd had this knife with him the night Sleipnir showed up, Odin might have been short one world-class champion for his band of not-so-merry men. Or could the knife have come to Gary from Oregon when he really needed it? Not, I realized slowly, that it would've done much good in a car wreck. Besides, there was something else clamoring for attention in my forebrain.

Who had sent this knife to me?

First Odin kills my best friend, then *somebody* sends me a supernatural knife by way of the grieving family? I narrowed my eyes, and tightened my grip on the warm haft. Didn't the one-eyed god of battle often present certain warriors with special, magical blades just before . . .

The knife seemed almost to squirm in my grasp.

This reeked of Odin's touch. I didn't trust the knife—

or the situation—any further than I could throw either of them. Even if the knife had just saved my ass, I wasn't about to make any more deals with Odin Oath-Breaker, much less accept his bribe. I'd seen what happened when men made a pact with Odin. He broke faith, and killed them.

I eyed the knife. It eyed me right back. I wondered if it could "hear" me.

"How about it?" I asked silently. "You know how I feel. Whatever you are, if you think I'm going to be a good little human now, you might as well go back where you came from."

Surprisingly it purred in my palm. Briefly the tail squeezed tighter.

Now what the hell was that supposed to mean?

I studied the—carved?—face of the dragon, and was forced to admit that there were exciting possibilities to owning such a knife. It could follow me anywhere, disappear when I couldn't afford to get caught with it, and in a fight wrap itself so firmly around my arm that no blow short of cutting off my hand would dislodge it. Why, with a knife like that I could even take on a god in one-to-one combat—

I caught my breath sharply.

Then stared at the weapon in my hand.

It fairly purred.

Alarm flooded through me, so deep I couldn't keep my hands from shaking as I released my grip. I didn't know what to think as I laid the thick blade across my other palm. The tail unwrapped obediently, resuming almost instantaneously its former rigid shape. Gently I returned it to its box and closed the lid.

"Put it back, will you?"

I thought that had come out sounding fairly normal.

The armorer glanced up, nodded, and put the book down.

"Thanks."

"Sure thing, bud."

Uneasily I watched him return it to the locked safe; then I retreated back out into the cold. I was so distracted, I damn near walked past the waiting troop transport. The guys gave up attempts at conversation well before we got back to the maneuvers site.

Chapter Eight

When I finally stirred, I was momentarily confused. I blinked at my surroundings for what felt like whole minutes until memory returned; then glanced automatically at my wrist. The watch gave me an utterly meaningless time; but I had a feeling I'd been asleep for several hours. I was so cold I could barely move. An angry, vibrating whine made itself known somewhere above my head, grating like fingernails on slate, just at the edge of hearing. That must've been what'd woken me. . . .

Groggily I rolled over. The cyalume still glowed brightly. Higher up, another greenish glow caught my attention.

Uh-oh.

I dragged myself up onto hands and knees and peered at the knife. It was embedded nearly to the guard in stone.

The eerie green light which I'd seen swirling through it during battle was back. A high-pitched sound resonated through the very rocks. I reached out hesitantly and touched the haft. The tail grabbed my wrist with

scalding strength. I yowled and jerked back. It felt like
I'd tried to move the whole mountain with my wrist.

"Ungh—"

There wasn't room to stand up, so I shrugged out of
my pack, and sat with both feet braced against the wall.
I grabbed hold with both hands, and *pulled*. Several vertebrae popped creatively; then the blade wrenched loose
from crumbling stone and my head cracked hard on the
opposite tunnel wall.

When the stars disappeared, I shook myself and sat
up.

The knife lay quietly in my grasp. The blade wasn't
even scratched.

It figured.

I rubbed my skull gingerly and didn't feel any blood,
although there was a lump growing beneath the skin.
Having determined that I was relatively undamaged, I
sheathed the knife and retrieved the cyalume stick, then
took a quick look around.

This passage was low and very narrow. Beyond the
glow of my lightstick it seemed to end in the utter blackness I'd learned to associate with deep passages. So far so
good. I eased up onto my knees and established that
there was just enough clearance to crawl with my pack in
place, so I strapped it back on and began to explore.

Presently the tunnel opened out into a larger chamber. Walls, floor, and ceiling had been smoothed from
centuries of flowing water. Soft green cyalume light
showed a vast circular pattern worn into a bowl-shaped
depression below me. Looking up, I saw a matching pattern on the ceiling, forming a dome above my head. It
looked as if a whirlpool had formed where the tunnel
opened out, carving the dome above and bowl below.
Beyond the depression, the passageway continued on,
wider and higher, through a black hole in the far wall.

Good. That boded well. But first, I had a little urgent

business to attend to. I was shivering so hard my elbows wanted to collapse beneath me. First came dry clothing. Fortunately, I'd packed my spares, including underwear and socks, in waterproof bags. I stripped off my wet stuff, shucked on dry clothes, and spent the next fifteen minutes doing calisthenics. When I stopped shivering and finally began to feel warm again, I sat down to deal with the rest of my soggy gear.

The sleeping bag was hopeless. I set it aside to form an "abandon" pile. Inside the pack, I found a waterlogged lump of former hardtack biscuits glued to the inside of their paper container. My stomach rebelled; but I'd eaten worse. I patted the mess into a lump, and divided it into three smaller "loaves." These I put to one side, along with my remaining bits of dried fruit and the last jerky stick.

Most of my spare ammo was wrapped in plastic against the dampness of the cave. I was pleased to find it still dry, despite my recent immersion. I set the wet plastic carefully aside and stacked ammo into a neat little pile, then removed the magazines from my belt pouches. They were soaking wet, of course, along with the ammo in them. I hoped the individual rounds were well sealed. I emptied the magazines and set the wet rounds to one side.

My meager supply of carbide was completely useless now, of course, since I had no way of burning it without the helmet lantern. I stacked that on top of the sleeping bag.

I then emptied every pouch and pocket of my gear, and spread everything out. I frowned and pulled at my lower lip. Two of my four twelve-hour lightsticks had broken their vials during my bout with the river, so I had plenty of light at the moment; but I'd run out one day sooner than I'd anticipated. I was down to two twelve-hour sticks, four six-hour units, and seven half-hour shorties, for a total of two days, three and a half hours of potential light.

Something told me I wasn't going to stumble across the gateway to Niflheim during the next two days and three and a half hours; but there wasn't much I could do about that. Spelunking in the dark ought to be about as much fun as scuba diving the Titanic.

Having established the condition of that gear absolutely essential to my survival, my next priority was to dry and clean the guns. They shouldn't have begun to rust yet, of course; but it didn't pay to take chances. Rummaging through my supplies, I found the little field cleaning kit I carried with me everywhere, and took the guns apart one at a time, drying, cleaning, lubricating, and carefully inspecting each part before reassembly. I checked the AR-180 aluminum magazines for damage. Thankfully, I found none, so I dried them and the rounds they had contained.

I took more care with the P-7 magazines, drying and very lightly oiling each one, both inside and out; then I dried each individual round thoroughly before returning it to the magazine. The only ammunition I had been able to buy for the P-7 had been some World War II German surplus 9mm Parabellum, which had steel-jacketed iron bullets rather than the civilian hollow-points I would have preferred. The caution I used in drying them out was well advised; there's always a risk of iron rounds rusting in steel magazines, even without submersing them in mineral-rich water.

Then, hungry enough to eat nails, I bit into the first of the three "bread loaves." It was awful: wet and doughy. But I choked it down and washed the taste from my mouth with water.

After drinking my fill—half emptying the canteen in the process—I grabbed a cyalume stick and crawled back to the river. Refilling the canteens left me with a full supply. I was relatively warm, relatively dry, and relatively fed. All in all, I felt relatively marvelous—only mildly battered, bruised, and bashed. Not bad for a guy who ought to have been dead a couple of times over.

Once everything was dry, I threaded the chain that held my gold Thor's hammer through carrying holes in the ends of my three functioning lightsticks. I couldn't afford not to have both hands free; hanging from my chest was a good place for them. Then I snugged the magazines back into the pouches on the web gear, repacked everything I was taking with me, and carefully strapped the rifle to the pack frame, with the stock folded so the barrel wouldn't scrape on the low ceiling.

The P-7 hung reassuringly at my waist, and the knife seemed to hum a pleasant little tune against my calf. My footsteps echoed above the distant sound of the river. I even whistled a Sousa tune, feeling remarkably well pleased with the world.

Which was probably a good indication that the bottom was about to fall out again.

It was Crater's fault we visited Frau Stempel in the first place. I'd never been to a fortune teller in my life, although I'd been to the circus as a kid, and had blown plenty of pop-bottle money on the sideshows. Crater got this wild idea that a fortune teller could warn us if the ragheads were going to hit us again, so after an argument, and several bets and counter bets, we decided to visit Frau Stempel. She had a place in the village, nice and discreet, and made a living selling books, candles, and advice. She could've been my grandmother.

As luck would have it, I drew lots for the first session.

"Sit down, won't you?" she asked with a smile.

Her "sitting room" smelled like a bakery, warm with scents of apples and cinnamon. There was no trace of mumbo-jumbo knickknackery, just a cozy little parlor for two, with comfortable, overstuffed chairs, and a little table with Belgian lace draped over it.

"You do not believe in what you have come for, do you?"

I glanced up, and met bemused blue eyes. I started to answer, reconsidered, and finally said, "Frau Stempel, I don't know what I believe."

Her eyes widened slightly; then she simply patted my hand, and sat down across the table from me. She didn't pull out tarot cards, or put a crystal ball between us. All she did was move a candle holder to the center of the table, and fish out a box of wooden matches. The candle was white, and covered with little squiggles and cramped words. She lit the new wick, fanned out the match, and smiled.

"Now, what would you like to know, my young friend? There is a girl, perhaps, or do you have a soldier's fears?"

What did I want to know? I didn't really give a damn about ragheads anymore, so long as they kept to their side of the fence. Even if they didn't, I could handle myself in a fight. Still, that's what we'd come to find out.

I opened my lips to ask about the ragheads, and said, "Tell me how to find Niflheim."

Her eyes shot wide, and her face lost color.

"What?" Her voice was breathless.

"Niflheim," I said with growing conviction. I leaned forward, with my elbows propped against Belgian lace. "If you're any good, Frau Stempel, tell me how to find Niflheim, without dying."

She blinked several times, and closed her hands in folds of the lace, then swallowed. "You . . . are playing with me, yes?"

I held her gaze. "I'm not crazy," I said softly. "And I'm not making a joke."

Frau Stempel wet her lips, then excused herself and poured a glass of water from a pitcher and drank it down in two rapid gulps. Then she returned to the table, and proceeded to ignore me completely. She concentrated on the candle flame, and whispered words, too softly for me to hear. The room seemed to grow darker, despite afternoon sunlight pouring through the curtains and the candle flame between us. The back of my neck crawled, and I found myself wanting to glance over my shoulder. Maybe this hadn't been my best idea ever. . . .

The candle flared wildly in the still air. For an instant, I thought someone must have opened the door on us—

Then a four-foot column of flame shot upward from the table. Frau Stempel screamed and I found myself on my feet, backing away from searing heat. Someone was yelling outside, trying to get the door open. Frau Stempel ran for the door, herself, but it wouldn't open. She whirled and faced the thing that was growing out of the fire. I had never taken my eyes from it.

It had fangs, and wild, angry eyes, and the lean, hungry shape of a hunting dog. Belgian lace ignited under its paws. Fire spread to the carpet, the chairs. Snarls filled the parlor, and the saliva dripping from its mouth as it advanced ignited new fires. Frau Stempel screamed again, and beat on the door.

There wasn't a dry spot anywhere on me, and I was having trouble breathing. . . . I hurled myself between Frau Stempel and the thing locked in the room with us.

It lunged.

I yelled, and threw one arm up—

A warm haft slid into my hand and wild green light flared brighter than the hellhound. Heat engulfed my whole body, and I yelled again. Momentum carried the blade right through the fiery apparition, muzzle to tail. I heard a sizzle as it parted to pass on either side of me. . . .

Then it was gone.

I stood panting in the middle of the rug, and clutched Gary's knife. The green glow vanished . . .

and so did the knife. Little fires scorched the rug all around my feet. I stamped them out, and grabbed the pitcher of ice water. That took care of the smoldering chairs and tablecloth. A moan reached me from near the door, then the knob simply turned, and the whole gang piled into the room.

"What the hell happened?"

"Get Frau Stempel!" I snapped. She was seated on the floor.

Wally picked her up, and carried her out of the room, while Chuck wrestled with the windows. The parlor was full of smoke. I followed Wally, who had found a couch in the next room.

"Frau Stempel? Are you all right?"

She looked up, and moaned. "Go away. . . ."

I crouched beside her. "I'm very sorry, Frau Stempel. I . . . had no idea. . . ."

She closed her eyes. "Please, go away."

Her face was somewhere between grey and white, and she was shaking uncontrollably. Wally covered her, and found a telephone. We waited until the doctor had arrived. I explained that the candle had overturned, and the room had caught fire, then I left him with some money to cover the cost of his visit and the damage to her home. I felt like a worm; but it was the best I could do.

Crater never did get his answer; but I'd gotten mine.

There was only one hellhound in all of Norse mythology. Its name was Garm. The cave it guarded was the entrance to Niflheim. Somewhere, that cave existed, and Odin didn't want me to find it. In less than three weeks, I'd have all the time in the world to hunt. Just three weeks . . .

If I could keep Odin from killing me first.

For the next three weeks, I watched my back and slept with one eye on the door, and generally was as edgy as an addict three days after his last blow. At any rate, I watched my step. *Every* step.

By the time my last shift on the towers rolled around (although I didn't know *then* it would be my last), I was beginning to wonder if maybe Odin wasn't saving up for a shoe the size of Manhattan to drop on me. Conditions had gotten back to relative normal—although nobody ever talked about Gary Vernon or Frau Stempel—and the guys had started in with the jokes about my being so "short" I'd have to start standing on a ladder to unzip my fly, and other equally crude quips designed to get me through my last few weeks as a U.S. infantryman. They were a good bunch of guys, and I knew I'd miss them.

It was a quiet shift from the start; but there was a new moon, which meant it was black as the inside of a cave beyond the lights. Bright sunshine the day before had started to thaw the frozen ground, leaving relatively warm, wet earth under a blanket of cool night air. Spring wasn't supposed to arrive in Germany until April, but the weather these days was every bit as weird as everything else in my life had been lately.

The nice part was not freezing to death in the towers, or having to slog through two feet of snow on patrol. The bad part was, cool moist air hitting the warm earth as it chilled had resulted in a sea of ground fog stretching across the whole countryside and hiding the terrain beneath a layer of thick white nothingness.

As luck would have it, I was stuck in Tower Three, facing the worst spot on the perimeter, a belly-deep washout that ended just outside the fence. It ended there only because we'd shoveled half a truckload of dirt into it on this side to keep it from running right into the compound. I couldn't see anything of the washout tonight, though. The fences rose from drifting fog, floating eerily above the wet earth as though we'd invented antigravity.

I hated nights like this. There was no way to see what might be crawling around out there, and I didn't have much backup from either direction if things got hot. Butler was over on my right, nowhere to be seen through his windows. Our resident doper was stretched out on the floor again, dead to the world, leaving me with double terrain to watch.

At least I didn't have to worry about watching over to my left. Johnson had really cracked that day I cut up the ragheads. Brass'd had to strip him of his security clearance and pull him off the towers. He'd kept babbling about "that knife. . . ." They'd given him a job filling ketchup bottles in the mess hall. At least he was off the guard towers and out of my hair.

(Every time I asked Sergeant Brown about the ragheads I'd cut up, he just said, "We're working on it," or, "The MPs are handling it." I finally quit asking.)

There hadn't been any more incidents since then, either. We'd put the fear of Allah into them; or at least made them more cautious. I hoped we hadn't made them *too* cautious—they'd always left traces before, warning us they were in the area; but things had been so quiet lately, everyone was getting too relaxed. I didn't like it; but there wasn't a thing I could do about it, except sweat.

I glanced over at the tower to my left, where Stanley was wide awake and fully alert. No; more like nervous and wound up tighter than my old childhood Timex.

I snorted. He still wasn't talking to us. His first day in the platoon—a week after Johnson left us—the guys had generously told him LAD meant Launch And Die, and the moron repeated it in front of the artillery officer. Five minutes of the best ass-chewing it had ever been my pleasure to witness was followed by fifteen minutes of intense one-on-one instruction on Launch and Dispersal tactics. . . .

I still marveled at Stanley's total lack of brains. He wasn't dangerously stupid, like Johnson; just amazingly gullible. The gods alone knew we had needed a few laughs by then. He'd been such an easy hit that first day, Chuck had really outdone himself, devising a plan to put Stanley to the test. And Stan, bless his teeny little brain, hadn't let old Chuck down.

The very official-looking orders required Stanley to attend the "Pershing Missile In-flight Maintenance Non-Commissioned Officer's Course," and included a typed description of said course, complete with parachute training, electronics training, promotion to sergeant, and extra pay for hazardous duty. All that was required of Stan was to show up with all his gear at the First Sergeant's office right before morning Physical Training (a full half an hour before reveille).

First Sergeant Pitt was One Serious Mutha from South Chicago. He'd been with us exactly one week longer than Stanley, and he already had a rep as someone you didn't, and I mean not ever, screw around with. So naturally, Chuck sent our lamb right into the new First Shirt's gentle care. Pitt read the orders, and asked Stan if he was ready to begin training, then opened his window, and tossed Stanley out through it. Into the middle of morning PT.

Poor old Stan. He promised to give the guys endless entertainment. I was almost sorry I'd miss it. Almost. Stanley just might make these last few weeks of mine more bearable than the months behind me had been. Brass had already told us we had to pull duty ninety days straight, so although I had leave coming to me before my discharge, I wouldn't be able to use it. We were short nearly half a shift, and there was no chance of getting any more new recruits security-cleared before summer. I had no idea what they'd do when I rotated out. No matter how you looked at it, it was going to be a long spring.

I sighed, watching the heavy fog stir into wisps and tendrils in the faint breeze, and tried not to think about the brunette I'd met on my last pass for the whole season. Ready, willing . . . and I was stuck with one raging appetite and no relief in sight. I glanced at the sky, and frowned at the heavy overcast I could just barely see. It might rain before the shift was up, and that'd be just great. Warm, wet—

I would *not* think about that brunette.

A hint of motion caught my peripheral vision and I looked sharply left. So damn dark out there, and with that washout running right up, hidden in pea soup . . .

The commander of the relief walked into sight between the fences on the far side of Stanley's tower, moving toward the washout. I relaxed. Stan yelled "Halt" and Corporal Brunowski called back the proper response. I wondered if Stanley would remember—or care—to follow custom and telephone us that the commander of the relief was headed our way.

A quick look right confirmed that Butler was still out cold. Of course. And—of course—there wasn't a peep from Stanley on the phone. Obviously he was way too pissed off to let anyone else know the corporal was making his rounds. I picked up the phone to warn Butler as well as the next tower down from him, where Monroe was on guard. Wally and Crater and the rest of the bums I normally hung out with were sacked out over in the bunkhouse between shifts. Lucky stiffs.

I got no response on the phone. I frowned, ringing it a few more times, still with no results. It was live; but no one was responding. Must be Sergeant Baker on the switchboard. It would be just like him to turn it off, to see who tried to call and who was sound asleep. Butler was still down and out. Well, Christ, I had to do something.

I went out onto the tiny back "porch" of the tower and

slammed the door a couple of times to wake Butler up. Nothing. I glanced over to see how close the corporal was—and saw nothing. Aw, nuts. He must've run past to get under my tower. The whole guard mount was playing stupid games tonight.

I peered under the tower—and found nothing. A prickle ran down my spine. Where the blazes was Brunowski? He'd been moving toward the washout. . . .

Thoroughly irritated, and more than a little worried about gigantic black hellhorses and one-eyed gods with a really perverted sense of humor, I slung my rifle over my back and climbed up onto the roof. I needed to gain an extra few feet of angle. With a slight grunt, I hauled myself up over the little walkway that ran across the back of the tower. The earlier faint breeze had picked up a little and felt cool in my face as I belly-crawled through roofing gravel over to the edge. Fog was blowing into eddies and clear spots, leaving the washout partly visible. I looked down between the fences . . . and found Brunowski.

Flat on his back, sprawled with arms and legs at all angles. Dark blood was still spurting from his throat.

They'd got Brunowski.

God*damn.*

A knot of something between fear and rage took hold of me, even as my eyes found the hole in the outer fence. Someone just outside the wire was holding the hole apart. Two guys were crawling belly-flat past the corporal, toward another man pulling apart a hole in the inner fence. Of all the times for sergeant of the guard to screw around with the phones . . .

I scooted back and pulled my rifle free, then eased back the bolt to cock it as quietly as I could manage. I checked to see if the magazine had fed properly, started a round in the chamber, knocked the forward assist into place . . .

And started to sweat.

Jesus God, let me not screw up. . . .

I put the rifle on semiautomatic, stood up, and took aim at the s.o.b. crawling through the hole in the inner fence.

Two shots rent the silence. Both caught the leading terrorist in the neck. He flopped awkwardly and slid backward to disappear into a stray patch of whiteness.

"HALT! DO NOT MOVE!"

I fired another quick burst of six rounds, two of which caught the second man in line when he jumped up to return fire. He slammed backward and I heard yells coming from Stanley's tower. Two down, eight shots gone; that left ten shots loaded. If the magazine had been full.

I caught motion with the corner of my eye and turned to see a fifth man running through the grass straight at us. I centered him and fired four times. He disappeared. I cursed. I'd hit him—where'd he go?

A burst of full automatic fire raked my position. I returned fire into the woodline, five shots, then dropped to my knee to change magazines. I heard fire to my right and saw flashes from Stanley's position, returned by fire from both the washout and the woodline. Jesus Christ, how many were we up against? I dropped the spent magazine, grabbed a fresh one from my pouch, and slammed it home.

I saw the flashes an instant before the roof exploded beneath me. Pain tore through my left foot and arm. Something slammed into my chest as I stared stupidly at a hole punched clean through the magazine. The carrying handle of the M-16 shattered in my face—chunks of flying shrapnel caught my jaw and cheeks with the force of knives shot out of a cannon. I think I yelled. Then I staggered backward, gasping, as pain and shock caught me like a fist.

My feet hit empty air as I plunged backward off the tower. I yelled like a stabbed sow, and windmilled stupidly all the way down. Twenty-eight feet is a long way to fall. Especially when you've just been shot multiple times. The firefight was still loud in my ears when I smacked into cold, wet muck. Sound vanished, and sight went with it.

When they came back, pain held me like a net, and tangled my arms and legs so that I couldn't move. I felt an icy breeze. A shudder shook my whole frame. I tried to get my eyes open. I could feel the ground, soft and oozing, under my back; but I couldn't see the stars that ought to be above me. Something blocking them? Another shudder tore at me and I tried to get my eyes focused. All I could see was a vague blackness. A thrill of horror nearly made me throw up.

Sleipnir had already come for me, dragged me to hell. . . .

I got myself to one elbow. For an instant, it was touch and go whether the vomit in my throat came up, or went down. Then I saw blurred motion in the fence not four feet from me. Someone in blackface, trying to get through—or two someones—

I groped for my rifle, but couldn't feel it. Couldn't begin to see it. I heard guttural curses in what sounded like Arabic. I tried again to focus my eyes, and saw two blurred hands trying to jam two magazines into two rifles. . . .

I groped wildly for my own rifle—then remembered it was shot to pieces—

DAMMIT—!

Sweat poured as I tried to summon that demon-bladed knife into my hand. Nothing. Son-of-a—

Goddammit, I wasn't going to just lie there and die while Odin laughed! I lurched upward. Two faces swiveled. Two rifles came up, two barrels centered me. . . .

Then nausea took hold and I collapsed onto my side, retching into the mud. I couldn't think with the pain in my head, and the knife hadn't come, damn its evil little black soul. . . .

I felt a tug on my shoulder. Sheer terror galvanized muscles I thought I'd lost use of permanently. I grabbed wildly—and found the rifle. I swung upward, hard. It connected with a meaty smack as someone tried to shove it aside.

"Randy, don't shoot—dammit, get his fingers loose— don't shoot—it's us—Crater and Wally—"

I finally managed to get my eyes focused. Crater's long frame leaned dizzily over me. The lower part of him seemed to be drifting in lazy white fog. . . .

Rage—sudden and terrible—spread a bloody film across that innocent white fog. I struggled to get up. Goddammit, if Odin wouldn't come fight me, fair and goddamned square, I'd show the bastard, I'd get up and walk all the bloody way to Valhalla—

A wave of intense nausea hit about the same time my head exploded in a twenty-megaton burst. I doubled up, and decided being dead would be a great deal more pleasant.

"Hey, man, don't move, you musta broken something—you shouldn't move 'til the medics get here."

They were pushing me back down. Pain drained the strength anger had brought. I sagged back into the mud. Then slowly I realized I didn't hear any more gunfire.

Crater blurred again. I muttered, "Hold still—you got two heads, dammit—"

"What'd he say?" Wally's voice asked from somewhere off in the fog.

"Shut up!" Crater hissed. Then, "Just hang on, Randy; the medics are coming."

"Did we get 'em?"

Had I actually got that out?

Crater answered, so I must have.

"We stopped the s.o.b.'s, Randy. We stopped 'em. There's a guy with a loaded rifle in his hand and four holes in his chest hanging right there in the inner fence, dead as a doornail. There's another dead one behind him, down in the outer fence by the washout. We found a blood trail off into the woodline. Sergeant Baker's out there with the rest of the relief, tracking it. Even Stanley got one, down by his tower."

Stanley? Good God.

"Did—you—get any—?" I tried to keep my eyes focused on a face that kept blurring out of shape, and heard Crater laugh.

"Hell, Randy, I got one in the head but you'd already killed him. He's the one who crawled off and got stuck in the outer fence. And Butler went nuts. Fifteen, twenty rounds out into the trees. I think he even hit a couple of rabbits, poor little bastards."

The laughter left his voice then. "Brunowski's dead. Stanley's dead, too. One hole in the front window, one in the back, and one clear through his head. His rifle jammed. You were one lucky s.o.b., man. There's holes in the floor, the desk, the radiator; not to mention the roof. Damn lucky all that wood and crap slowed 'em down. Medics ought to be here any minute." Then, dimly, "Dammit, Wally, aren't they here yet?"

I wasn't listening anymore. I was floating on a foggy sea of pain, thinking about a good noncom's death, and a newbie's useless one, and cursing a cowardly god who wouldn't show his face in an honest fight. The pain intensified. I wondered absently what they'd tell Stanley's wife back home—not that it made any real difference to me or anyone else—then I slipped into darkness and mercifully left the pain behind.

We never did find out who'd shot us up that night. Most of them got away, and the ones that stayed as corpses just disappeared, same as the ones I'd cut up with Gary's black knife. Nameless, faceless, they'd slipped away into the night to regroup somewhere else, while our officers figured out ways to keep the whole mess quiet. I never did find out what they told Stanley's widow.

I ended up in Frankfurt for a while, in the main hospital for the forces based in Germany. Actually, I'd been damned lucky. I'd been hit four times, and falling off the back of that stupid tower had netted me a concussion and several assorted nasty sprains and bruises. It was several days before I stopped seeing double images; but then, it was several weeks before I could walk on my shot-up foot, and even with crutches it hurt like bloody blazes.

One bullet had grazed my arm, just a flesh wound, not much deeper than a scratch. The second round had punched through the tower itself, then through my rifle's magazine before hitting my flakvest, leaving nothing more serious than a good-sized bruise, although it had hurt like I'd been kicked by a horse. The baby coronary I'd had in the ambulance on the way in had convinced me I'd been shot through the heart itself—and was just too slow on the uptake to go ahead and die.

The third round had shattered the handle of my M-16; quite a bit of flying debris as well as the spent round had slammed into my face. The stitches had left some very interesting scars that had proven surprisingly successful in rousing the nurses' sympathies. (So I'm an asshole—I'll take the attention of beautiful women any way I can get it.)

Of course, I was *really* lucky that my jawbone hadn't been shattered—which would've left me wired shut and sipping pizza through a straw for months—or that none of the shrapnel had hit my eyes. One handicap I could not afford was blindness. I figured Odin was going to be hard enough to find as it was.

The round that hit my foot had shoved all the bones aside on its way through, drilling through the boot sole, the fleshy muscles in my foot, and the top of my boot through the laces. Because of the concussion, they hadn't dared give me any morphine in the emergency room; but they had managed a local anesthetic in my foot while they cleaned leather and wool scraps out of it.

As for falling off the tower . . . I could easily have killed myself, or at the very least have busted up a leg or ankle to the point of being permanently crippled. My therapist—a sadist if ever I met one—had taken great glee in telling me about several of the guys he'd worked on, who'd fallen out of various buildings from the same height. I figured I'd gotten off one helluva lot luckier than I deserved.

By the time I was released from the hospital, I was officially out of the Army. Most of the guys I would have wanted to say goodbye to had called one afternoon from a pay phone while I was still in the hospital. They took turns telling me which Frankfurt whores to look up once I got back on my feet. Chuck even mailed me a box of rubbers, and a get-well card signed by everybody. A good bunch of guys . . .

When they finally pronounced me fit and discharged me, I packed up everything I owned, headed for the far north—toward good caving country—and hunted up a spelunking guide. I told Klaus what I needed, and good old Klaus outdid himself. He led me into a cave that had been discovered three weeks before my discharge, when a freak rockslide broke open the fissure. Professional spelunkers were still pushing it, and they hadn't found bottom yet. The first man to set foot in the cave had almost died in a nasty accident. When local kids saw him carried out, they said he looked like he'd been mauled.

Within days, everyone was calling the cavern "Garm's Cave."

Chapter Nine

My last cyalume stick was close to going out. So close, I very nearly didn't find the only way out of the blind end I had stumbled into. I had begun to hyperventilate, spraying sweat in every direction, before I finally noticed the opening. It was barely three feet high, down on the floor, so low I passed it at least twice.

I got down on my knees, shook the cyalume vigorously to coax the last of the light from it, and thrust the light-stick as far as I could reach. Although I couldn't see much, the hole didn't seem to narrow down any.

It was the only opening available.

For a moment I sat down outside the crawlway and stared into the darkness. No more light. Damn little food. Damn little water, either. If I went on, I risked getting stuck somewhere down that rabbit's hole. My fingers played with the flap of my holster, rubbing the smooth butt of the P-7.

—Well, if I got stuck, I could always end it quick.

I had an eerie feeling I wouldn't get stuck. I dragged Gary's knife out of the sheath on my calf and felt the warm tail wrap itself firmly around my arm. That was strangely reassuring; although I wasn't certain it should have been.

"Well?" I asked.

The blade tugged my hand toward the narrow opening.

"Huh." I cut a narrow headband from the hem of my shirt and tied it around my forehead. Then I resheathed the knife, stuck the nearly useless cyalume into my headband, rolled onto my hands and knees—and began crawling.

Within the hour, the damned crawlspace had gotten so narrow, I had to back up and unship the pack. From that point on, progress was slow. Shoving the pack as far forward as I could reach, I would dig in with fingertips and toes and painfully drag myself forward six inches at a time, flat on my belly, until I was close enough to the pack to shove it forward again. I had only scant inches of clearance above and beside me, leaving a space through which I could barely wriggle forward. I felt an aching sympathy for ants stuck in an antfarm.

The tunnel ran steadily downhill, at an angle of maybe ten degrees, so that my head was lower than my feet. The slope was painfully uncomfortable, with the increased pressure of blood in my head. My gloves were in ribbons and my hands were bleeding, and the rest of me was in little better shape. Since there wasn't a damned thing I could do about wrapping or even washing my injuries, I just suffered and kept inching forward.

Acute hunger pangs had finally subsided to a dull ache. God, but that last bite of rubbery apricot had tasted wonderful. I groaned and pulled myself forward another inch. I would *not* think about food. I had no idea how many days I been hiking, stumbling, and crawling through this accursed cave. I had lost track sometime after Bjornssen's death. Unfortunately my tritium watch dial—great for telling time, lousy for seeing anything but the glowing numbers on the watch face—didn't give anything fancier than a sweep second hand.

At least I didn't have to worry any longer about finding water. The fissure I dragged myself through literally oozed water. Provided I could find a wide enough space to get at them, I could fill my canteens again anytime I wanted.

I hoped to blazes the fissure widened out soon. I had dropped a lot of weight these past few days, or I wouldn't have gotten even this far. If I got stuck now, it was all over but the waiting. My hands were trapped above my head, and like a dolt I hadn't thought about shifting knife or pistol until it was too late even to think about scraping out backward and correcting the mistake. The rifle, strapped to the pack, was pointed barrel first, away from me. Of course.

The pack weighed a ton—several tons, in fact—and I was having trouble gripping anything with my hands. I didn't remember my last real sleep. I felt as if an invisible sadist had dumped a whole shaker can of Comet into my eyes. Even if there had been enough light, I probably wouldn't have been able to see where I was crawling. The final blow was having to pee worse than a Russian racehorse, in a spot so damn tight I'd soak myself in stinging ammonia and foul my drinking water at the same time.

Surely the fissure would open up soon. That old Greek guy, Atlas, had nothing on me—at least he'd been made of stone, so he couldn't feel the weight. I was flesh, and altogether too much blood, and was very much aware that the entire European continent rested on my back.

It was heavy.

I must have been shoving at the pack for a full five minutes before I realized it wouldn't budge. Frowning, my mind still dull, I pulled it back, rearranged it a little, and tried again.

Then said something profoundly foul.

I squirmed up as far as I could, hissing when I bumped my sore right knee, and shoved my hand over and under and around the sides until I found a low, sharp point in the roof (with a matching knobby bump on the floor). These had snagged the pack. I squirmed backward again, fumbling with the closures. In a couple of minutes I had managed to shove through the unstrapped rifle, ammunition, web gear and butt pack (which I'd been bright enough to take off when the tunnel narrowed), canteen, pump, and finally the empty pack itself.

I squirmed again, exhaled until I was as flat as I was going to get, and pushed. My arms went through, and my head, sideways, and my shoulders; but then the point of the stalactite stabbed painfully into my butt and the stalagmite bruised my belly just above the groin. I pushed forward and the pain ate deeper. I backed off enough to get the jagged point out of my flesh and lay still.

Once my pulse stopped racing, I squirmed far enough back to feel all the way around the fissure; then tried breaking off the offending projection. My efforts earned me two new slashes across the palms of my hands, right through what was left of the gloves. Grasping first the pump, then one of the ammo magazines, I tried hammering it loose.

I failed to dislodge so much as a single tiny chip.

Obviously it wasn't going to be that easy. I concentrated, and tried to summon the knife to my fingers. Sweat trickled—with a sting of salt—into the cut on my backside. I ignored it and gritted my teeth. The knife pouted in its sheath and refused to cooperate.

"Goddammit . . ."

My throat was so dry I couldn't even swear out loud. I coughed, spat, and tried again to summon it. No go. The blade would not come; and the hard stone point was still in the way. All right. If the knife wouldn't cooperate, I'd do it another way.

I dragged the rifle backward toward me, made sure by feel that it was loaded, and placed the end of the barrel against the stone projection. Easing back a few inches while keeping the invisible sights lined up on it as best I could by guesstimation, I eased off the safety and squeezed the trigger.

For the next several minutes I was deaf and blind. The flash brought involuntary tears to my eyes, and my ears rang painfully. Squirming forward again, I felt for the projection. There was a tiny scratch where the bullet had hit and ricocheted off. Emptying the magazine got no better results than the first round; it just left me blind and deaf longer.

All right—scorch his one-eyed hide—Odin hadn't won yet. If the blasted rock wouldn't be broken, I'd do this the *really* hard way. I shoved my stuff as far through the narrow spot as I could reach, and hyperventilated until I was dizzy. Then I exhaled and tried again. The point gouged agonizingly into the open wound it had already left in my flesh. I bit the inside of my cheek until it bled, while scrabbling and clawing at the rock like a crab pursued by a predatory fish. Shortly I was jammed in so tightly my balls were trying to retreat up against my spine. I shoved again and the stone point hit bone . . . my tailbone. Something like a sob stuck in my larynx. Just a little farther . . .

My muscles spasmed and gave out. All I could do was moan until multiple cramps along both legs and arms eased away. My fingertips were touching the pack; but the contents might as well have been on the surface of the moon.

I managed to squeeze backward just enough to ease my backbone free of the intruding stone point; then lay still. The air—damp and still and stale as it was—tasted sweet in my lungs. But breathing *hurt*, and blood was soaking into my pants, running down my hips from my back to mingle with the blood from cuts on my belly.

Maybe . . .

I shut my eyes, and let my muscles go watery. No. By the time I lost enough weight, I'd be too weak to move. I was dead. I just hadn't stopped breathing yet.

A crack above my head dripped steadily. Water splashed onto my nose and trickled down my cheek to mingle with a rivulet snaking past my fingers. That was what had caused it, of course. The blasted, innocent water, dripping and building a miniature stalactite and stalagmite that would eventually close off the tunnel altogether. The only tunnel left open to Niflheim—and it was closing steadily even as I lay here.

The knife could have cut through the stone; I was sure it could. But it wouldn't. Odin had thrown every obstacle he could think of in my way, and he'd finally found one I couldn't get past. He'd won. I swore softly. I was just too tired to fight any longer. Maybe I'd just go quietly to sleep, and the dripping water would gradually include my skull in the stone formation it was building so patiently.

Sleep nibbled at my consciousness. I couldn't remember what sleep felt like. I had no idea how long I'd been pushing myself without it, driven by the terror of not waking up. I sank into a delicious lethargy, my mind curiously alert. The faint sound of dripping water echoed down the impassable fissure.

I'd been injured before, lots of times—cut in fights, laid up in car wrecks, shot by terrorists—and I'd damn near drowned once, back in the glory days before I grew up and joined the Army. I'd been close to dying more than my share of times, even before swearing an oath no mortal in his right mind had had any business swearing.

But it had never been like this, waiting quietly in the dark for death to sneak up and say "Hey, what took you so long?" Exhaustion leached out of my bones and my brain fogged over, until my heartbeat had blended into the memory of angry waves crashing against the Oregon coast. . . .

I think I swore again into the stony darkness. I know I tasted salt on my lips.

Gary's knife grumbled now from my boot sheath, sending little tremors along my calf muscle. That made me angry. It had let Gary down, and now it had let me down, too. Maybe the cursed blade had played this same trick on other soldiers down through the ages, gathering more victims for its bloody master. Nice trick, neatly executed . . .

No, I hadn't been tricked into anything. I'd been the one to decide on this journey, every step of the way. I'd known the odds from the outset, and hadn't trusted the knife any more than I'd have trusted a rabid pit bull. None of that had stopped me from coming anyway. I didn't have much to be proud of, but I wasn't stupid, and I'd gone down fighting this battle on my own terms.

Admitting defeat left me feeling restive. I didn't like being beaten. Even as a kid, I'd been a lousy loser. The longer I lay there, the angrier I got, stuck like a fat roach in a skinny crack, all because I was too spineless to put up with a few seconds' pain. Meanwhile, somewhere beyond my fingertips, Sleipnir stood guard over the pawns of Valhalla—poor bastards like me—caught in eternal combat. Undoubtedly he was laughing through his great, wicked teeth, while men fought and died, only to stagger up and fight and die all over again.

And down in the worst stink of it was Gary, branding me coward. . . .

I hurled myself at that jutting stone point, and cursed the darkness, cursed death itself. If Odin wanted me dead, then by God, let him come and get me. Pain hit, and intensified until I floated in a reddened mist. I exhaled, forced every molecule of air out of my lungs. I gritted my teeth, gripped the rock beneath my hands, strained forward; and cursed the cold, wet darkness that rose and swallowed me whole.

Chapter Ten

My hands twitched. Cool air poured into my lungs. It seemed an odd sensation and took several minutes to register. I stirred in surprise, wondering if I'd died, and discovered that my cheek rested solidly on the rifle butt I had thought still lay a good foot ahead of me. I managed to flex my fingers and when they closed, one of the canteens was under them. For a moment all I did was lie there, touching first one piece and then another of my gear, foolishly, while salt water dripped off the end of my nose. Then I sniffed half sheepishly and forced my hands into action.

It took me fifteen minutes, by the fitful, faint glow of my watch's tritium dial, to stuff my gear back into the pack, and fumble with the closures. For several moments, I lay still again, gathering my strength. The initial euphoria had worn off. I didn't feel much sense of accomplishment, and thought I should have. All I felt was tired. Grateful; but so deadly tired. At least I was still alive and crawling. All I could do was keep moving.

Which I did, endlessly.

And then, maybe an hour, maybe a day, later, the pack

teetered and began to slide beyond my fingertips. For a split second I was caught by surprise; then I lunged forward and grabbed at a strap—only to have the whole floor skitter away beneath me.

For an awful moment I dug in with my toes and clutched at the pack while hundreds of tiny somethings bounced and slid and dragged at me in the dark. None of them seemed to be crawling, which was too bad, because I was hungry enough to eat anything that didn't eat me first. I had hoped to run across some of the blind fish or crabs I'd read inhabited deep caves; but so far had found nothing of the sort. Maybe live animals couldn't survive for very long in Niflheim's outer reaches?

The thought did not comfort me.

The movement around me finally skittered to a stop and I reached out a tentative hand. A shallow slope fell away directly in front of me, ending in another stone floor. This, in turn, fell at a sharp angle off to my left, and climbed just as sharply up past my right. Both surfaces—the little slope and the angled floor—were littered with chips of stone.

Squirming carefully onto my side, I felt for the roof that had lain fractions of an inch above my head for days. It wasn't there. I eased forward until I could roll over and brace myself; then sat up slowly, clenching my teeth as weight settled onto a tailbone that had seen entirely too much abuse. It felt like I needed stitches. I just hoped infection didn't set in.

Once my gear was secured, I crawled to my knees and braced myself with widely planted feet. Strapping on my butt pack hurt. I washed my cut knees and bandaged them with strips cut from underwear rescued from my pack.

A refill of the canteens slaked my raging thirst, although I was careful to drink gradually, to avoid bloating myself and getting sick. I finally refilled both

canteens again and put them back in their carriers. Then
I aimed as far out as possible to keep from contaminating
my water supply and emptied my aching bladder.

My immediate needs taken care of, I sat still and listened. All I could hear was water trickling away
downslope.

First question: Where was I now?

Second question: How big was the cavern I'd stumbled upon?

Third question . . .

No, better take things slowly and in order.

I scrounged for a bit of stone and tossed it straight up.
It arced up through the darkness, then—much later—hit
ground slightly downslope. Several more tosses—thrown
much harder—also failed to disclose the ceiling. Just
how big was this cave? Another barrage placed an
unbroken wall opposite me, sixty feet or more away.
Chips of stone tossed downslope to my left arced in
silence for a long way; then fell slithering into more
stone chips without hitting another wall.

I turned to my right. And very nearly slid off my
perch.

Light! Just a flicker, blue, and incredibly faint, but
unmistakably—

Gone.

I closed my eyes and reopened them. Nothing. I
swore shakily. Great, my vision was going. I closed my
eyes again, letting the muscles relax, and looked again.

Three pinpricks of white light . . .

Jesus, what was going on up there? I started to crawl
to my knees, still watching, and two of the lights winked
out. A moment later a reddish flicker appeared. I sank
down again, staring until my eyes dried out so painfully
they began to tear over. During the seconds it took to
blink and rehydrate, the lights vanished altogether.

Either my eyes were completely out of kilter, or there

was something weird as perdition going on at the far end of this cave. I allowed my eyes to rest for over two minutes, then while the lids were still closed, unholstered my HK P-7, brought it up into firing position, and looked. The tritium sights glowed eerily right where they were supposed to be, not flickering, not winking out, just sitting there doing exactly what they were supposed to. Nothing glowed anywhere else near them except my watch face.

I reholstered the pistol and gazed up at the far end of the cave, where everything remained dark. Had I stumbled into a mine shaft, maybe? Bjornssen hadn't said anything about mines in this area, and I'd never heard of blue or red carbide lamps. Besides, I didn't hear a thing, and mining sounds surely would carry over a great distance.

I thought about trying to hike up the slope, and even started out in that direction, but discovered almost immediately that climbing uphill through those stone chips was essentially impossible. For every step I took, I slid backward three. Then I noticed that my knife was rocking in severe agitation. I turned back, sliding carefully with one hand on the wall until I was back at the exit of my little tunnel. Weird lights or no, my journey apparently led deeper into the cave, not toward the surface.

Which only made sense. Niflheim had to lie farther down. And the knife was tugging insistently on my boot, urging movement in that direction. So I turned to my left, and noticed that the darkness wasn't quite as intense lower in the tunnel. There was no discernible light source, or even a hint of one; just an almost imperceptible lessening of the blackness.

All right.

I hauled myself to my feet, grabbed hold of the wall, and took an exploratory step.

Moving downhill proved almost as impossible as struggling uphill, with one notable exception. I quickly discovered that shuffling worked better than striding or even gingerly mincing along, a fact I discovered only after slipping and riding on my ass down a sixty-degree rock slide for nearly thirty feet.

That was the unhappy exception. I could always slide into Niflheim, so long as I didn't mind being slashed to ribbons by the time I got there. The whole floor was carpeted with stone chips, boot-lace deep in places, and each one was as sharp as an obsidian scalpel. My butt pack and trousers were slashed all to hell by the time I managed to stop that first wild skid. At this rate, I'd be bare-ass naked by the time I found Sleipnir.

I stuck closer to the walls after that, where the chips were shallower than out toward the center. The walls were nearly smooth under my hands. There was no noticeable variation in the angle of either the floor or the walls. I was moving down a near-perfectly straight, sharply angled chute through the heart of a mountain.

What were the odds against such a tunnel existing?

I supposed volcanic action might account for it; but I wasn't sure if there'd ever been volcanic activity around here. I wasn't a physicist, and certainly not a geologist, and I was far too exhausted to figure any of it out even if I'd had relevant data. At this point I was lucky to add two and two and come out with four.

—Hell, in this cave, *twenty-two* might be the correct answer.

The tunnel grew steadily lighter as I pushed deeper. I had no clue as to where the light source might be. The darkness had taken on a definite grey quality, vaguely reminiscent of the light on a hazy, overcast night, out away from any big cities. Not quite black, but not quite light enough to see anything clearly, either.

Who'd said Hell was murky? Probably Miss Wilkes, from sophomore English.

At least, it sounded like something she might've said.

Fifteen minutes later I could actually see the wall. It didn't look hewn or cut by any method I'd ever heard of; but it was straight as you please, and there was hardly a bump or snag anywhere. I stood still long enough to catch my breath and ease leg cramps; then pushed on, my curiosity building even more rapidly than the light.

A short time later a wide black crack appeared. Another fissure; only this one ran vertically, whereas mine had snaked in horizontally. I stood still and rested my hand on the smooth edge. I was aware that I was incredibly lucky to be out of that fissure alive.

Glancing back briefly, I saw more flashes of light. Blue, yellow; then darkness. I shrugged and started to turn away when a new set of flashes appeared, brighter than the others. The air began to vibrate, as with a half-sensed thunderstorm still out of sight over the horizon.

Bemused, I stood transfixed. The lights teased my retinas, dancing, swaying, flaring steadily brighter, while the air beat at my eardrums. Even when my ears popped it wasn't enough to cope with the rapidly building over-pressure. The lights were a kaleidoscope gone mad, shifting down the long dark tunnel, rushing closer as though space itself were collapsing.

The back of my brain whispered a warning to the front, and an urgent tugging at my calf clamored for attention; but I wasn't listening. What the blazes could it be? Landslide? Earthquake? Volcanic eruption? No, that'd have to come from below, not above. Wouldn't it?

I stood there beside the fissure with my mouth hanging open, staring as the flood of lights and noise rushed at me out of the darkness, and didn't have the sense to get out of the way. My ears popped again and a freight train noise roared in my ears, its thunder shaking the very walls. My teeth rattled and I squinted against brilliant light. It leaped off the floor as high as my head, showering in fountains and spurts like molten steel.

With the air a solid wall of sound beating at me, instinct finally took over and shoved me into the fissure, bruising ribs and tearing open my injured back and knees again. I yelled and heard nothing but the roar permeating the rocks. I found myself panting as terror took hold. Then I forced myself to face whatever it was that was sweeping down the cave.

Thunder hurt my skull. Stone chips stung my face.

Then I saw the eyes.

Thunder, lights, cave—all vanished into an ice-filled night, with those eyes gouging my soul as they hunted fresh prey. . . .

Thunder crashed back into my awareness. The bottom dropped out of the air pressure as Sleipnir tore past. Every footfall struck explosions of sparks. I stuck my head completely into the open, staring, while the wind sucked air out of my lungs.

He was *immense*; yet he was out of sight almost immediately, disappearing into the gloom downslope. The thunder gradually receded and the flying sparks vanished with it. When the wind of his passage finally died away, I took a long, deep breath and released it slowly.

Well . . .

The cave's ceiling had to be at least two hundred feet high, didn't it? Then I snorted. That was a stupid, irrelevant thought, for damned sure.

I chewed my upper lip thoughtfully, gazing down the tunnel after Sleipnir. Too bad Bjornssen wasn't here to see this. Niflheim couldn't be far away now, and at least I had graphic confirmation that Sleipnir did, indeed, visit the underworld.

I looked back up that impossible tunnel, which ran

through a cave where physical laws didn't work quite properly, and saw more flickers of light. I knew now that I could never have climbed up out of this tunnel, even if I'd fought the slope and the boot-deep stone chips until my lungs burst and my muscles gave out. This was Sleipnir's private passage to Niflheim, connecting the branches of Yggdrasil with the World Tree's great roots, in a link that only Sleipnir could cross.

Briefly I wondered where the fissure into which I was now jammed might lead; then decided I didn't care. There were nine worlds altogether, and not all of them were friendly to human life. Hell, some weren't even on speaking terms with the *gods*.

I glanced back up Sleipnir's great tunnel. The moist chill of the cave sank into my flesh and settled in my belly. How had I found my way into Sleipnir's private passage? Had I really gotten past that stalactite in the fissure? Or had Odin heard my angry challenge and answered it?

The chill deepened and I shook myself vigorously. It didn't bear thinking about. Besides, for a dead man, I hurt in a hell of a lot of places. I watched another light flicker into life at the top of the tunnel and wondered if those tiny lights were the stars, silent in the vault above the World Tree. It didn't matter. Nothing mattered, not even death. Dead or alive, I'd found my way into Niflheim.

Sleipnir was waiting.

Chapter Eleven

The glow that grew out of the darkness was green.

Not the warm, earthy green of gardens and mani-cured lawns; but a nasty, weird color somewhere between emerald and sickly yellow. Once, when I was about seven, I'd seen the whole sky turn just that color. When the storm was over, and the tornado gone, pieces of our toolshed, a neighbor's house, and three big live oaks were distributed all over one end of the county. I noticed that my feet had slowed and stopped by themselves, and after a moment's thought I decided they were right. I sat down in the stone chips. No sense just rushing in . . .

Not a waver of movement, not a hint of sound. Everything was utterly dead both behind and before me. Even the trickling of the stream was subdued; the water slid noiselessly along the wall. So what was I waiting for? An engraved invitation? I chewed the end of my thumbnail and rubbed my other hand palm-down against my trousers. It didn't do any good; sweat had already soaked what was left of my clothes.

I spit out bits of ragged thumbnail. I'd worked harder

to get where I was now than I'd ever worked at anything in my life. I couldn't just sit on my ass now that I was so close. Maybe striving for a goal *was* a lot better than reaching it. Now that I was this close . . .

Bull. The only thing wrong with me was a case of nerves like I hadn't had since Mary Lou Meyerson first showed me what the backseat of a Ford was for. I looked at the green glow ahead and discovered that I didn't have the faintest idea what to expect out there. Despite all my "research," I really didn't know what I was going to find. Fighting thirst and underground rivers and even terrorists—I was trained for that kind of battle. But how much would my training be worth in Niflheim, where even the gods went when they died?

I reached down into the stubborn core of myself, where I'd found the strength to haul my ass up out of that icy underground river, and lurched to my feet. Then I stumbled forward into the green light. I was barely aware of the hum against my calf where Gary's long knife rode patiently. The slope of the floor gradually leveled out until it was nearly horizontal again. The distant ceiling had long since disappeared into green gloom overhead. Muted echoes of my footsteps bounced back. The walls began to curve away as well, although not nearly as far as the ceiling.

The eerie glow brightened until I was bathed in ghastly green. Then I emerged from the tunnel onto the verge of a gravel beach. My feet stopped of their own accord and my eyes widened. And widened. I stood there long enough for both feet to go to sleep, just staring, and feeling awfully small. . . .

The cavern which stretched before me had *Journey to the Center of the Earth* beat all hollow, as it were. The "ceiling" was miles overhead; parts of it were dark, almost black, with streaks and splotches and whorls of brighter color just the shade of the green light. Bright patterns glowed with cold phosphorescence, like fire-flies, or those deep-sea fish I'd seen in *National Geographic*. As I watched, entranced, I could see the patterns moving, changing, sliding into darkness while the darkness blossomed slowly into light.

An odd sense of familiarity niggled at the back of my mind, but I couldn't place it, and soon gave up, lost in the eeriness on every side. The whole landscape was lit by that unearthly green glow, even my skin and finger-nails. My skin looked like algae, while my fingernails were a darker olive shade. My knife, peeping out of its sheath, still looked dead-flat black.

The rocky beach extended five yards in front of me. Beyond stretched a body of what looked like oil but smelled like water. The surface was as flat black as my knife, with peculiar green glints. Not a ripple disturbed it, as far as my eyes could see. It reminded me of some-thing, a place I'd read about, where oily pitch oozed to the surface of the ground to snare the unwary. . . . Heavy mist hung like curtains across patches of it, in places obscuring even the "sky." Whatever it was, it stretched off into infinity to both left and right, while directly across, so low it looked no more than a slight thickening of water, a dark smudge suggested a headland jutting toward me.

Just at the—water's?—edge stood a ruined structure of some sort, rising from the beach in a gentle slope to extend fifteen or twenty feet out over the lightless water. It had broken off—or something had broken it—leaving jagged edges to project above the smooth black surface below. The posts and ramp might once have been a dull gold; but now only hints of muted color clung to the grey stone. A bridge, maybe, that had collapsed?

Gauging the distance to the far shore, it must've been one hell of a span. I didn't see any sign of support pillars out there. Silence hung heavily in my ears. I could hear my breath rasping in my lungs. When I took a step forward to get a closer look at the ruined bridge, echoes of the loud crunch seemed to continue forever, disappearing across the misty horizon.

I stopped again, uncertain in the aftermath of that first loud noise, and scuffed a toe while deliberating on courage.

Blood froze in my veins, leaving my face stiff and cold. I knelt, and ran a disbelieving hand through the "gravel." Bones. Millions of them. Billions of them. Finger bones. Toe bones. Vertebrae. Wing bones. Tiny rodent skulls. Claws. Dull, greenish-white, and brittle as shale, the bones ran along the shore until it curved out of sight into the mist.

I thought some more about courage, wondering what it might feel like if I had any, and heard a faint sound, almost like a sigh of wind.

I looked up, glanced up and down the beach, then out across the water. I don't know what I expected to see; but when I saw it, I went very still. There was movement on the black surface, far out but approaching rapidly. I watched it come for some moments; then decided that staying on my knees would make me look entirely too overawed. Not that I *wasn't*; I just didn't want to give that impression. So I stood, and noticed I was breathing hard—and much too fast.

My fingers were gritty, so I brushed bone dust off my hands, wiping it onto my pants, where it clung like glue to the sweaty cloth. My boots were thick with the stuff, which coated the damp leather where I'd crushed brittle, dry bones into powder with my living weight.

Meanwhile, the object out on the water gradually took form, detaching from the black backdrop as it approached on a collision course with the ruined bridge support nearby.

Soon I could tell what it was: a flat-bottomed skiff,

propelled by nothing I could see. A series of gentle ripples patently at odds with its speed ran from the front, along the sides, and out behind the back. The prow rose into twin poles topped by human skulls. The sides were black, writhing with the intricately twined bodies of carved black snakes. Eyes and fangs gleamed silver throughout the hideous pattern.

Standing in the bow was a gaunt old woman with long, greasy hair that no comb in the world could have untangled. Her cheeks were hollow, her eyes were hollow, her whole body no more substantial than the bones I'd ground into dust. Her skin looked like the flaky piecrust from a TV commercial—but I didn't think a starving Ethiopian would've touched a piecrust *that* color.

The skiff stopped just short of the beach and we stared at each other across the intervening stretch of bones. Her eyes swept me at a glance, noting the bloodied knee wrappings, the weapons, the battered pack and heavily laden web gear, and stopped only when they caught my gaze. An expression that might have been the beginnings of a scowl or a laugh crossed her face, gone before it could really register.

"You're alive," she said. Her voice produced not even the whisper of an echo.

I repressed a spontaneous shudder and waited.

"Only the dead find their way here. Why have you come?"

The ball was in my court and abruptly I felt like a pee-wee-league runt going one-on-one against Kareem Abdul-Jabar. Confronting a pack of gods on their home court suddenly didn't seem like the great idea it had once been. . . . Under her penetrating gaze, I felt all too mortal, standing as I was on the bones of what might've been my own ancestors. I managed to check my virtually galvanic impulses, and—for a change—didn't answer flippantly.

There was no telling what this—woman?—might do or know.

"I'm looking for Odin." I winced at the thousands of echoes which bounced from water to "sky" and down again.

A grin split her face. She raised a hand and pointed to a spot behind me.

"Warriors looking for Odin find him by hanging on the tree."

I turned, already knowing what I would find but compelled to look anyway. A lightning-blasted oak had risen from the bone beach right behind me. The shattered trunk was rotten with the smell of death. Corpses swung from every twisting branch, ropes knotted tightly around decaying necks, spears plunged between the exposed bones of rib cages. Some had decayed until only the furs and helmets of Viking warriors clothed the bones; others had been strangled only last week, still clothed in flesh under uniforms of khaki, black, and olive drab. The congealed blood staining their chests looked black.

A moment ago there'd been nothing on that spot but beach, and now the stench sent me stumbling backward, trying desperately not to think about Hohenfels and Gary.

"And what will you say to Odin when you stand before him, human?" The old woman's voice called my attention back to the shore. "Will you ask to see Loki, where he lies bound?"

Loki! How in seven hells had the old witch known that? I stared down at my knife, suddenly aware of the focus of the old woman's keen interest. The knife lay quietly in its sheath, pretending to ignore me. Was the damned blade a mind reader? If it knew, Odin knew, and had maybe warned this disgusting old hag—unless *she* was the mind reader? Damn . . .

I tried to look unconcerned, and knew I failed utterly.

Meanwhile, the old crone just watched me, and her eyes glittered.

How had she known I was after Loki? Loki—who, for the sheer reckless fun of putting the rest of the gods in his debt, had turned himself into a mare to help the gods weasel out on a deal they'd struck with a frost giant. Odin and his crew had broken their contract, and Loki ended up giving birth to a baby horse—Sleipnir. The biology was impossible, of course; but I'd decided, not long ago, that I would never again say anything was impossible.

I glanced up. The old witch was watching me with eyes that glittered like polished bone. She might or might not know that I needed Loki's help to catch his son. Right? *Right.*

"Yes," I answered, meeting the old crone's eyes. "I do seek a word with Loki."

Hollow eyes narrowed to slits. I could smell the stink of my own fear sweat and hoped to god—to God?—that she couldn't smell it, too.

"And when you speak to Loki," she said, her voice bitter as wormwood, "will you tell him of life's pleasures?" Oddly her eyes had the look of a person who knows he is going to die, and is determined to take as many of his killers with him as he can. Fever-bright, they burned like coals in the deep black hollows of her face. I found myself clutching the P-7.

"Yeah. Sure."

A laugh ran like ice along my skin.

"It is worth the trip to see that one squirm," she cackled, my presence almost forgotten in her glee. I stood sweating on the beach. "Come, human," the old woman commanded, gesturing imperially. "Loki awaits your pleasure."

I glanced over my shoulder to look back up Sleipnir's great tunnel. Then I drew a quick breath, forced myself to let go of the pistol, and climbed over the broken bridge. I dropped carefully into the skiff. To my surprise, my weight didn't cause the craft to so much as bob in the water.

A chill crawled along my spine as the skiff moved silently away from shore, heading for the distant blur on the horizon. My hair lay glued to my head from what felt like (and might have been) weeks of accumulated sweat, oil, and dirt. The remnants of my clothes flapped loosely on my frame. The bow churned up no froth in the black water, just gentle ripples that caught the far-off green of the ceiling and flung it back into my eyes.

I turned to look at the crone. She was wrapped in a filthy black cloak. The tattered edges of the garment writhed in the wind like living snakes. A shudder caught me unawares, and I hastily turned to study the inside of the skiff.

It was black inside as well as out, and completely watertight. None of the strange black water found its way inside. I wondered what they'd used to waterproof the wood, and if the substance had caused the black coloration. That wouldn't explain the silver eyes and fangs, though, unless they'd been added afterward, applied like gold leaf.

Beside the ancient woman's feet, rolling slightly on the floor, rested a bowl made of dried, whitened bone. It looked like a human skull case. There were a few disks inside that gleamed dully metallic in the green light. A long pole lay beside it, one end decorated with a wicked iron hook and the other with the polished skull of a wolf, the dark brown color of museum bones. I hoped the old woman used the hook for mooring the skiff—it had lethal potentials I didn't even want to think about.

"What thoughts are in your head, mortal?"

Her raspy voice—snake scales slithering across dry rock—reached over the sound of the wind, apparently without effort. I turned reluctantly to meet her gaze.

"This sea—what is it called?" I gestured out to the horizon.

Her cackle filled my ears. "This is no sea, human. This is the River Gjoll, flowing out of the great wellspring Hvergelmir, which feeds all the rivers of Niflheim. Gjoll is Hel's river—it flows past her gate." She laughed again. "Living men are not welcome in her hall, little man. Hel prefers them newly dead. Shall we oblige her?"

Before I could even try to frame an answer, she was talking again.

"Loki's kin, she is, full blood daughter, and sent here by Them above as don't trust her. Give Hel the dead to satisfy her, They said, and she won't look to Asgard with greed in her eye." The old woman's laugh wheezed with every sentence. "Comes the hour when the sons of Muspell ride, and Hel will have Asgard; aye, in flames. And I, Modgud, will stand and watch as I've done through these long centuries."

Just when I thought the bombast had ended, Modgud's eyes caught mine and held them.

"I'll watch for Loki's fall in the Final Battle, I will, the great Ragnarok, and I'll laugh when I see him down. His groaning and fighting to be free of the Rocks shook the earth and broke my lovely bridge. . . ." Her thin shoulders were shaking, with visible rage. Spittle flew from loose lips. "Once I was Queen of the Golden Bridge of the Gjoll and now—nothing!—nothing but a slave, chained to this wretched boat. I'll watch him bleed and die on Vigrid's plain and I'll laugh as Surt burns the world. Aye, it'll be a fine day for vengeance when the sons of Muspell ride."

Modgud's eyes were glazed, my presence forgotten.

And I thought *I* was out for vengeance. . . ?

I hoped to hell—or was it Hel?—I did nothing to anger the old witch. Enemies like her I could do without. She began crooning to herself in a language I'd never heard, so I turned my gaze back out to sea—or rather, to the river. Christ, they didn't do things on a small scale in Niflheim. The opposite shore was closer; but not much.

What would I find on that inhospitable jut of land? Niflheim was where the old, the sick, and the accident-prone came when they died. From everything I could gather, it was supposed to be a pretty dull place. All the real fun was in Valhalla; although if Valhalla was supposed to be fun, maybe I'd settle for boredom and Niflheim.

The only thing I heard was wind in my ears. Given the way sound carries across the water, I couldn't imagine there'd be much happening over there. Maybe I'd find Hel's Hall, like Modgud had said. Would Loki's daughter tell me where to find her father? Or just casually squash the life out of me for daring to intrude into her kingdom? My fingers caressed my pistol and I thought I heard the old crone's snicker at my back.

A movement far off to port, almost on the horizon, caught my eye. The water was boiling. Great waves rolled off some disturbance. Plumes of spray shot into the air like a row of uncapped oil wells—angry foam bubbled and hissed for nearly a mile in either direction from the disturbance's center. A brief gleam tantalized my retinas, gone before I could name color or substance. The water continued to boil and spew for several moments more, then gradually subsided to flat black again.

I turned to look at Modgud; but she hadn't noticed or didn't care, and after her response to my last question, I didn't much feel like asking. The first rolling swell caught up with the skiff, lifting it slightly before the stern slipped into the trough. I thought the next wave would surely swamp us; but the skiff only repeated the gentle, lifting motion. Or was Modgud doing the lifting to keep her craft afloat?

I wondered if Death liked wet feet any more than the rest of us. Except she wasn't really Death; Hel was. . . .

I shook my head to clear it. Maybe it was something in the air, or just exhaustion; but my thought processes were beginning to resemble a well-scrambled egg. I turned my eyes back toward the far shore, which to my astonishment suddenly was only a hundred yards away.

There was no repetition of the bone beach. Instead, the ground was an odd, indefinable grey, somewhere between green and black, undercut at the water's edge to form a steep clay bank as high as my waist. The other side of the bridge had collapsed into stony rubble. From the river's edge, the land rose in sharp ridges, each higher than the last, blocking further view inland. Strewn across those ridges, and half buried in them, were jagged boulders, somewhat lighter grey in color, ranging from no larger than my fist to massive blocks that would've dwarfed a three-bedroom house. Some glinted oddly in the light, with occasional bright flashes of genuine color that made me wonder if they, too, were phosphorescing.

I didn't see anything that remotely resembled buildings. There was no sign of vegetation; but as we neared the bank, I could see that the top six inches of soil were extremely dark, forming a layer that looked richer, more organic than the clay below. The whole sweep of land was barren, utterly deserted. I wasn't sure if I should be relieved or apprehensive at the lack of habitation.

I had no more than these few moments for an impression of my destination because the boat had stopped dead in the water. The silence of the cavern rushed into my ears, replacing the roar of wind. We were still a good twenty yards from shore. I turned to look at Modgud. What now?

"You must pay the toll," she said softly, her eyes dancing.

I glanced at the intervening yards of water. I was a pretty good swimmer. A cackle interrupted my thoughts. She had picked up the braincase bowl and was scooping out a handful of silver coins. Modgud dipped the skull into the water, filling it; but carefully kept her gnarled fingers dry. She raised the braincase to eye level. Seconds later, water poured out the hole it had eaten through the bottom. I swallowed.

"You must pay the toll," she said again, with a grin that lingered as her eyes measured my braincase against the ruined bowl in her hand.

"Uh . . ." I fumbled through my pockets, fingers shaking despite my efforts to remain calm. I dug out a scant handful of change and saw mostly pennies, plus a couple of old "lucky" dimes I was never without.

I didn't have any gold, except the little gold Thor's hammer on a chain around my neck. I was awfully fond of that.

"I—uh—haven't got any gold coins—"

Modgud spat over the side. There was a quiet hiss as spittle struck the acid "water." Her lip curled. "Gold is for trinkets. Junk. Silver was the price of the bridge, and silver is the price of the ferry."

I scooped up both dimes and started to hand them over.

A disembodied voice reached across the water. "I wouldn't give her both, if I were you."

I spun. Pennies slid all over the bottom of the skiff. A man was rising to his feet, from a comfortable seat against a boulder.

"*What?*" I knew I sounded like a Vienna Boys' Choir soprano, and didn't care. I'd *looked* at that piece of ground, and hadn't even noticed him.

"I'd give her only one," he repeated, with a genial

smile. "How else will you pay for the ride back across?"

Good point.

If I lived that long.

I handed Modgud one dime. She curled bony, claw-tipped fingers around it.

The boat swept silently toward shore, and grounded gently a moment later. The owner of the disembodied voice had come down to the shoreline, and now stood looking into the skiff. Blond, with laughing blue eyes. He was surprisingly short, but compactly built and muscular. There couldn't have been an ounce of fat anywhere on him. Even at my best—which I hadn't been since getting shot full of holes—I was nothing but flabby standing beside him. And this guy was dead as a doornail. Dead people were supposed to look . . . well . . . decently dead.

He balanced lightly on the balls of his feet, arms loose, ready to grip my hand in friendship, or heft a weapon, whichever was called for. He wore a long sword, in a black scabbard worked with silver. His torso was protected by a ring-mail shirt, but he wore no helmet. Cautious; but not overtly threatening. Did he work for Mistress Hel? Or . . .

A bloodstain had dried across the front of his shirt, just visible beneath the mail. A curious little green dart was embedded in his chest, having struck between the circular links.

Green dart? The first dead person I met in Niflheim was a *god?* The "coincidence" made me sweat, despite the cool, damp air. The dart that had killed Baldr was Loki's doing. Though someone else had thrown the weapon, Loki alone had known that the mistletoe dart was the only thing in the nine worlds that could kill his foster nephew.

My next—irreverent—thought was how extraordinarily short Baldr was, for a god. I hadn't exactly pictured myself as a giant; it hadn't occurred to me that I might actually tower over any of the Norse gods. Vikings were supposed to have been tall people.

"How long are you planning on staying?" he asked, nodding toward Modgud.

With difficulty, I turned my attention back to the silent old crone. "I'll be finished here by this time tomorrow, or I should be, anyway, so how about you pick me up then?"

She just looked at me with those weird, hollow eyes.

My Nordic athlete spoke up: "Death has no concept of time, friend."

"Oh." Logical.

"Well, then, how about tides? We're at the bottom of Yggdrasil here, right? And Earth—I mean Midgard—is just above us here, so it's all part of the same tree, right? And this river is big enough to have tides, right?"

I really was going to have to stop babbling like a fool.

The blond laughed quietly, a nice sympathetic chuckle that somehow put me at ease despite my suspicions.

"Not necessarily; but it happens there are tides here. Two in about, oh, four-and-a-half songs. Roughly the same as Midgard. Earth," he added, smiling in deference.

Songs? Did they keep track of time by how long it took to sing a ballad? Without day and night, and no real need for sleep, it made some sense.

"Good. Can you be here, at this spot, in two tides?"

She held my gaze, and smiled slowly. "Can you?"

"Just be here, okay? I'll have the silver with me."

I knew I sounded petulant; but that old witch made me nervous, and Baldr—the dead god—was taking an interest in my affairs that I could have done without.

Modgud inclined her greasy head and I jumped ashore. I slipped in the clay, and slid toward the acid river. Before I could plummet feet-first into a messy

death, my benefactor grabbed my arm, and hauled me to
the top of the bank. I panted my thanks, which he waved
away, innately courteous, although I saw his eyes narrow
slightly.

He was probably wondering—with sudden apprehension—whether saving me had been the smartest thing
he'd ever done. Given who his father was, I wasn't so
sure—from his viewpoint—that it had been, either. Personally, I was pretty grateful. I had to watch my step
triply now that I was squarely in the middle of Death's
domain. I squared my pack and tugged my tattered shirt
back down into place.

His first question voiced what everyone must have
been wondering, myself included.

"What brings you here?"

The old woman's high cackle stopped any answer I
might have formed.

"He's come to torment your uncle," she wheezed gleefully.

Baldr's brows drew sharply down. My instinct was to
dive for my knife, even as I wondered whether a dead
god could be killed again. . . .

The skiff shot out into the river, disappearing into a
bank of mist, which left me no choice but to face Loki's
nephew—and Odin's son.

Chapter Twelve

It figured that Odin's favorite son—and one of Loki's worst enemies—would be on hand to greet me.

He stared out at the mist for a moment; then pulled himself together visibly. "I apologize," he said with a wan smile. "Thinking about my uncle is a little upsetting. I try not to, at all." He looked me up and down, taking my measure. "You didn't come all this way to torment Loki, surely?"

"No. That was her idea." I jerked my head toward where the skiff had vanished. "I'm really just looking for some information from him."

His face clouded somewhat. "I wouldn't advise that. Loki is dangerous, and not exactly cooperative." A pained expression crossed his face. "I ought to know."

"It must be rough, huh?" I asked, trying to sound sympathetic.

He shrugged, and smiled ruefully. "Well, it isn't great, no, and the mold growing on your feet can get to you; but it isn't so bad, really. Plenty of peace and quiet, no worries to speak of, so long as you avoid Loki. He's kind of bitter about the whole thing."

And Baldr wasn't? If someone had murdered *me* and dumped me in this gawdawful place for eternity . . . Maybe living in Niflheim *did* scramble a person's brain, or maybe dying was akin to gelding, because it was hard to believe that *any* Norse god could be *this* mellow, never mind a son of Odin who'd been *murdered*.

On the other hand, madness did take a variety of forms. I was convinced that Odin himself was 'round the bend and *gone*, so it was entirely possible that Odin's dead son was cheerfully mad in his own inimitable way. But while my current ability to judge relative sanity might be impaired (I was in hell, after all), Baldr didn't *look* insane. He looked hale, hearty, and sort of wistful around the eyes.

"What can I be thinking?" he said with a grimace. "I can only excuse my manners by pointing out that we get so few visitors, it's easy to forget courtesies. Baldr is my name."

He held out his hand. I started to take it and he clasped my forearm instead, in a firm grip.

"Baldr," he said again, "son of Odin, longtime resident of Niflheim. And you "—his eyes twinkled—"are something of a mystery."

I glanced over my shoulder in the direction Modgud had disappeared, and wondered if Baldr were lying. Everything I'd read about Baldr said he was the primal good guy. But if Modgud knew what was going on, surely Baldr did too? Or did Modgud know simply because she was in charge of the ferry, so it was her business to know? Or had she just made a very shrewd guess?

How the hell was I supposed to know which gods knew what?

I looked back at Baldr. "Yeah, well, everything that's been happening to me lately is kind of mysterious. I'm damned if I know how to explain it." I shrugged ruefully. "I'm Randy Barnes."

"Yes, I know."

My blood went cold and my eyes went hard.

Baldr chuckled and added, "Let me explain. A while back a Norwegian came through here, wrapped in ropes, cursing something awful, bones sticking out odd places—one hell of a mess, if you'll pardon the pun— and he said you were in a powerful hurry to get here. Of course, he thought he'd spoken figuratively." Baldr chuckled. "Then Hel heard your arrival—the living are so noisy in comparison with us dead folk; your footsteps echoed all the way down Sleipnir's tunnel and across the Gjoll—and we realized the poor man had inadvertently spoken literal truth."

Baldr was still chuckling; but I remembered Bjornssen's death scream. I didn't like the casual way these gods killed us off when it suited their game plan. Baldr's laughter died away, replaced by puzzlement.

"Why are you angry about this?"

"Why did you kill Bjornssen? It wasn't necessary."

He looked more puzzled than before. "I have never killed anyone."

"Yeah. Right. Tell it to the birds."

My knees had gone shaky—reaction setting in, maybe, or just plain rage—so I strode to the nearest boulder and sat down before I collapsed embarrassingly in front of him. I was whacked out, and bone-deep sore in more places than I wasn't, and standing there talking was a goddamn waste of time I probably didn't have to spare. I had people to see, and Gary Vernon to avenge.

"Sorry," I muttered. "I keep getting all you gods mixed up."

Baldr squatted beside me, and studied my face for several moments; then stared out across the Gjoll. When he spoke, his voice was distant, contemplative. "Each man's death is his own to meet, and each man must face it alone at the time decreed for him. That is one moment no one can take from him or assume for him. The fault of your friend's death cannot be yours, any more than it can be mine or any of the other gods'."

I glanced up; but couldn't tell whether he was talking about Klaus or Gary.

Baldr was still talking. "The Norns decree all that must be. They guided his footsteps up to the moment of his death, as surely as they have guided yours here while you still live."

Gary's death proved *that* wrong; but I didn't feel like arguing the point with Odin's son.

"All I want is to talk to Loki," I growled.

Baldr's eyes narrowed. "About what?"

"Sleipnir."

Baldr's eyes widened. "What in the nine worlds has Sleipnir to do with this?"

I glanced up from checking my P-7 for rust. "Got to do with what?"

He swept a hand around at the landscape. "Your presence here. Obviously the Norns have brought you here for a reason, and a very important one; but Sleipnir is Odin's horse, not Hel's. He doesn't live in Niflheim."

I met his blue eyes squarely. "I saw him just a few minutes ago, in that big tunnel of his. He was headed this way."

Baldr grinned, and shrugged. "I didn't say he doesn't occasionally visit." Then his expression sobered, and he pursed his lips. "Whatever's up, it certainly bodes to be interesting."

"Huh. You just said a mouthful, friend."

Living in interesting times was a curse I could've done without. I reholstered the P-7.

"You'll point out the way to Loki, then?"

He shook his head. Mistrust had crept into his eyes. Baldr was supposed to've been the trusting type. Clearly, he'd learned caution in the eons he'd been stuck in this slimepit of a world.

"No, I think not. This game is too serious for blundering about in the dark. My hostess will want to speak with you, at the very least."

"I thought Hel was only interested in dead men."

His smile was sincere enough. "True; but this is her world, after all, and we are but guests in it. She would not be pleased if you refused an audience. And believe me, no living mortal within her sphere of influence would want to anger her. I am not complaining, understand. She's a good hostess. But you are out of place here, so the same rules don't exactly apply to you."

I didn't bother to observe that so far none of the rules had applied to me.

"Come, pack up your strange belongings and follow me; I'll take you to Hel."

I didn't care for the sound of that; but didn't see that I had much choice.

We struck out along the shoreline. Baldr said conversationally, "I couldn't help noticing that the Sly Biter is with you."

"The what?" I glanced around involuntarily.

"The Sly Biter. Your knife. I'd always wondered what had become of it. Somehow, I'm not too surprised it wound up in your hands. It has a way of turning up precisely when and where it's needed. How'd it find you?"

I started to comment; then shut my lips. I shouldn't have been surprised.

"You recognize this thing, huh?" I slipped the knife out of its sheath and watched in satisfaction as the tail wrapped around my arm.

"Of course." He sounded surprised. "I used to see it frequently when I was younger. It disappeared, though," he added thoughtfully, "right before I was killed."

Interesting. Maybe I could finally get some answers.

"Where'd it come from? What exactly is it?" Green light caught the blade and sang gleefully along the invisible edge. The scaly haft was warm against my palm. It pulsed with an arcane life.

Baldr's voice warmed to his subject. "The Biter has *been* since before I was born. Some say it was carved from the living root of Yggdrasil." He gestured toward the cavern "ceiling," and the familiarity of swirling light patterns clicked.

"Others claim . . . Well, it just *is*. The Norns probably would know for sure where it came from. My father had it for a while; that's how I know it. But it's an odd creature, the Biter."

"Then it is alive?"

"Oh, yes, without a doubt. Well, not perhaps alive in the sense you might think; but it is not just a soulless artifact. It *chooses* those who will carry it, not the other way around, though I'm not terribly clear on why or how."

He grinned. "Father was furious when it deserted him. It's said that when the Biter chooses a mortal, only the mortal's death will break the bond." He frowned thoughtfully, and gave me a disquieted glance. "I'm also told it turns up whenever the Balance swings precariously. When that happens, it acts its will on those who are destined to tip the scales in the direction decreed by the Norns. Thus will it be until Ragnarok. The Destruction of the Worlds," he added, as if expecting me not to know what it meant.

"I know what Ragnarok is," I said dryly.

He smiled, unoffended. "Most of your contemporaries don't. It's sad, you know, being forgotten."

"Yeah, life's a bitch and then you die."

"How very Norse!" He chuckled.

I wasn't laughing.

Instead, I stared at the Biter. Worked its will on me,

did it? We'd just see about that. Light sang off its black skin, glinted in its black eyes. Something Baldr had said had begun to bother me. If the Biter did its own choosing—and had deserted Odin—what, precisely, did that mean to *me*? What did it want? And just whose side was it on, anyway? *Could I trust it or not?*

Whatever the answer, Odin had been upset to lose it. I grinned. The thought that the Biter preferred my company to his gave me a great deal of satisfaction.

"It's a temperamental little bastard," was all I said.

I carefully resheathed it. At Baldr's request, I related a few of my adventures with the Biter, leaving out key bits of information here and there. Baldr laughed merrily when I told him about the entrenching tool and the ragheads. I managed to keep the conversation light and humorous.

Then, as he took up the thread of conversation and began an improbable tale about the Biter and a frost giant, a biting wind picked up, seemingly out of nowhere. I shivered hard. Whether I wanted to admit it or not, I was just about at the end of my strength, and I wasn't dressed for freezing wind. Given the state of my clothes, I was barely *dressed*. When I fell behind, wheezing loudly in the cold air, Baldr slowed and stopped.

"I fear I must apologize again," he said ruefully.

Baldr assisted me over to a large boulder, which sported flecks and speckles of glowing yellow phosphorescence. It wasn't a warm phosphorescence, though, so I just sat wearily, shivering.

"Yeah? What for this time?"

"You are injured, tired, and undoubtedly suffering from hunger and thirst, and I've kept you walking all this time when there was no need."

A gust of wind caught us, and I wrapped both arms around myself, trying to get warm.

"And you are cold, as well. I really am sorry. . . ."

"I know, I know, it's just that the dead don't get tired and thirsty, right?"

"Well, yes; but that's no excuse when I'm responsible for your welfare. By the time you've caught your breath they should be here."

"Who?"

He put fingers to his lips and emitted an extraordinarily shrill whistle. It was the loudest sound I'd yet heard from an inhabitant of Niflheim, and I was surprised when it echoed off the distant ceiling.

I was just getting my wind back—and the racing of my heart under control again—when a low rumble of thunder shook the ground. Before I could open my mouth to ask what was up, two enormous horses burst into view from beyond a nearby house-sized boulder. Their sharp hooves churned up the dark soil as they slid to a halt in front of us. They were bridled, and saddled, and obedient as big, shaggy dogs.

They didn't appear to be breathing hard from their run. In fact, I couldn't detect any breathing at all. When I thought about it, I realized that—except for drawing air to speak—Baldr hadn't been breathing, either.

I eyed our mounts. "Dead horses?"

"What else? Several of your ancestors were thoughtful enough to bury horses with themselves, which has provided us with a wide variety of excellent mounts and draft animals. These were once war horses." He grimaced, and sighed. "Their unfortunate masters died of old age in their sleep. Poor souls; no man deserves such a fate—but we can't all die in glory, can we?"

"No," I said dryly, "I don't suppose we can. The species wouldn't survive it, if we did."

He grinned. "I like the way you think. It's . . . refreshing. Here, let me introduce you to your mount so there'll be no misunderstandings. He hasn't carried a live rider in hundreds of years."

Baldr urged one of the horses forward, and I wondered what I was supposed to do. I'd never been on a horse in my life.

He glanced at my face—did a quick double take—then halted the animal several paces away. He rested one hand casually on the animal's—shoulder?—and lifted one shaggy blond eyebrow in apparent surprise.

His question came out sounding droll. "Not a horseman?"

"Uh, no."

He gave me a look that seemed to ask what the hell we learned on Earth these days. But he didn't say anything; just patiently explained how to mount, steer, start, and stop. I struggled aboard, envious of Baldr's graceful leap to his animal's back.

"We'll go at a slow trot," he said, urging his horse forward. I followed suit, and my horse obeyed, tossing its head briefly in irritation before settling down to the job of nursing me along.

Riding was marginally better than walking, except for the cold wind; but I couldn't grasp properly with my injured knees, so I just sat loosely, hanging on to the reins *and* the mane, and flopped along as best I could. Each jolt sent agony through the tear across my tailbone. Gradually the seat of my pants grew warm and sticky. I'd almost *rather* have walked.

My horse didn't like it much better than I did; but he was surprisingly cooperative, for a war stallion. Dying must've taken all the spirit out of him. We got along well enough, at any rate, and the horse's longer legs covered the ground in mile-eating strides. We approached a massive bend in the river, and Baldr turned his horse slightly inland, urging the animal up the flank of the nearest boulder-strewn ridge.

I followed, having absorbed enough basics to avoid sliding off backward when the horse started up the steep slope. My knees hurt from trying to grip; but I stayed on and, within moments, we reached the crest. Our new vantage point revealed a long, shallow valley, with headlands that jutted out on either side of the bend in the river. The result was an enormously broad, sheltered harbor.

I pulled up sharply. Baldr stopped his horse to let me look, innately courteous. Below us, situated some fifty yards inland from the river's edge, stood a building that would've dwarfed anything but the Pentagon. A gate the size of a football goalpost had been set in a massive wall that ran right around the structure. Spread out as far as I could see, squatting right up the slopes of the ridgelines to either side, were houses, mud streets, and what looked astonishingly like farms.

I felt like a high-desert plainsman astride my shaggy war horse, looking down from my barren wasteland onto civilization.

We had arrived at Hel's Hall of Death.

Chapter Thirteen

The panorama below was one of the dreariest I'd ever seen; it was dark and dull, in shades of green, grey, and black, with a very little bit of dirty white and yellow shining up briefly whenever the eerie phosphorescent lightplay in the ceiling flared brighter directly overhead.

There was movement in the "fields," and along the narrow clay roads. I couldn't identify the crops growing in the farm rows. There was no cheerful sound of bustle and activity, no warm firelight from hearths or windows; just a slow, ponderous sense of heavy, endless work to be done by people dead long before I'd been born.

The farms and the miserable town must furnish Hel with foodstuffs and goods. She hadn't been dead when Odin had banished her here; so presumably she still needed to eat, drink, and make merry in her own gloomy fashion. In that context, it made sense to put to work the legions of dead under her authority. I wondered if she gave them any choice. Somehow I doubted it; but even hard work must be a somewhat attractive alternative to eternal boredom.

As I watched, a curtain of dull mist swept in off the

river, obscuring the hall, so Baldr led the way down the slope and I fought to keep from sliding up my horse's neck. When we finally touched level ground again, we were near a hard clay road. It led from a black dock on the river to the massive gate of Hel's hall. The dock seemed to be for Modgud's skiff—I saw no evidence of any other craft.

We rode toward the gate, and were swallowed by dark mist. I shivered under a blast of sleet, which was condensing within the mist to fall on anything miserable enough to be caught below. The gate was closed, and—judging from the looks of the fortress—probably barred from inside.

The closer we rode, the bigger it loomed, until I had to crane my neck, shielding my eyes with one hand against the sleeting mist. The wall itself was built from massive chunks of utterly black stone, mortared with what looked sickeningly like dried blood.

The gate was metal, dull and colorless until a blast of wind opened a rent in the mist, admitting a glare from a bright swirl directly overhead. The brighter light revealed it to be badly tarnished silver. The surface was utterly flat, with no patterns; but the massive posts at the corners were topped by human skulls, coated inside and out with silver, also badly tarnished.

The gate swung ponderously open at Baldr's approach. It groaned like something out of a really bad horror movie. I could've done without the theatrics. If I hadn't been so jittery, I probably would have laughed out loud. Baldr rode straight through. I followed nervously, craning my neck to see what had opened the massive gate so effortlessly. There was nothing there, of course.

Instinctively I rebelled at the idea that it opened by magic; but I was dealing with gods and goddesses, and I'd already seen several sciences go out the window, at least partway. Gary's death alone had tossed out physics and biology. It would have made me feel slightly better to believe there were hidden weights and pulleys concealed inside that massive wall, the better to awe superstitious peasants. But I couldn't really bring myself to believe it.

However she managed it, the gates swung wide to admit us, then closed solidly again. The heavy thud sounded muffled behind us. My horse shied, and I grabbed at his mane to keep from falling off.

"Stupid animal," I muttered, wondering why my rock-steady beast would turn abruptly skittish. The fact that Baldr was also having trouble with his mount made me feel slightly better—until I thought through the implications. . . .

"Better dismount while you can," Baldr called back, jumping lightly to the ground.

I tried to imitate his style; but my knees gave out and my feet slipped on the ice coating the stone road. I landed in a painful lump under my horse's belly, and the blow jarred the wind from me. The horse snorted and bolted sideways, leaving me to scrape my much-battered self off the road.

Baldr lent me a welcome hand. I swayed for a moment, feeling as though all my bones had jellied under this last insult. Baldr kept me from falling, and I leaned on his arm for support until the worst had passed.

"What's got into them?" I wheezed, jerking my thumb at the horses, who stood huddled against the gate. Obviously they wanted out again very badly.

"Even a dead horse can smell death."

Oh.

We stood on a paved flagstone road that led to enormous double doors. Huge grooves, six inches deep, slashed into the flagstones just beyond the gate. I remembered reading—somewhere back in the world of yellow sunlight and warmth—that Sleipnir had jumped this gate, when the gods sent him to ask Hel to return the newly murdered Baldr. Sleipnir's hooves had cut those grooves; but his mission had failed. Baldr was still Hel's guest.

Hel's hall was made of extremely dense wood, coated black as Modgud's skiff had been. The closer we approached, the harder the sleet fell. I found myself shuddering uncontrollably. I maintained a tenuous grip on the ice, which coated everything, and was glad I'd worn my combat boots. I concentrated on not falling a second time. I was too proud to ask Baldr for help walking this last little bit—although by the time we got to the doors, I regretted it.

A rectangle of blackness loomed; I looked up to see the huge hall door swinging silently open. *Come into my parlor. . . .* Baldr stood waiting. I tried to hurry; but just as I reached the threshold, he grabbed my arm.

"Take care," was all he said. He reached out with one toe and tapped the broad flagstone in front of the door. It dropped dizzily out of sight, instantly lost into a yawning black chasm.

I swayed. He steadied me. "The entry stone of Hel's Hall is called Drop-to-Destruction—never forget that."

That wasn't bloody likely.

The stone slid up out of the depths, grinding back into place. Baldr stepped carefully over it; then turned and gave me assistance I badly needed. By the time we were inside, I was leaning pretty heavily on his shoulder, pride be damned. The door swung shut with a hollow bang. I looked around Lady Death's home.

"What's this place called?" I muttered, trying to adjust my eyes to the extremely dim light.

"Eljudnir," Baldr answered. "That means Damp-with-Sleet," he added, glancing at me to see if I'd take offense at the translation.

"Huh. Appropriate."

An enormous fireplace across the room boasted the oddest fire I'd ever laid eyes on. It flickered eerily in the semidarkness, its flames an odd blend of greens and yellows as some unknown, glowing vegetable matter burned on the hearth. I could feel the heat from where I stood, though, and leaned imperceptibly toward it, wishing I had the strength to walk closer. Baldr guided me slowly across the room.

The air was thick, the light foul and disturbing. It distorted the shapes of stone furniture scattered around the immense room. I looked for the source of the strange lighting, and found—hanging from the ceiling in enormous nets—twisted fungi. They glowed balefully in the shadows near the ceiling. Great loops of chain ran between the nets, and held suspended in midair large, glowing boulders. Their rusty red and orange phosphorescent minerals added a touch of alien color to the room.

I noticed queasily that the boulders had been carved into horrifying shapes. The impression was of a torture chamber bathed in bloody light.

"Ugh, how can you bear this?" I muttered.

Baldr shrugged, and helped me to a stone chair near the fire. "It's better than a dank hovel out in the sleet. And I told you, Hel really isn't a bad hostess. Just a little grim."

Grim wasn't the word for this nightmare room. If her house were this bad . . . Decor usually reflected the owner's personality. Well, she *was* Death. At least the fire was warm. An extraordinarily old man was making his way toward us from a shadowed doorway, moving so slowly, it looked as if he were swimming through blood.

Baldr addressed him before he could get very far into the room.

"Ganglati, please inform your mistress that her guest has arrived, and ask Ganglot to send my wife to us."

The ancient man nodded, took five minutes to turn around, and slowly disappeared.

"Twins, he and his sister. They serve Hel, and do their best; but they're aptly named."

I just looked at him, too tired and too busy swallowing back nausea to answer.

"Slow-moving. Both their names mean slow-moving."

I nodded. Fortunately, the message reached Baldr's wife faster than the old man moved—he must've called ahead. The woman who swept into the hall was stunningly beautiful. A look of gentle concern on her face made her presence the most welcome thing I'd seen since arriving in hell.

"Baldr, whatever have you been doing to this poor dear? Didn't you even think to take a cloak to warm him through the sleet? Of course not; it was never your worry to see to such things." The words were not accusatory, just solidly practical. Women took care of details like food and clothing, her tone suggested, so how could a mere man be expected to remember?

She touched my forehead with the back of her hand, reminding me of childhood and Mom standing next to my bed in the middle of the night. Her hand was cool and gentle. She frowned.

"Fetch warm furs and go rescue some of that hot soup Ganglot was preparing for Hel's dinner. It should be nourishing for a mortal."

Baldr surrendered me to her care without a word, and she smiled reassuringly. "My name is Nanna, if no one's thought to tell you. I understand you are Randy Barnes?"

I was beyond surprise. I just nodded.

She slid the backpack off my shoulders, fussed with the web gear until I showed her how it unhooked, and shortly had me out of my ragged clothes. Baldr returned with several fur rugs, and wrapped me in them; then handed over a steaming mug. I peered into it suspiciously. I was revolted by the thought of drinking anything that glowed that shade of green and had floating lumps of iridescent yellow in it; but the stuff smelled wonderful and I was much too hungry to argue. I shut my eyes and drank slowly. The taste wasn't bad at all.

When I had finished the first mug, Nanna produced another, and I drank that; then I consumed an entire loaf of dull grey bread spread with a thick, crumbly green substance that tasted like cheese paste. It was wonderful. I ate slowly and carefully until my shrunken stomach would hold no more. Baldr produced a mug of incredibly potent ale, and shortly I sagged in the chair. My last thought was that I really ought to remain on my guard.

Waking up took a long time, with various parts of me clamoring for attention as I slowly became aware of them. There was an ungodly burning in my knees, a dull ache in the muscles of my arms and legs, sharp pain across my tailbone and back, and a matching pain across my belly. Other than that I felt wonderfully refreshed. I even managed to sit up on my own.

I was in a small room with no windows, dimly lit by a net full of bloated puffball fungus. I accepted the illumination gratefully; but avoided looking directly at the mottled "light fixtures."

Under fur coverings, I was naked and undeniably scrubbed. Even my hair felt squeaky clean. Smears of ointment had been daubed on the worst of my injuries. I actually blushed. Who'd bathed me while I was unconscious? I couldn't credit Baldr's doing it, and wondered if a goddess had the strength to pick up and carry a grown man.

Someone had obviously given my battered wardrobe as much attention as they'd given me. My boots stood on the floor beside me, cleaned and polished, and the remnants of my pants hung on a nearby chair. While badly stained, they were patched and repaired with some sort of heavy grey cloth. My tattered shirt was missing. It had been replaced by a coarse peasant-type shirt of non-descript grey. Socks and underwear lay on top of this, laundered somehow. The rest of my gear was piled beside the chair, and from here it looked like nothing had been disturbed.

Easing carefully out of bed, I found that someone had also thoughtfully provided a chamber pot. I grinned. They might not be accustomed to living guests; but someone had remembered. I relieved myself gratefully; then slowly dressed. I was hungry again, and wondered if I could wrangle another meal before having to meet the mistress of the hall. A soft knock sounded at the door and I hastily zipped my fly.

"Uh, yeah, come on in; I don't think it's locked."

The door opened and Baldr stuck his head in. He grinned when he saw me.

"Good, you're up and about." He came in, leaving the door ajar, and nodded in satisfaction. "Much better. I hope you're feeling better as well as looking it?"

"Much, thanks. When's supper?"

He chuckled. "You really must have been half-starved."

"I was." I thrust my hands into my pockets, and regarded him seriously. "Do you have any idea how long it took me to get here?"

He shook his head. "No; I couldn't even guess. None of us can quite believe you managed it at all. Hel is most anxious to meet you."

"Huh. I'll bet she is."

She had to figure Odin was behind this. I just hoped I could convince her I wasn't a threat, to her, at least. Unpleasant as it sounded, she and I were mostly on the same side—against Odin. I hoped Baldr hadn't guessed the truth of that.

"Let me get my knife, and I'll be ready to go."

I strapped Gary's knife to my calf and felt a hum of approval go through my leg. Good—I wanted the Biter's backup in case things got unpleasant.

Baldr led the way through immense corridors, past closed and barred doors, until we came to a wooden door decorated with silver filigree. I didn't even try to make sense of the ghastly scenes depicted in that metalwork.

Baldr knocked, and a woman's voice, low and gravelly, answered, "Enter."

Baldr pushed open the heavy door and motioned for me to proceed. I stepped through, glad when Baldr followed. The room was lit by even ghastlier carvings than the main entrance hall. I carefully averted my gaze, not wanting to spoil her first impression of me by throwing up on her carpet. There were indeed carpets on the floor, knotted in intricate patterns from what looked like plaits of human hair.

The walls were hung with tapestries—also woven from hair—and with heavy furs of animals I didn't recognize. Strange carvings of bone and ivory stood on smaller tables and shelves, and one massive piece of furniture seemed to be a wardrobe for clothing. Briefly I wondered what Death wore. Another ghostly fire blazed in a fireplace which must've required regular harvesting of giant sequoias. A heavy table stood beside it, laid with one place setting.

The central fixture of the room, however, was a bed on a raised platform. Silver skulls—human ones—topped stout posts at all four corners. Hangings of shimmering cloth obscured the occupant I could just barely see. Death reclined at her ease.

"So, you are the man who dares enter my kingdom before his time."

Her Bette Davis voice didn't sound angry; just intrigued.

"Come closer. I would look at you."

Baldr nodded toward the bed, so I moved across the carpets and approached the shimmery hangings, not without considerable trepidation. Unlike Baldr, Hel was very much alive. Her voice came again, chill as the wind and sleet outside.

"My home appears to distress you. What would you have me dwell in? A shining, fairy-tale palace full of warmth and light? Once those things were mine; but those who banished me made certain such were taken from me forever. Instead I wield a terrible power, and do not miss such trivialities."

She moved behind the hangings, nothing more than a shadow and a voice.

"My table is set with Hunger and Famine. I repose at my leisure in the Sickbed you mortals dread. My draperies—do you not admire them, the way they shimmer and lure you? They are Glimmering Misfortune, shining with elusive promise until you are ensnared. Come closer, mortal—or have you already come too near and tangled yourself forever?"

The hangings billowed out. For an instant, I was engulfed in a smothering cold stench, like a slaughterhouse. I lunged backward, and found the Biter in my hand. The stench vanished, and I was free.

"*Very good*," she purred.

The draperies subsided. A slim white hand pulled them aside. A fetid smell of sickness assaulted my nostrils and sent me back still another step. The goddess rose gracefully and let the hangings drop back into place. I tried not to stare. Then sternly repressed an idiotic urge to grin. I seriously doubted she would appreciate being laughed at.

But . . . *honestly* . . . !

She was half black, half white. The colors split right down the center, from head to foot. And—God help me—she looked as if she'd stepped right out of the hammiest *Star Trek* episode ever filmed. Her dark right side was the deep ebony of southernmost Chad, with long, black hair intricately braided and knotted in an arrangement that fell to her waist. Her left side was fairer than Baldr, with masses of silvery-blond hair braided just as intricately as the right side. Where the two colors met at the crown of her head the braids were interwoven, forming a banded pattern that reminded me unpleasantly of snakeskin.

The gossamer thin veil she wore left absolutely nothing to the imagination, and was held in place only by a snarling wolf's-head brooch at one shoulder.

Her gaze caught mine, and all trace of amusement drained away, leaving me clutching the Biter with a sweaty hand. Her eyes were crimson. They glowed hot like coals. When she smiled, her teeth were sharp, white fangs. She was beautiful, in a terrifying, compelling fashion. I understood, deep in my gut, why men throughout the ages had been repelled by—yet fatally attracted to—the angel of death. I found myself wanting to embrace her, to stretch out on her pallid bed and let her come to me. . . .

The Biter flared in my grasp. A flash of brilliant green light reflected the anger that flashed abruptly through my whole being. *Hel was playing games, and I was cast in the role of toy.* I blinked sudden sweat from my eyes.

Hel smiled, and gestured as if to say, "You can't blame me for trying." I discovered that I was shaking.

Her voice was a sultry purr, like a self-satisfied cat, and her eyes glinted briefly.

"Enough amusement, for now. I can see that you are a strong hero, so there is little to gain by deception. Come, sit at my table."

"Unh-uh." I stayed right where I was.

"Baldr," she said, a trifle wearily.

"It's all right to sit down," he said from the shadows. "Just don't accept anything from her table and you'll be fine."

She gave Baldr a pained glance; then gestured us to chairs. We sat; she joined us. I kept my grip on Gary's knife, and it kept its grip on my arm. Hel lifted a goblet and drank deeply; then set it down and contemplated me again. Her expression was impossible to interpret, shadowed here and highlit there by the eerie glow of an orange sculpture suspended above her table. I glanced at it only long enough to determine that the carving showed something utterly unspeakable being done to a pregnant woman, then hastily averted my gaze.

Hel's eyes narrowed slightly. "What I must know is why you have come to Niflheim. Can you answer that?"

I cleared my throat, and was irritated with myself for having to do so. "I want to speak with Loki."

Hel sat back slightly, which left her face in deeper shadow.

"That is what Baldr said. I did not believe him."

Hel fell silent. I had no idea what to say in response to that. I'd only been telling the truth, after all; sitting here was not *my* idea. The longer she remained silent, the more I sweat. I caught a glint in her eyes as her look sharpened, and the brief flash of sharp teeth as she licked her lips with the tip of a pointed tongue.

"Precisely what did you want to discuss with my father?"

"I have reasons for wanting information about Sleipnir."

"And those reasons are?"

I had to clear my throat again. "Private."

Her blond eyebrow rose. "I see." She picked up a knife—its handle was carved with scenes of blasted crops, skeletal men and beasts—and cut into a slice of meat on a dish shaped like a starving child's bloated belly. My jaws worked. I clamped them shut on nausea when she bit into the bloody meat and chewed thoughtfully.

"You realize that I am vitally interested in anything to do with Loki?"

I was aware of the reasons, and nodded.

"Good. You do understand why?"

I nodded again. Odin had imprisoned her father. He had also imprisoned her and her two brothers, simply because they were supposed to make trouble at some future, unspecified time. Given the gods' unshakable belief in predestination, I supposed it made sense from their point of view, despite the fact that they themselves believed the action would prove futile. Eventually the siblings—Fenrir and the World Serpent—were supposed to escape. Their wretched treatment ensured a well-whetted appetite for revenge. It looked to me like self-fulfilling prophecy; but then, given what I now knew, it was easy for me to point out what looked like flaws in Odin's thinking.

An idea nudged the fringes of my awareness then; but Hel spoke again, and I couldn't devote any attention to it.

"You are indeed an odd mixture of signals and portents, mortal. I wonder whose side you choose in this conflict? Mine? Or *Odin's?*"

The name was spat out. Her eyes flashed, daring Baldr to protest. He held silent. Wise man.

I sympathized with her, truly I did. The part of me on the side of justice cried out for the wrong done her to be righted.

Unfortunately, the day Hel's wrongs were redressed, everything I had ever known and loved was supposed to come to a fiery end; a consideration that tended to push me toward Odin's side of the bargaining table—where I emphatically did not want to be.

"Let's say I'm on my side," I answered, forcing a tight smile. Truth, Justice, and the American Way . . . Gary would've been proud.

She looked at me with astonishment. "Your side?" she echoed. Baldr looked equally baffled.

"Well, my world is caught in the middle, isn't it?"

She started to speak; then stopped and looked thoughtful. Taking another drink from her goblet, she studied my face for a long, tense interval before answering. What she finally said left me cold, sweating, and on my feet.

"I think," she purred, glancing up at me from beneath her eyelashes, "that you are entirely too dangerous to leave running about loose. It has been a long, long time since I took a hero of your strength to my bed, mortal. I think you will find my hall . . . less unpleasant . . . once you are dead."

I knew she had a thousand ways at her disposal to do me in right where I stood. And the wonderful knife in my hand wouldn't be the slightest bit of help against most of them. You can't fight off bubonic plague or a heart attack with a knife. Not even a supernatural one. I had to move fast. . . .

"Look, Hel, before you kill me, there's something you ought to know."

She paused in the act of lifting one slim white hand.

"Yes?" Her red eyes reflected morbid curiosity.

I wanted to glance at Baldr, and didn't dare. "Baldr," I growled, "get the hell out of here, will you? This is between me and her."

He hesitated. Then went without a word spoken. I heard the door thud softly shut behind him. I was alone with Death.

Hel had risen to her feet. She moved around the table

toward me; I backed up involuntarily, and swung the knife up between us.

Her lips quirked in amusement. "You are certainly entertaining, mortal, and uncommonly brave; or perhaps merely foolhardy. It is hard to decide which." Her eyes actually twinkled for a moment, looking like flame-shot rubies. "What is so secret that you do not wish Odin's son to hear it?"

Cut the crap and get straight to the point. . . .

"I don't plan to die yet, Hel, and it's not in your best interest to kill me."

Both her brows soared this time. "Oh?" That came out softly dangerous.

Sweat dripped into my eyes. "You want something I can give you."

Her voice filled the room with threat. "And what can you possibly know of Death's desires?"

I forced a laugh. It sounded one helluva lot braver than I felt. "What does every goddamn god and goddess in the entire stinking Norse pantheon want? Revenge."

"Revenge?" Her eyes narrowed. After a moment, she turned away to pace toward the hearth. Firelight glowed behind her, casting green luminescence through the filmy gown she wore. Firelight highlighted exquisite thighs and hips through sheer cloth rendered virtually invisible. I swallowed hard, and tightened my grip on the Biter. It squeezed back reassuringly.

She turned without warning and fixed me with a cold stare.

"Yes," she hissed quietly, "I do want revenge. Odin tortures my poor brother Fenrir, who did him no harm, and denies me my rightful place in the ruling councils of heaven. I have the dead"—she laughed coldly, and the bitter sound made my flesh creep across my scalp—"but the dead do not swell to near bursting with the lust for life, as I do. Cold lot of miserable, ambitionless slaves . . ."

She regained her composure and blinked in surprise for a moment. Then her brow furrowed deeply. "You *are* dangerous."

She reminded me of a cat about to pounce on a hapless beetle.

"Yeah." I grinned, still sweating. "I do believe I am. But not to you."

Her glance swept me from boot soles to crown. "Are you trying to tell me you won't fight to the end of your strength when I come for your soul?"

I managed a nonchalant shrug. "Who says *you* are going to collect it? I've got several deities vying for that right. Personally speaking, I'm not done with it just yet."

She actually gaped. Then laughed aloud. "*Not done with it yet* . . ." She wiped genuine tears from the corners of her eyes. "So tell me, little man," she said, still chuckling, "just what is it you intend to do with your soul while it is still in your possession?"

She hadn't killed me yet. If I could just keep her talking . . . I remembered somewhat desperately bargaining with Frau Brunner for that knife I'd given Odin. Gary'd told me, "If you could bargain that way when it really counts . . ."

"You want revenge on Odin. So do I. That makes us allies, not enemies. You're the goddess of death, yes; but only death from accident and sickness and old age. I've got a lot of fight left yet, which means Freyja and Odin both have a stake in me, too. Who knows, I've been so much trouble I might end up getting thrown into Niflhel with all the *real* badasses."

She smiled coyly. "That could be arranged."

"Huh. I'll bet it could. My point—my first point—is this. You've only got a one-in-three chance of getting hold of me. And if I'm dead, I can't finish what I set out to do."

She nodded impatiently. "Get to your real point. Why should I let you live?"

"Because I'm going to kill Odin for you."

She just stared. Then blinked once. Then she said, very quietly, "You aren't meant to be the instrument of his death."

I smiled into her eyes. "Are you sure?"

Hel frowned.

I pressed my slight advantage. "How many dead has he stolen from you already? Dead he shouldn't have been able to take?"

Her eyes widened, and she blurted, "How did you—?" Then Hel clamped her lips, and narrowed her eyes. "All right. You've made your point. Just how do you propose to kill him?"

I grinned. "Are you kidding? Tell you my plans with his son listening on the other side of the door? Besides, those goddamned, tattletale ravens of his could be hiding anywhere."

She started, and looked suspiciously into the shadows for Hugin and Munin. Odin sent that pair out daily as spies to the various nine worlds, to learn what was going down. Then she scowled and turned a baleful glare on me. "If you know so much, mortal, you should realize full well that Odin will die in the final battle! My brother will devour him."

I murmured again, "Are you *sure?*"

She paused. Then she licked her lips with a narrow vermilion tongue, and chewed absently at her lower lip with a sharp white fang. I sweat some more, and waited for her to think it through.

Finally she muttered to herself, "You seek a word with my father about Sleipnir, and say you wish to slay Odin." She looked up and held my gaze. "I can certainly guess why you need Sleipnir." Her tone was droll. I had no doubt whatever that she had. "And the Biter comes willingly to your hand," she mused aloud. "I am probably a fool. . . ."

She caught and held my gaze with a glittering ruby stare.

"Do you swear to me on your immortal soul that you will harm neither of my brothers in this mad quest of yours? Be warned—go back on this oath, and you are mine forever, regardless of the manner of your death."

I, too, was probably a fool. . . .

Slowly I shook my head. "I'm not stupid, Hel. I'm not after your brothers, but no one can swear that kind of an oath and be certain of keeping it. Accidents happen. Innocent bystanders get in the way. I'll promise to do my damnedest not to injure either of them, but I won't swear an oath like that."

I expected her to kill me on the spot. Instead she smiled.

"You drive a hard bargain, mortal. And you are shrewd." She shrugged her smooth shoulders, which lifted her breasts tantalizingly beneath the gauzy gown. "Can you blame me for trying?"

I snorted. "Not really. Lady, you're about the farthest thing from stupid I've ever seen."

Her chortle was surprisingly warm. "Why, thank you." She reached out a long finger toward my chin. I stepped hastily back, swinging the Biter up between us. She halted, and looked hurt; then sighed. "And you are a very wise man. I really do regret this; you'd have been such fun in bed."

I wrapped my other hand around the wrist holding the Biter, not only to brace my arm, but to keep both hands from shaking so badly. Damn her. . . .

But she didn't kill me. She said only, "It is a bargain, then. I allow you to keep your life as your own—for now," she added with a winsome smile that left me dripping sweat, "and you agree to spare my brothers—if possible—" she amended graciously when I opened my mouth to protest, "when you go after Odin on this mad quest of yours. Agreed?"

I reviewed the wording of that contract with microscopic care. "You agree to allow me to keep my life as my own, period, no strings attached and no interference, and then you can haggle with me and with the rest of the gods and goddesses for my soul when my time to die eventually comes around in its own due course. And I agree to try not to injure or kill either of your brothers in the course of hunting and killing Odin, but make no promises that I might not accidentally kill or injure one or both of them, since I can't predict the course or outcome of any fight with a god or anyone or anything that might support him." I thought about what I'd said again, decided I was happy with it, and added, "Agreed?"

I saw her lips moving silently as she, in turn, reviewed the potential contract. At length she pouted in sheer annoyance and muttered, "Agreed."

I began breathing again; cautiously.

She turned aside, and toyed with the scraps of food left on her plate. "I suppose I should wish you luck in capturing my traitorous half-brother. Sleipnir is notoriously tricky. Of course," she flashed a grim smile, "he *is* our father's son."

I'd never quite thought of Sleipnir in terms of Hel's half-brother. I thought about the terms of our agreement, and wondered which two brothers I'd ended up swearing to try not to hurt. Of course, that knife cut both ways—I could always claim that she hadn't stipulated which two, and therefore I wasn't bound by any kind of oath regarding Sleipnir. Of course, she could then declare the whole thing null and void and kill me anyway. . . . I decided I'd better not hurt Fenrir, the

World Serpent, *or* Sleipnir if I could possibly help it.
Who would we get to judge a contract dispute?

"I think perhaps you *are* none of my affair, mortal,"
Hel was saying. "And since you wish to speak to my
father, you are going to have to arrange for your own
transportation to him." She glanced up at me. "He lies in
Niflhel, mortal, not Niflheim, and no one enters Niflhel
without the express permission of the Norns themselves."

I didn't know whether or not she was telling the truth.
It didn't make sense that the goddess of death wouldn't
have access to that part of the underworld where the
truly evil dead were sent. Even psychopathic monsters
sometimes died accidentally, or of old age. But then,
someone had to judge the dead, and the Norns seemed
as likely a candidate as anyone.

"I'd rather not make another detour," I said dryly.
"It's nothing personal, but I'd just as soon spend as
little time as possible in this world of yours, and I've
got other people to call on. So why don't you just give
me directions—"

She slammed her fists down on the table. The plate
jumped, and the knife clattered to the floor. I'd never
seen sparks literally fly out of someone's eyes. . . .

*"Impudent little man! I have been patient enough with
you!"*

The Biter flared wildly green in my hand. I snarled
right back, "Going to forswear yourself so soon, lady?
Isn't that *Odin's* specialty?"

She bit down on whatever it was she had been about
to say.

The next thing I knew—even before I could take in
what had happened—I was standing in a driving sleet
storm, dizzy and shivering. The Biter was in my hand;
but I was utterly alone outside Hel's miserable hall of
death. And all my gear was locked behind doors and
walls I could never hope to penetrate.

Chapter Fourteen

For a long moment I stood gaping stupidly at the high, ice-coated wall; then rage swept through me. What actually went through my mind I don't know; but abruptly Gary's knife was glowing even more fiercely in the gloom. I launched myself straight at Hel's tarnished silver gates. The Biter sank deep, cutting a gash downward like a blowtorch. The silver on either side melted and dripped away, freezing an instant later into sharp points and rounded globules.

The Biter cut deeper. Then a ponderous groan reached my ears above the sleet-heavy wind. The gates moved toward me. I stumbled numbly back out of the way to avoid being crushed by several tons of solid silver.

I did not expect the sight that met my eyes. Baldr appeared, riding one horse and leading another. My gear was slung over the second animal's back. The Biter went dark in my hand. I blinked. The heavy gates groaned shut behind him again and came together with a dull thud. He glanced over his shoulder, saw the damage I'd inflicted, and whistled between his teeth.

"Im-press-ive. Stupid, but impressive. What were you going to do if you got in?"

I gestured at the second horse. "I needed my gear."

"Uh-huh. Ready to go?"

I didn't let go of the Biter, and was pleased when it remained poised for battle. "I have no intention of going anywhere near the Norns. Like I said, I've got things to do, and I'm a little shy on time."

Baldr shook his head. "For one thing, you're in no shape to reach Loki. One meal and a few hours' rest won't do it. For another, you haven't the faintest idea which way to go. —Wait, hear me out," he said as I started to interrupt.

"All right," I growled, "say your piece."

Baldr inclined his head in mock thanks. His voice came out a little flat. "You're finally learning courtesy."

"I'm courteous enough," I countered. "Tolerance for assholes, I've never had."

Baldr's brows shot into his hairline. Then he laughed—and, notably, his breath did not steam in the freezing air, the way mine did. "I've been called many things, Randy Barnes; but you are the first to give Odin's son *that* title."

"Huh. Good to know I'll be famous for something."

He chuckled. "Indeed, you will. I am sorry, you know, but you really must see the Norns. Hel was right. You're none of her affair, which means you shouldn't be in Niflheim at all. Either you're here by my father's design—which I'm seriously beginning to doubt—or you're here because the Norns want you here."

"I wouldn't bet on that," I muttered.

Baldr frowned; but refrained from comment.

I wiped ice crystals off my eyelashes so I could see him better, and took my horse's reins. Mounting took only a moment, then I swung my horse's head around to face Baldr. I kept the Biter in my free hand, between me and

Odin's son. "If it's all the same to you, Baldr, I don't need a nursemaid. Especially not Hel's. Nothing personal."

His frown deepened furrows in his cheeks. "I am not here at Hel's instructions."

"Oh?"

For the first time, Baldr looked tired and . . . well, dead.

"No. I'm not." He paused; then met my gaze levelly. "It's clear I don't understand what's happening here, any more than Hel does; but I rather like you, Randy Barnes, and you may believe it or not, I admire you very much already. I'd hoped to extend my hand in friendship."

"You'll understand, I hope, if I have trouble believing that."

I expected him to get angry, and abandon me to my own devices—which was exactly what I wanted. Instead, he paled, and looked troubled.

"I am not accustomed," he said very quietly, almost inaudible above the sleet-filled wind, "to being so mistrusted. Whatever drives you, it is clear you have little love for us." He glanced up from his horse's mane, and shivered in an errant blast of icy wind, the first indication he'd given that Niflheim's weather affected the dead.

"Perhaps," he mused, "you have good reason. I would give a great deal to know what you said to Hel. In all my centuries here, I've never seen her in such a towering temper. Frankly, I'm astonished she let you live."

"As someone else has found out recently"—I smiled tightly—"I'm not so easy to kill."

He stared levelly into my eyes. "That may be. But Niflheim isn't exactly hospitable to someone who's still alive. Please believe me, if you want to survive much longer, you will have to accept some help. Without food, water, or a sense of direction, you won't last another four songs."

"Twenty-four hours, huh? You don't know what a

tough bastard I am. And the Biter can get me where I want to go."

—Unless where I wanted to go conflicted with its notion of where *it* thought I should go, a possibility I had to consider.

"It's your funeral." He shrugged. "I'd thought you were more intelligent than that. I would be more than willing to guide you to Loki, and you would travel safely in my company. I swear that on whatever you consider sacred; but only if we visit the Norns first. I, at any rate, would like to know what I've let myself in for, befriending you. Hel was not amused when I left her hall to come after you."

I studied him narrowly; but found no hint of guile in his troubled blue eyes. Had Odin's son really put it on the line for me? It didn't seem likely. On the other hand, Baldr's reputation argued that he was telling the truth. I found myself wanting to believe him. I liked this stocky, blue-eyed god who'd been dead before mankind learned to turn iron ore into weapons. Baldr waited in silence, while I sat astride my dead horse and tried to decide what to do.

I was already ravenously hungry, especially now that I was away from Hel's unappetizing home. I had no food of my own, and there wasn't much water left in my canteens. If the River Gjoll were any indication, none of the water in Niflheim might be drinkable. I might be able to steal some of the weird mushrooms I'd seen growing nearby; but I couldn't be sure which ones were safe. Nanna had known, and Baldr probably would, too, but I might end up poisoning myself, especially if they had to be specially prepared to get rid of toxins. I'd be no good to Gary dead of starvation and consigned to Hel's hall for eternity.

On the other hand, visiting the Norns might not be such a bad idea. If they called the shots—or once had—I might get valuable information from them. The more I thought about that, the more it made sense. Predestination had gone screwy. So who better to consult than the three old witches who were supposed to preordain everything? For all I knew, maybe they'd gotten so senile they'd simply lost track of what they were supposed to be arranging. In which case, I might be able to do a helluva lot more than I'd hoped.

I glanced over at him, and scowled. "Dammit, Baldr, you know I haven't got much choice."

He grinned and tossed me a fur overjacket slung across his lap. "Then get into that before you freeze—and see if you can guide your horse out of this ice storm without breaking your fool neck. Whatever do they teach warriors these days?"

"Yeah? Well, I'd like to see you try and drive an M-113 armored personnel carrier," I muttered. I slid the parka on and closed it up, then turned in the saddle and checked my gear. Everything was there. I slipped the web gear on; then adjusted the pack straps to fit over the fur jacket.

"Okay, pal o' mine, lead the way."

Baldr smiled, friendly and relaxed again, then turned his horse's head and set off at a walk. I wondered briefly what I'd let myself in for this time, then wondered what Hel made of all this. Probably was gnashing her pointed teeth. I shivered in a stray blast of wind, and hoped I never saw Hel again, before death or after.

We skirted the enormous wall and headed inland.

Once past the wall, Baldr glanced back curiously. "What, exactly, did you say to Hel back there?"

"What Death didn't want to hear."

He favored me with a long, keen stare; then shut up. I heard him mutter to himself, "It's going to be a long ride."

Then both of us fell silent.

✧　　✧　　✧

He was right—it was a long ride. I developed saddle sores the size of dinner plates on my butt and thighs. He produced some sort of ointment that healed them into calluses. The food Baldr had brought along was edible— barely—but it kept body and soul together, a fact that undoubtedly displeased Hel tremendously. I thought a lot about Gary Vernon, and what Valhalla might be like. I hoped to God it was better than Niflheim. If it wasn't . . . Well, that's why I was here, wasn't it?

Baldr did most of the talking. He had an endless stream of stories to tell, but I no longer found the exploits of murdering gods amusing. Letting him talk, though, proved easier than shutting him up, so I let him ramble, and hoped I might eventually learn something useful. Most of the stories were little more than braggadocio. At least most of them weren't about Baldr. My new friend really was a self-effacing kind of guy. Despite my vow to remain cautious of him, I found myself ever more grateful for his company. For a Norse god, he was a decent guy.

The horses plodded on untiringly. It still bothered me that they needed neither food nor water. There was no way of telling time from the environment; the lighting never changed. Only my watch hands, moving faithfully around the luminous dial, told me time was, indeed, passing. I was halfway surprised my watch still functioned. I'd always figured Hell would be a place where time stopped. Not even the dead were immune from the inexorable sweep of years.

As we continued riding, for what felt like days, I began to grow suspicious again. There was no end to the barren wasteland we had entered upon leaving Hel's gates. The ridges had grown steeper, and the valleys colder and more desolate. That was about it. We could have been riding across the surface of the moon and found more life. There weren't even any more of the strange fungi Baldr had harvested along the way.

With our supplies running low, and sources of neither food nor water in sight, I was beginning to wonder if Hel had sent Baldr to lead me into the desert to die. The opposite side of the cavern was still lost beyond the horizon. The ceiling was unchanged, still swirling and flickering in random, abstract patterns of darkness and light. There were times when the overwhelming alienness of Niflheim pressed in like a boulder on my sanity.

Gary Vernon's face, floating in my memory, and the image of Sleipnir's wild eyes, kept me going.

Eventually—when we topped another ridge and I saw nothing except more of the same nothingness—I stopped my horse and planted my fists on my thighs.

"Okay, Baldr, don't you think this has gone on long enough?"

He turned in the saddle. Surprise flickered through his blue eyes. "What do you mean?"

"You know damned well what I mean. We're going nowhere. There's nothing out here but more nothing, and pretty soon you're going to watch me die of dehydration. I let you talk me into this against my better judgment, so I guess it's my own damn fault; but I didn't come this far just to wander around Niflheim's Outback until I drop conveniently dead."

The Biter came unbidden to my hand. I tested the edge casually with one thumb. "I wonder how dead horse tastes."

My mount grunted in distress. He tossed his head, and danced sideways; but my riding skills had improved steadily, and I not only stayed with him, I brought him under control. "Not you, stupid, the other one."

This time Baldr's horse pranced sideways, away from me. One eye rolled white at the Biter. The dead god brought his animal up short, and said, "Randy, put the knife away. There's been no trick. We're almost there."

"Yeah, and I'm the President of the United States. Try again."

"Did you think the Norns would sit out in the open?"

I hadn't really thought about that. If I were a Norn, would I want eavesdroppers watching me manage the Macrocosmic All?

"They're very private beings, by choice and necessity. Believe me, Randy, you could get within a hundred yards of them and not know it. Unless you knew exactly where you were going, you'd walk right past. I do know where we're going—I've been there many times, after all—and we're truly almost there."

He seemed sincere, and he'd saved my ass before, although I still couldn't be sure of his motives. Hell, I couldn't be sure of anyone's motives, except my own. All I wanted to do was get on with my hunt. Find Gary, kick cosmic butt . . .

Everything and everyone in Niflheim seemed to be conspiring to sidetrack me.

"This is the last time anyone distracts me," I answered shortly. "We get this over with, then I'm on my way. Not you, not Hel, not anybody else is going to stop me. Got it?"

He frowned. "As it must be, so it shall."

"Cut the fate crap. I don't buy it. Are you ready?"

His eyes were troubled; but he nodded. "Yes."

He turned his horse and started down the steep slope into a much broader, wider valley than most. I followed, and slipped the Biter carefully back into its sheath. My horse's hooves touched level ground. Baldr, several paces ahead, rode past an enormous rock, larger than any of the other gigantic boulders I'd seen so far.

His horse shimmered once, and vanished.

Mine rose on his hind legs. He screamed; then lunged sideways and tried to bolt. I cursed long and loud, and clung to his back while he sunfished and tried to hurl me straight into the jagged boulder.

Chapter Fifteen

It took longer than usual to get my spooked mount settled. When he finally stood quietly, I was more than ready to find out if a god could be killed twice.

"BALDR!"

I wasn't expecting an answer, and was nearly unseated again when the head and shoulders of a horse appeared out of nowhere in front of us. Baldr peered curiously through a shimmer in the air while I struggled to keep my horse from dumping me and bolting. Baldr placidly ignored the scalding stream of obscenity I sent his way while fighting my mount.

"Finished?" he asked when the horse stood still and I sat panting for breath.

I growled something physically—and probably metaphysically—impossible.

"I told you we were close. See if you can get that nag of yours to follow me through."

He vanished again; but this time I was ready. Grimly I forced my mount back to the ground. A great deal of swearing and kicking later, I had him moving forward, toward the end of the great boulder. I thought about all

the times Gary'd told me horseback riding was fun, and
glowered. When I found that grinning idiot, I was going
to tell him exactly what he could do with his fun, his
horses, *and* his gods.

The air shimmered around us, and we stepped onto a
carpet of lush, green grass. The horse snorted, threw his
head up, and stopped short. I let him.

The unrelenting, soulless green light had been
replaced by the warm light I'd known all my life. Color
sprang up on all sides of me, real color that soothed the
eyes. Overhead, an unearthly glow, the color of fire,
caught my eye. Startled, I tilted my head back to stare,
and nearly fell off my horse's back. Directly overhead
were great rivers of blood and fire, gold, sapphire and
emerald, and a violet so intense it hurt the eyes to look at
it. . . .

Arching up and up, finally vanishing from sight miles
overhead, the ghostly, brilliant spans of Bifrost radiated
their colors across the whole sky. Only it wasn't sky; it
was a roof, just like Niflheim's, broken into three enormous arches by the immense crack Bifrost climbed
through on its journey to heaven.

These were the three great roots of Yggdrasil itself,
spreading out to encompass the netherworlds. The
unearthly green glow was still there, but paled into
oblivion under the brilliance pulsing out of Asgard's
sacred rainbow bridge.

I closed my mouth with an effort of will, and lowered
my gaze back to the humble ground, where I sat even
more humbly on my dead horse.

Below the bridge lay a pool of shimmering white
flame which at second glance resolved itself into shining
water so bright it hurt my eyes even more than the rainbow bridge did. At the edge of that pool was an
incredibly beautiful young woman.

My mouth fell open again.

I hadn't expected them to be so . . . *young*.

Baldr murmured unnecessarily—although I couldn't get my mouth to work properly enough to stop him— "This is one of the Three Sisters, the Norns, maiden keepers of the spring called Urd. I believe you would translate that as Destiny. Urd waters the three roots of Yggdrasil"—he gestured to the immense roof overhead—"the ash tree that spreads its branches and digs its roots through all the nine worlds, tying them together."

I knew about Yggdrasil, and its branches and roots. Nidhogg, an immense snake, was supposed to feed on one of the great roots; but I hadn't seen anything like that, thank god. Unless that disturbance in the river Gjoll had been Nidhogg?

Baldr added, again unnecessarily, "Some say the ash will wither, maybe even die, from the many enemies conspiring to kill it; but others believe it will be the only living entity in the nine worlds to survive Ragnarok." Staring up at the immense roots above us, I couldn't imagine anything powerful enough to harm it. Then I thought about the nuclear missiles Gary and I'd guarded for the past few years and changed my mind.

I yanked my thoughts back to the Norns. They were more than the guardians of this spring and the weavers of Fate; they were supposed to be the most powerful forces in all the worlds connected by Yggdrasil. Even Odin feared them. I wondered what they would make of my pragmatic free-will attitude. The only Norn in sight stared at me with an expression I couldn't begin to interpret.

I closed my lips with difficulty, and concentrated on reminding myself that these women were *dangerous*. The glorious creature standing in the spring didn't look dangerous. My gut drew in sharply, and my hands started to sweat on the reins. I hadn't expected them to be so . . . *beautiful*.

Baldr moved forward, and I urged my horse to follow.
The brilliant pool that welled up from the great spring
lay directly beneath Bifrost. It shimmered like a sheet of
molten silver; but as we approached, I saw that despite
its appearance it wasn't actually flame; the surface
danced in the still air, tricking the eyes like a heat mirage
on an asphalt road. The play of light in the water had
nothing to do with Bifrost's radiance. It somehow welled
up from within the spring's crystalline depths, and
reflected off the underside of the surface then refracted
into a thousand shifting, shimmering colors. I could
almost *hear* those colors. . . .

The far shore was lost in the trembling white light;
but near our side, the surface reflected the brilliant
bands of color from the great bridge above. On a small
rise nearby stood a magnificent wooden hall. The long,
gabled roof was covered with gold, and rose to peaks at
either end—peaks carved to resemble the reaching
trunks and branches of golden trees. The structure was
enormous, dwarfing even Hel's sinister abode; but
here there was no wall surrounding it, no gate, no icy
blast of wind. In fact, I found myself growing warmer
by the moment, and stopped long enough to shrug out
of the pack so I could peel off my fur jacket. I draped
the coat over the horse's neck, and looped the pack
over one arm.

The sides of the Norns' hall were alive with intricate
carvings that almost breathed and moved across the
walls. I had the eerie feeling that if I looked too closely at
the patterns, I'd see living men and animals in those
designs—or worse, myself, walking toward the carved
wall. Would that wall show me where Gary Vernon was
right now? If the Norns carved men's lives on the walls of
their hall, shaping and reshaping the patterns to suit
their aesthetic desires, that building had to be the ulti-
mate sculpture.

—Or was my overloaded brain just imagining the movement in those carvings?

Reason reasserted itself. The walls would've needed to be miles thick, or they'd have been carved to matchsticks by now. Unless, of course, the building itself was growing, like the tree arching above it. The hall's heavy golden doors stood wide open; but the interior lay in deep shadow, hiding the contents from sight. Close to the nearest corner lay what looked like rusty tools, piled into a discarded heap. *Rusty tools?* I wondered just how old the newest carvings on that building were.

Then, as I watched, another breathtakingly beautiful young woman appeared from inside the hall and made her leisurely way toward us. Baldr dismounted, and I followed suit, finding myself ankle-deep in soft grass. My horse swished his tail nervously, so I placed one hand on his neck; then strapped the pack to the saddle, in case I needed both hands to control the idiotic beast again.

The goddess nearest us—the one in the spring—eyed me steadily and ignored Baldr altogether. That was simultaneously unnerving and flattering, since she was not only one of the true immortals, but also the most radiant creature I'd ever seen. She'd hitched up her simple white dress to reveal flawless knees. Spring water lapped at exquisite ankles.

Her hair was as white as her skin, as white as the feathers of the swans that glided up to nuzzle her legs with long, graceful necks. The trailing ends of her hair brushed the surface of the spring. Yet she didn't look pale; rather, she glowed with light, and when she moved, shining sparkles hovered in the air around her, dancing and glittering as brightly as the spring in which she stood. I caught a glimmer from inside the silver pitcher she held. The vessel's gently flaring lip dripped shining beads of water back into the spring, reminding me how thirsty I was, and how hungry, and how filthy from head to toe.

Movement nearby distracted me. I looked up to see the second Norn walking toward us. She had come down from the hall, and when she moved, her stride was the essence of *woman*. My eyes—even my nostrils—widened.

God . . .

Balanced on one hip was a bowl of carved green stone, swirled like malachite. It was filled with white clay, evidently dug from the earth at the edge of the spring. I wanted desperately to *be* that bowl, riding her hips. . . . Her emerald-colored dress was cut low, allowing sight of the aureolae as well as the swell of full, ripe breasts the color of new honey. But the material hid what I wanted to see, clinging tantalizingly to curved hips and long, shapely thighs. That simple green dress teased more sensually—and far more mercilessly—than Hel's near-nudity.

Her glorious hair was the deep, still green of a pool hidden in an ancient forest, and framed a face of pale honey gold. While her sister's features were fragile as rare porcelain, this goddess' exquisite face invited a man to take it between his hands, to press his lips against her softly inviting mouth, to watch those brilliant green eyes shift from sparkling laughter to the smoldering heat of passion. . . .

Her hair rippled with her movements, as still water ripples when a leaf drops onto its glistening surface. Silky strands clung to her arms, her breasts, her thighs. . . .

She met my stare, and her lips slowly parted in a knowing smile of welcome. She returned my gaze frankly, appraising me as openly as I appraised her. When her eyes rested on my crotch she smiled again. I suppressed a groan, and dug my fingers into my horse's mane. Her eyes flashed with laughter again. A low, sensuous chuckle reached my ears, compounding my agony. She had a voice men dreamed of hearing in bed. I had to force my gaze away—

And saw the third Norn.

She had appeared apparently from nowhere at all.

She took a step directly toward me, her stare intent— and when my eyes focused on her, the blood drained from my face, the lust from my loins, and the courage from my bones. My horse screamed, rearing high, and suddenly I was busy fighting to keep him from bolting with everything I owned in this world, or any other. I finally wrestled him down, and got him to stand still. He laid his ears back, and sweated down his neck, but he stood where I held him.

Reluctantly, I turned to face the third Norn. I'd rather have faced Hel again.

Her gown billowed like windblown flame. It crackled hotly in the perfectly still air. The very earth scorched where her bare foot stepped. Her hair was so bright, looking at it brought streams of tears to my eyes. Long strands of fire danced around her shoulders, and trailing tongues of flame brushed the earth to leave smoking trails in the soft white clay. Her whole body shimmered in the heat that hung about her, distorting the slender figure, obscuring the features of her face.

She stepped closer and raised long, smoky lashes to look directly into my eyes. Hers were smoldering embers, flashing with white-hot sparks that shifted and glinted in their glowing depths. Hel's eyes had disturbed me. Looking into this Norn's eyes made my confrontation with Hel seem like a schoolboy's apprehension of a scolding.

Heat engulfed me. It stifled my lungs until drawing breath was agony. I tried to stumble backward, tried to break the gaze that held me prisoner, but was unable to move. I was caught by her gaze like a moth drawn to the very scorching edge of a candle flame. My horse screamed again; but I was powerless to stop him from lunging free and bolting as fast as he could run.

She reached out with slender, flame-tipped fingers. They crackled in the hot air. Sweat drenched my clothing in rivers. I watched, waiting for the pain that would come when my skin blistered under her touch, and wondered if the Biter would even come to my hand. . . .

A smile teased her lips, blurred slightly by the heat haze between us. A smoky, sultry voice reached through the heat roar in my ears. "No mortal has ever dared my gaze so long. You are brave beyond telling."

She turned her gaze to Baldr. A draft of cool, sweet air rushed over me, filled my lungs. I staggered, and just managed to avoid collapsing to my knees. I was trembling from head to foot and couldn't stop.

A cool hand touched my brow. I yelled, and jumped about three feet straight up. When I landed, my knees folded, dumping me ignominiously to the ground. I managed to look up. The goddess in green, her bowl of clay discarded, stood beside me. Her expression wavered between contrition and amusement. She was holding the silver pitcher of water her sister had been filling from the spring. Wordlessly, she placed it in my hands. When she curled hers around mine to steady them, a shock of energy sped through me. Strength raced up my arms and spread throughout my whole body. My ragged breathing slowed, my hands steadied, and the tremors eased out of my muscles.

When I looked down into the pitcher, I saw the same eerie play of light I'd seen in the spring. I nearly dropped the whole thing in my lap. My benefactress caught it deftly. She wrapped my hands around the sides, and overlapped my fingers warmly with hers; then lifted the rim to my lips. I drank deeply, and closed my eyes as the shining water sank into me.

The sensation was utterly indescribable. The shock of energy from her touch was nothing compared to the feeling that raced through me now. I could feel flesh closing, healing over wounds that until now had mended only with painful slowness. Scars disappeared, and bitter, bone-weary exhaustion vanished. My mind cleared. A sense of strength and energy I hadn't known in years flooded through me. When I opened my eyes, the pitcher was empty and dark.

I stared at the beautiful woman beside me. She smiled, taking the pitcher from my hands, and touched my brow. A flush ran through me. I reached out, unthinking, wanting only to touch her, to take her in my arms and drown in the soft warmth of her. . . .

She placed a fingertip against my lips and shook her head slightly. I kissed the warm flesh touching mine; then closed my eyes in ecstasy when she traced the outline of my mouth with her fingertip. I felt her lips brush mine; then she was gone. I swayed drunkenly.

Something nibbled warmly at my ear. I opened my eyes. My horse stood over me, lipping my hair and looking contrite.

"Goddamn stupid nag," I muttered. Baldr had averted his gaze; but he was smiling. In an attempt to regain my composure, I tightened the girth, and made sure my pack and its contents had suffered no damage.

Sneaking a glance over one shoulder, I saw that the woman of my dreams had returned the pitcher to her sister. Where her footsteps crossed trails of char—left by the fiery Norn's feet—new grass sprouted thickly, covering the blackened scars with a carpet of tender green shoots.

The white Norn refilled the pitcher, and where she trod, the earth withered into fine white ash that blew away on the breeze of her passing. I noticed trails and patches of grass, char, and ash all around the spring, crisscrossing each other all the way to the open doors of the hall.

"Baldr . . ."

The fire Norn breathed his name into the smoky stillness.

When I looked, Baldr was pale to the lips. He held the Norn's gaze with obvious difficulty. Suddenly I didn't feel quite so bad.

"Skuld." He sketched a courtly, archaic bow which I suspected was designed solely to break her gaze. It gave him a moment to compose himself. "Pray forgive me for intruding on your private affairs. My apologies as well to Urd," he bowed to the white Norn, "and Verdani." Each nodded in turn, acknowledging the apology.

I wondered briefly if Urd was named for the spring or the spring for her. Destiny. History. How were maiden and spring interwoven, I wondered, these two who watered the Tree of the Worlds? I thought about the ashes of her footsteps and felt a chill run through my bones. Even if these three *weren't* still in charge of the universe—something I was beginning to doubt, despite what I'd seen so far—they were clearly the most dangerous trio I'd ever encountered. Not even Sleipnir instilled the same fight-or-flight terror Skuld did.

As though she'd heard my thoughts, Skuld glanced my way. I stiffened. She smiled, then turned a stern gaze on my companion. I felt as though I'd been granted a reprieve. Baldr stiffened in turn.

"Yes, Baldr, this one is assuredly our private affair. Why have you chosen to interfere?"

Sweat broke out across the dead god's forehead; a healthy dose of fear shone in his eyes, mingled with stunned surprise.

"You *ask*?" His voice actually broke.

She inclined her head slightly. A tremor caught him.

For a goddess who was supposed to know every-thing—including, obviously, Baldr's very thoughts—her question was decidedly odd. A cold, murderous smile started somewhere at gut level and stretched its way across my lips. Skuld's question—and Baldr's white-faced reaction—confirmed what I had already known.

—And what Odin's favorite son was just beginning to guess.

Come Niflhel, come high water, Odin was mine.

Baldr was in deep distress. He closed his eyes, and his fists; then he met Skuld's eyes. Sweat poured off him. "I seek only guidance, lady."

She gazed at him in stony silence for a moment. "There are things stirring that even gods may not know, Baldr."

I thought he was going to be sick. Then Skuld turned, and the heat of her gaze caught me unawares. I reeled and fought to return it.

"Have you told your somewhat foolish—although undeniably loyal—companion why you came?" she asked me.

I straightened. Sweat rivered off me. I managed to draw one scalding breath to reply. "I want to talk to Loki. And that's all I'm telling anyone."

I fully expected to be incinerated for my insolence. I wasn't. And if her laughter astonished me, it stunned Baldr speechless.

"I fear that will have to be enough for you, Baldr," she said, still laughing, "and for your grim hostess, as well. This mortal keeps his secrets well."

Baldr started to protest; then fell uneasily silent. He eyed me warily. I could see clearly that he bitterly regret-ted his impulsive act of friendship, made back at Hel's hall.

Skuld sighed, and said, "Things are not as they once were, Baldr; but if it makes you feel any better . . ."

She closed her eyes, and stood perfectly still inside the crackling aura of heat that surrounded her. Skuld began to speak, in words wreathed with smoke and flame:

Helblindi's eye from heaven sees
The battle grim which heralds doom,
And fearful of His dreadful fate,
He strives to halt what must transpire.
Does Fimbulvetr lurk beyond
The madness He himself has loosed?
What guilty thoughts Helblindi hides,
Such deeds, the valkyries abhor,
And Frigga hangs her head in shame.
A mortal's eyes and mortal's heart
See all with other eyes than His,
And mortal lips pronounce a doom
That drives no bargain save with Death.
Helblindi sees, Helblindi snarls,
And all the worlds await the hour,
To see if mortal blow can break
The chains which hold Muspell at bay.
Will all that rages for revenge
Be loosed upon the tree of ash?
Or will the dour hall of Hel
Receive another guest tonight?
The force Between is now unleashed
For good or ill upon the Worlds,
And mortal gods do well to fear
The Midgard hand unbound by Fate.

She stopped speaking.
Thank God . . .
Every hair, from my scalp to the dark hairs on the tops of my toes, stood on end. Only when I started breathing again did I realize I'd stopped. Skuld had raised more questions than she'd answered—in point of fact, she

hadn't answered *anything*—and I wasn't sure I *wanted* some of her questions answered. All I wanted was a couple of words with Loki, a quick ride on Sleipnir, and a quicker end to Odin. Visiting an oracle hadn't been my idea in the first place; and Skuld's "prophecy" was decidedly enigmatic, even for an oracle.

Skuld opened her eyes and turned again to Baldr. "Do you begin to see?"

The look Baldr awarded me was filled with . . .

I could not interpret the emotion in his eyes. Probably akin to the look in Dr. Frankenstein's eyes when he realized what his creation had done.

I gave myself a rough mental shake. I had to clear my head again, think . . .

"No," Baldr whispered. "But I thank you for the Sight."

"Stand with him, if you will, or send him on his way, with all due warning. He has chosen this path, and not even you may turn him from it, without his consent."

I stared hard at her, nerving myself to ask, to confirm it. She had turned away, and gazed pensively at the rainbow spans rising high above our heads. Colors of fire and blood pulsed hotly in the still air, overriding the other hues in Bifrost. She looked inexpressibly weary, almost vulnerable. . . .

Baldr's hand touched my arm. I jumped, and yelled; then turned to meet the blue of his eyes. They were dark with inner trouble. I glanced away, back to where Skuld stood. I needed to ask—needed to *know*, not just guess—but I could not. I couldn't force my mouth to shape the words.

Mostly, I couldn't stand the thought of withering under her burning gaze again. Skuld was a killer. I knew one when I saw one, and I was certain she did too. Hel, I could fight. Skuld, I wasn't so certain. The future arrives inexorably, second by relentless second, and there's not much any man can do to stop it. I didn't even plan to try. My business was elsewhere.

"Come," Baldr said, his voice and whole bearing exhausted, "the interview is over. We have another journey to make before I . . . leave you."

He'd almost said "before I can escape." The words all but hovered in the clear air between us. I didn't know what to say. I unstrapped my backpack from the saddle and slung it across my shoulders, then we mounted and rode away in silence. I didn't give Skuld so much as a backward glance.

Chapter Sixteen

Baldr led the way around the shore of Urd and rode off in a different direction from the way we'd entered. I followed without protest. Whatever his reasons, Baldr had chosen to lead me where I wanted to go, which was better, I supposed, than being abandoned to Skuld.

I didn't quite know what to make of my interview with Skuld. Had she been trying to warn Baldr? Or me? Why? And of what? I narrowed my eyes, and tried to recall exactly what she'd said.

Helblindi was another name for Odin: "He who blinds with death"—a fitting title if ever I'd seen one.

I snorted, which earned me a curious glance from Baldr. I held his gaze, but declined to enlighten him. He grunted once, then turned back around in the saddle; but not before his facial muscles tightened. From his expression, it was obvious he was beginning to view me as a decided threat.

As well he should. Not that I meant Baldr any harm. I wondered briefly if seeing Loki about Sleipnir was the smartest thing I could have tried. Probably not. Unfortunately, I'd gone to a lot of trouble to set this hunt in motion. I could hardly back out now. Besides, it was still the only way I knew to get my hands on Sleipnir, and without Sleipnir, there wasn't much purpose to anything I'd accomplished so far. So I worried and rode and worried some more, and didn't even notice when Baldr and his horse vanished. My horse did, though. I grabbed wildly at his mane when he reared and danced sideways.

" . . . stupid, walking lump of Purina Dog Chow . . ."

I went on in this vein at some length; but I managed to haul the animal's head around and forced him in the direction I wanted to go. I promised myself solemnly that when I caught up with Baldr, I was going to arrange a trade in mounts—forcibly, if necessary. This greenbroke nag was determined to get me killed. Probably another present from Odin. If the witless animal pulled another stunt like this one, I'd serve him to Odin for his goddamn dinner.

A shimmer swallowed us. My horse's hooves rang on solid stone—and bone-chilling cold knifed through my light clothing. I experienced a massive bout of shivering before I managed to get the pack off and the fur jacket on. Even then, I couldn't get warm.

There was damn little light anywhere. My horse quieted down uncertainly while I peered through the darkness to get my bearings. Crossing the spatial bubble the Norns lived in had accomplished more than just crossing a section of Niflheim—it appeared we'd left Niflheim altogether.

A dully glowing wall of maroon rock rose just ahead. A wide lip curved outward, forming a deep overhang. It was almost a small cave. The overhang was bathed in ghastly, rust-colored light. Enormous boulders glowed like bloodstone on all sides. Inside the overhang I could see movement; but couldn't quite discern what was moving.

Baldr dismounted. I followed his example. As my feet

touched the ground, I noticed an odd trembling underfoot, almost like the rumble of heavy machinery felt through a concrete floor—except I didn't *hear* anything.

Or did I? Yes, there was a sound, almost too low to hear. A sort of rustling, scraping noise, like leathery scales crawling across straw. . . .

A chill crept up my spine. "Baldr, where in God's name are we?" I whispered.

Baldr ignored the metaphysical gaffe. He didn't quite whisper, but his voice was low when he answered. "We're in Niflhel."

A world of eternal darkness and ice, where murderers and other evil men were sent for punishment.

"Loki is chained here. And this," he added, "is as far as I go." Baldr's expression was unreadable. "Family killing family is terrible. I will not seek Loki's company for any reason. Nor am I . . . allowed to remain." A strained expression crossed his face; he said quietly, "'Brothers will fight and kill each other . . . an axe age, a sword age . . . a wolf age . . .' Do you understand me?"

I didn't have to answer. I understood exactly what he meant, and didn't want to talk about it. Fimbulvetr, the three-year-long Terrible Winter that would come just before Ragnarok, and the end of everything . . . These were the portents that heralded its arrival. Skuld—and Odin—were afraid I might be the one to bring it down on their heads. Baldr gripped my arm—very hard indeed for a dead man—and met my gaze squarely.

"Be warned. Loki is master of lies and trickery. His moods are more changeable now than ever before. He may be chained; but he is still very, very dangerous to a mortal man. Do what you must, for Fate will have it no other way, but guard your life if you value it."

That struck me as an odd statement for a god who believed wholeheartedly in predestination. I wondered if Skuld's predilection for strange behavior was contagious.

"I must leave you now. Remember—caution. . . ."

My mouth was dry and my palm was wet when I clasped his arm.

"I . . . uh . . . thanks." I wanted to say more but had no idea how to say it. I owed Baldr my life. Killing his father wasn't much of a thank you, which made the moment more awkward than it should have been. "Guess you ought to take this worthless nag back with you, huh?" I jerked my thumb at my horse.

Baldr shook his head solemnly. "Keep him for a while. If you don't need him, he'll find his way back home. But if you do need him . . ."

"Yeah."

Baldr gripped my arm one last time; then turned, mounted, and galloped away without another word. The Norse weren't much on prolonged goodbyes. Either that, or he was as scared as I should have been. I watched him disappear into the shimmer marking the boundary with the Norns' world; then I leaned against a nearby boulder and contemplated my situation. I had a horse that bolted at the sight of its own shadow, but I was in better physical shape than when I'd started out, thanks to Verdani and that marvelous drink of water.

I was about to meet Loki face-to-face—with no guarantee I'd survive the interview. Well, I was armed to the teeth, and then some. Meet Loki? Nothing to it. Just walk right up and introduce myself. I'd survived Hel and Fate; what was a little chat with Loki?

I shrugged out of my battered pack and started getting ready. The soil was so cold I wondered whether it might be made of frozen hydrogen. On further reflection, I decided that if the temperatures here were cold enough to freeze hydrogen solid, I'd be a Han Solo-style popsicle by now. I was, however, still alive and functioning. Well, mostly. I wasn't too sure the end of my nose was ever going to regain feeling.

Despite the numbing temperatures, I took my time getting ready. No sense rushing in half-assed. Half-asses got killed a little too quickly to suit me. I did *not* want to die in this frozen wasteland.

I loosened the Armalite from the pack and restrapped it so I could pull it loose with one quick jerk. Then I checked my spare magazines and stuck them into various convenient pouches on my web gear where I could get at them in a hurry. There were six extras for the rifle and two spares for the P-7. I had some good civilian, soft-point hunting ammo in the rifle, but had been able to get only military "hardball" ammunition for the pistol. I regretted again that I hadn't had enough cash to buy a large supply, and so had picked up some old World War II surplus stuff—armor-piercing German rounds— priced to sell. It'd tested okay when I shot some; but I didn't like it as much as the hollow points I would rather have had in the P-7.

It occurred to me presently that I was letting my preparation become procrastination. I couldn't afford to let my courage get cold. Caution was one thing—but too much thought bred inaction and that would probably prove fatal. So. The guns were set, the ammo was set, and Gary's knife . . .

The Sly Biter had grown deadly quiet in my boot sheath. I didn't care much for that portent, but I wasn't going to let it worry me. I loosened the Biter's sheath snap, and shouldered my pack. Then I drew a deep breath, mounted my horse, and set him to a brisk trot. The frigid air got blood and adrenaline flowing again.

I headed toward the distant overhang, keeping the larger boulders between me and the source of that low scraping sound, which had already started to set my teeth on edge. My horse was growing more nervous with every step. I had my hands full keeping him under control. We rounded a corner—

Loki!

Before my horse could scream, I whirled his head back around. We retreated behind sheltering rocks. Freezing air knifed my lungs with each gulp. Gripping the reins firmly, I risked another look—and found myself overcome by a rapid, shrinking sensation that reduced my ego to its proper insignificance.

Loki . . .

One of the few names from Norse mythology most people had at least heard . . . It was a name full of dark madness. Only who was madder: the god, or the fool seeking him out?

I had thought I was ready for this interview. Now I knew why Baldr never came here. Loops of slender chain bound Loki to three flat slabs: one under his head and shoulders, one under his hips, and one under his knees. It looked hellishly uncomfortable. I couldn't guess what the chains were made of; but they were damned (as it were) strong. He writhed like an epileptic in grand mal seizure and all they did was creak a little. No wonder the ground trembled constantly.

He was a dark god, in more than just reputation. Long black hair, plastered by centuries of sweat and grime, hung across dark skin and deep-set black eyes. An aura of darkness hovered around him, tantalizing the eye and blurring details I needed to see. If he'd been clothed when the gods bound him here, the fabric had long since rotted away. Or maybe it'd been eaten away. . . .

Acid burns and half-healed scars covered him, turning a face that might once have been very handsome into a grotesque parody of human features. Only the eyes remained human—and they burned with an endless rage.

Prospects for a productive interview looked poor.

Likewise, I wasn't thrilled with the idea of getting any closer to those slabs of rock, because the entire rest of the space beneath the overhang was filled with seething, half-seen movement. Rounded boulders of dark, coppery bronze surrounded Loki on three sides, hellishly lit by the glowing rock of the overhang. Covering those boulders—swarming on and around them by the tens of thousands—were vipers. Big ones. Little ones. Colored like the rainbow and writhing in a solid mass toward the chained god. All of them hissed and dripped venom.

Onto Loki.

And if I went in there . . .

A huge head reared above the tangled mass of snakes—and my mouth went dry as dusty kitty litter. The "boulders" weren't rock at all. They were the coils of the biggest, scaliest snake I had ever had the misfortune to encounter. It leaned over Loki and spat. Drops of venom the size of basketballs splashed across him and splattered over the ground.

He screamed. The ground heaved. My horse's groans were drowned by the roar coming from Loki's rocky prison. The horse stumbled sideways, and I came loose. The ground was a long way down; but I kept my grip on the reins, even when I couldn't get my breath, or see anything but stars. My nag—bucking and rearing—all but dislocated my shoulder. When the ground tremors finally died away, I found my horse sprawled beside me. It didn't look like either one of us was interested in getting up.

Did I say getting *up*? Hell—I ought to be getting *out*. Except I didn't exactly *remember* the way out. . . . And I still had this little problem with Odin. . . .

I had to talk to Loki. No way around it.

I finally crawled back to my feet and risked another quick peek. A woman had stooped over the chained god. She held a large bowl in trembling hands. I couldn't remember her name; but I knew she was Loki's wife. She, too, had once been beautiful. You could almost see it shining through the wreck of her face. Now her whole universe was the bowl she held, trying unsuccessfully to catch all the drops of venom before they could splash onto her husband.

As I watched, a slow rage began to simmer through me. What was she doing here? No man was worth this. But then, I was a twentieth-century man and she was not a twentieth-century woman. Viking goddesses had been models of archaic honor, sacrificing themselves for family whenever sacrifices were called for. Nanna had voluntarily died to join Baldr in Niflheim, and Loki's wife had willingly gone into exile with her wretch of a husband. Some of the assholes I'd known over the years would have cheered. I wanted to throw up.

Having nearly convinced myself of my moral superiority, and argued almost convincingly that now was better than never, I girded my metaphorical armor. I wished intensely for a sword and magic helmet like Elmer Fudd's, and hoped my rifle and Gary's knife proved as effective. If all else failed, Loki did present the classic sitting target. And if things got nasty, I might find out the hard way if a living god could be killed. I mounted with far more confidence than I had any right to feel, and rode boldly out into the open.

Nothing happened.

Loki continued moaning, and Mrs. Loki continued stooping, and the snakes continued spitting at them both. So much for moral superiority. At least the really big snake seemed to have lost interest for a while. Or maybe it was just recharging its venom supply for another blast. Be that as it may . . .

"Uh—hello?"

Stupid, stupid . . .

Several thousand heads swiveled to stare at us, and my horse caught sight and scent of *snake*. He screamed louder than I'd ever heard before, and abruptly I had no time to evaluate the startled glance Loki and his wife shot in my direction. I nearly came unseated several times, but even a dead horse can be handled if you're forceful enough. By the time I'd gotten my mount under control again, Loki had lifted his burned, scarred face. He watched through mad eyes. My breath rasped in my ears, loud as a freight train as I recovered from wrestling the stallion.

"Well." His voice was a ragged croak. He probably hadn't said a word in a thousand years, and screaming is hard on the throat. "It would seem, my dear, that we have a visitor."

His wife glanced distractedly my way again, then returned to her task. When I looked back at Loki, I nearly fell from my horse. He had transformed. . . . Rather than a scarred wreck, the god bound to the rocks now appeared to be a robustly handsome young man. Wavy black hair fell across smooth fair skin, and twinkling dark eyes seemed to suggest that his chains were a mere inconvenience. No sign of the hideous damage remained.

I swallowed hard. Baldr had warned me Loki was tricky. If I hadn't seen him from hiding, I would never have guessed his true appearance. I watched narrowly for the least sign of treachery. What was it Gary had told me about bargaining? Sweat froze under my shirt and inside my boots.

Loki smiled, all pleasantries and curiosity. "Now what would a plucky young mortal like you be doing seeking out an old wreck like me?" Even his ravaged voice had smoothed into a mellow tenor. "I'll wager it's been two thousand years since anyone came my way. —No, no, I take that back. What was his name, Sigyn, that delightful fellow who came around for a chat, oh, four decades or so back? Higre? No . . . Hister? Eh, what was that, my dear?"

She whispered something too low for me to hear.

"—Oh, yes, *Hitler*. Yes, that was his name. Entertained me for days. Bright chap. Too bad he killed himself, though. Seems the talented ones always do. Had some good ideas; but he wasn't ruthless enough. Killer instinct is so important in his line of work. I must say, though, I really am impressed with you, young fellow. However did you manage to get here alive, of all things?"

I opened my mouth. Nothing came out. It wasn't that I was *scared*—although I was, down to my socks—I just didn't know what to say. Loki found me more impressive than Hitler? I narrowed my eyes, and shut my lips. Tricky wasn't the word. It wasn't even close. *Let him talk? Or say my piece and get the hell out of here?* Not even the Sly Biter had any useful suggestions.

My inclination was to let him talk. Flattery is generally more productive than petulance.

"It wasn't easy," I answered him truthfully.

"Didn't quite catch that, son. Could you come a little closer? I'm afraid I'm going a little deaf in that ear. Old age is dreadful."

I kneed my horse one step closer—but no more.

He smiled genially up at me. "Now, then, what was your name? I don't believe you said."

"Barnes."

"Barnes," Loki echoed flatly. "That's it? Nothing else? Odd names they're giving humans these days. Well, Barnes, what was so important, you had to ride all the way to Niflhel?"

I forced myself to sit back in the saddle, and relax my death grip on the reins. "I'm looking for Sleipnir. Have you seen him?"

"*Sleipnir?*" Loki broke into laughter, which startled me considerably. He let his head fall back while he wheezed. Only then did I notice something dark spattered on his chest and belly.

"Have . . . I seen . . . " He finally managed to control his hilarity, although tears seeped from the corners of his eyes, and froze on contact with the stone slab. "Oh, yes,

I've seen my bastard son, my friend. He left his calling card, as you can see." One hand waggled fractionally in the direction of his bespattered chest. "I never did understand where I went wrong with that youngster. Turned myself into a mare—a *female*, mind you, which is not as easy as it sounds, let me tell you that—just so the ungrateful little wretch could get himself born, and what did he do to thank me?"

"Ran away from home?" I suggested.

Loki sighed, and nodded. "Got himself into bad company, then didn't have the good sense to bite the hand that fed him. I suppose I was just too preoccupied with other matters to take him properly in hand. Pity; he'd have been such an asset." Loki shook his head mournfully, looking very much the part of a bereaved father. Then he spoiled the effect. "Not that Sleipnir'll be much help when Fenrir gets hold of Odin. I do look forward to that."

The Father of Monsters chuckled, clearly relishing the moment when his other son gobbled Odin alive. Not that I objected to Odin's demise. I just didn't want the aftermath of Loki's revenge destroying *my* world.

"So, tell me, lad, what is it you want with my eight-legged freak of a son?"

"I plan to—"

"Speak up, son; I can hardly hear you. Damned snakes hissing so loud I can't hear myself piss anymore. Come closer—I don't bite, you know. I can't even move." He shrugged his shoulders in apparent resignation, which I didn't buy for a second. His eyes glittered with malice, and with hope.

I eyed him darkly, and kneed my horse one small step closer.

"I plan to catch Sleipnir."

Loki's eyes went round. "Catch him? Wel-l-l-l now, that's an interesting bit of strategy, isn't it? Where were you planning to go with him? Must be Asgard itself—only place you really couldn't get without his help."

Loki was smart, all right.

"The thought had crossed my mind," I allowed cautiously.

Loki grinned. "Has it, now? And what would you be wanting in Asgard, little friend?"

I wasn't little, and I wasn't his friend, and I wasn't about to answer him straight out, not until he'd given me something in return.

"We've got a saying on Earth these days," I said with a tight smile, "that seems appropriate."

He lifted one brow. "Oh?"

"You scratch my back, I'll scratch yours."

His lips went slack with shock. "Audacious little maggot, aren't you?"

I grinned. "Hel and Baldr thought so, too. So'd Skuld."

Loki blinked; then narrowed his eyes, and gave me a chilling smile. "You *have* made quite a little journey, haven't you? Hel and Skuld both, eh?" He dismissed Baldr without comment. "Catch Sleipnir. Well, now." He seemed lost in thought for a moment; then grinned quite suddenly. He looked like a mischievous schoolboy. "I suppose I might be able to give you a pointer or two. Of course, you'd have to make it worth my while. You scratch first, eh?"

I held his gaze, but refused to be stampeded into offering anything. If Loki wanted to name a price, let him. I could always try for Sleipnir without his help. It was obvious the horse visited here occasionally.

Loki studied my silent form. Then his voice came again, a silky whisper of approval. "Very good. I begin to see why you have made it this far." He cleared his throat, and got down to the serious business of bargaining. "Now, what kind of price would I be wanting, you're asking yourself. There is the obvious, of course."

I waited, affecting the posture of a stone gargoyle.

"I could really use a bath."

"A *what*?"

I was nearly as startled as I'd been when Baldr first spoke to me from the bank of the Gjoll.

"A bath, man. A bath. You do know what a bath is?" he added dubiously, staring at my filthy, mended clothes. "Do you have the slightest idea how many centuries it's been since I was clean?"

I thought about the effect of freezing water expanding inside the links of that chain, and shook my head.

"I'm afraid not. Even if I could find any, water'd freeze solid before I could get it here." It was a small lie, since I could probably have managed to douse him before it solidified; but it was a good excuse.

"Ah, well, I suppose it might, at that." His eyes glinted. I hadn't fooled him for an instant. "You might give me a shirt to keep off the worst of the chill."

"I might. But I couldn't get it onto you under those tight chains, could I?"

"No, I don't imagine you could. Pesky things, really. I should've broken them long ago; I just didn't bother. I don't suppose you could sort of shift them a little, scratch under them and maybe let me ease a few muscle cramps?"

The chains around his shoulders wouldn't move any farther down across the broad expanse of his chest, and to move them toward his head would've given him room to wriggle loose.

I shook my head. "I'd rather not come any closer to those snakes. This nag of mine is nervous enough—and if I dismount, he'll be gone before I can grab him."

Loki's eyes narrowed savagely. "Well, now, it's an uncooperative sort you are, isn't it?"

Sigyn turned to dump her bowl. Venom splashed onto his nose, burning a bloody path across his cheek. The illusion of youthful beauty vanished abruptly. His scarred face and body were even more repulsive by contrast. Loki shrieked. The ground heaved. How my horse kept his feet was beyond me. At least the last time venom had hit Loki, I'd still been safely hidden. What had Baldr said about wild mood swings?

"Get out! Get out!" echoed somewhere behind my eyelids.

Unfortunately, Loki chose that moment to raise his head. He didn't even bother to project the illusion of health this time.

"All right, mortal"—his voice was again a harsh rasp—"you don't seem to want any of my bargains. Strike one of your own, if you want my help. I do not think you have much hope of succeeding without it."

Hel was every inch her father's daughter—and something told me that Loki was a thousand times more dangerous than Death.

I considered my very few options, and settled on, "Help me trap Sleipnir, and I'll kill your worst enemy."

"*Odin?*" he gasped. His laughter shrieked nearly as loudly as his screams had. It bounced off the overhang and set the vipers to agitated motion. Venom poured onto him. Loki's screams and struggles threw my horse into blind panic. I had my hands full trying to stay on his back while he slipped and slid on uneven, icy ground.

By the time he stood quietly—blowing and sweating and trembling—Loki's laughter had subsided. I took as a bad sign the withering glare he turned in my direction.

"And what good is that bastard's death if I'm not there to relish it? Damn you to an icy tomb, mortal, if you think I'll give up one precious second of that revenge. I'll see him torn to shreds before my eyes if it's the last thing I do while still breathing!"

My brain demanded immediate retreat from this

worse-than-hellish place. I held my ground stubbornly. I was determined to get as much information out of Loki as possible before abandoning my initial plan. So maybe lack of adequate food and sleep had made me terminally stupid.

"I'll tell you what good it is," I countered. "With Odin dead, *before Ragnarok*, who's to say you'd have to die, either? Seems to me a chance at freedom and revenge— with the sure knowledge you don't have to die to get it—beats lying there on that slab of rock, cursing till your voice bleeds."

Loki's wild eyes reflected shock. "You really believe you can kill him."

I gave him a short, hard laugh. "Would I be here if I didn't?"

"You're mad. Madder than I. Stupid little man, do you think you—a groveling worm in the dust of the earth— can hope to succeed where I, the great Loki, failed? Have you any brain at all in that shriveled, shrinking body of yours? Without my help, you and your pitiful kind would be animals rutting in the dust, grubbing for maggots! Having created you, given you brains, must I think for you as well? Can you even piss on yourself without help?"

"What, name calling? Point for point, Loki, I'm already doing one helluva lot better than you did. I'm not the one chained to a rock."

"SILENCE!" Loki was literally frothing at the mouth. "When I am free, your puny race will be squashed like the dung beetles they are! Why that one-eyed fool gave Midgard to the likes of *you* . . ." He spat out the final word, and seemed almost to choke on it, he was so overcome with rage.

I forced a feral grin. "I'd say we earned it. I've made my counteroffer, Loki. Give me Sleipnir, I'll give you Odin, on a platter. What about it?"

He said nothing at all. His eyes were mere slits of darkness. When he spoke again, his voice was cold.

"Go to the dwarves for Ur metal, fool. Get chains of it. Nothing else will hold my traitorous offspring. Trade them silver, or daughters if you have them. Then take yourself from my sight and wait for Sleipnir to return." A wheeze of mirth broke from him again. "If you can out-live the wait! There's no living food in Niflhel. None but your own flesh. How hungry will you get?"

I laughed. "No living food? Broiled snake's a real deli-cacy. Didn't you know?"

"*Snake?*" Loki's eyes had shot wide again. "You would—?"

"Hell, yes, I'd eat snake. It doesn't taste half bad. Okay, I go find some dwarves, and wrangle a few yards of Ur-metal chain from them, then wait for Sleipnir. Great plan. There's only one flaw."

A look of insane rage was creeping into his eyes.

"Care to point out the direction to the nearest dwarves?"

Venom seared his left leg. A howl broke from Loki's lips. It took the form of a single word: *"Die!"*

I groped blindly for the rifle; but nothing happened. That didn't matter. I yanked the Armalite clear, anyway, and reached for the release on the pack straps, thinking to ditch the bulky nuisance—

I stopped . . . and stared.

Sigyn had gone rigid. She glanced at her belly. I did too. Both of us stared. She was pregnant. And growing rounder by the second. Her tattered shift split and fell from scarred shoulders, revealing breasts that once had been smooth and round as honeydews. A contraction rippled visibly across her swollen belly. Then she fell to the ground, giving birth right there amidst screams of pain and falling venom.

The child flopped onto the ground. I gaped, unable

to believe what I was seeing. It looked like a bear. Sort of . . .

The goddess was screaming mindlessly. In less time than it took to think about it, another child flopped on the ground beside its—brother? Which was already the size of a brown bear and rapidly approaching that of a king grizzly.

A croaking grunt diverted my attention back to Child Number Two. That one was scaly as a snake, but shaped more like a Tyrannosaurus, with a badger's heavy, clawed forearms. It stood slowly up—and dwarfed its older brother. It looked like death on the hoof.

My death, his hoof.

My horse gave one wailing screech, and contorted in a maneuver that dumped me headlong into disgusting, icy slush. It vanished in a drumming of hoofbeats. I shook my head, and scrubbed frantically at my face to wipe off the slush, which burned like acid. Even as I dragged my furry sleeve across my face, I scrambled to my feet, snapping open the folding stock of my rifle and bringing the weapon to my shoulder.

I clicked off the safety. A grin stretched the skin of my face. It wasn't a smile—I was scared shitless—but it beat hell out of slobbering all over myself. The lizard took a big step forward and I fired. And hit it. Six times.

"Ow!"

I shook my head. That single, human word echoed impossibly about the hellish terrain. The big lizard had stopped and was looking at six neat holes in its chest. No sway, no buckled knees, not even much blood. It poked a claw into one of the wounds and licked it while Br'er Bear squinted curiously through nearsighted eyes. Just as impossibly, the lizard chuckled—a ghastly human chuckle—then it said, "Lead and copper. And just a little tin—gives it a nice flavor."

This amused both of them greatly; Loki just watched.

His wife lay panting out of my line of sight. I glanced at the Armalite and made sure the magazine was in snugly.

"This just won't do."

Prickles ran up my spine at the sound of that voice issuing from jaws which weren't designed for human speech.

They lunged simultaneously. I think I yelled. I know I emptied the magazine. Bullets might not kill them, but bullets seemed to hurt the bastards, and slow them down. I threw myself behind a big boulder and tried to reload. The unwieldy pack encumbered me. Before I had time to even think about reaching for the pack release, Br'er Bear was snapping his jaws at my shadow. I scrambled wildly away. My hand shook as I released the spent magazine. I cursed my clumsiness. Shit! Doubleshit! The bastards wouldn't die. . . .

Baldr had warned me.

A premonition of danger caused me to jerk my head up. I dove simultaneously backward. Br'er Bear landed in a sprawl right where I'd been. He spun around. A snarl blasted into my face with a stench of incredibly bad breath; then a giant paw arced viciously toward me. I skidded backward again on solid ice. His paw caught the rifle instead of my side. The blow swatted the Armalite from my hands with such force, the barrel bent and the receiver was crushed as it smacked into rock. The rifle's plastic forearm shattered into hundreds of pieces.

I went down hard, and kept rolling in a backward somersault. When I came up into a crouch, the bear's hindquarters were disappearing—away from me—around the corner.

What. . . ?

I grabbed my P-7 and eased around the corner—and came nose-to-nose with T-Rex.

"Yahhh!"

I lunged sideways, out of jaw range, and shot wildly into the lizard's face; but in the critical half-second it took me to bring up my arms and fire, he'd dodged sideways, too. The shot went harmlessly past. I rolled and twisted around, managing to keep my hold on the P-7. Two-foot badgers' claws missed my legs by inches. T-Rex overbalanced, and rushed harmlessly past, then skidded in the ice, and went down in a spray of acid slush.

I scooted backward on my ass, scraping the butt pack across sharp stone, and tried to gain my feet. Br'er Bear lunged out of nowhere. I was out of position to do anything but shoot. Smothered under an avalanche of fur, I fired one shot point blank into the bear's belly, and waited to be mauled. He screamed, jerked once, and collapsed heavily on top of me.

Br'er Bear was very dead. At least he was warm. . . .

I heard confused shouts of "Iron!" as I fought my way out from under the grizzly corpse pinning me down.

I thought I heard Sigyn screeching, "I don't care whether iron kills you or not—you can't go back—" but I was pretty dazed. . . .

A thirty-foot snake had coiled itself around us. I emptied the pistol into it. One half fell across the bear. I climbed desperately over the other half while dropping the empty clip and slammed a second into the butt of the pistol. By the time I was free of the corpses, the dead snake's twin was slithering down on me.

How many of these things were there?

T-Rex leaped out of nowhere. I fired a few quick shots at its unprotected throat, savagely satisfied when it went down in a spray of blood. Then I wondered how many shots were left in the clip, and how long before I had to fumble for the last magazine.

Something sank claws into my pack. I snatched at the release, letting whatever it was have the whole pack, harness and all. Momentum dumped me to my knees. A second set of claws closed on empty air above my head.

Even as I lurched sideways and rolled over, I hissed. Acid slush was eating right through my pants. I managed to writhe away from the snapping jaws of a six-headed God-only-knew-what, with foot-long teeth grinning out of each feathered head. One head went flying after I emptied the clip into its neck.

I jammed home my remaining clip—wondering in acute panic how many monsters were left—and saw Loki's wife giving birth again. Whatever it was, it glistened and oozed a slimy pus that sizzled where it dripped onto the ground. It had lots of teeth. Its mouth and eyes were already open, homing in on me.

I gritted my teeth and fired at it before it could get completely born. *Please*, I prayed, *let its corpse block the way to whatever else is in there waiting to get out*. My hands were shaking so hard I had trouble controlling the aim. I heard a scream of agony as most of the rounds hit the obscenity being born. Then I froze, sick to my bones. A couple of rounds had torn right through Sigyn's pelvis. God, I hadn't meant to kill *her*. . . .

That instant's horror damn near cost me my life.

Smothering scales tightened down so fast I couldn't even yell. The useless, empty pistol dropped from my grasp. Gleefully the snake began squeezing air out of my pores.

A frantic thrumming against my calf shrieked for attention. I closed my eyes, willing the Biter to come. Gary's knife slid warmly into my grasp, and its tail wrapped securely around my wrist.

There was a flash of blinding green light. I slid into a crumpled heap at the base of the Mother Viper's coiled body, thirty feet from where a very dead snake lay severed in the dust.

I shook my head to clear it, trying to see—then

howled as venom burned through my shirt sleeve. I ripped the rest of the tattered cloth away and scrubbed at my skin even as I threw myself away from the snakes. Loki's unconscious—or dead—wife lay nearby, unmoving. I felt bad about her; but I didn't have time to grieve.

My pistol was missing, my rifle broken, but the Sly Biter hung in my hand, radiating an evil green glow. I was still surrounded on three sides by more monsters than I'd killed already. I backed up until I ran into stone—a rough, ten-foot-high chunk of it. It was the only way out I could see. I whirled and climbed. It took both hands. I grunted in appreciation when Gary's knife hung curled from my arm, refusing to resheathe itself for even a few seconds. I swarmed up the rock, waiting for claws or fangs to tear me back to the ground; but nothing hit close enough to do damage.

I'd just gained the top when a tremendous roar beat the air. It knocked me flat against stone. Thunder rolled through Niflhel. Semidazed, I looked up to see Sleipnir—all eight hooves flying—headed straight for Loki.

Startled, I looked down—and time stopped dead.

One link of the slender chain was partially bent open. A stray round—probably one of the wild shots I'd fired at Loki's wife—had struck it at supersonic velocity. Nothing on Earth had been capable of that kind of speed, that much force, when those chains had been forged.

All it had taken was one very desperate fool to blow open the chain that stood between Earth and Ragnarok. . . .

I couldn't force myself to move, wasn't sure how I might repair the damage. All I could do was watch in morbid fascination as Loki struggled to jerk the trapped link through the open one. He was howling at his children to help him.

Then Sleipnir skidded to a stop on all four haunches right in front of him. His rear hooves cut inch-deep grooves in the rock. Sleipnir reared to full height under the overhang.

It came to me very slowly that Sleipnir wasn't two hundred feet tall any longer. Of course, he wouldn't have fit under the lip of rock if he had been. . . .

I wondered if the other gods could change size at will. Maybe Loki'd tried it and those chains expanded with him? Or maybe they just cut into his flesh without breaking? Or maybe . . .

I stopped thinking altogether. All four of Sleipnir's front hooves struck the open link in rapid succession, like jackhammers in tandem, striking sparks that scorched Loki. The mad god howled and shrieked, and fought harder to jerk the link free.

The monster nearest the stallion—whose dark coat was flecked with foam—leaped for his throat. Crocodile jaws gaped, propelled by eleven feet of heavily muscled panther body. Sleipnir screamed in rage, and slithered back onto his rearmost haunches. The crocodile jaws missed, and Loki's offspring landed at Sleipnir's feet. Sleipnir pounded it into a bloody pulp.

Odin's hellhorse slid back another few feet, and half-reared for the leap back to the nearly closed link. His backward momentum carried him directly beneath my boulder.

Suddenly I was looking down at the broad, sweat-stained back of my transportation to Odin—but right now he had urgent business with Loki, which I didn't dare interrupt. . . .

Quick movement flickered in my peripheral vision. I slewed around. A twelve-foot wolverine hurtled in midleap across the top of the boulder. Its dripping jaws were agape, wider than I was.

I didn't think—I just jumped.

My legs closed around Sleipnir's sides. The Biter slid into its sheath. I grabbed at the long black mane instants before the enraged horse screamed. My head snapped when Sleipnir shot skyward and bounced on four hind legs. The wolverine's leap carried him well past Sleipnir's shoulder. My would-be killer landed on Loki's legs. Its claws dug huge, bloody gashes across the god's shins. Loki screamed obscenities.

I had no more time for anything except staying with Sleipnir. I clasped my legs harder as the stallion rose higher and higher on his hindmost legs—then my head snapped back, the other direction. Sleipnir didn't try to throw me—but he did grind the wolverine into the slush. I clung, bruised and shaken breathless, as the enraged stallion methodically killed each and every one of Loki's monstrous children.

If I fell off, Sleipnir would pound *me* into a red stain, and that would be the end of that. No avenging Gary, no killing Odin . . . Did death by Sleipnir count as murder, accident, or battle? I stuck on that stallion's back like a sandspur in dog fur. Sleipnir tossed his head, screaming defiance. Loki screeched back, cursing as the great warhorse hammered the link down again. Sleipnir flattened it shut with his forefeet while I jolted and groaned.

I could tell at a glance that Sleipnir's jury-rigged repair job wasn't going to hold Loki long. The god was too powerful, despite the passage of centuries, which should've left him with atrophied muscles. But Sleipnir's temporary fix would buy Earth time. And maybe—if I stayed with Sleipnir—it would even be enough.

Sleipnir pivoted on his rearmost set of legs. I lurched sideways, barely hanging on. He switched around on his forehand and pivoted the other direction. Overbalanced to compensate for the first pivot, I came loose. I clung one-handed to Sleipnir's mane, with my leg hooked around his neck and my boot stuck in the coarse hair. The

Sly Biter—still sheathed—had grabbed hold of Sleipnir's mane with its own tail. I hauled myself back aboard at the expense of strained shoulders. The stallion screamed again, craning his neck to snap at my leg. He missed by a fraction of an inch, then shook himself like a dog coming out of water. My legs bounced as I lost my seat—

Instantly the bastard launched forward into a dead run.

Again, my grip on his mane was all that saved me. I managed to get my feet hooked around his sides again, and gripped harder than I'd thought possible as he picked up speed. We raced through the freezing blackness of Niflhel—straight at a solid wall of rock.

I yelled and screwed shut my eyes.

We burst through a barrier of solid stone. I received a fleeting impression of bone-chilling, smothering cold; then we lurched into green light. Niflheim again . . .

Wind whipped tears from my eyes. I was nearly blind. Sweat from Sleipnir's coat drenched my legs. His muscles surged, and his breath whistled in my ears like a freight train. Sleipnir's hooves pounded against stone, casting sparks that blasted upward and smoldered in the remnants of my trousers. The wind blew the embers into ash. I could feel their burning sting by the hundreds. I gritted my teeth.

We roared past a sluggish, bubbling green river that poured over a cliff face like oozing lava. What looked like a serpent had reared up out of it. Enormous fangs had gouged black scars in the ceiling. Then we were airborne, in a leap that nearly slid me off Sleipnir's haunches. By the time I'd dragged myself back into a halfway secure position, we were hell-and-gone from sight of the snake.

I was ready for the leap across the black-acid Gjoll. I stayed on, and the long tunnel I'd found a lifetime ago tilted wildly toward us. Then the world again turned into darkness. The cold of the mountain blasted into the wind of our passage. Compared to Niflhel, it was almost balmy.

Sparks white as burning magnesium erupted toward my face. I tried to shield my eyes, and ignored the ache in my teeth where my jaws had cracked shut during Sleipnir's latest tremendous leap. My ass was growing numb from the eight-legged gait, and still the horse swept on through the darkness. My fingers froze in his mane until I couldn't feel them. I couldn't breathe real well, either; we were going too fast. Dizziness became the next threat to unseat me. I clasped my knees tighter, praying to whatever was listening that I not fall off while we raced through the heart of a living mountain.

Abruptly Sleipnir skidded sideways. His tight turn would've done a barrel racer proud. It damn near unseated me. Then he got all eight feet under him and was off again. Moments later his muscles bunched— *here we go again*—and he leaped forward. Light exploded into being. We were in clear air. Gale-force wind snatched my breath away. Brilliant—*ruby red*— light blinded me.

Where—?

Sleipnir bucked. I sailed toward his ears, damn-near airborne. Then I came down hard on bony double withers. The shock jarred what little breath I had left out of me. I started to slide sideways, and knew I was in trouble. Then he began to grow. His mane swallowed my arms, and I dangled from a neck that was suddenly larger than I was, and getting bigger. . . .

He sunfished midair, and I was gone. I fell away beneath eight churning hooves that receded with frightening speed. I had time to scream one obscenity at the bastard, then twisted and hurtled into the glinting surface of a bloodred ocean.

Chapter Seventeen

I came to in bits and pieces: first my butt, which felt like raw meat; then my scalp, which felt detached. My clothes were soaking wet, and my nose and throat burned as though I'd tried to breathe water—which, I thought groggily, I probably had.

My ears woke up a moment later, to a howl that chilled me to the marrow of my living bones. At least, I hoped they were still living. Compared to this unearthly sound, Loki's bellows were nothing but the mewlings of a newborn infant. Every hair on my body stood on end as the cry died away into silence. It was neither human, nor quite animal. . . . I tried to roll over—wanting rather urgently to find out where it had come from—but was too stiff and sore even to get my eyes open. So I lay where I was, and decided the best course of action was playing dead.

Human voices reached through the reverberating vacuum left behind by that howl. The voices sounded excited, laughing and shouting in anticipation. Of what? Given my possible location—land of the frost giants, or the dark dwarves' realm, or even *Muspell*—whatever fun was anticipated probably didn't bode well for my immediate future.

One voice emerged, distinct from the general babble: "This is gonna be great!"

"Great! Ha-ha!"

"Five flagons says he soils himself!"

"You're on!"

"Ten says he pisses first!"

My immediate future was getting rapidly bleaker. Warm liquid splashed across my face. I peeled back one eyelid—it felt bruised—and saw fur. I managed to pry open the other eyelid, and confirmed it. A vast expanse of matted, grey-black fur rose above me, to the silver-furred throat of the biggest damn dog I had ever seen. A little wearily, I wondered if the Norse gods ever did *anything* on small scale. Then I decided they did: humans.

I was sprawled between Big Daddy Doggy's forelegs, on my back. My throat was bare to the world—and his fangs—but given his size, he wouldn't need to tear my throat out. All he had to do was step on me. His nearest paw was the size of my head, with claws like railroad spikes digging into reddish-black mud. Like the child who sees an elephant for the first time, all I could think was "Big . . ."

I wondered what Garm, the hellhound, was doing away from the entrance to his cave. Had Odin dragged him off duty? Garm certainly wouldn't hold me in high regard; not after chopping him in half with the Biter in Frau Stempel's parlor.

I lifted my gaze to glittering green eyes. They met mine without flinching. Lock gazes with a dog long enough, and he'll either flinch, or attack. . . . I dropped my gaze to the animal's jaw. His teeth glittered; but the saliva that splashed onto me was streaming crimson. The cruel point of a sword stabbed into the roof of his mouth. The hilt was lodged in the lower jaw.

I swallowed once. This wasn't Garm.

In fact, it wasn't a dog at all.

A stab of ice-cold adrenaline was enough to wake up my brain, but not enough to run. *I needed to run.* . . .

The Fenris Wolf crouched lower. He watched me intently, head cocked to one side. Fenrir's eyes glittered with a madness born of unbearable pain, and even worse betrayal. The faint beginnings of a growl rumbled in his throat, half deafening from my vantage point. His green eyes were—like Sleipnir's—more than animal, but not quite human. One blow from his paw would crush my skull. After a convulsion of muscles that were far too abused to obey, I relaxed. There really wasn't much point in being afraid. Either he'd kill me or he wouldn't, because the unending abuse to which I'd subjected myself had finally caught up. My body was on strike.

A chain around the wolf's neck held him. He'd stretched as far as it would reach. Breath rasped in his throat against the pressure. The far end of the chain disappeared into the earth, pinned there by a huge, jagged boulder. Gleipnir, the chain created from six elements: " . . .the noise a cat makes when it moves, the beard of a woman, the sinews of a bear, the breath of a fish, the roots of a mountain, and the spittle of a bird."

I hadn't considered precisely what that list of components meant until now, but seeing how very slender the chain was—in fact, almost invisible, when the light fell on it just right . . .

The Fenris Wolf was held by . . . nothing.

And the day he learned it, the nine worlds would fall, all living men and gods would die, and everything I had ever loved would become as ashes before Surt and the sons of Muspell.

(Whoever the hell *they* were.)

Unless, of course, I killed Odin first. That was, I

reflected drolly, what I was here for; though my chances of pulling it off were looking slimmer and slimmer.

"Uhhh," I said, unable to articulate anything more profound.

Fenrir cocked a pointed ear, and listened. More bloody saliva splashed across my torso. To my astonishment, now that I'd decided fear was a useless reaction, I found myself pitying the cruelly gagged wolf. He certainly hadn't done anything to deserve this, any more than I had. The only "crime" he'd committed was somebody else's prophecy.

"Poor bloody bastard," I muttered in his direction. I propped myself on one elbow, and was only marginally aware that I spoke aloud. "They got you pretty bad-off, too, don't they, old boy? And damn it all, you didn't deserve it."

The growl disappeared. Fenrir cocked his head the other way, and both ears came forward. I gave a mental shrug; then reached up to scratch at that magic place located on all dogs at the base of the throat, just above the sternum. I could barely reach, even sitting up. The wolf was damn near as big as the murderous black horse I'd browbeaten into carrying me the length and breadth of hell's scenic wonders. Fenrir's eyes glazed momentarily. He lowered his head. His lower jaw scraped my belly, then he snuffled across my clothes and hair, getting my scent.

"Poor old fellow, you and me got troubles, don't we?"

I stopped scratching. To my amazement, the immense wolf whined, and nudged my arm. I crawled unsteadily to my feet and stretched to scratch his muzzle. He leaned into it, eyes half closed. The laughter behind me had died away. The moment I'd recognized Fenrir, all thoughts of my captors had slipped from my mind; now I glanced over my shoulder to see who was behind me.

Fenrir whined again, head lowered as far as the chain would permit.

Screw them. Whoever they were.

I stretched full length, and resumed scratching vigorously behind his ear. "Poor old fellow, poor old boy, your mouth's cut to pieces, isn't it? I'll bet Odin would just shit if I were to get this sword out of your mouth. . . ."

Of course, I had no intention of freeing Fenrir, since that would be even more disastrous than freeing Loki— and I'd already done enough damage in that department. But I couldn't repress a sneaking admiration for the powerfully muscled animal, and I figured nobody around here was going to scratch his ears for him, so I stood there and did just that. I did wonder how I'd gotten here instead of drowning, and how I was going to extricate myself from this mess without getting killed. The Biter was conspicuously absent from my boot sheath.

"That's quite enough."

The new voice was icy cold and full of authority. I turned around, and found at least forty archers standing in a rough knot behind me. They'd fully drawn their bows; two-score arrows pointed straight at my chest. Maybe I was just tired, or maybe I was just so sick of these stupid games it didn't matter anymore, but I didn't even blink. What were a few archers, anyway, compared to Loki's brats? I glanced around for the source of the voice I'd heard. A tall, one-eyed man in furs strode through the ranks.

A very slow, very cold smile started somewhere in my gut, and ended turning up one corner of my lips.

At last.

Odin.

He was no taller than I was. That startled me, almost more than Baldr's lack of height had done. His remaining eye glinted like a pigeon's blood ruby. The ruined eye was a hideous mass of scar tissue. He hadn't bothered to cover it with a patch. He was probably proud of the scar—after all, he'd sacrificed the eye to gain wisdom, hadn't he?

Too bad the trade hadn't worked.

His face was deeply lined, the color and texture of very old, very dry leather. He was heavily bearded, and his long hair was grey. In fact, all he lacked was the stereotypical horned helmet to look every inch the seasoned Viking warrior.

Power rolled off him in damn-near visible waves. His every movement, every gesture, proclaimed someone accustomed to blind obedience to his slightest whim. I narrowed my eyes. Any chink in the armor was welcome; Odin wasn't likely to have very many. How much would it take to provoke him beyond his normal caution? My smile deepened. Given the look in his eye right now, not much.

An enormous raven sat on each shoulder. Bright little black eyes watched everything the way a starving vulture hovered over a road kill. I knew that one of the pair was Hugin and the other Munin; but I didn't have time to study birds just now.

The men near Odin followed his movements with adoring eyes. Many wore heavy gold rings. Was that how he retained loyalty? Bribery? No, it was more than that. Odin possessed a compelling, hypnotic charm that reminded me of a cobra. I got the distinct impression that of all the lethal things I'd met so far, the one I would have least wanted as my enemy—had I been given the luxury of choosing—was this one-eyed, gloating old bastard.

I'd just have to make the best of my perilously meager resources. Before our fight was over, one of us would be dead. Being a betting man, if I'd been placing money on the outcome, I'd have bet every cent I owned on Odin. I grinned. I always had nurtured a sneaking admiration for underdogs.

Fenrir had leaped into the air at first sight of Odin. He fell as the chain jerked him back. The wolf snarled deep in his throat and thrashed wildly to be free. Even as I stepped clear of his maddened struggles, I marveled that the slender chain didn't shatter.

Odin laughed, head thrown back. "You'll not break Gleipnir just yet. The dark elves forged it well, eh, Fenrir?"

Malevolent green light crackled through the depths of Fenrir's eyes. The look in Odin's eyes told me he knew only too well that someday Fenrir would have his revenge.

The look he gave me a moment later was even more chilling. Obviously Odin had wanted Fenrir to kill me; but—once again—something had gone wrong. Maybe Fenrir was smart enough to figure out that Odin wanted me dead, or maybe he knew I was a prisoner, too—or maybe he'd just wanted his ears scratched.

Whatever the reason, I was still alive and kicking and damned glad of it, because my prey was finally within reach. Meanwhile, I was surrounded by a pack of unwashed, walking corpses. The leader of the pack glared at me through one narrowed ruby eye. I grinned into his face—which caused a ripple of mutters to race outward from where we faced off—but before I could demand a showdown at high noon, or something equally Gary Cooperish, he turned without speaking a word and strode off.

Now what?

I planted both fists on my hips and caught the eye of the nearest guard, who—judging from his furs—had been dead several centuries. He looked uneasy.

"What's the plan?" I demanded. "An arrow in the eye, or a sword in the kidney?"

He didn't bother answering; or maybe the guttural grunt he belched in my general direction *was* an answer. Anyway, I found myself herded away from Fenrir, who had fallen onto his side, thrashing to be free. Odin himself strode ahead, handing out heavy gold rings as he went. What did this unwashed pack of warriors spend their treasure on in Valhalla?

Again it struck me how slavishly Odin's men followed him. Maybe he could out-propagandize Goebbels? Or were conditions here vastly different from my suppositions? Could these men really enjoy hacking each other to pieces?

I might buy that for a comparative handful of Viking Berserkers, or even a slightly larger handful of Mongol hordesmen; but most of the soldiers who'd died down through history were just scared farmboys sent off to die in battles they didn't understand against people they'd never seen, much less hated. Either Odin genuinely commanded their respect and loyalty through wise leadership—something I seriously doubted—or he was the most charismatic madman since Adolf Friend-of-Loki Hitler.

I squared metaphoric shoulders. I'd come unscathed through interviews with Hel, Skuld, and Loki, I'd actually managed to filch a ride on Sleipnir, and I'd brought Fenrir to his knees. What was one more pissed-off god?

We followed the course of a bloodred river that flowed away from Fenrir's prison. This had to be the River Von—"Expectation"—which flowed from Fenrir's jaws. Valhalla itself, the actual building which gave this world its name, must lie across the lake up ahead, where the river emptied into a bloody delta. A couple of football-field-sized barges were drawn up on the bank, to transport the "Viking Retreads." As we approached the delta, they began jostling one another like rowdy truants waiting in line for a roller coaster. They eventually got themselves sorted out and loaded.

Sleipnir stood waiting beside the boats. At his side stood another stallion, the same rusted-iron color as the river. This horse's eyes were amber and his mane and hooves were glittering gold. It made for an odd-looking beast. A heavy gold war-helmet hung from his saddle, beside a long, wicked sword.

Then I noticed *her*.

Tall, self-assured, with thick blond hair, icy blue eyes, and a figure that heavy, gilded chain mail couldn't disguise, she was far plainer of face than the Norns would be at their absolute grubbiest; but far more earthy and real. Hers was a beauty born of inner fire and pride. She reminded me of someone; I couldn't imagine who. She was maybe six inches shorter than I was. She stood beside her war-horse with the air of a woman who knew exactly who and what she was, and needed no outsider's flattery to tell her she was good at it.

My guards—some of them had managed to remember their duty—marched me through the grumbling crowd and delivered me into her delightful hands. She looked me over as I studied her assets. When she had finished her own frank perusal of *my* assets, she met my gaze. When she smiled, her teeth flashed whitely. Death looked from her eyes. (But what a way to go. . . .)

Odin leaped to Sleipnir's back. The eight-legged stallion tossed his head, pawing deep gashes in the earth with both right forefeet.

"Rangrid," Odin called.

The woman turned his way. "Yes, lord?"

God, her voice was as sultry as the rest of her. . . .

"Bring him."

Sleipnir leaped away, and vanished in a crack of thunder. Nice trick. I was reminded unpleasantly of the night Gary had died. Behind me, the interminable loading of the barges continued. I wondered where Gary was. Somewhere in that crowd? I wanted to see him again, almost as much as I wanted to kill his murderer.

Rangrid mounted her warhorse in one fluid, graceful vault. I followed the motion as she sprang easily to the saddle. I found myself insanely jealous of a dumb animal as she gripped with perfectly shaped thighs. . . .

She turned in the saddle to face me, and held out an imperious hand. I stood my ground, and grinned up at her. I kept my weight balanced on the balls of my feet—while hoping that I didn't look as dead-tired as I felt—and planted my fists solidly on both hips.

"No way in hell, lady."

She laughed, a delightfully intimate sound. A wave of her hand dismissed the guards. To my surprise, they obeyed, leaving us alone on the shore.

"You are truly provocative, hero," she smiled.

"Huh."

"Oh, but you are," she objected. "You have defied the Valfather time and again, and lived." The implied "so far" hung on the air between us. I didn't bother to comment. "Your touch tames Fenrir. And you, alone of mortals, have caught unawares and ridden the great Sleipnir." Genuine respect, and what sounded suspiciously like wistful regret, colored that last observation. This lady wanted to ride that murderous black fiend?

"Sleipnir," I said deliberately, "is dog food. His gaits are lousy, he bucks, and he bites. His sole saving grace is jumping between worlds, and that's not a joyride, either. Give me a Harley Davidson any day."

She gasped.

While she was off balance, I pushed for information. "How come I wasn't left to drown?"

Surprise deepened in her lovely eyes. "You don't remember?"

"Remember what?" I snapped.

"Coming ashore in Valhalla?"

I just looked at her.

The rust-red stallion moved restively; she brought him up short. She studied me minutely, then shrugged, a delightful motion, even in armor. I would have given a lot to have seen her without that chain mail. Enough was visible to make my blood pound.

She kept her voice low. "When Sleipnir tossed you into the River Von, you swam ashore and came staggering out onto the riverbank. Some of the Einherjar saw you collapse, and had the sense to realize you were still alive, not just one of their number. They called Odin at once."

She paused, and a smile hovered about her lips. "You should have heard him. Even I was impressed. He hasn't used that kind of language since Baldr died."

"Huh."

She shrugged again. "Valfather thought maybe Fenrir would enjoy your company."

"He thought Fenrir would tear me into pieces!" I corrected harshly.

She flashed me a genuine smile. "To be perfectly honest, yes. And can you blame him? No one wants to die—and you did nearly free Loki. I can't imagine what else you'd expect him to do."

"Huh." My vocabulary was deteriorating rapidly. I sighed, and looked her square in the eye. "You're right about one thing, lady. No one wants to die. Not even unimportant little mortals like me. So why don't you tell me what he's going to do with me, so I can plan accordingly?"

She smiled again, revealing toothpaste-ad teeth. "You know, you're the most excitement I've had in decades. Too bad I have to take you straight to Valhalla. I'd enjoy a tumble with you first."

I grinned. The mere suggestion of sleeping with this

valkyrie—and I assumed by "tumble" that she didn't mean hand-to-hand combat—left me with a sudden raging desire to strip off that chain mail.

She noticed the bulge and smiled. I replied with a wolfish grin, "Then why don't you ask him to postpone things?"

She laughed. "Thank you for the compliment. You've courage, hero. I admire that. You'll make a fine addition to the Einherjar, Skuld willing. I might just ask him, at that. Come," she held out her hand again, "the Valfather intends to meet you in personal combat."

I glanced back at Fenrir. *Beware Norse gods bearing gifts?* Odin was giving me exactly what I wanted—a chance at him—so naturally, I started looking for the shiv up his sleeve. There was no way this would be a fair fight. I returned my gaze to the lovely Rangrid. "Do I have a choice?"

She laughed merrily. "I do like you. No, you do not have a choice. Not unless," she correctly interpreted which choice I'd meant, "you can walk on water? It's rather a long swim."

I chuckled. "So it is. After what I've been through, Rangrid, I'm starting to think I could do just about anything."

She didn't laugh. Her brow arched, and a troubled look came into her eyes. Good. I had at least one of Valhalla's permanent residents worried.

I grasped the proffered hand, expecting her touch to be cold as death, since that was what she brought. I was pleasantly surprised at her warmth. She lifted me easily to her stallion's back, behind her. Fenrir howled in the distance, a lonely sound that caught at my throat. I knew how the poor bastard felt.

Her horse leaped into a gallop that sent us speeding across the surface of the subterranean lake. Wind tore my breath away. I was proud of riding skills I'd accumulated the hard way; but I still took advantage of the opportunity to wrap my arms around her golden-armored waist. Rangrid didn't seem to mind. I gave a quick squeeze, and heard a chuckle float back to me on the wind.

The horse's golden hooves touched the far shore and he slowed to a walk. We had entered the outer fringes of an array of fighting men that dwarfed even the cast of *The Longest Day*. These fighting men, however, were all dead: the Einherjar, Chosen Heroes of Odin.

They constituted a solid mass, moving toward a vast, dark hall set on an open plain. The corners of the hall were lost beyond the horizon in either direction. Rangrid urged her horse through the crowd; soldiers gave over with surprisingly little grumbling. I wondered how many of them she'd personally collected. I saw men dressed in battle gear from every culture back to the dawn of time itself, all crowding against the bloodred stallion's flanks. Many of them were badly wounded; but they were mending before my eyes. The effect was dizzying, utterly alien.

All of us—dead warriors, horse, Rangrid, and I—were making for a massive doorway. I couldn't begin to grasp the size of the Valhall.

I could see only one side of it from our position, and not even the whole side at that, since the wall receded into apparent infinity. The door stood wide, dwarfing every other doorway I'd seen. Men streamed toward it, turning the bloodred plain black with their numbers. I knew from my studies there were six hundred thirty-nine doors in the Valhall. And this was just one of them? Sometimes, an occasion arises when a man fully appreciates how puny his imagination truly is. At a conservative guess, close to a thousand men would fit through that massive opening ahead without jostling. I glanced back.

We'd just ridden through a solid mass of humanity that stretched from the doorway all the way down to the water's edge.

The stallion's golden hooves rang out on hard stone flooring as Rangrid urged him on through the dark opening. Tables that looked like they'd been hewn from an entire forest of giant redwoods stretched away into the distance, covered with preparations for a great feast. An enormous goat stretched on its hind legs, nibbling at the buds of a tree growing within the Hall. Ale flowed like amber milk from the animal's heavy teats, falling with a pleasant splashing sound into strategically placed buckets.

I snorted: convenient.

Hundreds of thousands of men, women, and children—billions and billions, for all I could tell—scurried between the tables, bearing trays of goblets, and heavy pitchers of what smelled like beer but was probably mead.

More staggered under loads of roasted meat, trenchers of steamed vegetables, stacks of hot, freshly baked breads. I couldn't imagine where all these people had come from. None of the materials I'd read had mentioned slaves in Valhalla, even though many of the Vikings had kept captives to serve them. Slaves had sometimes been put to death and buried with their masters—especially young girls—but those few burials wouldn't account for the thousands of men and women of every conceivable age here.

"Rangrid, who are all these people?"

She twisted slightly in the saddle. "Those are the ones who die in war but are not warriors themselves."

"You mean they're the innocent victims? And you *enslave* them?" My hands had balled into fists. I missed the Biter's dark presence badly.

"Where else would you have them go? To freeze in

Hel's dour worlds? No, they belong here, in Valhalla, where they are at least warm and treated well."

A child of no more than eight staggered past with a heavy tray. I ground my teeth. "You call that good treatment?"

"You've been to Niflheim!" she snapped. "Would you rather see her slaving for the creature called Hel?"

Recalling Hel's tastes, I couldn't help wondering if she wouldn't have preferred eating the child—but that didn't excuse what was being done to these people. It was bad enough that Odin was snatching people like Gary—but innocent women and kids and men who'd only got caught in the crossfire . . .

Back in Germany, I'd fought ragheads on behalf of people just like these. Now I had another reason to kill Odin. I couldn't blame Rangrid for this latest outrage—she was just a soldier following orders, which was something I knew about—but Odin was another story. What was being done to these people was unforgivable.

I didn't respond to Rangrid's angry retort, and she didn't press me further.

At the far end of the vast room, almost lost in distant shadows, was the High Seat of the Valhall. The carved throne stretched into the darkness that hid the rafters from view. Rangrid's stallion danced toward it, picking his careful way between the scurrying slaves.

Valhalla's High Throne was occupied, and I didn't have to ask by whom; that vermilion eye glowed balefully from the shadows as we approached. Two slavering, gaunt timber wolves chained near Odin's feet raged, first at one another, then at anyone foolish enough to get too close to them. The two black ravens still sat on Odin's shoulders. Having slightly more leisure to study them, I realized they were virtually identical. I *thought* the one on the left was Hugin and the one on the right was Munin; but my memory wasn't entirely clear.

In my ear, Rangrid murmured, "Beware of Geri and Freki, hero. These wolves are called Greedy and Gluttonous for good reason. Not even Odin's own portion from the boar Saehrimnir's eternal flesh is enough to satiate them. Living mortal is a treat they have never seen."

"Thanks for the warning," I said dryly. It was only appropriate that Odin's pet wolves reflected his own personality. Most pets did.

Rangrid drew her mount to a halt and we sat waiting for Odin to speak. He sat in silence for a moment, just staring. I returned the look with an outward semblance of calm. Inside . . . My hands *ached* to close around his throat.

"So, you have come living to Valhalla."

His gravelly voice reminded me surprisingly of Hel's—an observation which startled me into some interesting conjectures.

"You will find my hospitality generous, mortal—but once I have entertained a guest, I am constrained to continue his entertainment. Eternally."

He laughed uproariously.

I growled, "I'll bet you're dynamite at a party, with a lamp shade."

Rangrid giggled; Odin looked grumpily puzzled.

The wolves' jaws gaped expectantly.

Odin recovered his composure to gesture at the ebony birds on his shoulders. Their little black eyes hadn't left me.

"Hugin and Munin also bid you welcome. Thought and Memory advise me of all that happens in the wide, wide worlds."

Briefly I wondered if these feathered tattletales were the source of "a little bird told me."

He added, with a tight, feral smile, "They have kept me well informed of your treason, mortal."

"Treason?" I barked. "That's rich."

Odin scowled at the interruption. "You have provided some measure of entertainment, despite your colossal presumption. Now—having been amused for so unexpectedly long—I return the favor. Have you any questions before you die in honorable combat?"

"Sure. I got a million of 'em, but I'll settle for just one answer before I turn your ugly ass into wolf chow."

He narrowed his eye; but nodded. "Speak."

"Okay, buddy. *Why?*"

Surprise lifted his shaggy grey brows. Rangrid turned in her saddle to look at me. Odin's voice was flatly puzzled.

"Why what?" It came out sounding almost petulant.

I enumerated my points by ticking them off on the fingers of one hand.

"Why are you murdering men who never knew you existed, wouldn't have worshiped you if they had, and could care less about you, your Valhall, or your petty squabbles with Surt?

"Why did you try to kill me *before* I'd done you any harm?

"Why are you meddling in affairs which are none of your business?

"And why the blazes did you start snatching recruits out of traffic accidents? You know as well as I do who you're supposed to take. Traffic accidents do not constitute battle."

His eye had widened further with each enumerated point. It narrowed savagely on the final one. I folded my arms with an air of assurance I was far from feeling, and added, "If you don't want to explain it to me, maybe you'd prefer explaining it to Skuld?"

Rangrid stiffened; her stallion's muscles turned to iron beneath my legs.

Uh-oh.

I braced myself.

Odin, however, merely looked thoughtful.

"You do have a way of getting to the heart of the matter, don't you?" he mused, stroking Memory absently. Or was it Thought? "Perhaps Skuld has granted me the boon at my request?"

I got the crazy impression that *he* was stalling.

I shook my head. "Unh-uh. In the first place, why should she? A few extra corpses to toss into a battle you can't win isn't a good enough reason to throw the whole order of the universe into chaos. *You* might feel better about a few more men here and there; but that's no reason for *Skuld* to change the laws of metaphysics. There's no percentage in it, if it doesn't gain anything. Besides"—I grinned nastily—"I already talked to her. Try again."

Strike one . . . Odin still at bat . . .

A sharp intake of breath into the shapely torso in front of me told me I was really pushing it. I didn't care. I was here to push it.

Like a politician dodging the press, Odin started talking without answering. "Your people have forgotten so much. Some, like you, recall the old stories just a little, perhaps; but most, no. They forget, and sleep soundly, feeling safe. There is no way to avoid what must be. The sons of Muspell will destroy your world as surely as you breathe, whether I lead the armies against them or not. Is there no rage in your breast that this must be?"

He sounded like a schoolboy reciting the only lesson he knew. I wanted to throw up.

"We are doomed, all of us; but we will kill as many of our murderers as we can, in just vengeance for the loss of everything we hold dear. Surely you know it is not for the dead themselves that we mourn. We grieve for what we, ourselves, have lost. This is what drives us to strike out in vengeance."

I wasn't arguing that point—I'd lost my best friend, and look where that had gotten me—but Odin wasn't through orating.

"Perhaps your world's mad drive for peace in these last few years has blinded you to the fate that awaits you all. Death is inevitable. Personal death . . . world death . . . even your modern science admits this is so, does it not? Life itself lives on death, and all is doomed, all is the same in Skuld's eyes; and no living creature can stop the march from Muspell. We can only fight until we fall, and take with us into oblivion as many of the enemy as we can kill, so that the price of their victory is high."

The doom-and-gloom clichés didn't impress me. I had as much respect as the next soldier for that old adage, but there were better ways of dealing with enemies. Even when you were outnumbered. *Especially* then . . .

Odin acted as if all he had to fight with was his muscles. A tiny lightbulb flickered in the back of my mind. I carefully stored the half-formed thought so I wouldn't lose it. I hoped I got a chance to mull it over before Odin and I came to blows.

Odin was shaking his grizzled head. "In the short decades you have lived, mortal, the numbers of men entering this most hallowed of halls has fallen to the merest trickle. We need warriors badly and take them where we find them, battle or no. The end is upon us, and there is little time to recruit more.

"In your grandfather's time we had some great heroes, oh yes, and many men came to us; but now your politicians tremble, and your young men bleat of peace and cringe in the face of bloodshed. You fear death so greatly, you will not even risk your lives to defend what is already yours."

I hit the floor running. The wolves scattered out of my way. I snatched him up by the shirtfront, and shook him so hard, the ravens flapped into the air, squawking objections.

"Listen, you fat-assed old bastard! Don't talk to me about putting it on the line! I've been there and damn near didn't come back. And what's more, we don't play with knives and spears anymore; we play with bombs that would turn your precious Valhalla into slag and you along with it! Don't you *dare* sit on your murdering ass and whine to *me* about bleating for peace and being too goddamn terrified to start a war. What the hell do you think I'm here for, you lying, cheating son-of-a-bitch, to dance a minuet and sip tea? You want a war, Odin, you've got one. With me.

"And if you can get *that* through your thick Neanderthal skull, try *this* on for size—we don't need Surt to burn up the world anymore. We're more than capable of it ourselves, and we sure as *hell* don't need you helping us do it. Frankly, if we're going to blow ourselves to the stars, we'd like to do it by our bloody, goddamned selves! And *that*, my fat little friend, is why I'm going to kill you."

He stared at me, in utter wide-eyed shock. His mouth was slack. His throat worked against the pressure of my grip. I was weaponless; but so was he. A collective roar went up behind me, and hooves rang out on stone.

"You want a duel?" I asked softly, too low for anyone but us to hear. "Fine. Under code duello, I get to choose the weapons. How would you prefer to die, old man? Fifty-megaton hydrogen bombs at ten paces? That ought to do the trick, eh? Or maybe just swords at dawn? How about recoilless rifles? M-1 tanks?"

Odin hung in my grasp still, mouth working. "You . . . impudent little . . ."

I laughed easily. I was cool . . . incredibly, clear-headedly cool. "You don't know the half of it."

I shoved him back into his chair. "Tell you what.

You've got the home field advantage. Give me the Biter back, and I'll fight you here and now."

Odin came out of his chair. I didn't back down, which left him teetering precariously on his heels. He overbalanced, and landed on his backside.

"What do you take me for?" he rasped. "A fool?"

My lip curled. "Actually, yes."

Deliberately, I turned my back, and strode past Rangrid, who sat stunned, a frozen statue on the back of her stallion. She'd wheeled around to put herself between me and the Einherjar. Ranged along the endless tables, thousands upon thousands upon multiple thousands of warriors listened in absolute, dead silence. Even the slaves had stopped to stare. The wolves at Odin's feet continued to cringe.

I stalked to the nearest table, grabbed a flagon of mead from the nearest hand, and tossed the potent brew down in one gulp. I managed not to cough and wheeze—it was gawd*awful*—then grabbed another. Less than twenty paces away, I noticed a red-bearded giant of a man, standing poised with one arm uplifted. He hadn't thrown the short-handled hammer in his hand. I lifted my mug in a silent toast, and grinned at him.

Thor's eyes widened, and he lowered his arm; then scowled deeply, and glanced toward his boss for orders. Whatever Odin signaled, Thor's scowl deepened, but he didn't make any further moves toward me.

"Thanks," I muttered to the guy I'd deprived of a drink, then turned to lean against the edge of the table. The nonchalant pose kept me from falling down as a case of very serious shakes set in.

I figured Odin would personally dismember me any second. He was certainly welcome to try. I narrowed my eyes, and waited for Odin's response.

I didn't have to wait long.

Chapter Eighteen

Odin exploded to his feet, fists clenched. His flame-red eye blazed. Released from momentary paralysis, the wolves leaped to the ends of their chains, snapping and snarling in belated efforts to reach me. I ignored them. I didn't bother even to glance over my shoulder—when you're that badly outnumbered details don't matter.

The one-eyed god snatched up an enormous war axe and raised his arm to hurl it. Bunched muscles on his throwing arm flexed, and I prepared to dodge—

And an outraged bellow rose from thousands of throats.

Odin paused. I resisted the temptation to glance around. What was going on? His eye flicked over the assembled host, which peripheral vision told me had surged to its collective feet. Then his gaze returned to me. He regarded me the way a man might watch a rattler he'd accidentally roused in the grass—only to discover that it was a cobra instead.

His expression reminded me of the hopelessly mad Loki. Slowly, and with the reluctance of a man forced to surrender at gunpoint, he lowered the axe again.

"Now is the time for feasting," he growled unpleasantly. "No battle is joined in Valhalla while feasting continues."

Ahh . . . No wonder the Einherjar had protested earlier. It wasn't *personal*; they'd just been enforcing the rules, with Thor acting as Sergeant-at-Arms.

"Never let it be said," Odin muttered, "that I have dealt dishonorably in my own hall."

Huh. He could deal dishonorably all he wanted *outside*; just not at home, eh? Made sense—he'd lose the loyalty of the Einherjar if he broke that particular oath in front of them.

"Rangrid." Odin's voice had gone oily smooth. "See that our guest is properly entertained for the evening. This is his last mortal night. I would not have it said he spent it unhappily under my roof."

"Yes, lord," she answered, her voice uncertain.

I hadn't taken my eyes off Odin, despite his apparent capitulation. He had resumed his seat and was stroking his ravens to calm. He still watched me narrowly; but he had relaxed back into the throne. I concluded that—for the night, anyway—I was probably safe enough. I began warily to relax. Odin noticed, and accorded me a nasty little smile, but kept petting his birds. I turned my attention to the valkyrie. She was supposed to "entertain" me, eh? This might not be such a bad deal, at that. . . .

Rangrid twisted around in her saddle. "Coming?" she asked.

"Oh, I do hope so," I answered with a slow grin and a raking stare, "but that'll probably depend on you." I leaned easily back against the edge of the table.

A great bellow of laughter spread in a receding wave as the joke was repeated down the length of Valhalla. Even Odin roared appreciatively. Rangrid actually turned scarlet under her armor.

I heard her mutter, "Just wait until I get you alone."

The laughter redoubled when she grabbed me by the wrist and hauled me across her lap. One shapely hand smacked against my ass with enough force to sting.

"Rangrid," I said in mock surprise, "do you like spankings? For shame, and here I thought you were a nice girl." I twisted around, and grinned up at her. "Do I get to return the favor?"

She seethed in silence. The nearest warriors fell over each other laughing. My discomfited valkyrie put heels sharply to her stallion's flanks. The warhorse snorted and bounced once; I grunted sharply and decided to cease and desist—until I was in a better bargaining position. We rode out through a side doorway big enough to drive a Clydesdale forty-horse hitch through, and left behind the hooting and cheering.

To my vast relief, the first thing Rangrid did was send away her horse. She removed his tack, slapped him on the rump, and sent him trotting down an interior hallway toward a slave who waited with a bucket and halter. The saddle and bridle she dumped onto a rack; then she led me through yet another door into a suite of private rooms. These chambers were delightfully free of the scents of spilled mead, unwashed corpses, horse sweat, manure, and hay dust—of which the outer chambers and corridors reeked.

"I didn't know Viking halls were laid out this way," I observed wryly. "I thought it was a free-for-all in one big room."

She smiled. "Oh, we valkyries haven't lived out in the main chamber in centuries; not since separate bedrooms were invented."

She peeled off layers of armor, and I watched in fascination as tantalizing bits of her became visible. Once she was down to a linen undergarment that clung sweatily, she pulled her long hair up, and tied it in place, lifting her breasts delightfully beneath the nearly transparent linen. Then she turned to me.

"First, a bath."

I glanced down at myself. My clothes were in tatters, I was filthy from head to foot, and there were acid burns on my skin.

I grinned. "Sounds good to me. Got a hot tub hidden somewhere around here?"

She laughed delightedly and turned to lead the way into an adjoining chamber. The sway of her hips under the short linen shirt was hypnotic. I followed her like a mesmerized rat chasing the Pied Piper. Once I'd stepped through the doorway, I stopped abruptly.

"Well, I'll be damned. . . ."

She crooked a brow and her lips twitched. I laughed out loud. Sitting in the center of the room, raised a few inches above a bed of glowing coals, was an enormous oaken barrel full of steaming water. I dumped battered web gear and skinned out of my shirt. She unfastened my pants, and once she'd stripped off my boots and a pair of socks that stood stiffly at attention when she dropped them, she peeled off the rest of my clothes. Her hair fell in wisps out of the ribbon she'd used to fasten it up, and her skin was damp and flushed.

"There." She eyed me critically from where she knelt. "Yes, a good hard scrubbing will work wonders, I think. I do believe there's quite a man underneath all that dirt."

At the very least, there was quite a bit of me saluting her enthusiastically at her current eye level.

She rose gracefully and pulled off the damp linen in one smooth motion, treating me to a shapely back, trim waist, and firm buttocks. I groaned, and staggered after her.

"Unh-uh, not till we're both squeaky clean," she scolded when I reached out. "In you go." She pointed imperiously at the waiting tub.

I settled into the hot water with a delicious sigh. I closed my eyes, and let the heat soak into my bones. I heard her slip in beside me, and made a pleased sound deep in my throat as she began rubbing me from one end to the other with soap. When her hands roamed between my legs, my breath hissed out between my teeth. She laughed softly, and water flooded my eyes and nose. I coughed and spluttered as she dumped another basin of water over my head and went to work on my filthy hair.

"Witch," I muttered, trying to lean close enough to kiss her.

"Close your eyes before you get soap in them," she commanded.

I obeyed, and she rinsed my hair until it squeaked to her satisfaction.

"All right, lover; your turn."

She handed me the soap, leaned back, and waited.

I rose to the occasion.

Rangrid was soft and warm and slippery. I caressed every inch of her, teasing until she moaned. I soaped the length of her lovely back, and delicately nibbled at the base of her neck. She shivered. I licked her earlobes, then tugged gently on them with my teeth. Her head came back against my chest, and I reached around to trace her lips with one wet finger. She kissed it dry.

I trapped her against my chest and reached around to move my soapy hands across her until her breath came in soft little gasps. She shuddered once, and closed her eyes. A smile played across her lips. I ended by turning her around, and kneaded each foot in turn. I rubbed the insteps, digging in hard with both thumbs, and gently pulled on the toes, until she lay limply against the edge of the hot tub, head back and eyes closed.

Cupping my hands, I rinsed the soap from her breasts and shoulders, then covered her lips with mine. Her hands slid down to caress me, until I was crushing her against me and she was wrapping herself even closer. Her skin moved against me like silk. I sought her, and she pulled slightly away. I gave a heartfelt groan; then my breath shuddered when her fingernails traced lightly down me.

Then, moving decisively, she unwrapped her long legs and stood up, dripping onto my skin. I rose with her. Wordlessly, she slipped out of the tub and reached for a large, soft towel laid conveniently nearby. She tortured me mercilessly with that towel, until I splashed out of the tub toward her.

"No, you're all wet." She laughed, pushing me away. "Get the other towel."

"Where?" I looked and didn't see another.

She pursed her lips; then smiled. "Oh, silly Gerta, she's probably left it on the bed instead of in here."

Rangrid disappeared into an adjoining room, and I followed, still dripping onto the floor. "Yes," I heard her say, "there it is. Go dry yourself while I brush out my hair."

She had wrapped the towel around herself and was hunting for a brush on a nearby table. I spotted the towel in the center of her enormous bed, and leaned over to retrieve it.

She tackled me from behind.

I sprawled, exhaling sharply as her weight pinned me on my stomach.

Blind survival instinct kicked in. I heaved upward, spilled her onto her side, and rolled fast, pinning her flat on her back before she could move. An involuntary snarl escaped as I pinned her wrists and looked for weapons. Her eyes widened as she realized this wasn't just rough foreplay. Abruptly she lay very still.

"I'm sorry," she whispered. "I meant only to tease—"

Warily I held her gaze. Suspicion still flared; but I

could find no trace of guile in her eyes. When I let go and sat up, there were red marks on her wrists. I scrubbed at my eyes, then stood up and found a wall to lean against.

"Look, Rangrid," I said wearily, "I've been through more than you'll probably ever understand. You're a goddess. I'm just Randy Barnes, the dumb troopie. It's your boss who's trying so hard to kill me. Not twenty minutes ago he was ready to split my skull wide open with his war axe."

I glanced up to see how she was taking this. Her eyes reminded me of a puppy somebody's recently kicked. Her lower lip actually trembled. I felt angry, betrayed, stupid, and loathsome, all at once. I'd never hit a woman in my life, and hadn't meant to start with Rangrid.

"Dammit, don't look at me like that! I'm not some low-life scum who gets his rocks off beating women! Think about this, Rangrid. Odin's called Oath Breaker for good reason, and you work for him. What else am I supposed to think when you attack me from behind?"

She came off the bed in one fluid movement. "I am a valkyrie! Not a coward! Those who have fallen to me in battle have died honorably. I have never taken a mortal outside of combat—never!—and certainly not with the *coward's* blow!"

Proud, furious, naked in a way that made her strangely vulnerable . . . How many of the "heroes" in that hall out there had seen Rangrid like this? Something told me, not very many. God help me, I didn't trust her; but I wanted her. I scowled and thumped the wall absently with one bare heel.

"Yeah, well, maybe you've got a sense of honor; but that bastard out there misplaced his. If he ever had one to begin with."

"I am not Odin!" she said sharply.

I gave her an equally sharp stare. "Meaning. . . ?"

She looked as if she wanted to lower her gaze; but she was too proud to look away.

"I do my job. I do it well, even when I do not like it. All soldiers face this; do they not? But I am not Odin, and I do not wish your death, and it is not I who will collect your life on the field of battle tomorrow."

Her eyes were bright with unshed tears.

Rangrid's expression shifted, then, into a terrible fear which chilled me. What could frighten a valkyrie? Whatever it was, it scared hell out of me.

She whispered, "There are so few like you. . . ."

Her eyes met mine. A cloud of soft gold framed her face. Her voice was velvety, persuasive. "You are safe so long as you remain with me. And we have the night to enjoy. Please, for a few hours, at least, try to put aside your suspicions. You have a right to them; I will not argue that. But I am not your enemy. I never have been. Tonight I wish only to enjoy your company. As I hope you will enjoy mine."

I don't normally sleep with the enemy. But she was soft and warm, and my skin remembered the feel of her, and wanted more. And there wasn't much use ruining what might well be my last night as a living, breathing man. Even condemned murderers get a last meal. Besides, I wanted to believe her.

So call me a fool.

I nodded, unsure how to break the tension that had flared between us.

Rangrid took care of that. "Come, lie down. Please. Let me rub your back and shoulders. You look like stone."

"Huh. I feel like it." My shoulders were so knotted, I could've earned a merit badge with them.

I crossed to the bed—one eye still on her—and lay down, slowly. She knelt above me. Then, as promised, she went to work on my shoulders. She kneaded and stretched out the hard knots, slowly working her way up my neck, down my back, across my hips, and down each leg, until I lay relaxed and glowing beneath her touch. She could've gotten a job at any whorehouse this side of the planet Neptune, just giving backrubs.

"Mmm," I sighed. "Nice."

Her lips touched my shoulder blade, like sun-warmed rose petals. Lazily, I hoped this boded well for the rest of the evening. Rangrid was a lady I wanted a long time to get to know. More time than Odin might give us.

"Shh . . ." she urged. "Don't think of tomorrow. Think of my hands, and lazy, sunlit afternoons. . . ."

She continued on in that vein for several minutes. As she worked over me, her breasts tickled and teased my sensitized skin. Her hair brushed my back with the softness of butterfly wings.

She even rubbed my feet.

Then she worked her way slowly back up my legs, running her thumbs up the insides of my thighs, stretching the sensitive skin in rhythmic circles. I hissed softly.

"Keep that up," I murmured into the bedding, "and you'll undo all your good work."

"We mustn't let that happen, then, must we?"

There was low laughter in her voice. When she turned me onto my back, I rolled willingly, returning the smile she sent from beneath a cascade of golden hair.

"Now," she said with a wicked smile, her fingers doing soft, tantalizing things, "what was it you said out there about your coming depending on me?"

"Oh, no," I groaned.

"Oh, yes," she replied, leaning over me until her hair tickled my chest. "Really, you should never tease a valkyrie; especially not where the Einherjar can hear."

Her hair trailed tantalizingly downward. . . .

My eyes crossed and I moaned. When I could speak again, I croaked hoarsely, "Really, I didn't mean it that—"

I grunted when she sat on my chest. The witch leaned over my face until her breasts just barely skimmed my lips. "Oh, yes you did!"

I was too distracted to deny it. It was true, anyway.

Eagerly I licked. "Mmm," I said in my throat, nursing and nibbling with my teeth.

She pulled back, smiled demurely; then turned around.

I gasped; my torture had begun.

For the first half-hour, she never even touched the one part of me that demanded to be touched; by the end of that time I was thrashing and grinding my teeth. Every time I reached for her, she moved my hands aside, and continued tantalizing me.

"For gods' sake, Rangrid," I gritted, "have a . . . little mer-*cy* . . . !"

My voice hit soprano. Cold air a moment later was a shock.

"Mmm," was all she said.

"Oh, *god* . . ."

When she started a slow, rhythmic dance my eyes rolled back into my head and I convulsed. "Oh, god!"

My whole universe contracted, centered on the exquisite agony at my hips. I could endure no more, and did, and cursed and begged. Warm breath from her low laughter teased me as much as her actual touch. I lost all sense of time. When she finally turned and slid down over me, I actually lost consciousness in the throes of orgasm.

When I woke, the room was dark. The scent of her filled my nostrils. This time I took the initiative, and before I was even halfway finished with her, she was crawling backward up the wall, clutching my head and screaming with every shudder.

I brought her down, took her up again, and brought

her down until she quivered. When I slid inside, she gasped, pulling me close and raking my back with her nails. She was reduced to little more than panting groans when my mouth sought hers.

And then we fought a battle few—if any—other mortals had ever fought with Rangrid, and survived to tell the tale.

This time she was asleep before me.

When I woke the second time, I found her gazing at me. Her long hair spilled across both our bodies. I smiled, and she answered. Then she leaned closer to kiss me.

Ahh, what I wouldn't give . . .

But I was utterly relaxed, my body warm and tired, and I didn't want to move again for the rest of my life.

Her eyes crinkled nicely when she smiled. "Are you hungry?"

"Mmm; but I don't think I could manage it again."

Her eyes twinkled. "Not that, silly. I meant, would you like some dinner? Gerta did bring in a platter of food while we slept."

"Oh, so there really is a Gerta? I thought she was a convenient fiction."

She laughed. "Don't tell me you didn't enjoy every second."

I held up three fingers of one hand in a Boy Scout salute.

"I cannot tell a lie."

She kissed my fingers; then rolled over and sat up.

I groaned. "God, how can women have so much energy?"

"Lie still, then, and I'll drop grapes into your delightful mouth."

I grinned. "That sounds good." Every great hero is

entitled to a couple of grapes from a beautiful woman; isn't he?

She reappeared with a heavy tray, and proceeded to fill my "delightful mouth" with all sorts of wonderful delicacies. I fed her in turn, and we laughed like children and drank strong, dark mead until we were both tipsy.

Then I surprised myself, and made love to her again, slow and gentle; and we made it last for more than an hour.

Sometime thereafter I gradually awoke to a sensation I hadn't experienced since I was four years old. The mattress was cold and wet. I struggled up onto one elbow.

"Oh, no." I flopped back down.

"Mmm?" Rangrid opened her eyes, and looked worried. "What is it?"

"Somebody spilled." My mother's favorite phrase returned to haunt me.

We had managed to spread the contents of the dinner tray with remarkable thoroughness across the bed. The overturned pitcher had been responsible for waking me; mead was soaking its way coldly beneath us.

Rangrid rolled over, and eyed the mess askance; then turned and unexpectedly licked the inside of my right knee. I jumped. Her tongue tickled. Especially after . . . what . . . *three*? Gad, a personal record. . . .

"Tasty," she approved.

"Oh, yeah? Let's see."

She shrieked as I pinned her down, licking and tickling mercilessly. About an hour later, we managed to stumble into the hot tub again, where we scrubbed away the sticky remains.

Gerta arrived to say she'd freshened the bed. Rangrid smiled her thanks. We lay in each other's arms in the heated water for a long time without speaking. I listened with surprising contentment to our mingled breaths and the soft hissing of the coals beneath the tub. I could get used to this. . . .

But then, Loki probably was on the verge of getting loose . . . and I still hadn't done anything about Gary . . . and Odin was just waiting for morning. . . .

And Rangrid's softness was more distraction than a man could bear.

I had to concentrate on Odin. He never had given me the answers I'd asked for. He'd given me a speech—and a bad one, at that—but no answers. Certainly not an answer to why he'd been snatching folks like Gary. Killing me made sense; at least it did after I'd sworn to wring his neck and proved I was dangerous enough to be a real threat.

Odin was afraid to give me back the Biter, which meant he was afraid of the knife, at the very least. Had he kept trying to kill me because I owned the Sly Biter? Was that why he'd killed Gary? Because of a knife? Baldr had said the Biter turned up when the balance hung precariously, and he'd confirmed what Gary's grandmother had said, about it choosing who carried it. Maybe Odin was systematically eliminating everyone who owned the thing. I should've asked Skuld about the Biter; but talking to Skuld, even for a few seconds at a time, was a soul-shaking experience.

Still, I should've asked.

The idea that Odin might have murdered Gary Vernon over a *knife* . . .

That brought me squarely back to tomorrow morning. Why had Odin challenged me to a duel—instead of just murdering me—when he knew I wanted to fight him? Was he that confident? Or that skeptical of my chances? I worried over that like a rat with a bone, looking for a trap I knew had to be there. All my plans hinged on whether or not Odin *could* be killed. I didn't mind taking the risk—or I wouldn't have been where I was—but I would've felt better, knowing. It would have helped to know for sure whether I'd killed Loki's wife, or just injured her. I suppose that made me callous; but certainty beats blind speculation any day.

What if I couldn't kill him?

I wasn't normally so philosophical. All that mead was having an effect, and I wasn't certain it was a good one. I'd accomplished what I had by charging in feet first, and counting the cost later. Changing tactics now might be fatal; but I couldn't afford to ignore the possibility that Odin might not be killable.

I narrowed my eyes, and considered alternative tactics. Maybe I could defeat him without killing him? I snorted. Right. He wasn't about to quit fighting until I was very much the deceased Randy Barnes.

This wasn't getting me anywhere.

I tried to come up with some sort of battle plan, and instead found myself thinking about Skuld, and Loki, and predestination. Maybe it was just the major events that were planned out in advance. Maybe nobody understood the game plan when it came to details. If everything were predestined, then maybe Ragnarok *was* inevitable, and maybe Loki being freed was inevitable, and I'd merely been used as a tool of convenience.

I didn't much care for that scenario. Nor did it fit known facts. Obviously, Odin knew at least some of the rules were off; perhaps he knew, too, that *everything* was changeable. Given his spy network, even Odin could have figured that out, eventually.

I began to feel a little better. Not much; but a little.

I'd have felt better yet with the Biter in my hand. Funny, how naked I felt without it. I wondered if Gary had felt the same way. He was out there, somewhere, in that vast, dark hall. I wondered if he was awake, too, and what he was thinking. I missed having him around to bounce ideas off, or to offer advice. Right now, I *needed*

Gary Vernon's advice. Nobody on Earth realized it, but I was the only thing standing between them and Odin's version of Ragnarok. That left me holding several billion lives in my water-wrinkled hands.

My lips quirked wryly. If I were Earth's best chance, Earth was in big, big trouble.

Rangrid stirred, and lifted her head. She saw me, and made an unhappy sound in her throat.

"It's time, isn't it?" I asked.

She nodded silently.

"Rangrid—"

"Don't. Please."

She left the tub quietly, and dried herself; then turned and held a clean towel for me. She kissed my lips again, with tears in her beautiful eyes; but she didn't shed them, and her chin came up resolutely, reminding me of someone, from long ago. . . .

She hugged me fiercely. I held her for long moments, with my heart thumping so hard it hurt. I wasn't sure whether she hugged me for comfort, or to offer it, but I wasn't ready to let go yet when she finally pulled away. I cursed Odin and followed her into the bedroom, where she dressed me in battle clothing. It felt alien and awkward. Heavy leather pants and shirt offered minimal protection. Over these went a sword belt, to which I supposed I would hitch some sort of scabbard. I certainly didn't have a sword of my own, and wondered darkly if Odin intended to offer me one. Last came my own boots, carefully cleaned and laced with new leather laces.

"Neither of you will wear armor," she said softly, "for this is a duel of skill, to test your cunning and strength. You will carry a sword; Odin will carry sword and spear."

"Isn't that a little lopsided?"

She bit her lip; then nodded.

"Dammit, Rangrid, this isn't a duel; it's a goddamned execution, and you know it. I've never carried a sword in my life; yet Odin's got his favorite weapons, and twice as many, to boot. Why? He's already got the advantage. Is he that goddamned scared?"

"We need you," was all she would say.

Like bloody hell.

I didn't answer at all. After a moment she crossed the room to a heavy cabinet, where she took out a sword and sheath. She squared her shoulders; then turned and held out the weapon. The gesture was familiar. . . .

Abruptly I knew.

Knew, and hated the very sight of her. The pride in every line of her body was the same. Although the hair that tumbled around her shoulders was golden instead of silver, and lines of age and grief had been erased, all the little familiarities had clicked into place.

It was her.

Ingrid Vernon.

I had spent the night with my best friend's grandmother.

And she worked for Gary's murderer.

"*You*—"

I couldn't even get the curse out past my throat. I wanted to strike her, punish her for such a cruel deception, for playing games with my life, and Gary's. Everything I'd felt while holding her, while making love with her, burned to ashes in an instant.

"*You . . . murderous . . . bitch. . . !*" I stalked forward, fists clenched—

She whipped the sword up between us. Its flashing point stopped me cold. Angry as I was, I wasn't about to get myself killed before my chance at Odin came.

I narrowed my eyes to slits, and calculated my chances of ducking under her guard. *Not very damned good . . .* She held her distance, but that wicked sword hung poised to strike.

"What's wrong, Rangrid?" I gritted. "Aren't you going

to press the attack? Oh, sorry, I forgot. You're saving me for the boss, aren't you? Just exactly what was your assignment, *Mrs. Vernon?* Keep the fool busy screwing his brains out half the night, so he'll be nice and tired for the grand finale? Damn you to hell, *did you kill Gary yourself before Sleipnir took him?"*

I thought for an instant she *would* strike. I hoped she did, so I'd have an excuse to kill her. Rangrid was trembling. Her eyes flashed like the edge of the sword between us.

"I did not kill my grandson!"

"Blow it out your—"

"I DIDN'T KILL HIM!"

Something broke inside her. I could see it snap. The sword point dropped about six inches. She heaved one great sob, and caught it back again, then squeezed shut her eyes. In that instant, I could've taken her. I was ready for just that kind of opening. Ready, and more than capable of snapping her lovely neck in about a quarter of a second. In that moment, killing her would have been easy.

I almost lunged. Almost.

A faint, high moan, and the convulsive swallow that followed it, stopped me. Her hand was shaking despite the steadying weight of the sword. She opened too-bright eyes, and found my gaze. Something told me she knew how close I'd come to testing her speed with that sword. Something else told me she wouldn't have struck.

Which was crazy.

Rangrid was one of Odin's closest allies.

Her voice came at last, so choked I could hardly hear her.

"Did you think the old stories weren't true? Of course we lead mortal lives, take lovers and husbands, give birth to strong warriors, fiery daughters. Your race is stronger and better for it. Not all our sons bleed for the Valfather. . . ."

Her voice strangled.

Mine came out cold, each word a piece of ice dropping into the silence. "Gary wasn't supposed to die."

"No! He was not! I still don't know why Odin took him! It wasn't the right *time*. There should have been a wife, children. . . ."

There were no words to express what was inside me. There was nothing in striking range for me to kill. So I bit down on it, and stored it up to give to Odin when the time was right.

"I even went to Skuld," Rangrid said harshly. "I demanded an answer. She wouldn't say anything! Wouldn't *do* anything. She just looked right through me, like it wasn't my affair. . . ."

Her laugh hurt me.

"Can you imagine," Rangrid said, her voice shattering again on a semihysterical note, *"not my affair?"* Her eyes met mine again. "And *you*," she snarled—the sword came up again—"how could you *possibly* say such things to me? I should have *made* Skuld take back the Biter, rather than let it fall to the likes of *you*—"

"*Skuld?*" I interrupted. "What do you mean? Why would you give the Biter to Skuld?"

Rangrid blinked. "My God. You really don't know what I gave you, do you?"

I very nearly exploded. Instead, I counted to thirty— in German, English, and Spanish, then started over in German, just to be sure—and said, "No. How could I?"

The tip of her sword dropped just the tiniest fraction. Rangrid frowned. "Skuld carved the Biter with her own hands, before the Valfather was born."

That explained why it was black. Whatever it had started out as, her hands had burned every millimeter of its surface. A chill settled over me. If Skuld were the living personification of the future, which burned away each second of our lives, what in God's name was the Sly Biter?

Rangrid's voice went bitter again. "All of us, all the valkyries, share that in common with the Biter. All of us are older than Odin. We rode to battle at Skuld's bidding long before he took over Asgard, long before he tried to banish the Vanir."

She shook wildly tumbled hair across bare shoulders. "He did not succeed! No more than he succeeded in stealing the Biter for himself. I've kept it hidden away in my mortal family for centuries, where not even Hugin and Munin thought to look. After all the centuries we've spent in Valhalla, Odin trusts us valkyries, and never suspected." She sniffed, with a long, long lifetime of disdain in that single sound. "Besides, Skuld is my elder sister. Naturally, when the last of my family died, I took the Biter back to her for safekeeping."

I tried to digest all these bits of news. Shook the wrinkles out of them and put them in perspective with everything else. "And just what did Skuld say when you tried to return it?"

Rangrid frowned. "It didn't make sense, then." She met my eyes, and scowled. "Although it makes too much sense now. Skuld told me a stubborn young fool was going to need it, because he was probably on his way to making some serious enemies."

"Huh." That was putting things mildly.

A tiny vertical line between her brows marred perfection.

"It was so unlike Skuld to say that, too. Strange things are happening in the Worlds. . . ."

"You bet your sweet . . . life."

Skuld's blade—Skuld's!

How had they known the way I would react to Gary's murder? Actually, that was no great mystery. Given the circumstances of Gary's death—and my own peculiar personality—it wouldn't have taken a genius to figure that out. Skuld had made a couple of logical guesses, and tossed the knife into my likeliest path. The Sly Biter had simply hopped aboard my bandwagon, and come along for the ride, lending a hand now and again when I got myself inevitably into trouble.

Quite unexpectedly, I felt a whole lot better. The Biter might not be in my possession, but it wasn't part of my enemy's arsenal. That had to count for something. And Odin was terrified. Rusty tools, abandoned at the foot of the Norns' carved hall, flashed through my memory. I smiled—

And Rangrid shuddered.

I glanced into her eyes and a plan took form. "Rangrid, I'm going to ask you a question—and you'd better think very, very carefully before you answer. I'm here for one reason. I doubt I have to tell you what. Odin murdered your grandson, maybe even your son and your husband—are they here, too?" I asked abruptly.

The flinch in her eyes was all the answer I needed.

"Dammit, he's killing the whole world. All nine of them. No more. I'm going to stop him. One way or another. If you support him, then you'd better leave right now. But if you aren't lying to me . . . Well, last night *you* were the one who pointed out you're not like him, right around the time you started gushing about honor. Just now . . ."

What could I possibly say about just now?

"You've put up with his bullshit longer than anybody should ever have to. If I were in your place, I'd want his head on a platter, for what he's done to your family, not to mention all the other people he's murdered—yes, dammit, murdered, don't pretend it's anything else."

She closed her lips over a protest she didn't finish.

"Support me, Rangrid. All I want is a fair chance. For my world."

She stared at me. Then slowly, she lowered the sword. Its point dug into the floor. Maybe my plan was working. When she spoke her voice was so soft I had to strain to catch her words.

"I admired you—wanted you—from the moment you came to his grave. You were . . . afire. From within. But held so tightly in check . . ." She shivered. "It terrified me to think what would happen when you let that fire loose. Part of me wanted to see you take on Odin face-to-face; part of me . . ."

She looked up, met my gaze. "I didn't want you to die, too."

I believed her—despite everything—and felt like a heel. There had been that moment, in her living room, when my gaze had locked with hers. . . . For a couple of heartbeats, it was almost like I'd never left Oregon. I found, to my intense shock, that I was still willing to die to give this woman—this *valkyrie*—what she wanted. But not until I'd given Odin what was coming to him.

Rangrid whispered, "My sisters ride for accident victims now. Men who die of poison gases. Earthquake and flood and fire victims. Hel hates us. We—at least I—hate ourselves, what we've become. But what are we to do? Skuld no longer speaks with us, and Ragnarok is upon us, and we are not ready—"

"Would you be ready anyway?"

"Yes, I—"

I interrupted wearily. "Rangrid, you wouldn't be ready if you had another thousand years. Odin's hell-bent on dying in a blaze of glory and gore. He's dragging you and everything else down with him. Do you really want to die with a sword through your guts? Or drown in your own blood from poison, or have Surt's bully boys burn you alive, and do it so fast you still have time to hold your skin as it falls off—"

"*Stop!*" Rangrid was ashen. "Please, stop, I know what Ragnarok will be like, and I know it's hopeless—"

"*Then why keep doing Odin's dirty work?*"

She flinched, and didn't answer.

"My God," I said, utterly exasperated, "and they call the human race shortsighted, blind, and stupid."

That earned me a hot glare. "I am not shortsighted, blind, *or* stupid!"

"Oh?" I asked softly. "Then prove it, Rangrid."

Her voice broke on desperation. "I can't! Ragnarok can't be changed! Odin will die *then*. Nothing I do can stop him from killing you, *because you can't possibly kill him!*"

"Yes I can."

I said it quietly, reasonably, with the assurance of unassailable fact.

She stood gulping for several seconds, unable to find words. Finally, she whispered, "How can you know?"

Good question; but I wasn't quitting now. "Because the rules are off. You still don't see it, do you? You went to Skuld for answers, because Odin shouldn't have been able to take Gary from that wreck. Skuld didn't have any answers, because she *can't* answer. All bets are off. Odin's been operating under free will, and so have you, but you didn't know it. Can *you* explain why Odin's so scared of me? Just because I *might* have freed Loki?"

I laughed. It was an ugly sound. "Sorry, Rangrid, it won't wash. If I'm just part of the grand scheme, what's to fear? I'd be just a cog in the wheel—and not a very big cog, at that. No, Rangrid , he's scared because the grand scheme's in tatters around his feet. Odin knows damned well I can kill him. That's why he's stacked the deck so badly against me. *You* can make the difference. You can do whatever you please, Rangrid, choose whatever side you want, be a loose cannon he's not expecting. And think about this. Odin has no honor. You lose whatever honor you ever had, following his orders."

That really shook her. Rangrid's face went pale, and a tremor came to her hands. Getting a goddess who had thousands of years' worth of conditioning to predestination to swallow free will was tough; getting her to swallow treason was tougher. But then, treason always has been defined by the winner. John Adams and Tom Jefferson were traitors on one side of the Atlantic, patriots on the other.

I did sympathize with her. I knew how I'd feel if some green-horned, mealy-mouthed little alien showed up and tried to convince me that the law of gravity had stopped working—and calmly invited me to jump off the western rim of the Grand Canyon just to see for myself. I also knew exactly how I'd felt the day that slimy little German bastard had offered me ten thousand dollars for our code book.

I'd put him in the hospital. *Then* I'd reported him. Last I'd heard, he was still in prison. At least Rangrid didn't look like she planned on dismembering me. That was something.

"If," I continued very gently, "what you said about the final battle being so close at hand is true, then you've got precious little time left to make a decision. You can either die stupidly—uselessly—with Odin, or you can do something about him. I know I sound crazy as hell. But what in the world do you think drove me to go through all the agony I went through to get here? It took me weeks to convince *myself*, and I started out with an even bigger handicap than yours—I didn't even believe Odin was *real*."

Her lips quirked in a ghost of her former smile.

"The more I learned—and the more times Odin tried to kill me—the angrier I got, until the only sane thing I could do was find him, and stop him. Somebody *has* to stop him, Rangrid. It's a whole new, unpredictable ball-game out there; and the way he's running this war, it *is* already over, because your general's convinced himself he's already lost."

She studied my face earnestly, and chewed at one thumbnail for a moment. Then stared at the thumb self-consciously and dropped her hand to her side.

"Go on, please," she said very quietly.

I drew a deep breath. "Rangrid, if you can't—or won't—stand up to one outdated old tyrant, then you don't deserve to survive, either. He may well kill me out there today. Hell, he might kill me so fast, I won't even have time to yell. But I'll go down kicking and biting every step of the way. And I'll try to rip out his throat with my teeth as I die, because I know how desperately he's got to be stopped. And if I win . . ."

Her eyes widened.

I added softly, "If I kill Odin, then *everything* changes. At the very least, I think I'm a better soldier than he is. I don't lie to people, and I keep my promises—and don't make promises I know I can't keep. I may be nothing but a mortal man, Rangrid; but I think I'm a better man than he is a god."

The tears in her eyes spilled over. I couldn't quite bring myself to add that I didn't want to die still thinking of her as my enemy.

Rangrid whirled, and flung the sword. It embedded itself point-first in the wall, and hung there, quivering. My eyes widened. Good God, she was strong. . . .

An instant later, I was engulfed by one hundred thirty pounds of valkyrie. For at least five minutes, neither one of us spared a single second for breathing. When we unclutched, I had to gulp for oxygen. Her eyes blazed.

"Odin," she hissed, with a look in her eyes that made

me very glad she *wasn't* my enemy, "will take your life only if he kills me first! And I am very much harder to kill than you."

It was not a boast.

I grinned and said, "Got any last words for your hero?"

She didn't; but then, she didn't need any.

And I'd thought that previous kiss explosive. . . .

When we finally came up for air again, I held out one hand, a little shakily. "Better give me that damned silly sword, Rangrid."

She managed to free it with one emphatic grunt, then handed it over hilt first. I examined it appreciatively. Being hurled into the wall didn't seem to have done it any harm. It wasn't ancient work, because the blade and hilt were quite obviously made from modern materials; but whoever had made it had put months of loving work into it. I wasn't a fencer; but I was a weapons buff, and a perennial haunter of military museums. I'd never seen craftsmanship like it in my life. I repressed a wistful sigh, then resheathed it and fastened the sheath to my sword belt. I got it right only after she shook her head and showed me how.

"It's hopeless," she murmured, watching me make awkward practice swings. "He'll cut you down where you stand. It isn't fair."

I flashed her a confident grin that had nothing to do with the way I felt. "Darling Rangrid, he didn't intend it to be fair. I'll just have to fight dirty."

She laughed, and threw her arms around my neck, kissing me again until we were both dizzy. I finally broke my lips free. "I don't suppose you've got a machine gun stashed anywhere around here? I'm a damned fine shot, if I do say so myself. . . ."

She shook her head slowly. "Odin fights only with tra-ditional weapons."

"Huh. Figures. How the hell does he aim to fight a

modern battle that way? Don't answer; I already know.
He intends on losing. Stupid way to plan a war. . . ."

Her eyes went dark. "I don't want you to die," she
whispered. "We need you to fight Surt and the sons of
Muspell; but it's alive we need you. If he kills you, Randy,
you'll just be one of his millions—and be wasted, along
with the rest of them."

"Then I'll just have to take care not to get killed, won't
I?" The breezy bravado in my voice barely masked the
dread I felt. "You, uh, better get dressed; I think we're
late."

There was a fearful pounding at the door. Rangrid
threw herself into armor faster than I'd have thought
possible without doing injury to sensitive spots. When
she opened the door, another incredibly beautiful
woman in full battle armor stood outside.

"He is ready?"

"Yes, sister. We are ready."

Rangrid's reply warmed me to the bottom of my terrified cockles. I threw her a smile; then resolutely squared
my shoulders, grabbed my courage in both fists, and
marched out to meet Odin.

Chapter Nineteen

The great hall beyond the private chambers was a shambles. Broken dishes and tables, clean-picked bones, unidentifiable bits of garbage, spilled mead, and a few unconscious warriors were strewn randomly across the floor. Those warriors on their feet were swaying badly. The civilians I'd seen the previous night were conspicuously absent.

Odin waited on his massive throne. His single ruby eye followed our progress through the stench and the mess. My escorts saluted him, although I noted that Rangrid's was sloppy. I simply waited, poised lightly on the balls of my feet, one sweating hand on the hilt of my silly sword. I'd rather—far rather—have been holding Gary's knife, or even my lost AR-180 rifle.

Odin's glance swept me dismissively. "Are you prepared to die, mortal?"

I grinned. "Even the gods die sometime. Maybe this is *yours*, eh, Odin?"

Rangrid drew a sharp breath. The other valkyrie made an abortive move toward her sword. I ignored them both. Odin's face had lost color. The hall was so quiet, I heard a faint belch from at least a mile down the tables.

His attempt at a sneering grin was a dismal failure. "This should be uncommonly entertaining." It came out sounding forced.

I was, perhaps, more relaxed than I had a right to be. "I hope you sold lots of ringside seats. It isn't every day a god gets the immortal shit kicked out of him. Hell, after today, my future's in the bag: cereal endorsements, sportswear franchises, maybe even a shot at a commentator slot on *Monday Night Football*."

His stare was vacuous. Beside me Rangrid made a strangled noise that sounded suspiciously like choking laughter.

Odin scowled. I guess even Neanderthals catch on eventually when someone scores off them; he obviously didn't have the faintest idea how to score back. So he settled for an uncreative curse and a speech that was beginning to sound like a broken record.

"You have come living to Valhalla"—I never said he was genius material—"and you have feasted under my roof and partaken of the pleasures reserved for the Einherjar alone.

"You now must demonstrate that you deserve the right to join our ranks, or forfeit not only your life, but also your soul, to everlasting torment in the darkest, frozen wastes of Niflhel. The choice is yours: Die fighting and join us; or die shamefully, as a coward dies. Which do you choose?"

I stood watching him for a moment; then deliberately folded my arms across my chest and spat to one side. I'd fight him, all right—and die if I had to—but I wasn't about to buy into that ridiculous pair of choices. The way I had it figured, I had three options: fight and win, fight and die, or fight to a draw. If it turned out I couldn't physically kill him, then I had only one slim chance. And that depended on two things: Was Odin a betting man? And could I trust his sworn word to honor a lost bet?

Yeah, right.

I didn't have much choice.

So I looked him up and down; then spat on the floor again, and launched into it.

"Who the hell taught you to make speeches? Professor Bigwind at Pompous University, Bombast 101? If I thought you could fight as well as you talk, your offer might actually be tempting."

The vacuous stare returned. Hell, it wasn't nearly as much fun scoring off someone too stupid to appreciate your wit.

A murmur of laughter ran through the crowd behind me, though. Odin might not get it; but the Einherjar did. Odin's face and neck began to turn red under all that hair. A little slow, our boy, but not entirely dim. Maybe he was just getting senile?

I added with a drawl, "You realize, of course, getting killed isn't in my game plan. I came here to kill *you*. Tell you what: I'll fight you. And if you can kill me, I'll join up with the boys. If you can't, or if I strike a killing blow—"

He interrupted me with a snort. "You know well enough you cannot kill me. Fenrir is fated to bring my death; not you, nor any other *man*." There was worry in his eye, though, and his bravado didn't dispel it.

"—or," I went on, as if he hadn't spoken, "one that would *be* a killing blow if you were an ordinary man like me, then the fight ends, and I win."

"Your point, mortal?" he asked testily.

"Just that. I win; you lose. I'm free to go my merry way—and you will step down forever as head of the gods and general of the armies of the Einherjar."

Odin gaped. Even Rangrid gasped. A low mutter spread through the hall as dead warriors passed along my challenge. The only thing Odin seemed capable of was sputtering.

I nudged a little harder.

"What's wrong? It's just a sporting little bet, between rivals. A minute ago, you were all set to tear my living heart out and eat it for lunch. Don't tell me the great Odin's a chickenshit? You'll break my heart."

Rangrid gasped. The muttering became a muted roar. Odin's face went slowly purple, out to the roots of his hair. For a moment I thought I wouldn't have to fight him, because he looked like he was about to have a stroke.

I decided to give it one last shove and twist. I glanced at Rangrid. "Hell's bells, Rangrid, I thought you were just paying me a compliment when you said I was a bigger man than Odin."

She flamed scarlet. I winked. The other valkyrie gasped audibly, and stared. I noted peripherally that she *wasn't* staring at my face. As for the Einherjar . . .

Laughter erupted at the front tables and spread in spastic waves. Odin looked dazed for an instant, resembling a hairy, purple, dumbstruck virgin caught with his pants down.

The nearest Einherjar howled and pointed; Odin was losing them, and he knew it.

His mouth worked, and his Adam's apple bobbed convulsively, then his harsh voice rang out across the hall. "It is a fool's bargain! Done!"

I grinned. "Yo, fool, you just made yourself a deal."

Laughter exploded out of control. I thought for an instant Odin would jump me right where I stood. Rangrid tensed.

Instead, he spat, "Rangrid Shield-Destroyer! Take this . . . this silver-tongued son of Loki to the battlefield!" He stabbed a pointing finger at a distant door, which looked like it was about a mile away. "I'll be waiting!"

He spun on his heel so fast, both ravens squawked and took flight. He vanished through a side door. A moment later, I heard his voice raised in bellowed curses.

Rangrid looked a little round-eyed as she met my glance. I winked again, and gestured grandly. "Shall we?"

A slow smile lit her eyes. "You," she said succinctly, her lips twitching uncontrollably, "are a thoroughgoing, unrepentant bastard."

"Oh, without doubt." I grinned. "After you, dear lady."

Rangrid had other ideas, however. She got her sister to lead the way, and chose rear guard herself. It was probably just as well; the other valkyrie was so white-lipped, she might've been tempted to skewer me, if she'd been presented with a convenient target like my back. I certainly didn't bank on the other valkyries possessing anything like Rangrid's motive for defecting.

They escorted me into the press of crowding Einherjar. A swelling roar gathered as men beat empty flagons on tabletops. I heard shouts of encouragement and last-minute advice. The noise level mounted deafeningly, beating against us with near-physical force, and still we moved down endless lines of tables. When at last we gained the cavernous doorway, the maelstrom of noise died away behind us, and a mad scramble for the best vantage point came in its place.

I blinked and paused for an instant on the threshold.

"What is it?" Rangrid asked tersely.

"Uh . . . nothing," I muttered. Hastily, I strode forward before the Einherjar—jammed into the doorway behind us—could trample our heels. Yesterday, when we'd come in through a different door, we'd ridden up across a broad plain. Beyond *this* door were rocky hills, muddy valleys, and twisting, treacherous little gorges with angry white water snarling through stony riverbeds. The size of the Valhall staggered the imagination. Useful for battle training, though . . .

Odin waited atop a barren ridge, seated on Sleipnir. The horse bore the brunt of his temper. Sleipnir tossed his head fretfully. There was blood in the foam at his muzzle. Odin constantly jerked the bit in his mouth. It was a lousy way to treat a valuable horse. I was a little surprised Sleipnir stood for it. Even from here, I could see the war-horse's eyes rolling white.

I narrowed my own eyes. Did he mean to fight from Sleipnir? A man on foot was at a bad enough disadvantage against a man on horseback; but Sleipnir's little trick of popping in and out of reality left me with sinking apprehension in my belly.

Well, I hadn't expected a fair fight, and I knew a trick or two that might just startle a cavalryman into a fatal error.

When I heard a familiar, spine-chilling howl, I turned, badly startled. Further down the ridgeline, where the vantage was best, was Fenrir. He snarled wildly at the end of his chain. A one-handed man held grimly onto the quivering fetter. Each time the wolf lunged, Tyr's shoulder and arm strained to hold him. I wouldn't have thought Tyr would get anywhere near Fenrir again. The wolf had bitten off his other hand the day they'd chained him.

Just beyond Fenrir's slavering reach, Thor swung his short-handled maul as though it were a jackhammer. He was busy driving the boulder that pegged Fenrir's chain deep into the earth.

Tyr, struggling to hold the wolf, bellowed, "Hurry the hell up, Thor! The bloody fight's about to start."

Thor grunted sharply and finished the job. He stepped back, and nodded once. Tyr let go the chain. Fenrir's snarled cry set up a nearly subliminal resonance through the sword blade jammed into his jaws. I pressed a hand against my skull bones and shook my head against the painful sound. Tyr lunged out of Fenrir's way, then strolled closer, chatting animatedly with Thor. The red-haired god, I noted dourly, watched me narrowly and caressed his war hammer Mjollnir. Fenrir gave one final snarl, then turned his baleful green eyes on me.

He whined piteously.

I growled under my breath. Odin was one sadistic son-of-a-bitch.

I turned my gaze away, sickened. We'd stopped in a broad, shallow valley below the Fenris Wolf's vantage point. Rangrid turned to me.

"Fight well, hero," she murmured. She drew me close. Her lips were warm and trembling against mine. "Take the kiss of Rangrid Shield-Destroyer into battle." I thought for an instant she was going to cry. Then she shook her hair back, lifted her chin in the motion I'd come to recognize, and stepped back.

I stood alone in the valley.

As alone as a live human can be surrounded by more dead men than Genghis Khan had left in his wake.

The air trembled with the swelling noise from tens of thousands of throats: "O . . . *din!* O . . . *din!* O . . . *din!*"

Tyr had squatted down comfortably on his haunches up on the ridgeline. Thor was beginning to grin. Odin shook a heavy war spear above his head in a gesture of confidence. Numbing sound rolled over us, stirring the blood—his hot, mine cold.

I knew, of course, what he held. It wasn't just a spear, any more than Sleipnir was just an eight-legged horse. The weapon was called Gungnir. The dwarves had presented it to him as a gesture of obeisance.

Gungnir never missed its mark.

Never.

As Odin held Gungnir on high, the tumult gradually died away. Silence stretched taut.

"Einherjar," Odin said. He spoke without raising his voice; yet I knew that even the farthest, dimmest ranks lost in the misty distance heard him clearly, so profound was the silence.

"There has come to Valhalla a living mortal"—cripes, was that the only speech he knew?—"who has challenged your Valfather to personal combat. His courage is great."

Odin's sneer revealed what he really thought of me; but he was wary of saying it after his comeuppance in front of these men.

"Before the sun sets on our feasting, he will join you as brother. Honor to him! Honor to you all! Let battle be joined!"

A shock wave blasted through the valley, a spontaneous, inchoate deluge of noise from the Einherjar. Odin hooked his leg over Sleipnir's withers and slid easily to the ground. He was fighting on foot, thank God. With sweating fingers I dragged my sword from its sheath. Odin might call me a silver-tongued son of Loki, but I was one helluva worried one. I knew all too well what my odds of success were. Somewhere behind me, I heard some poor fool betting money on *me*; and abruptly felt better.

Then there was no time left to worry about anything.

Odin strode down the ridgeline, not quite loping. I considered whether to let the bastard come to me, or carry the fight to him. He had the reach of me, armed with a spear against my sword. Odin held his weapon in the classic bayonet assault position as he closed the distance. His right hand gripped the haft just above the butt, with the butt end tucked between elbow and hip. He grasped the haft farther toward the deadly iron point with the other hand, ready to jab or charge.

I watched his narrowed bloody red eye for any betraying movement that would telegraph his intent. He squinted slightly. . . .

And charged.

I shifted into a classic right guard, with my right side toward him, sword ready in front of me. Odin drove forward, like a freight train on full steam. The iron spear point never wavered a millimeter from true. He was driving Gungnir straight toward my center of mass. At the last possible second, with the glittering sharp tip a hairbreadth from my skin, I shifted hard left. Gungnir's point passed harmlessly behind my shoulder.

Before I had time to be shocked that Gungnir had missed, I seized the haft. I shoved the spear point down hard, driving it into the ground with Odin's own momentum. Odin stumbled. I leaped clear. A booming wave of sound rolled over us.

Odin ripped the point free and charged again.

I dropped into left guard, left side toward him.

This time when he rushed past my shoulder, I deflected the spear haft upward with the flat of my sword. I dropped the blade instantly, and grabbed Gungnir with both hands. Again using his own momentum, I shoved the spear shaft straight up and back over Odin's shoulder. Gungnir's razor-edged point windmilled in a circle. Odin was forced to let go. He howled in pain as his arm was wrenched beyond its normal range of motion.

I couldn't hear my own panting breath above the thunderous noise. The point came down hard behind Odin. The spear which *could* not miss, had. Twice.

And now it was mine.

He twisted blindly around, his mouth agape as I grasped the haft and swung the point around at his exposed side—

A tornado-force wind slammed me backward. I sprawled flat, badly winded. A shadow fell toward me. . . .

I jerked sideways, dragging the spear with me. Odin slammed into the dirt. His sword blade sank into the mud all the way up to the guard. I rolled to my feet and so did he, wrenching mightily on the buried weapon. Before he could evade, I charged.

Two steps from achieving Odin shish kebab, I staggered. A cloying stench hit me wetly in the face. A decaying corpse—its rotting flesh falling away in gobbets and chunks—rose out of the ground and grappled me. The damned thing tripped me up and clawed its way higher as it pulled itself up out of the muddy earth. Its hands were slimy and cold, its flesh disconcertingly solid. Its grip was as tenacious as an alligator snapping turtle's.

I stabbed and clubbed at it with Odin's spear, knocking off hunks of dead meat; but the decaying hands clung like leeches. A bony skull leered blindly through empty eye sockets. Nearly liquid brains the color of dead algae oozed out through them. The apparition shifted its grip. Bile rose in my throat as some of the stuff dripped across my hands. I set my jaws, and shattered the skull case with the butt of the spear, but still I couldn't pull free.

Feet consisting mostly of bone tangled with my own and we crashed backward. The obscenity fell with me, smothering me in slime and rotted flesh.

I'd lost my grip on the spear. I was left with nothing but my bare hands. Tearing with fingers, kicking with booted feet, I wrenched my way clear of the mess, sufficiently to see Odin—spear once again in hand—bearing down on me. I rolled violently aside. Abruptly I was as free of slime and gore as though it had never existed.

The spear point buried itself in the earth where I'd been.

I scrambled to my feet. A gibbering, five-foot-high skull with fire shooting from eye and nose sockets sailed through the air at me. I dodged under the lower jaw, snatched up my discarded sword, and threw myself at Odin again.

Now I knew why they called him Helblindi, he-who-blinds-with-death.

Too bad for him the "helblindi" ploy wasn't working. I began to feel hopeful—which was a damnfool thing to do.

Odin fell back, feinting left; and I whirled to face him.

And suddenly a hot flush spread through me. Whatever it was, it hit my brain like a fifth of whiskey gulped neat. I was abruptly—reelingly—drunk out of my mind. The horizon tilted wildly. I staggered, trying to stay on my feet. A large blur lurched forward, toward me. I had to remind myself that I was the one doing the lurching, not the blur. Then I realized my eyes were blurred, not the shape barreling down on me like a bull elephant.

I tried to move out of the way, which was a mistake. I tangled my feet together and landed flat on my face, breathing mud. Wet earth splattered into one ear as a foot thudded into the ground right beside me. Gradually it occurred to me that my drunken mistake had saved my life.

I crawled to my hands and knees and shook my head in an attempt to clear it. I willed the ground to quit heaving and billowing like ocean waves. Then I reminded myself that Odin was somewhere behind me, charging at my exposed back. There was no way I could get out of his way. So I fell flat again—and a spear point whistled across my back. The draft of its passage left goose bumps along naked flesh where it had split open my leather shirt. The Einherjar's cheering shook the very ground.

Someone—it had to be Odin—was swearing nonstop. I shook my head again, still trying to clear it. These sensations were Odin's doing. They weren't real.

I remembered First Officer Spock muttering, "The bullets are not real . . ." while the Earps blazed away, and I giggled drunkenly. Yeah, that was the ticket. *This drunk is not real. . . .*

It occurred to me, in my befuddled state, that somewhere in this valley, Gary was watching me crawl around on all fours while Odin finished me off at his leisure.

That made me mad. Hatred colder than the ice in Niflhel spread through me. As the hatred grew stronger, the drunken stupor faded. My eyes focused sharply. With a prickling of the hairs on my neck, I lunged to my feet. Blind instinct prompted a twisting, sideways motion. An animal shriek struck my ears. I felt more than heard the passage of something massive just behind my left shoulder. I snapped into a diving forward roll. I came up scanning wildly for my lost sword and Odin's current position.

Movement overhead caught my eye. I snapped my attention skyward. Silhouetted against the bloody skies was a gigantic eagle, big enough for a starring role in a Harryhausen Sinbad movie. It clutched Gungnir in great, curved talons. The bloodred light from Valhalla's skies glinted off those curved daggers as the huge bird of prey dove fast and hard. I scurried backward and sideways—

My ankles sank into something cold and wet. My foot twisted under me as I stumbled over a buried rock. I windmilled wildly and fell flat again, back into a deep snowdrift. The eagle was diving at my belly, screaming out of a pulsing vermilion sky. . . .

I was helpless to move. Irresistible surges of sexual bliss left me shaking and weak. I groaned aloud. My eyes rolled back in my head, and I felt a warm stain spreading across the inside of my heavy leather pants. . . .

Then my right thigh cramped. My foot cramped even worse. I rolled over in agony. I tried to rub the spasmed leg muscles with one hand while I forced the foot out straight with the other. That brought on an even worse spasm, and left me doubled over and rolling around like some demented pillbug.

A mass of feathers and bone slammed into the snow

with meteoric force. Abruptly I was engulfed in a smothering cloud. One huge wing buffeted me, with enough force to stun. Then, as the eagle struggled to right itself, it backwinged to regain its balance. The leading edge of its wing caught me in the side. The force of the blow rolled me along the snowbank like one of those cartoon characters bouncing along at the center of a rapidly growing snowball.

By the time I slithered to a squishy halt, all thought of cramped muscles had left me. In fact, the cramps had vanished as quickly as the corpse. I struggled to my feet. Odin was back in man form, literally spitting mud where his beak had plowed deep into the muck. His furs were askew. He was cursing so hotly, sparks crackled spontaneously in the air about him.

Odin yanked the great spear free of the mud with one Herculean pull. He kicked at the snow. It vanished. My lost sword reappeared, buried halfway to the hilt in the muck like Arthur's sword in the stone. Odin spat one final mouthful of muddy saliva, bent my sword downward, and stepped on the blade with one foot. Then he yanked up hard on the hilt.

Rangrid's sword broke with a snapping sound that brought a hush to the onlookers. I thought I heard a single sob, cut short.

My eyes narrowed. I flexed my fingers, watching coldly as Odin flung away the useless hilt of my sole weapon. He stepped forward, and raised the spear.

"Now," he snarled, "we end this little game!"

I watched him begin his lunge. Time slowed. I tensed, ready to meet him with nothing but my naked fingers. Sweat poured from me. My fingers twitched, wanting the feel of the black-bladed weapon Odin had stolen from me—

Its warm haft slid snugly into my palm.

The Biter's tail lashed firmly around my wrist. The

Biter met Gungnir's iron point and shoved it upward. The blade slid along Gungnir's iron socket with a shrieking whine that sent sparks flying in every direction. The Sly Biter's long blade pulsed with an aura that looked black in the bloody light of Valhalla's skies.

The spear point whistled harmlessly past my shoulder. I grabbed the haft in my free hand and wrenched it aside—

And Odin lunged straight onto the Biter's waiting blade.

I gritted my teeth, and braced my wrist with my other hand, then wrenched upward with all my strength. I cut through muscle and bone. I heard an immortal, gawdawful scream. . . .

Then Odin was past me. He crouched on one knee, huddled in on himself. I gasped for air, deafened by the screaming Einherjar. The Biter hung expectantly in my hand.

Slowly Odin straightened. He turned to face me, holding his belly. Blood oozed from between his fingers. Not gushed—oozed. Slowly. And fell off to a mere trickle while I watched. Odin swore, tearing off ruined furs to reveal a long, nasty gash in his abdomen. It was healing before my eyes. He scratched a scabbing scar that obviously itched, passed wind, and worked one shoulder as though it had twinged a little.

Too winded to do anything else, I just stared, first at the healed wound, then at the blade in my hand, which had failed me. I got an impression of deep dismay from it, and decided that this time, at least, the Biter was not at fault.

Brunowski had warned me there'd be days like this.

I scrubbed my face with the back of one hand, and waited. There was still our bet. And if he didn't honor that, I'd try cutting off his head. What worked against Dracula . . .

"I did warn you," Odin wheezed. He wagged a finger in my direction. "It is not my time to die. The Biter knows that. Did you truly think Skuld's favorite blade would harm me before my time?"

I didn't bother to answer. He didn't want one, in any case.

"I must confess some small jealousy. The blade was once mine. I had thought it loyal when I relieved you of it." He shrugged. "I grow weary of this nonsense, mortal. You have fought well. Your end shall be quick, and well rewarded."

Paralysis hit before I could protest. I couldn't move, not even my lips. I'd expected him to break the bet; but not this. . . .

An angry roar went up from the Einherjar; then Rangrid sprawled into my line of vision. Her lips were bloody. The side of her face was already bruised.

Odin shouted, "This is none of your affair, traitorous bitch!" He added a kick to the ribs when she tried to drag herself to her feet. She doubled up, and lay still. "I'll deal with you later!"

Exerting all my strength only brought rivers of sweat into my eyes. I quickly discovered I couldn't even blink to clear them. At the very fringes of my peripheral vision, I saw movement. With an effort that cost me burst blood vessels in my nose, I managed to blink until I could see.

Off to my right, an oak tree was growing. Its gnarled trunk split the wet earth as its diameter swelled from sapling to water-oak-sized monster in less time than it took to think about it. Darkness engulfed me. The huge tree spread heavy branches and thick leaves between me and the bloody skies. A massive branch dipped invitingly a few feet above my head. Its leaves rustled quietly in the breeze.

Odin strode into view, all trace of humor gone from

his craggy face. In one hand he held a coil of thick rope; tucked under his other arm was the spear.

He drove the spear point into the soft earth, and kicked viciously again at Rangrid when she tried to cut his legs out from under him. Then, using slow, deliberate motions, he knotted a hangman's noose. Sweat flooded down me. Blood streamed from my nose; but I couldn't move anything. I remained frozen as a marble statue, and watched—raging and helpless—while he slipped the heavy rope over my head. He grinned into my face.

"A bigger man than Odin, eh?"

He tightened the noose cruelly around my throat. A quick flick of his wrist sent the free end sailing over the waiting branch and back into his hands.

He pulled hard, taking up slack. Coarse, thickly twisted fibers cut into my windpipe and carotid artery. I swayed into the air. He hauled me up until just the tips of my toes remained in contact with the earth. Then he tied off the end, pulled his spear free, and moved directly in front of me. I fought to move, and gurgled obscenely. No air got past the back of my mouth. Blood pounded agonizingly in my ears. Pain bit deep into my throat. My chest heaved—but nothing got into my lungs, save spittle.

Odin watched with a leering grin. He was savoring every second of this. . . . Rasping, gargled sounds and the thunder of blood filled my ears. Pain seared my throat, burning inside and out. My tongue felt thick as old shoe leather. Pounding agony filled my head, lay like stones in my heaving chest. . . .

The entire universe seemed to collapse. It shrank in on itself until all that remained was one blazing crimson eye, burning in the air before me. Then even sight of his eye vanished into a red mist. Searing, icy hatred shook through me. It coursed like a drug through my veins, exploded through my entire body. . . .

Abruptly I was moving. I clawed at the rope above my head, before the front of my brain had time to register what the lizard back of it already knew. Freedom might be short-lived. . . .

I hauled myself upward to ease the pressure on my throat, and tore madly at the choking noose. Some instinct screamed at me to kick out. I did so, blindly, with both feet. My boot soles connected hard with something solid.

Air whistled into my lungs. I hung by one hand, and wrenched the noose wider. My vision began to clear with agonizing slowness. The Biter still hung grimly from my wrist, by its tail. The moment I realized that, it slid back into my hand. I slashed through the rope with one cut, and fell heavily. I landed flat on my back.

Hearing began to return. The Einherjar were screaming mindlessly. I neither knew nor cared who they cheered. My whole concern was to get the clinging noose off. I tore again at the rope around my throat, dragged it over my head, hurled it away. Then I staggered to my feet and faced Odin. His face was a bloodied mess. His nose was shattered. It streamed gore where I'd kicked the living shit out of him, point blank.

My tongue didn't want to work right. "Old man . . ."

I coughed, and tried to swallow. I wiped sweat from my eyes with an arm that weighed more than a mountain.

" . . . Old man, you can't even kill me when you cheat. You're finished. Done. It's my turn, and my world's. Nothing you do will stop us. Nothing, do you hear me?"

I advanced on him. He gave ground at every step I took. I lifted the Biter and pointed it at him, stabbing the air to emphasize every syllable: *"You . . . lost . . . your . . . bet!* Now pay the hell up and get the hell out."

He didn't reply. He just roared and rushed me, spearpoint foremost. My muscles were sluggish; but the Biter came up, dragging my arm with it. The spear point threw sparks as it scraped along the length of the Biter's black blade. I stumbled to one side, off balance, and tried to get the tree trunk between us as the enraged god charged again.

The screams of the Einherjar shook the earth. The very air trembled. Odin came at me, and I evaded, again with the Biter's help. He came again. I foundered, fell, and rolled aside. Odin drove the great spear into the mud. I tripped him up with my feet and he fell heavily against the spear shaft.

A terrible splintering crack rent the air.

Gungnir split down the shaft, breaking off completely just above the heavy iron point. Odin looked almost ready to cry.

The Einherjar fell utterly silent.

Then Odin shrieked. He whipped his sword out of his scabbard, and swung like a madman. I dodged under the blow, and slashed across the hilt. The Biter sang in my hand. There was a moment's terrible shock. . . . Odin was left holding a hilt, and two inches of broken blade. He hurled the ruined weapon at my face, and leaped. Odin sought my throat with his bare hands. We rolled. I stabbed blindly with the Biter. I heard a grunt of pain, and stabbed with all my strength. Hot blood drenched my knuckles.

The Biter's hilt went slippery—then a grip of unbelievable strength fastened onto the Biter's tail. It lashed madly as Odin forced it slowly to uncurl from around my arm. The tail came completely loose and he wrenched it bodily away from me. I cursed, and got clear. Odin hurled my knife with all his might. I dropped to the ground. It whistled past my ear as I fell, and landed quivering, its point buried deeply in the trunk of the great oak tree.

Odin slammed into me. We rolled in the mud, unable

to get a killing grip on one another. I squirted out of his grasp like a watermelon seed at a spitting contest. I scrabbled my way up a muddy slope. Odin followed, grabbing at an ankle. I kicked backward and slammed my foot into his teeth. I felt several break off; then he let go and I sprawled forward into shadow. I squirmed forward on my belly.

Again he closed, wrestling me into the mud. We rolled in several directions at once, flailing about ineffectually, with arms and legs sticking out every conceivable direction. We fought for fatal grips, lost them, and squirmed for new ones.

He finally got his hands on my windpipe. I couldn't break his hold. He was twisting my head around, toward the snapping point. I jabbed my thumb into his good eye.

He screamed and let go. I wriggled free. Odin groped blindly for a weapon—

I froze. His questing hand had found the hilt of a sword—*a sword jammed into gaping jaws*. He wrenched it free. I had time to roll aside, then the bloody point stabbed into the earth millimeters from my ear.

I slid backward, willing the Biter into my hand. A flare of frantic motion blazed in my peripheral vision, then the Biter slid firmly into my palm. The tail got a death grip of its own around my wrist. The Biter was literally buzzing with rage. I slashed blindly. The Biter met Odin's swordpoint and turned it. The weapons grated against one another. Then sword and Biter strained sideways, smashing against a taut length of chain.

Both weapons rang and scraped noisily along it, drawing sparks without nicking the fetter. Fenrir was howling like all the demons of hell combined. His chain was caught on our weapons—and I stood between him and his prey.

As our locked blades slid down the length of chain, toward Fenrir's jaws, I yelled in a last-ditch effort.

"Fenrir! This chain is made out of nothing! Nothing at all! It's a goddamned illusion! Break it!"

The Biter pulsed with baleful black light.

Then sliced through Gleipnir's magical links like a blowtorch through butter. Either that, or the whole chain just disintegrated into dust.

And Fenrir was suddenly free. The sword that had held his jaws open for centuries was now clutched in Odin's sweating grip. Odin was frozen in place. He was staring—horror-struck—at the Fenris Wolf.

I came around with a deadly slash. It laid Odin's throat wide. He reeled. Brought up his sword with a fumbling motion . . .

I slammed the Biter through his black heart.

"Die, damn you!"

I don't know what the Biter did, inside him. But he stumbled backward. Shock and pain turned his face grey. I fell off balance, pulled forward as he jerked himself free. He started to crumple. . . .

I was buffeted to my knees by a massive, grazing blow from behind. I heard a blood-gurgling scream through the spurting mess from Odin's jugular. A huge shadow fell across us. Odin's scream ended abruptly in a strangled whimper. Then something slammed into me again from above and rolled me aside. When I managed to lift my head, Odin's body lay strangely twisted on the muddy, bloody ground.

He had been bitten in half. His legs and hips were missing entirely. He was still alive.

I caught a glimpse of murderous light dying from his single red eye. It had fixed on me with a look I knew I would see in nightmares for the rest of my life.

Then Fenrir opened his great bloody jaws one more time. . . .

And the rest of Odin vanished forever.

The silence was so still, I could hear the individual breathing of tens of thousands of men above my own labored gasps.

Fenrir raised his muzzle to the bloody sky and howled once, a drawn-out victory cry that chilled the blood. Sleipnir thundered toward him. The stallion screamed, and reared; then unaccountably settled again, and pawed restlessly with two right front hooves.

Twenty paces away, Thor—his face ashen against his flaming hair—lifted Mjollnir. Mouth working, eyes blazing with homicidal rage, he hurled his massive war hammer. It flew at my head with all the speed of his immortal strength.

I moved blindly. The Biter whipped up. The shock against my arms lifted me off the ground and hurled me fifteen feet backward. Then I lay panting on my back, both arms completely numb. The shattered pieces of Mjollnir lay scattered in the mud all around me.

The Biter purred in my grasp. If it'd been a kitten, I'd have rubbed its ears.

No one else moved, and I remained where I'd landed.

I still was unable to take it in.

Mjollnir was broken.

Fenrir was free.

And Odin was dead.

Chapter Twenty

I looked at the Biter, and wondered—somewhat stu-pidly—what I should do. I couldn't think of anything. Neither, evidently, could anyone else. The entire com-pany stood frozen like a crowd of statues.

Then Fenrir moved. Toward me, the man who'd freed him. I raised the Biter halfheartedly, pleased that it still moved at my summons, even more pleased that my *arm* would move. I still couldn't feel it.

Then, dumbfounded, I lowered the Biter again. The great wolf whined. He dropped his head to where I lay sprawled in the mud, and butted against my leg in the timeless gesture of canine submission.

Uh . . .

"Good, boy?" I croaked uncertainly.

An eager whine broke from the creature. He lifted his head. A blast of blood-foul breath choked me; then his tongue slathered across my face like a wet towel. Fenrir panted happily, and moved to my side. I managed to wipe off my face without gagging. The Fenris Wolf sat on his haunches and turned a snarling visage to the assembled company.

"He's mine, so don't try it," was the clear message.

Nobody seemed inclined to try anything; much less Fenrir's temper. . . .

Except Sleipnir, who tossed his head, and snorted. That murderous black fiend sidled and danced his way to my other side, flanking me, then bared his teeth at the nearest Einherjar.

Uh . . .

Unsteadily I rose to my feet. I almost fell. Instinctively I put my arms out, and found rough fur on one side, sleek muscle on the other. . . . I hung supported between them, with the Biter still in one hand. The wolf stood every bit as tall and broad as the horse. Allies . . . brothers . . . who moments before had been bitterest enemies . . .

I took a deep breath and searched for Rangrid. Her eyes were dull with shock.

"You okay?"

She put the back of one hand to a bleeding lip, looked absently at the blood; then nodded, staring up at me.

"A little bruised. But, yes. I'm okay." That fact seemed to overwhelm her. "You. . . ?"

"Yeah."

We looked at one another across the churned battle-field; then I shook my head, and muttered, "Jesus Christ."

A familiar voice said, "Wrong church *and* wrong pew."

I snapped around. Gary Vernon strolled out of the crowd, stopping well clear of my threatening compan-ions. He'd thrust his hands into his pockets, and just stood there, a grin on his face fit to crack his jaw.

"Well, Barnes, you certainly know how to shake things up."

My guardians never had a chance to react. I was hug-ging Gary and pounding him on the back before Sleipnir could do more than snort. Both of us were laughing, and he was hugging and pounding me until I nearly fell. I had to wipe tears with the back of one arm.

"Goddamn, Vernon, goddammit, it's good to see you. You wouldn't believe what I've been through. . . . "

I babbled for a couple of minutes, and he let me; then I finally grasped his arm. "Let's get *out* of here."

Before he could say anything, a flare of brilliant light drew our attention. I squinted into the glare; then stiffened.

—Aw, shit . . .

Sleipnir screamed a shrill warning and reared to his haunches. Gary glanced sharply at my face; then peered at the new arrival. A stallion had appeared before the Valhall—a stallion wrapped in flame. Fire defined its muscles, flickered from its mane and tail, and exploded from the prancing hooves in gouts of sparks. The glare was so fierce, I had to lift one arm to shield my eyes.

Skuld rode him like a seasoned pro. Her thighs clamped his sides. She controlled him easily as he reared high in answer to Sleipnir's challenge. Her hair whipped out behind her, each strand writhing like a living thing in the wind of the stallion's passage.

She brought the horse back to earth and held him firmly in check. The reins in her hand flickered like lightning. Skuld glanced around with a satisfied air . . . then turned her fiery gaze toward me.

I'd thought the heat of her gaze staggering before. . . .

Even Gary flinched.

One fiery brow rose slowly. I thought I saw the corner of her lips quirk. "Not bad. Not half bad."

Then she reached out a flaming hand. Her fingers closed around my wrist. Before I could even draw breath to scream, Skuld had pulled me astride her stallion. I heard Sleipnir's trumpeting neigh; then the bloody landscape of Valhalla was fading around us. As we transferred between worlds, I realized there was no pain, and wondered whether—if I *were* in the process of being burned to death—I'd notice.

We came out beside the shimmering spring Urd. Skuld slid gracefully to the ground. I jumped down with considerably less finesse, but a great deal more enthusiasm. I eyed her warily, and ascertained that I was, in fact, uncharred.

"I'm glad you survived," she said, by way of greeting.

Finding myself still alive and unincinerated seemed somehow to have caused difficulty with my breath control. I suspect I sounded more than a little petulant as I replied, "I'm glad you're glad—couldn't you have told me that back there?"

Her lips twitched and her eyes sparkled; but all she said was, "Yes; but not the rest of what I have to say. First, let me offer you a gift."

She lifted her hand. I heard a distant squawk; then two midnight-black ravens swooped down from the eaves of her golden hall. They alighted on my shoulders. I stood very still. Sharp little claws dug into my flesh as they found their balance.

"Hugin and Munin returned to me a few moments ago," Skuld explained. "I daresay you will find them useful."

I glanced cautiously from side to side. "Yeah, they'd be great for reconnaissance—better than spy satellites—but what does that have to do with me? I mean . . ." What the hell *did* I mean? What did *she* mean, offering them to me? I studied her through narrowed eyes. I wasn't sure I liked the implications here.

"How do you know they'd even report to me?" I stalled.

I was frantically searching for a way to broach the more delicate questions in my mind. Somehow, I didn't feel quite like blurting out, "What are you up to now?" Instead, I managed to sound like a truant little boy. "I mean, I—um—sort of killed their former owner."

Her glance was as droll as her tone. "I sort of noticed." But her eyes sparkled with white-hot highlights.

Skuld had a sense of humor?

She smiled. "Hugin and Munin were raised by my hand. Odin begged the gift of them long ago, and I obliged."

I eyed her the way a bird eyes a hungry snake. "I don't have to give up my eye or something, do I?"

Her gaze left my clothes soaked with sweat under a crust of dried mud.

Despite what she was, her voice came out cold as a German blizzard. "I would have you know, Randy Barnes, my sisters and I gave up a great deal of power, on the barest *chance* someone like you might come along someday and win a duel with Odin. I'm not about to sabotage the man who managed to kill that dithering old fool."

Just what was that supposed to mean? Other than the obvious, which was that Skuld's opinion of the late, unlamented Odin Oath-Breaker seemed no higher than mine.

I wondered if accepting the birds would be something like signing a contract in blood. I'd just managed to wriggle out of my contract with Hel, by killing Odin; I didn't feel like striking any more deals with any more deities. But Skuld was waiting for me to do *something*.

I reached up a tentative hand. Hugin—or was it Munin?—let me stroke his glossy feathers. I glanced up at Skuld again. "Would you, uh, mind explaining that, please?"

I thought it was a reasonable request, considering.

She sat down on a white limestone bench carved with vines and flowers. The stone blackened. If she sat there

long enough, would the limestone turn to marble? She
patted the bench gently. Reluctantly, I sat beside her.

Skuld sat poised for a moment, as though lost in
thought. I waited politely.

"You have already puzzled out the most important part
of it," she began, gazing wistfully at the magnificent
rainbow bridge that arched out of sight overhead. "My
sisters and I have not been . . . controlling things . . . for a
long time, now. Quite a long time. Ragnarok, of course,
approaches. We foresaw long, long ago that no matter how
we three meddled, we were going to lose the war. So. We
introduced free will and stopped meddling. Permanently."

"Couldn't you just have prophesied victory or something?"

She offered a wan smile. "No. We had the power to
shape men's lives, yes. But the power to stop the sons
of Muspell from riding against the rest of the Worlds?
You credit even us with too much power, my friend."
She pursed fiery lips. "Perhaps I had better explain
further. We three—Urd, Verdani, and I—controlled
men's lives through our little sisters, the lesser norns. I
do not speak of the valkyries, although they, too, are
our sisters. There was one lesser norn for each man,
woman, and child born in all the Nine Worlds, and
when their host died, so did they. Some were good,
some evil, some mixed in varying balances of the two.
But look around you, Randy Barnes. What—or rather
whom—do you see?"

I studied the immediate vicinity. Violet-eyed Urd
stood knee-deep in the misty spring that bore her name.
She was filling a basin with brilliant white clay from the
spring bottom. Verdani sat beneath a shaded tree with a
wide bolt of iridescent cloth in her lap, sewing what
looked like rainbow-colored feathers to it. Besides the
two swans that nipped playfully at Urd's shapely ankles,
there wasn't another living thing in sight.

"You. Urd. Verdani. A couple of birds."

"Exactly. There are no more lesser norns. You may think it ruthless; but we killed them all long ago."

I had no idea what to say. *All of them?*

"Would you prefer centuries of us killing your kind?" Her voice dripped sarcasm.

I didn't have an answer.

"When the last of our little sisters died without issue, the final thread tying us to your race was severed forever. No longer did we decide who lived, who died, who murdered whom, who bore the child that would become king, who would start a war, and who would finish it. We did this, in the hope that your creative, inventive race would eventually produce exactly what it did—you. A free agent no one could control, angry enough, strong enough, determined enough to change the balance of power in the Worlds."

I swallowed hard. Was that what I'd done? I didn't *feel* much like a hero. I felt much more like a terrified kid confronted with a motorcycle gang after his bag of candy.

"Great." My voice cracked a little. "Just what am I supposed to do, now that you've got me?"

She regarded me with a mixture of apprehension and pity.

"You must stop Surt and the sons of Muspell from destroying the Worlds. If you can. There is no one in the nine worlds with a better opportunity. That is what you wished; was it not? To save your world?"

I gazed out across shining water. I hadn't exactly thought about what I'd do after I won. Hell, I hadn't really expected to win.

Stop Surt and the sons of Muspell?

Impossible.

I snorted. Killing Odin had been impossible, too, and I hadn't let that stop me. The fact remained, however, that all I really wanted to do was grab Gary and get back to something resembling a normal life. I didn't want to be a hero. I was too damned muscle-sore and bleary-eyed to be a hero. What I wanted was about a hundred years of sleep, and a hot bath, and about a ton of rare T-bone steaks. . . .

I did *not* want to start another madman's war.

Before I could draw breath to answer, I heard the thunder of hoofbeats. I whirled, dislodging Hugin and Munin. They squawked indignantly—it occurred to me they did a lot of that—and took wing briefly, then settled back onto my shoulders moments later.

Skuld rose gracefully to face the intruders. Rangrid sat Sleipnir like they'd been carved from the same block. Gary rode Rangrid 's golden-maned stallion. I had to repress a grin. Gary was green around the gills and hanging on for dear life.

Rangrid pulled Sleipnir to a sliding stop just in front of us.

"Give him back!"

She wore full battle armor, complete with dings, sweat marks, and bloodstains, not the gilded ceremonial stuff she'd worn to collect me from Fenrir's island. Odin's eight-legged hellhorse snapped at Skuld with long, bony jaws and wicked yellow teeth.

Skuld raised a brow in amazement. "You would defy me?"

Rangrid 's sword rang out of its scabbard. "Burn me to ashes if you can! But give him back!"

"I'm already dead," Gary gritted out, dragging his horse around to face her. "What's left that could be worse?" The question was an appropriate one, all things considered.

The fiery Norn glanced my way and—to my everlasting astonishment—dropped a wink. "Your friends are loyal, Randy Barnes." She turned, then, to stare haughtily at Rangrid. My darling valkyrie went rigid; but held her ground. It was amazing how cold Skuld's gaze could be.

"Rangrid Shield-Destroyer, it is not your place to decide what this mortal does. Nor," she added, holding up a warning hand when Rangrid started to protest angrily, "nor is it *my* place."

My beautiful, furious valkyrie faltered. "You mean . . . you didn't . . . you aren't going to . . . "

"The only one who may decide this mortal's fate is the man himself." She turned her burning gaze on me. I stiffened, swallowed hard, and tried not to flinch as sweat broke out all over me again.

"What do you choose, Randy Barnes?"

I looked at Skuld. Her expression was as inscrutable as a Chinese mandarin's. Rangrid looked tense. Gary sat calmly in the saddle, and waited for me to speak.

I caught his eye.

"Let's get *out* of here. I'm homesick as hell."

His facial muscles tightened. He bowed his head for a moment, and his hands tightened whitely on the reins. Then he met my gaze and slowly shook his head. "No, Randy. I'm afraid I won't be leaving."

The tremble that hit me left my face white and my fists even whiter.

"*What?*"

It came out more squeak than question.

"I'm staying here."

I don't know what I was going to say. Probably would have involved his mother and grandmother and her grandmother before her—momentarily forgetting Rangrid's presence—and then I would have called him traitor and other less flattering names.

But before I could do more than open my mouth, he barked, "Shut up, Randy!" in a tone I'd never heard from him. "God damn you, at least let me explain *this* time."

I rocked back on my heels. Then I clapped my lips

shut. There was a cold, sick feeling in my stomach. I couldn't look at him. I'd forgotten—in the emotional high of beating Odin, and seeing Gary again—that it was my fault he was dead.

"I'm sorry, Gary," I said quietly. "I'm sorry. For a lot of things. You know I didn't mean . . . "

"I know, Randy."

I heard him sigh. Then he muttered, "Let's go somewhere private for a minute. We need to talk."

That was the understatement of the century. I nodded toward the open doors of the Norns' hall. "Mind if we go thrash things out, Skuld?"

"You would not feel comfortable inside," she said with gentle warning. "Human senses do not . . . work properly, there. But the shade outside is cool, and the grass is sweet and deep. You are welcome to a moment of privacy if you wish it."

"Yeah. I wish it." I turned on my heel and stomped in that direction. Behind me—after a noticeable pause—I heard Gary jump to the ground and follow. I stopped beside the intricately carved wall, and quickly averted my gaze. The closer one got to the building, the harder it was to see clearly. I was glad I hadn't tried to go inside, after all. Gary stopped behind me. He squeezed my shoulder. I couldn't look at him.

"Okay," I ground out. "Convince me."

He said quietly, almost as though speaking to himself, "You always did do things the hard way, Randy." I made a rude noise and he chuckled. "You know I'm right."

I shrugged, mostly so I wouldn't have to admit that he was, as usual, right once more.

"Look, RB," Gary said patiently, "I really can't go back. Think about it. I'm dead. They buried me. Took me off the tax rolls, cancelled my Social Security number, gave my old clothes to Goodwill."

I finally looked at him. Despite grief in his eyes, his

expression was, I don't know, almost amused. Gary always had possessed that knack of adjusting to circumstances. I didn't. I wanted desperately to go back—but only to a world with Gary Vernon in it.

Something in Gary's eyes told me he understood. "Honestly, Randy, what have I got to go back to? I wouldn't have a physical body even if I tried. Here I have substance. There . . ." He grinned. "You know me, Randy. Hanging around like some vaporous Hollywood spook isn't exactly my style."

My lips twitched despite my determination not to let him sway me on this one.

"Besides, it really isn't so bad here. You know how I feel about stuff like this. It's kind of like a five-year-old kid dying and waking up in a candy factory." His voice took on a diffident tone. "You ought to understand—I feel like what I'm doing here is important."

"And what we were doing back home wasn't? In case you hadn't noticed—"

"Nothing we did back home meant squat. We were nobody there. You have a choice, Randy," he said in a hard voice. "You can go back home, find some nice girl to marry, and have a couple of hell-raising rug-rats with her; maybe save enough money to buy a piece of land, build a house."

He turned away, but not before I saw a suspicious film brighten his eyes.

Then, slowly, I saw the tension drain from his face, and he looked over his shoulder to where Skuld and Rangrid stood watching us. Rangrid looked as though she wanted to shake some answers out of Skuld, and didn't quite dare try it. Skuld ignored the valkyrie.

"Or," he added in a lighter tone, "you can stay here. I get the feeling Skuld had made you an offer just before we showed up."

I scuffed a booted toe into the thick grass and dug

up a divot; then guiltily tamped it back into place. The Vernon charm had done it again, curse him. I didn't have to like it—but he was right. Everything I'd fought and damned near died for was useless. The s.o.b. was staying. I scowled; then sighed.

No, not entirely useless. Odin was dead. That counted for a lot. Without him around to screw things up, maybe the world would get along all right.

Then I remembered Surt and the sons of Muspell, and kicked another divot out of the grass.

And what about the rest of the gods? They weren't likely to take Odin's murder lying down. Thor had already tried to kill me once. If I went back to the world I'd been born in, I'd be a sitting duck for any potshot the gods cared to take.

But in Valhalla, with an army at my back . . .

Hell, maybe I could even convince the Aesir they were better off without Odin, and get them to throw in with me and the Einherjar.

Crazier things *had* happened.

I looked up at Gary. He stood with his arms folded patiently, waiting for me to think things through.

"So," I stalled, "I always knew you'd be an officer someday, Vernon. I guess you'll get to be a general here, huh?"

His eyes glinted briefly as he acknowledged my surrender—on one point, at least—then he grimaced.

"No, we don't run that kind of a military organization here, Randy."

"Huh? Why not? What do you do, for Christ's sake?"

He shrugged. "Mostly practice hacking at each other. The invasion is expected soon, so we just fight it out every day in one great big horde until it gets here."

I looked at him in disbelief; then snorted.

"Jeez, Vernon, that's the dumbest thing I've ever heard. Didn't you learn anything? And you were going to be an *officer*? I thought you guys learned strategy, and battle planning, and all that crap."

Gary raised one eyebrow in my direction. "You got any better ideas?"

"Well, sure. You could start training programs. I mean, those guys are pitiful. Pitiful! Hacking at each other like a bunch of Stone Age numbskulls. I mean, if you really want to beat someone in a war, there are lots of better ways to go about winning it. Christ, Gary, even the newbies we got stuck with were better than *that*."

He grinned. "Well, yeah, that's a good point, Randy. But who's going to do it? There's no one to lead this ragtag army—and they sure aren't going to listen to me!"

I shot him a dark look. "Vernon . . ."

He waited.

"You set me up, admit it."

He grinned; then sobered again almost immediately. "Randy, look at it this way. The whole time we were in the Army back home, you spent more time bitching about the system than any man I know. You complained about stupid officers; you moaned about how things *should* be done; and about what you'd do if you had half a chance. Well, dammit, you've got more than half a chance right here, handed to you on a silver platter."

A faint breeze stirred my hair.

He chuckled nastily. "It's almost poetic justice, wouldn't you say? You actually went to hell to prove your point. Well, good buddy, you got rid of Odin. And now you've got a chance to rewrite the rules. You've got a whole army ready to let you tell it what to do next. The Einherjar already think you're the hottest thing since bottled beer." He shrugged then. "You've already proven you *can*. All you have left is to decide whether or not you *will*."

I didn't care for the implications.

If I left Valhalla now, I'd end up feeling for the rest of my life like I'd run out on him. On the whole world.

Which would only be the truth.

Besides, what would I ever amount to, back there? Shopkeeper? Short-order cook? Even if I went to college, even if I managed to make a ton of money . . .

Surt and his cronies weren't about to call off their invasion just because it might inconvenience Randy Barnes, Odin-Slayer. In fact, if I were Surt, I'd make damned sure I *did* invade; especially if Odin's killer was a big enough fool to leave Valhalla and the Einherjar in disorganized chaos.

Gary had made his point.

I didn't know if the Einherjar would follow me if I stayed, although he seemed to think they would, and he knew them. Hell, if I were a soldier in the employ of a god, and somebody with balls enough to kill him came along . . .

Maybe they would follow me, at that.

I just *might* be able to make a real difference.

At the very least, I'd have a job. That thought almost made me grin. I met Gary's eyes. And he, of course, knew my decision before I did.

"Right," I said briskly.

Gary *did* grin. "Right. We can work out the, uh, details later."

I nodded.

He clapped my shoulder. "Welcome to Hell, RB!"

I gave him a sour grin and jerked my head toward Skuld.

"I've got a little unfinished business over there."

He chuckled. "What's one goddess, more or less, for the guy who killed Odin?"

I snorted disgustedly and started toward Skuld. Obviously, Gary had not spent any amount of time in Skuld's company. She still scared me spitless.

I plunged feet-first into it before I lost my nerve.

"Okay, Skuld, you gave me these birds, and they'll be

useful. But what about Fenrir and Sleipnir? Can I trust them?"

She laughed, a tinkling, crackling sound in the super-heated air around us. "My dear hero, it's a free universe. I have absolutely no idea. You'll just have to take your chances, I'm afraid."

To my surprise, I grinned, heartened by her honesty. "Yeah. I guess I will. And so," I added grimly, "will *Surt*."

I thought I detected a glint of satisfaction in her burning eyes. "Yes." She smiled through the heat haze. Her teeth glowed like embers. "Do not doubt your strength of will, Randy, nor doubt that you possess that which makes a man a hero. You have made yourself what you are." Her smile widened. "Your children with Rangrid will be something truly to behold. I look forward to them with pleasure. Provided, of course, the plans of our southern friends don't interfere."

I nodded.

Rangrid looked from Skuld to me and back again. "I . . . don't understand . . . You're not going to—"

I came to Rangrid's rescue. "Skuld wanted to return Hugin and Munin to Valhalla. She figured I'd find them useful. What's the matter; don't you think feathers become me? Come to think of it, birdshit doesn't. How the hell did Odin clean it off his clothes?"

"Birdshit. . . ?" Rangrid was looking a little round-eyed again.

"You'd best explain things after you get her back to Valhalla," Skuld suggested dryly.

"I think you're right. Thanks. For, um, everything."

The Norn nodded gravely.

Rangrid gave me a hand up. I settled myself on Sleipnir's forward set of withers. Skuld lifted a hand in farewell; then we were transferring between worlds with a blur and thunderclap.

Chapter Twenty-One

When we emerged in Valhalla, the Einherjar were milling around, clustered into little knots of intense conversation; but no one had left the scene of battle, except—notably—Tyr and Thor. Fenrir snarled at Sleipnir, who trumpeted a challenge right back.

"Hey." I punched Sleipnir's arched neck. "Chill out."

He shook his neck, but subsided. Fenrir was still growling; but not as loudly.

"You, too," I muttered.

The wolf whined; then yawned, and settled back on his haunches again.

"How did you do that?" Rangrid demanded.

I glanced around. "I dunno."

She grinned. "That's what I like about you."

I'll steal a kiss anywhere, anytime. Especially Rangrid's.

Unfortunately, the Einherjar caught sight of us right about then. A howling tumult assaulted our ears. Gradually the noise resolved itself into discernible syllables: "Ran . . . dy! Ran . . . dy! Ran . . . dy!"

I didn't much feel like repeating Odin's pompous salute. I just grinned tiredly, and slid to the ground. It

was a long way down. Rangrid was right behind me.
Fenrir damn near knocked me off my feet. He licked my
face half off, and whined joyously in the back of his
throat. Wolves don't bark; but Fenrir uttered a shrill little
yip, and took my whole shoulder very gently in his teeth.

A love bite from the Fenris Wolf . . .

I stretched on tiptoes to rub his ears, which evidently
placated him, because he settled to his haunches and
didn't appear to have the slightest intention of moving
again until I did. Which brought up a very good question. Now what?

"Well," I began in a practical fashion, "I'm hungry. I
could eat a horse—"

Sleipnir snorted indignantly.

"—Make that a cow. Sorry, Trigger. And if I'm going to
do anything constructive with this army, I'd better get
some sleep first. I'm just about out on my feet." I was,
too. My whole body weaved drunkenly at each step.

"Let's get you inside," Gary suggested firmly. He
caught his grandmother's eye. "Got him?"

Rangrid responded by picking me up bodily.

"Hey—"

Gary got my legs, and I found myself sprawled
between them like a limp carpet. I was ignominiously
carried into the looming Valhall. Shouts and cheers followed our progress. My face burned. Fenrir and Sleipnir
trailed suspiciously, while Hugin and Munin sailed into
the Valhall ahead of us.

I had no idea what the Einherjar thought of all this.
For once, I found that I was too bloody tired to care.
By the time they'd carried me the seeming miles to
Rangrid's bedroom, I was already so relaxed the Valhall
had blurred into one confused image of endless,
overturned tables. I remembered vaguely mumbling
to Gary that I'd see him in the morning, to muster the
troops. Then they lowered me into the bed, and I

relaxed with a self-satisfied sigh. My new pets winged into the chamber and alighted on the headboard. Gary disappeared at some point, I wasn't sure when.

I lay where they'd dropped me and let Rangrid pull off my clothes. They were filthy—mud-caked, blood-stained. But then, so was I, from scalp to toenails. I closed my eyes while she sponged off the worst of the muck. She seemed to understand that I was too tired to face a full bath. When she crawled in beside me, I curled against her softness under a warm fur, and listened to her breaths.

I didn't fall asleep right away, though. I couldn't. My body was inert—I was too tired to move—but my brain was still revved up and going full speed. All I could think about was that horde of dead humanity waiting for me to do something useful with it. What, exactly, did I have to work with? I considered with growing dismay the list of possibilities. Surely there were a few generals in that motley mess I could rely on?

Would Patton be here? He was another traffic accident, like Gary. But when had Odin begun to pilfer the "wrong" men? And—for another instance—how about Caesar? He'd been murdered by a bunch of civilians. The problem with the Einherjar was, only so many of them were going to be real "heroes," the kind who died doing a good job, or were just unlucky enough to be at the wrong place at the wrong time. How many more were there who simply hadn't dodged fast enough, or ignored orders, or were too damn stupid to avoid trouble?

The kind of soldiers I wanted were the ones smart enough to live through it and go home to die of old age.

And what about my two self-appointed guardians, Fenrir and Sleipnir? Tomorrow morning they might tear each other's throats out—or mine. I had no idea whether I could trust either one of the murderous beasts.

At least I had Hugín and Munin. I would need the kind of information they could provide. I had to know what was happening, where it was happening, and who was making it happen.

I fell asleep thinking this must be what it felt like to be an officer—I was worried about everything.

When I woke up, I was almost too stiff and sore to move—even after Rangrid rubbed an evil-smelling ointment into my muscles. I sat up, but only with a great expenditure of pain, and getting my feet onto the floor took an act of supreme will. My throat was so hoarse I could barely whisper. Ugly bruises and raw marks from Odin's noose circled my neck. If I was going to take Odin's place, it would've been nice to have inherited his healing powers.

At least I was alive.

Rangrid fussed over me like a worried mother. She helped me dress when I couldn't lift my arms high enough to get them into the tunic she'd found for me to wear. Then she sat me down on the edge of the bed and laced my boots for me. When I was finally clothed, Rangrid rested her arms on my shoulders, and stood between my knees. Her long, unbound hair tickled my face.

"Ready to turn Valhalla upside down, hero?" she murmured.

Her tone was unconvincingly demure.

I laughed rustily, and drew a strand of her hair across my fingertip.

"I thought I did that yesterday, Rangrid. I think today I'll just start with breakfast and see how it goes from there."

She bent to kiss my lips softly and smiled. "In that case . . . last one to the table's a rotten egg." She bolted. Rangrid was out the door before I could even struggle to my feet.

"No fair!" I yelled after her. A tinkling laugh floated back my way.

Showoff.

When I arrived in the main hall, the scene was one of complete chaos—worse even than the previous morning. There was a lot more broken furniture. Unconscious bodies littered the filthy floor as far as the eye could see.

At the nearest table, Gary had cleared away a spot in the general grime, and had nudged aside several slumbering—no, passed-out drunken—companions to provide a seat for the three of us. He and Rangrid had already helped themselves to breakfast, and were eating when I sat down. Rangrid scooted over to sit beside me. She glanced contentedly from her grandson to her new lover—me, I thought with an amazed flush of realization—then back at her grandson again. She grinned and bit into something that looked and smelled wonderful.

Gary looked so chipper, I wanted to hit him. I felt like a recently mashed potato.

"Have some eggs," he said, dumping about seven fried eggs onto my plate from a nearby serving platter. "And bacon."

"Good God, Vernon, *I've* still got to worry about cholesterol."

He grinned unrepentantly. "Here, try these, too." He dumped several small, round lumps of greasy fried dough beside my stack of eggs.

His expression was entirely too innocent for my liking. I glanced apprehensively at Rangrid. Her eyes twinkled, but she wouldn't talk.

"What the hell are those?" They didn't smell like hush puppies.

"You always were a grouch before breakfast—when's the last time you had any coffee? Don't ask what they are; just eat 'em. They're great, if you don't know what's in 'em."

"Vernon . . ."

He grinned, and waved an empty fork to forestall me long enough to chew one up and swallow it. "Deep-fried goat testicles."

I turned green, and carefully nudged them to one side of my plate. Gary laughed. Rangrid chuckled, then lifted a pitcher and snagged a cup.

"That smells like coffee!"

She threw me a reproachful look. "It *is* coffee. We're not entirely in the dark ages here, you know. Some of our best guests grew coffee before they joined the guerrillas and got . . . uh . . . collected."

Her look was uncertain, so I just nodded. "Speaking of the, er, collectees, I'm going to need help. You two are my officially appointed general staff. The first thing we need to do is get the men sorted into some sort of order, and I'll need a list of potential officers, men with command experience, sound judgment. How soon do you think we can get that done?"

Gary looked thoughtful.

Rangrid answered. "I'll get my sisters busy on it right away. They were a little stunned yesterday; but I did a lot of talking last night after you fell asleep, and they've come around." Her eyes twinkled. "It's funny, isn't it, how you can change attitudes overnight by giving folks hope? They're ready and willing to do whatever you think needs to be done. Some of my sisters can form the Einherjar into groups. While the men are being assigned by time period, or weapons expertise, or whatever, others can poll them about command experience. Best suggestion for sorting them out?"

"By weapons expertise," Gary suggested, "but only for the last one hundred years, or so. Then divvy them up by when they were born, about one hundred years per group, on back to however far back you've been collecting them. That sound about right, Randy?"

"Yeah, that should put men with roughly similar technology and tactics into approximately common groups. We can refine assignments later, after we have a better idea what we've got under arms out there."

"Anything else for today?" Gary asked.

I considered; then shook my head. "Not for you two. Rangrid, get your sisters together, and get that list of commanders back to me as soon as possible. Gary, I'd like to see a list of available weapons systems. Then we've got to get the mess in this building cleaned up, and figure out how to get some discipline established. Without discipline, we'll lose the first skirmish. Where the hell are Hugin and Munin? I need information, stat." A young boy of about eleven slipped in beside us, and retrieved our breakfast dishes. He grinned at me, then vanished into the crowd. I scowled. "And what the hell am I going to do with all these civilians?"

Nobody had an answer to that one. Not that I'd really expected one. Command responsibility is a bitch. My ravens flapped in from outdoors somewhere, and listened very gravely as I gave them instructions. First: what were the Aesir doing? Second: what was Loki doing? Third: what was Hel doing, and did she consider my contract with her fulfilled? Fourth: what was Surt up to in Muspellheim? And fifth: what was everybody else in the rest of the Nine Worlds doing?

The ravens looked a little awed by my demands; but obediently flew off on their mission. Rangrid left Gary and me huddled in conference—while the civilians I didn't know what to do with quietly cleaned up the hall, roused the slumbering warriors, and got them organized for breakfast. When the noise level rose to that of a minor tornado, Gary and I moved outside. We found a quiet spot under the eaves, and got busy with paper, pencil, and the calculator he'd been carrying the night of the accident.

The two of us made a good team. Compared to getting here in the first place and getting Odin out of the way, this was going to be a snap. All I had to do was organize my troops, figure out how to retrieve the generals I needed from wherever they'd ended up, learn what kind of enemy I was really up against, set up training programs, procure modern weapons systems, figure out what in the world to do with those wretched, inconvenient civilians . . .

By the end of the week I was beginning to think we might actually have a chance. Gary and I had decided to organize our forces along the lines of the most sensibly run military model we had ever run across—Robert Heinlein's *Starship Troopers*. We split up the Einherjar, putting modern military personnel in temporary command of each section. Our theory was simple: modern personnel had a better grasp of a wide range of weapons systems, and a wide range of strategies and tactics. Under their watchful eyes, the troops were being run through weapons drill.

Gary and I sat down for twenty-four solid hours, poring over the list of commanders Rangrid compiled. We muttered, gnashed our teeth, and pulled our hair.

"Have we got Patton anywhere?"

"No, dammit; is Lawrence of Arabia on any of your lists?"

"Hell, no. Christ, where's Rommel?"

"We've got Genghis Khan's third nephew."

"Great. Isn't he the one who jumped onto what's-his-face's sword when he was drunk?"

"Yup."

"Get rid of him."

After we'd figured out who to keep, who to dump, and who to bargain for, I made arrangements with a balky Hel to meet with her. I wanted to trade three of my discards for each of the worthwhile generals and other command-grade officers in her domain, which would cull most of the crazy-ass Berserkers from my ranks.

What I wanted to do was eliminate the "die-for-glory" crowd and leave a solid "kill-for-glory" core, which I felt possibly could be hammered into a legitimate fighting force. I didn't really want to do any more bargaining with Hel; but she had what I wanted, and I thought I could offer her something *she* wanted in return.

All in all, I was pretty well pleased with progress. Hell, I was even beginning to look forward to the coming challenge. We had good men, and good plans. We were even planning to pilfer a few nukes here and there, along with the other equipment I intended to steal. If the enemy had the World Serpent to blow poison, well, we'd just hit them with a few multimegaton devices before they could bring their complete arsenal into play.

A lot of my preliminary plans were going to depend on what Hugin and Munin brought back. I was vitally interested in the sons of Muspell and their allies the Frost Giants, and moderately concerned about Odin's kith and kin back in Asgard. Every couple of days I'd look up at the vermilion sky and wonder what was taking them so long; then shrug and tell myself that a really detailed report took time to assemble.

I asked Gary once, between reviewing pike-thrusting demonstrations from ten different cultures, what—exactly—a Frost Giant looked like.

"You remember the Jolly Green Giant?"

"Yeah."

"Not like that."

"You're a big help."

"I do my best."

Rangrid and I made love several times a night. I marveled at her recuperative powers—not hers personally, her ability to restore *me*. Once I had finally satisfied her, she would snuggle beside me, and drift off to sleep. I would lie awake in her arms far into the night, going over in my head everything Gary and Rangrid had reported to me; reviewing plans to increase esprit de corps and discipline; and still wondering what I was going to do with all the civilians in Valhalla.

I didn't want to send them to Hel—and wouldn't, unless she insisted on taking them as "payment" for the generals I needed. I didn't like the idea of turning over any of those people to someone like Hel. But I didn't know what I *could* do with them. I certainly couldn't send them back to Midgard. None of them seemed inclined to leave. Maybe I could train them to fight. Morale was certainly picking up, and everyone was likely to have real motive to fight, if the rumors I'd heard about Surt and Muspellheim were true.

A faint scritching at the door brought me to full alertness. I rose carefully to my feet, and groped for the Biter; then tiptoed to open the door. Hugin and Munin sailed in and perched on my shoulders. I relaxed. The Biter disappeared back into its sheath.

"Well, you're finally back," I whispered to my feathery spies. "So tell all."

Taking turns, first one and then the other, they whispered into my ears. Before the first raven had gotten three sentences out, I was groping for a seat.

"Whoa—back up—how many did you say they had?"

"Wait—how many is a beejillion?"

"How *many* more than a googol?"

"And they look like what? Muspell has *what* for weapons?"

As the birds whispered facts and figures into my ears there in the dark, I listened in growing horror. The Frost Giants, the Dark Elves, Niflhel's denizens in revolt, civil war in Asgard, a real barnburner of a mess developing on Earth, and Muspell—holy cow, what was I supposed to do about Muspell?

We were in deep shit. But damn, if it wasn't going to be one roaring helluva fight. And victory . . . ?

Well, stranger things *had* happened!

About the Author

Linda Evans was born on Christmas night, carrying the family tradition of first-born daughters into its third generation. Ms. Evans achieved national attention as 1991–1992 president of the North-Central Florida Sportsman's Association, the NRA's Outstanding Club in America for 1992. Ms. Evans has volunteered many hours as a firearms safety instructor, and delivered speeches at the 1991 Gun Rights Policy Conference and across the country on the subject of firearms safety and civil rights.

Ms. Evans is also a volunteer at the Florida Museum of Natural History, and an amateur jeweler. She shares living quarters with, among other sentient beings, an inherited cat named for Jack the Ripper.

If you enjoyed this adventure, you should try *The Bard's Tale*™ novels, also from Baen. Here is an excerpt from *Castle of Deception* by Mercedes Lackey and Josepha Sherman.

0-671-72125-9 * 288 pages * $5.99

As the minstrel troop rode and rattled along the wide dirt road, the day was as bright and cheery as something out of a story, full of bird song and pleasant little breezes.

Kevin hardly noticed. He was too busy struggling with his mule to keep it from lagging lazily behind.

"Here, boy." One of the musicians, a red-clad fiddler with instrument case strapped to his back like Kevin, handed the bardling a switch broken from a bush. "Wave this at him. He'll keep moving."

The fiddler's eyes were kind enough, but it seemed to Kevin that his voice practically dripped with condescension. *Thinks I've never ridden before,* Kevin thought, but he managed a tight smile and a "Thanks." It didn't help that the man was right; as long as the mule could see the switch out of the corner of an eye, it kept up a nice, brisk pace.

The North Road cut through brushland for a time, then through stands of saplings, then at last through true forest, green and lush in the springtime. This was royal land, not ceded to any of the nobles, and the road was kept clear, Kevin knew, by the spells of royal magicians. But those nice, neat spells hardly applied to the wildness on either side. The bardling, trying to pretend he'd travelled this way a hundred times, couldn't help wondering if bandits or even dark creatures, orcs or worse, were hiding in there.

Oh, nonsense! He was letting his Master's fussing get to him. It was forest, only forest. No one could see anything sinister in that tranquil greenery.

He'd let the switch drop and the mule was lagging again. Kevin waved it at the beast yet again. When that didn't seem to do any good, he gave it a good whack on the rump. The mule grunted in surprise and broke into a bone-jarring trot, overtaking the wagons and most of the riders. The equally surprised bardling jounced painfully in the saddle, lute banging against his back. For a moment Kevin wished he'd kept it in its case rather than out for quick playing. Struggling to keep his stirrups and his balance, he was sure he heard snickers from the troop.

Then, just as suddenly, the mule dropped back into its easygoing walk. Kevin nearly slammed his face into the animal's neck. This time, as he straightened himself in the saddle, he *knew* he'd heard muffled laughter. Without a word, he pulled the mule back into the troop.

Although the minstrels kept up a steady patter of cheerful conversation and song all around him, Kevin clamped his lips resolutely together after that. He had given them enough entertainment already!

It wasn't helping his increasingly sour mood that every time someone looked his way, he could practically hear that someone thinking, *Poor little boy, out on his own!*

"I'm *not* a baby!" he muttered under his breath.

"What's that?" A plump, motherly woman, bright yellow robes making her look like a buttercup, brought her mare up next to his mule. "Is something wrong, child?"

"I am not a child." Kevin said the words very carefully. "I am not a full Bard yet, I admit it, but I am the apprentice to — "

"Oh, well, bardling, then!" Her smile was so amused that Kevin wanted to shout at her, Leave me alone! Instead, he asked, as levelly as he could:

"Just how far away is Count Volmar's castle?"

"Oh, two days' ride or so, weather permitting, not more."

"And we're going to stay on this road?"

"Well, of course! We can hardly go cross-country through the woods with the wagon! Besides, that would be a silly thing to do: the North Road leads right to the castle. Very convenient."

"Very," Kevin agreed, mind busy. He hadn't dared hope that the castle would be so easy to find, even for someone who'd never been there before. Even for someone who just might happen to be travelling alone.

That night, the minstrels made camp in a circle of song and firelight that forced back the forest's shadow. Dinner had been cheese and only slightly stale bread from the inn, water from a nearby stream, and rabbits the older children had brought down with their slings. Now Kevin, sitting on a dead log to one side, nearly in darkness, watched the happy, noisy circle with a touch of envy. What must it be like to be part of a group like that? They were probably all related, one big, wild, merry family.

But then the bardling reminded himself that these were only minstrels, wandering folk whose musical talents just weren't good enough to let them ever be Bards. He should be pitying them, not envying them. Maybe they even envied him . . . ?

No. Two of the women were gossiping about him, he was sure of it, glancing his way every now and then, hiding giggles behind their hands. Kevin straightened, trying to turn his face into a regal mask. Unfortunately, the log on which he sat picked that moment to fall apart, dumping him on the ground in a cloud of moldy dust.

Predictably, every one of the troop was looking his way just then. Predictably, they all burst into laughter. Kevin scrambled to his feet, face burning. He'd had it with being babied and laughed at and made to feel a fool!

"Hey, bardling!" Berak called. "Where are you going?"

"To sleep," Kevin said shortly.

"Out there in the dark? You'll be warmer — and safer — here with us."

Kevin pretended he hadn't heard. Wrapping himself in his cloak, he settled down as best he could. The ground was harder and far colder than he'd expected. He really would have been more comfortable with the minstrels.

But then, he didn't really intend to sleep . . . not really. . . . It was just that he was weary from the day's riding. . . .

Kevin woke with a start, almost too cold and stiff to move. What — where — All around him was forest, still dark with night, but overhead he could see patches of pale, blue-gray sky through the canopy of leaves and realized it wasn't too far from morning. He struggled to his feet, jogging in place to warm himself up, wincing as his body complained, then picked up his lute. Safe and dry in its case, it hadn't suffered any harm.

Stop stalling! he told himself.

Any moment now, one of the minstrels was bound to wake up, and then it would be too late. Kevin ducked behind a tree to answer his chilly body's demands, then tiptoed over to where the horses and his mule were tied. One horse whuffled at him, but to his relief, none of them whinnied. Although his hands were still stiff with cold, the bardling managed to get his mule bridled and saddled. He hesitated an uncertain moment, looking back at the sleeping camp, wondering if he really was doing the right thing.

Of course I am! I don't want the count to think I'm a baby who can't take care of himself.

Kevin led the mule as silently as he could down the road till the camp was out of sight, then swung up into the saddle.

"Come on, mule," he whispered. "We have a lot of ground to cover."

The minstrels would be discovering his absence any moment now. But, encumbered with their wagons and children as they were, they would never be able to overtake him. Kevin kicked the mule; frisky from the still chilly air, it actually broke into a prance. The bardling straightened proudly in the saddle.

At last! He finally felt like a hero riding off into adventure.

By nightfall, Kevin wasn't so sure of that. He was tired and sore from being in the saddle all day, and hungry as well. If only he had thought to take some food with him! The mule wasn't too happy with its snatches of grass and leaves, but at least it could manage, but the few mouthfuls of whatever berries Kevin had been able to recognize hadn't done much to fill his stomach.

Overhead, the sky was still clear blue, but the forest on either side was already nearly black, and a chill was starting up from the cooling earth. Kevin shivered, listening to the twitter of birds settling down for the night and the faint, mysterious rustlings and stirrings that could have been made by small animals or . . . other things. He shivered again, and told himself not to be stupid. He was probably already on Count Volmar's lands, and there wasn't going to be anything dangerous this close to a castle.

He hoped.

"We're not going to be able to go much further today," he told the mule reluctantly. "We'd better find a place to camp for the night."

At least he had flint and steel in his pouch. After stumbling about in the dim light for a time, Kevin managed to find enough dead branches to build himself a decent little fire in the middle of a small, rocky clearing. The firelight danced off the surrounding trees as the bardling sat huddling before the flames, feeling the welcome warmth steal through him.

The fire took off the edge of his chill. But it couldn't help the fact that he was still tired and so hungry his stomach ached. The bardling tried to ignore his discomfort by taking out his lute and working his way through a series of practice scales.

As soon as he stopped, the night flowed in around him, his small fire not enough to hold back the darkness, the little forest chirpings and rustlings not enough to break the heavy silence. Kevin struck out bravely into the bouncy strains of "The Miller's Boy." But the melody that had sounded so bright and sprightly with the inn around it seemed thin and lonely here. Kevin's fingers faltered, then stopped. He sat listening to the night for a moment, feeling the weight of the forest's indifference pressing down on him. He roused himself with an effort and put his lute back in its case, safe from the night's gathering mist. Those nice, dull, safe days back at the inn didn't seem quite so unattractive right now. . . .

Oh, nonsense! What sort of hero are you, afraid of a little loneliness?

He'd never, Kevin realized, been alone before, really alone, in his life. Battling with homesickness, the bardling banked the fire and curled up once more in his cloak.

After what seemed an age, weariness overcame misery, and he slipped into uneasy sleep.

Scornful laughter woke him. Kevin sat bolt upright, staring up into eyes that glowed an eerie green in the darkness. Demons!

No, no, whatever these beings were, they weren't demonic. After that first terrified moment, he could make out the faces that belonged with those eyes, and gasped in wonder. The folk surrounding him were tall and graceful, a touch too graceful, too slender, to be human. Pale golden hair framed fair, fine-boned, coldly beautiful faces set with those glowing, slanted eyes, and Kevin whispered in wonder:

"Elves . . ."

He had heard about them of course, everyone had. They were even supposed to share some of King Amber's lands with humans — though every now and then bitter feelings surfaced between the two races. But Kevin had never seen any of the elf-folk, White or Dark, good or evil, never even dreamed he might.

"Why, how clever the child is!" The elvish voice was clear as crystal, cold with mockery.

"Clever in one way, at least!" said another.

"So stupid in all other ways!" a third mocked. "Look at the way he sleeps on the ground, like a poor little animal."

"Look at the trail he left, so that anyone, anything could track him."

"Look at the way he sleeps like a babe, without a care in the world."

"A human child."

"A careless child!"

The elf man who'd first spoken laughed softly. "A foolish child that anyone can trick!"

So alien a light glinted in the slanted eyes that Kevin's breath caught in his throat. Everyone knew elvish whims were unpredictable; it was one of the reasons there could never be total ease between elf and human. If these folk decided to loose their magic on him, he wouldn't have a chance of defending himself. "My lords," he began, very, very carefully, "if I have somehow offended you, pray forgive me."

"Offended!" the elf echoed coldly. "As if anything a child such as you could do would be strong enough to offend us!"

That stung. "My lord, I — I know I may not look like much to someone like you." To his intense mortification, his empty stomach chose that moment to complain with a loud gurgle. Kevin bit his lip, sure that those keen, pointed elf ears had picked up the sound. All he could do was continue as best he could, "But — but that doesn't give you the right to insult me."

"Oh, how brave it is!" The elf man rested one foot lightly on a rock and leaned forward, fierce green gaze flicking over Kevin head to foot. "Bah, look at yourself! Sleeping on bare ground when there are soft pine boughs to make you a bed. Aching with hunger when the forest holds more than enough to feed one scrawny human. Leaving a trail anyone could follow and carrying no useful weapon at all. How could we *not* insult such ignorance?"

The elf straightened, murmuring a short phrase in the elvish tongue to the others.

They laughed and faded soundlessly into the night, but not before one of them had tossed a small sack at Kevin's feet.

"Our gift, human," the elf man said. "Inside is food enough to keep you alive. And no, it is not bespelled. We would not waste magic on you."

With that, the elf turned to leave, then paused, looking back over his shoulder at the bardling. With inhuman bluntness, he said, "I hope, child, for your sake that you are simply naive and not stupid. In time, either flaw will get you killed, but at least the first can be corrected."

The alien eyes blazed into Kevin's own for a moment longer. Then the elf was gone, and the bardling was left alone in the night, more frightened than he would ever have admitted.

He's wrong! Kevin told himself defiantly once his heart had stopped racing. *Just because I'm a bardling, not a — a woodsman who's never known anything but the forest doesn't make me naive or stupid!*

Deciding that didn't stop him from rummaging in the little sack. The elvish idea of food that would keep him alive seemed to be nothing more exciting than flat wafers of bread. But when he managed to choke one of the dry things down, it calmed his complaining stomach so nicely that the bardling sighed with relief and actually slipped back into sleep.

Kevin stood with head craned back, sunlight warm on his face, feeling the last of last night's fears melting away. How could he possibly hold onto fear when it was bright, clear morning and all around him the air was filled with bird song?

Maybe the whole thing had been only a dream?

No. The sack of wafers was quite real. Kevin gnawed thoughtfully on one, then gave another to his mule, which lipped it up with apparent delight. He saddled and bridled the animal, then climbed aboard, still trying to figure out what the purpose of that midnight meeting had been.

At last he shook his head in dismissal. All the stories said the elf folk, being the nonhuman race they were, had truly bizarre senses of humor, sometimes outright cruel by human standards. What had happened last night must surely have been just another nasty elvish idea of a joke.

"Come on, mule. Let's get going." At least he wasn't hungry.

The road sloped up, first gently then more steeply, much to the mule's distaste. When it grew too steep, Kevin dismounted now and again to give the animal a rest, climbing beside it.

But at last, after a quiet day of riding and walking, they reached the crest. Kevin stared out in awe at a wild mountain range of tall gray crags, some of them high enough to be snowcapped even in spring. They towered over rolling green fields neatly sectioned into farms. On the nearest crag, surrounded by open space stood:

"Count Volmar's castle!" Kevin cried triumphantly. "It has to be!"

The castle hadn't been built for beauty. Heavy and squat, it seemed to crouch possessively on its crag like some ancient grey beast of war staring down at the count's lands. But Kevin didn't care. It was the first castle he had ever seen, and he thought it was wonderful, a true war castle dating from the days when heroes held back the forces of Darkness. Bright banners flew from the many towers, softening some of the harshness, and the bardling could see from here that the castle's gates were open. By squinting he could make out the devices on those banners: the count's black boar on an azure field.

"We've done it," he told the mule. "That is definitely the castle of Count Volmar."

He forgot about elves and hunger, loneliness and mocking minstrels. Excitement shivering through him, the bardling kicked his mule forward. Soon, soon, the real adventure was going to begin!

INTERLUDE THE FIRST

Count Volmar, tall, lean and graying of brown hair and beard, sat seemingly at ease in his private solar before a blazing fireplace, a wine-filled goblet of precious glass in his hand. He looked across the small room at the woman who sat there, and raised the goblet in appreciation. She nodded at the courtesy, her dark green eyes flickering with cold amusement in the firelight.

Carlotta, princess, half-sister to King Amber himself, could not, Volmar knew, be much younger than his own mid-forties, and yet she could easily have passed for a far younger woman. Not the slightest trace of age marred the pale, flawless skin or the glorious masses of deep red hair turned to bright flame by the firelight.

Sorcery, he thought, and then snickered at his own vapid musings so that he nearly choked on his own wine. Of course it was sorcery! Carlotta was an accomplished sorceress, and about as safe, for all her beauty, as a snake.

About as honorable, too.

Not that he was one to worry overmuch about honor.

"The boy is safely ensconced, I take it?" Carlotta's smile was as chill as her lovely eyes.

"Yes. He has a place among the squires. Who, I might add, have been given to understand that he's so far beneath them they needn't bother even to acknowledge his presence — that to do so, in fact, would demean their own status. By now, the boy is surely thoroughly disillusioned about nobility and questioning his own worth."

"He suspects nothing, then? Good. We don't want him showing any awkward sparks of initiative." Carlotta sipped delicately from her goblet. "We don't want him copying his Master."

Volmar's mouth tightened. Oh, yes, the Bard, that cursed Bard. He could remember so clearly, even though it was over thirty years ago, how it had been, himself just barely an adult and Carlotta only . . . how old? Only thirteen? Maybe so, but she had already been as ambitious as he. More so. Already mistress of the Dark Arts despite her youth, the princess had attempted to seize the throne from her half-brother.

And almost made it, Volmar thought, then corrected that to: We *almost made it.*

Amber had been only a prince back then, on the verge of the succession. His father had been old, and there hadn't been any other legal heir; Carlotta, as the court had been so eager to gossip, was only Amber's half-sister, her mother quite unknown.

But there were always ways around such awkward little facts. Once Amber had been declared dead — or so it was believed — in heroic battle (when actually, Volmar thought wryly, Carlotta's magics had turned him to stone), the poor old king would surely have . . . pined away. Volmar grinned sharply. Why, the shock alone would have finished him; Carlotta wouldn't have needed to waste a spell. The people, even if they had, by some bizarre chance, come to suspect her of wrong-doing, would have had no choice but to accept Carlotta, with her half-share of the Blood Royal, as queen.

Ambitious little girl . . . Volmar thought with approval. *What a pity she didn't succeed. Sorceress or no, she would have been too wise to try ruling alone. She would have taken a consort.*

And who better than one of her loyal supporters? Even one whose role in the attempted usurpation had never become public.

Volmar suddenly realized he was grimacing, and forced himself to relax. His late father had been an avid supporter of the old king, and if he had ever found out his own son was a traitor . . .

But he hadn't. And of course if only Carlotta had safely become queen, it wouldn't have mattered. The only traitors then would have been those who failed to acknowledge her!

If only . . . Bah!

Carlotta *would* have become queen if it hadn't been for the boy's Master, that accursed Bard and his allies. . . .

"Forget the past, Volmar."

The count started, thrown abruptly back into the present. "You . . . have learned to read minds . . . ?" If the sorceress suspected he planned to use her to place a crown on his own head, he was dead. Worse than dead.

"You must learn to guard your expressions, my lord. Your thoughts were there for anyone with half an eye to read."

Not all *my thoughts,* the count thought, giddy with relief.

Carlotta got restlessly to her feet, dark green gown swirling about her elegant form. Volmar, since she was, after all, a princess and he only a count, stood as well: politic courtesy.

She never noticed. "Enough of the past," the sorceress repeated, staring into the flames. "We must think of what can be done *now*."

Volmar moved warily to stand beside her, and caught a flicker of alien movement in the flames. Faces . . . ah. Carlotta was absently creating images of the boy, the bardling. "Why do you suppose he sent the boy here?" the princess murmured. "And why just now? What purpose could the old man possibly have? You've convinced me the manuscript is merely a treatise on lute music." She glanced sharply at Volmar. "It *is,* isn't it?"

"Of course," Volmar said easily, hiding the fact that he wasn't really sure which of the many manuscripts stored in the library it might be; his father had been the scholar, not he. "My father collected such things."

"Yes, yes, but why send the boy *now*? Why is it suddenly so urgent that the thing be copied?"

"Ah . . . it could be merely coincidence."

"No, it couldn't!" The flames roared up as Carlotta whirled, eyes blazing. Volmar shrank back from her unexpected surge of rage, half expecting a sorcerous attack, but the princess ignored him, returning to her chair and dropping into it with an angry flounce. "You're the only one who knows how I've been in hiding all these years, lulling suspicions, making everyone think I was dead."

"Of course." Though Volmar never had puzzled out why Carlotta had hidden for quite so many years. Oh, granted, she had been totally drained after the breaking of her stone-spell on Amber, but even so . . .

"Maybe that's it." Carlotta's musings broke into Volmar's wonderings. "Maybe now that I've come out of hiding, begun moving again, the Bard has somehow sensed I'm still around. He *is* a Master of that ridiculous Bardic Magic, after all."

Volmar was too wise to remind her it was the Bardic Magic she so despised that had blocked her path so far. "Eh, well, the bardling is safe among the squires," he soothed. "I've been debating simply telling him the manuscript isn't here and sending him away."

"Don't be a fool!" Sorcery crackled in the air around Carlotta, her hair stirring where there was no breeze. "The boy was sent here for a purpose, and we will both be better off when we find out just what that purpose might be!"

"But how can we learn the truth? If the boy becomes suspicious, he'll never say a thing. And I can hardly order the imprisonment or torment of an innocent bardling. My people," Volmar added with a touch of contempt, "wouldn't stand for it."

"Don't be so dramatic. The boy is already quite miserable, you say. No one will talk to him, no one will treat him kindly, and he's faced with a long, boring, lonely task." Carlotta smiled slowly. "Just think how delighted he would be if someone was *nice* to him! How eager he would be to confide in that someone!"

"I don't understand. An adult — "

"No, you idiot! Don't you remember what it's like being that young? The boy is only going to confide in someone his own age."

As usual, Volmar forced down his rage at her casual insults. *Ah, Carlotta, you superior little witch, if ever I gain the throne beside you, you had better guard your back!* As innocuously as he could, he asked, "Who are you suggesting? One of the squires?"

"Oh, hardly that."

Her shape blurred, altered . . . Volmar rubbed a hand over his eyes. He'd known from the start that Carlotta was as much a master of shape-shifting as any fairy, but watching her in action always made him dizzy.

"You can look now, poor Volmar." Her voice was an octave higher than before, and so filled with sugar he dropped his hand to stare.

Where the adult Carlotta had sat was now a cloyingly sweet little blonde girl of, Volmar guessed, the bardling's own age, though it was difficult to tell age amid all the golden ringlets and alabaster skin and large, shining blue eyes.

"How do I look?" she cooed.

Honest words came to his lips before he could stop them. "Sweet enough to rot my teeth."

She merely threw back her head and laughed. *Her* teeth, of course, were flawless. "I *am* a bit sickening, aren't I? Let me try a more plausible form."

The sickening coyness faded. The girl remained the same age, but the blonde hair was now less perfectly golden, the big blue eyes a bit less glowing, the pale skin just a touch less smooth. As Volmar grit his teeth, determinedly watching despite a new surge of dizziness, he saw the perfect oval of her face broaden ever so slightly at the forehead, narrow at the chin, until she looked just like . . .

"Charina!" the count gasped.

"Charina," the princess agreed. "Your darling little niece."

Too amazed to remember propriety, Volmar got to his feet and slowly circled her. "Marvelous!" he breathed at last. "Simply marvelous! I would never know you weren't the real — But what do we do with the real Charina?"

Her voice was deceptively light. "I'm sure you'll think of something."

"Ah, yes." Volmar smiled thinly. "Poor Charina. She always *has* been a bit of a nuisance, wandering about the castle like a lonely wraith. How unfortunate that my sister and her fool of a husband had the bad taste to die. Poor little creature: too far from the main line of descent to be of any use as a marriage pawn. No political value at all. Just another useless girl."

"Not so useless now." Carlotta/Charina dimpled prettily.

"Poor Charina," Volmar repeated without any warmth at all. "So easily disposed of. She never *will* be missed."